Jumping in Sunset

JUMPING
IN
SUNSET

DAWN
RINGLING

Multnomah® Publishers *Sisters, Oregon*

JUMPING IN SUNSET
published by Multnomah Publishers, Inc.

Published in association with the literary agency of Janet Kobobel Grant, Books & Such, 4788 Carissa Avenue, Santa Rosa, CA 95405.
© 2003 by Dawn Ringling
International Standard Book Number: 1-59052-227-3

Cover image by Getty Images/Sean Justice

Multnomah is a trademark of Multnomah Publishers, Inc.,
and is registered in the U.S. Patent and Trademark Office.
The colophon is a trademark of Multnomah Publishers, Inc.

Printed in the United States of America

For information:
MULTNOMAH PUBLISHERS, INC.
POST OFFICE BOX 1720
SISTERS, OREGON 97759

Library of Congress Cataloging-in-Publication Data

Ringling, Dawn.
  Jumping in sunset / by Dawn Ringling.
      p. cm.
  ISBN 1-59052-227-3
  1. Divorced women—Fiction.   I. Title.
  PS3618.I54J86 2003
  813'.6—dc21

                                        2003013983

        04 05 06 07 08 09—10 9 8 7 6 5 4 3 2

To my mom, Adela, who has nearly died twice—
and wanted to once.
She has shown me that forgiveness is a process—
often painful, usually slow, but always healing.

Acknowledgments

So MANY PEOPLE have read and contributed to the publication of this book that I could dedicate pages and pages of thanks to all of them. Unfortunately, I can do no more than list them. There are a few people, however, that deserve special recognition.

Jim and Diane Huber, for encouraging me to seek publication for a manuscript that, at the time, was intended as a vehicle for my own healing. They each read countless versions of *Jumping in Sunset* and made suggestions that enhanced the final product.

Donna King, for loving my first draft—and for talking me through so much of the pain and questioning of my life.

Glenn Pickering, for his Godly wisdom and professional advice.

David Himlie, for the caring manner in which he provided legal assistance.

Julie Cayemburg, for never walking away. For reading and reading and reading. For sharing my occupation with me and all the intense conversation that goes with being a writer of Christian fiction. For Christ-centered commitment. For friendship that is never afraid to confront or to love.

To Janie, my wonderful, constant friend who is teaching me the facts of friendship.

To Rod Morris, my editor, whose expertise has polished my work until it shines. I've learned so much from you in the past few months—and believe me, I won't ever forget RUE!

To Janet, my agent. You have been an amazing source of encouragement. Your faith in my writing kept me going during the dry times—and your persistence was the greatest blessing of all.

My children, Austin, Jace, and Natalee, whom I love with every ounce of my being. Your patience during the crunch times was amazing—especially Austin, who set aside sibling rivalry and played with his brother and sister so I could meet deadlines!

To all of the other readers who read and critiqued my manuscript: Beth and Mark, Patty, Jon, Roxane, Colette, John, Jennifer, Carol, Lori, and Tammi. You'll never know how much I appreciate your time!

One

"I'm really not up to doing anything for my birthday this year, Pam."

Paul had mentioned it twice. The first time he'd said it on the fly, late to some meeting, back door slamming before she even registered the last syllable of her name. And Pamela didn't take him seriously in the least. His second protest, however, had been on the way home from church just this past Sunday, when she'd asked what time he could be home Thursday night.

But even then she'd ignored him.

For May 28 in the Thornton family had grown to be more celebratory than Christmas. Paul's greatest occasion to shine, to put on a show, mingle and flirt, and be king for the day. It was always a party—lots of people, great food, champagne, sometimes entertainment or dancing. Last year had been the biggest of all: Pamela had invited over a hundred of their friends, relatives, and business acquaintances to his forty-fifth birthday dinner aboard a rented yacht. And Paul hadn't stopped gushing about it for a month!

After nearly two decades of marriage, Pamela had finally developed just the right panache to pull off the type of social event her husband craved. He *couldn't* have been serious about wanting to stay home and do nothing this year, could he? More likely it was just Paul's subtle way of letting her know he didn't expect something enormous like last year. So what about an intimate dinner for just the two of them? Though it wasn't his thing, it might be a nice compromise. They had so little time together these days just to talk.

In the end, Pamela played it safe and invited another couple, Harm and Liz Jenson—church friends from way back—to share the evening with them at Bella's, one of Paul's favorite restaurants. The Jensons were in their early fifties, and though Liz and Pamela weren't extremely close, she and Paul had found out early on that, as couples, they made an enjoyable foursome.

Not that tonight was exactly typical. To Pamela, it became increasingly obvious that Paul would rather not be there. And she bent over backward to cover for his uncharacteristic introversion, forcing a bright look to her eyes and smiling at the anecdotes Harm shared—painfully aware of the absent expression on her husband's face. As if he wasn't even listening.

"Okay. Okay. Comedian I'm not." Harm laughed and accepted a glass of wine from the waiter. "How about I stick to something I'm good at? May I propose a toast in honor of Paul's birthday?" He raised his goblet a bit higher and winked at Paul, who looked touched. "Here it is my favorite holiday of the summer...and I'm not talking Memorial Day! To you, Paul, for the fun-loving, all around great guy you are. To a man who gets things done—one whose generosity and drive we all admire. Happy Birthday, my friend."

Everyone clicked their glasses against Paul's and nodded agreement.

"Thanks, Harm. Your words mean a lot," Paul said. "And thanks to both of you for sharing this evening with us. I have to apologize, though. I'm a little beat. Lots going on, lately."

"Don't blame you a bit," said Harm.

Pamela smiled with relief. But after those few words of justification, Paul again left the burden of conversation mostly up to Pamela and the Jensons—nodding or squeezing out one- or two-word answers when necessary. His apathy even bordered on rudeness at times and was nothing like his usual, congenial take-charge mentality. Pamela caught his eye while the waiter refilled water glasses and silently questioned his tight-lipped demeanor. But he turned away from her probing eyes.

"I sure do like your haircut, Pamela," Liz said after the waiter left them to their meals. "You're the only person I know whose hair changes every month. I always look forward to seeing what you've done with it!"

Pamela laughed and tossed her slightly blonder, shorter waves. "My beautician should have been a salesman. I've never been able to say no when she suggests a new look."

"You women and your hair. Oh, to be so vain, huh, Paul? Lost all mine before I turned forty. Have to say, it's easier without it. Though I wouldn't complain if God had seen fit to have slowed down the ol' aging process a bit. I mean, look at that head of hair on you, Paul! Tall, dark, and handsome to boot? Some guys have all the luck!"

Luck may have had something to do with some of it, but Paul's dad had died of a heart attack when Paul was a boy, so Paul was a stickler for exercise and a low-fat diet…minus the occasional hamburger and fries he just had to have.

"I'll bet it's lonely around the house without Angie," Liz was saying, her plate licked nearly clean of the walnut-encrusted salmon and couscous their waiter had claimed was "to die for."

Pamela sighed. "That's an understatement. I think I'm finally letting myself feel again. It's been such a whirlwind this past week—first graduation and Angie's reception, then the all-night party at school Paul and I chaired. And then getting her packed and off to Mexico…"

"At least it must be good to breathe again," said Hal.

"I didn't mind the busyness really. And it was all for Angie. Sort of a last hurrah. Right Paul?"

He nodded. "She had a good time, so it was definitely worth the effort."

"And the team got off to Mexico okay?" Liz asked. "I just dropped off my support check for Angie at the church office today and was hoping to get an update from somebody in youth ministries. But nobody was around."

"No major problems," said Paul. "Other than navigating the mess at the airport."

"Second summer of construction. Hear it's even worse than last year," Harm said.

"No doubt about that," said Paul. "Then you add the kids from church and their baggage, and a bunch of emotional mothers. Not sure what was worse: the traffic or the tears."

Pamela smiled. "Yeah…well. When all was said and done, the flight to Mexico City left pretty much on time and I got the allotted two-minute phone call from Angie last night. They got all checked in to the places they're staying. The Hoyt Covenant kids are all staying at homes in one area, and I guess that other church from downtown is in another place. Angie sounded so happy, but when I got off the phone, I sat down and cried all over again."

"Don't you think you're overreacting, Pam?" Paul said. "It's a great opportunity for her. Chance to see a little bit of Mexico and do a few good deeds in the process."

"I don't deny that. It's just that…"

"It's just that she's your baby," said Liz, casting a stern look Paul's way before turning her empathy on Pamela. "Your baby *and* your only. And after she gets back from Mexico, she's off to college. I know all about the emotions that go into that kind of letting go."

"That's it exactly," Pamela said. "But I completely agree about the opportunity. After all, we're used to Angie being gone. She's signed up for short-term mission trips since junior high. It's more that…well, this is pretty much it."

"The motherhood chapter of your life is drawing to an end," Liz said.

"Was it like this for you when your boys left home for good, Liz? I just can't seem to shake this sad feeling of finality."

"It was, and I still miss them." Liz rested her hand on Harm's forearm. "But if there's one thing I've realized, it's that God didn't give us children to hold on to. That's what that husband of yours is for." She smiled in Paul's direction. "You'll be amazed how much fun the two of you can have now! Trips. Dating all over again. It's a whole new life."

Pamela eyed her husband, whose mouth had drawn into a tense line beneath his mustache. It was pulling teeth to get him to go out with her alone, let alone take extended vacations. He always had business to attend to. She'd finally coerced him into booking a trip to Europe in the fall and couldn't help but wonder if he'd back out at the last minute.

"You're how old, Pamela? Forty?" asked Harm.

Pamela nodded.

"Just a baby! Get your mind off Angie and onto something new. Tennis maybe—or rollerblading. Or rock climbing! You should give *that* a try! I hear climbing is quite an experience."

"I don't think extreme sports are quite up Pam's alley," Paul said, a hint of a grin turning up the corner of his mouth.

"Oh, I don't know. Maybe I—"

"Maybe you should both take a little vacation—get on a plane and head to Aruba or Hawaii or wherever else people go to get their minds off stuff," Harm said. "You look like you could use a break, Paul."

Paul grunted at the back of his throat. "May be true, but I've got some major changes coming up at the bank that pretty much make vacation an impossibility right now. And Pam committed to a full schedule with the magazine."

"You're going back full-time, Pamela? That's great!" Liz said.

Harm laughed. "Finally letting her off the ol' chain, eh Paul?"

"Actually, it was his idea," Pamela said.

That was the ironic part. She had been chained to the house in some ways. Harm's words may have been meant as a joke, but in reality, Paul had never really *wanted* her to work outside of their home. Not even when opportunities for a career in photography were dropped in her lap.

"So when do you start your new schedule?" Liz asked.

"Not until Angie leaves for school. And right now I'm not even working at all. I'm using up some vacation time to get stuff done at home."

"Good timing," Harm said. "Liz was a wreck after our youngest left for college. I remember her sitting on the floor of Tim's bedroom crying her eyes out because she missed him so bad."

"I, for one, think Pam's gonna be just fine," Paul said, sending another bland smile Pamela's direction. Then he pushed his chair away from the table and stood up. "It's not as if Angie is never coming home again. Chicago is a hop and jump from Minneapolis. And they run those ninety-nine-dollar airfare deals on ATA all the time. Excuse me for a bit, would you?"

Pamela watched her husband wind his way through tables filled with laughing, talking patrons toward the back of the restaurant, then slip his ever-present cell phone out of his suit coat pocket. What was so important that he needed to call on a Saturday night? That must be part of his problem tonight. More going on at work than he'd let on.

Liz was patting her hand and saying something.

"I'm sorry, Liz, what was that?"

"I was just saying that men don't always get it. Even Harm, well-intended as he was, couldn't quite see why I was so lost. And it does help, but there's a lot more to it than just keeping busy." She grinned at her husband's protest. "Sorry dear, but it's true. The reason I was in Tim's bedroom was because I *needed* to do all that crying. It was part of the separation process."

When Paul came back, he was far more animated. More

himself, but champing at the bit to escape, despite the waiter's pass-by with the dessert tray. It was loaded with chocolate creations and several other destructive sweets Pamela would have loved to sample.

"Looks great, but I think I'll pass," he said, checking his watch. "It's getting late…"

"We should probably get home, too," Harm said, rising to pull his wife's chair out for her. "I need to be at the station tomorrow by five for a taping. That reminds me, Paul, Jack Larson left a message today that he can't work the sound board at church tomorrow. Any chance you can fill in?"

"Well…actually, I've got to meet with the Lifelines staff before the first service."

Pamela stared at her husband. "But yesterday you canceled the—"

"You know, final decisions before summer and all."

Harm looked from Paul to Pamela. "Ah, well, no bother. I'm sure I can nab Mel or one of the other guys in the morning."

Paul signaled for Pamela to rise and when she did, he pressed firmly on her back—guiding her toward the door. Harm and Liz followed. Two sets of heels clicked across the parking lot, echoing into the cool blackness of the night.

Harm unlocked the door of his and Liz's car. "You two have plans next Friday night? We're trying to get tickets for *Buddy*, that new Broadway show at the Ordway about Buddy Holly's life."

"Hey, that sounds fun…" began Pamela, but Paul put his arm around her shoulder and ushered her toward their car.

"Have to take a rain check. We've got a board dinner I forgot to tell Pam about. But thanks again for tonight, guys."

The warning chime dinged until Paul buckled his seat belt, then all was silent as he wove through the restaurant parking lot to the road. Pamela could feel the earlier tension creeping back into the darkness inside the car. Though she suspected he wouldn't answer, she had to ask.

"Are you okay, Paul? Something happen at work?"

Her husband was still silent.

"Paul? You've been off all night. What's wrong?"

He looked at her for a moment before turning his eyes back to the road. "We should've stayed home."

"I'm sorry. I should have listened…it just seemed so unlike you."

Paul clenched his teeth, a habit he demonstrated when he was disturbed about something.

"Paul, talk to me. Please? Is it work?"

He swiveled toward her again, and just as quickly he looked back to the road and drummed his fingers on the wheel. "Okay. I didn't want to do it like this. I hoped we would be at the house."

"For what?"

"Oh, Pam," he huffed. "Oh, heaven help me, there's just no easy way to do this. I've waited as long as I could…And, well…I might as well spit it out."

Her stomach jumped. "What…"

"Pam, I'm leaving you."

She was quiet for more than a few seconds, wading through the onslaught of confusion.

"Did you hear me?"

She looked at him then. Paul's profile was tight, unfeeling in its straight-ahead glare. And he was suddenly removed (*was* it suddenly?) from her.

"Yes. You said you're *leaving*."

Paul's expression lost its tenseness for a moment. "I…we…I'm moving to Los Angeles. But I know you'll be fine—better even. Really. And you don't have to worry because I'm leaving you with plenty. I've taken care of everything. You're getting more than half, more than the state even says I have to give. We'll divide what we have in savings, investments, and…and on top of that, the house is yours. All of it. It's yours."

"Mine? What are you saying!" she yelled. Paul flinched as if she'd slapped his face. "Where are…What?…Why are you saying this? Are you crazy! You're ruining everything! Los Angeles! Why now?"

And then she stopped and just looked at him, grounded herself in the familiarity of twenty-one married years and closed off the rest. "Did you accept the job with Liberty Financial after all? You're going ahead of me to find a house. That's it, right?"

"Yes. I am taking that job. But no, Pam, I'm not going *ahead* of you…I'm going *without* you. I…I just can't live like this anymore."

Paul looked at her then, and she saw tears. Never once in over twenty-two years of knowing this man had she seen such a thing. And that panicked her more than the rest had. Suddenly comprehension struck like an earthquake, tremor after tremor shaking her with implication.

"Who is it, Paul?" Her voice thudded to a dead stop inside her ears. She already knew, didn't she? Somewhere…deep down.

"Dana," he said.

Did Pamela imagine the momentary softness that he wrapped around that one, horrible name? But then all hint of it was gone and the rest just spilled out, burning her with caustic calculation.

"She's going to Los Angeles with me. They need me at Liberty. And we'll be married as soon as the divorce is final. I'm sorry…but I just don't love you, Pamela. I've tried. I really have. And I don't want to hurt you…but I need you to know this now because I don't want to talk about it again. You'll be all right, you just see. Without me. We'll talk, work things through for you as much as possible tonight. I've got it all arranged. And then I'll leave first thing in the morning."

The headlights illuminated the driveway and the garage door—an oasis of sameness. Unshed tears stung her eyes, but there was no way she was going to cry. Not in front of him. The burgeoning hatred was strong enough to keep her emotion in check.

Paul reached to the visor above her to open the garage door, and she flinched as his suit coat brushed against her. The sensation, in the wake of his rushed explanation, was nearly a burn. Her husband was running away with another woman and somehow he thought it was all okay because he was leaving her with "plenty"!

"No, Paul, you're leaving tonight. Take what you want and go."

Pamela got out and turned her key in the lock, went straight to the darkroom in the back of the house, and slammed the door. Then she sat and listened to his sounds of departure above her.

The grinding closet door, the suitcases thumping off the shelf, drawers opening and closing, his steps. When, twenty minutes later, she heard the garage door vibrate closed again, she broke down and wept for hours, perhaps. Days, really.

Two

FOR THE LAST TIME, Paul backed out of his driveway, the Lexus's headlights shining on and then fading from the brass plate that announced the street number of his home. And though it struck him that this was the final time he'd call the place his own, he didn't mull it over or feel any sort of nostalgic prick of emotion. In fact, he exhaled his relief at finally being able to stop living such a divided life.

He hit redial on his cell phone. "Hi." His whisper, a smile. "I'm free, angel…Call the Hilton. We don't want to spend our first night on a mattress in an empty house…" He laughed at her surprised exclamation on the other end of the line. "*Yes, now…You better believe I'm serious…Really! I'm coming over now.*"

He clicked off the phone and released a deep, even sigh. It was over! And he was ever so relieved Pam hadn't put up a fight. He couldn't have shouldered an emotional outburst much worse than the one she'd offered. The end had come, and he had no intentions of returning to that house—not to rehash it, nor to fight with Pam over worldly goods. Somehow without her knowing, Paul had been able to secret away enough of his clothes over the past few weeks—mostly suits—and the few possessions he wished to keep. The rest she could have.

Other than absolutely necessary communications concerning Angie or the divorce he'd already begun to pursue, Paul intended to avoid talking to Pam. The less contact the better. His attorney warned him of that. Her emotions weren't his to soothe any longer.

It wouldn't be easy for Pam at first—the embarrassment, the stigma. Paul guessed that much. But he hoped the money would help see her through to a better place. She would live comfortably without any interruption in the style of life she'd grown accustomed to. She could stay in the house they'd raised Angie in.

In addition to the half he was taking, Paul had squirreled away quite a bit extra for himself over the years—investment profits buried in spots no one would unearth unless things got messy. But then, it wasn't like Pam to hire an attorney of her own to dig for such things. Anyone she asked would tell her 50 percent of Paul was plenty.

Paul yawned and waited for the light to change. The last stop before the freeway. It felt good to know he'd soon be in bed, curled up next to this woman he loved so much. Especially since he'd planned on being up all night—poised for hours and hours of Pam begging him to stay, nagging at him, blaming herself, crying, and then blaming him, picking at the details of issues from the past he'd thought were buried. Oh, how he hated to waste valuable time arguing over incidentals that had nothing to do with why he was leaving.

But for once Pam had taken him completely off guard. Not

that she was wrong in asking him to leave right away. This cold break was the only way to go, of course. Closure. Not wasting another year of his life with a woman he had no feelings for.

But tonight he had wrestled with second thoughts. He had started to get cold feet at dinner, especially when Pam and Liz started talking about Angie. Maybe he should have waited until *after* Angie left for college. Let Pam get more settled into the newness of it all.

But he couldn't push Liberty off any longer. And Dana was counting on him. Her car and most of the furniture they had picked out together over the years had already been shipped to the new house in California, and she'd flown back and forth a few times getting settled in her new law firm. So Paul went ahead with the original plan—and refused to worry about how Pam would handle the next few weeks. He *had* to do this for himself now or it would never be over.

Pam would manage. She'd call her best friend, Starla. He figured that much. He could picture the two of them now: Starla would *love* the drama and go out of her way to smother Pam with attention and sympathy. Talking constantly with her hands, putting on the little Jewish princess routine he detested so much. And then, Starla would launch some sort of moral attack on Paul—or worse yet, question his faith.

That had been that woman's way since the get-go…since he and Pam and Starla had first met at that small-time Assembly of God church he'd once ended up at by mistake. Starla (a hefty, gabby girl who hooked his elbow before he could escape down the aisle) took offense when he happened to mention that the worship was a little too "Spirit-moved" for his preference. She'd had some self-righteous chip on her shoulder ever since.

Around her, Paul felt weak. Unspiritual. But he knew the Bible through and through from his long-ago days at Central Avenue Presbyterian in downtown Los Angles. Though he'd never said much about it, his experience with church was one of the few things he actually valued from his childhood. Central's congregation had been a haven to him since the day his father had first put him on the Sunday school bus when he was in the second grade. Unfortunately though, Paul's beloved church was all too connected to the *rest* of his past—to the stuff he wanted to bury and never deal with again.

If Starla wanted to question his faith, let her. She just didn't see it the way he did. God had been the force that kept Paul pointed in the right direction and who ultimately held everything in the palm of His hand. And the God Paul understood best was hungry for good deeds to put balance back into a precariously pitched world.

Sure, he'd done enough to upset that balance himself...Paul would never claim that what he'd done with Dana was morally right. As questionable as having an affair was, though, he had done all he could to offset the sin. God demanded that of him, and he was more than willing to give back. His commitment to Lifelines—and all his other church and community involvements—was mostly about that.

And wasn't the smoothness of this transition out of his marriage a sign that the scales were now balanced—that God smiled upon his and Dana's love? Divine approval was a good thing, because Paul had finally reached the end of deception. The stress was beginning to take its toll upon him. He couldn't deny his feelings for Dana any longer, nor could he confine them to secret trysts that demeaned the truth of what they shared. He needed Dana in his life just as much as she needed him. And though divorce was nothing to brag about, Paul knew that, for him, it was necessary.

His situation was entirely different from the others he'd witnessed: fifty-five or sixty-year-old weasels sporting trophy wives after leaving their exes nearly destitute. For one thing, Dana was not a "trophy." To Paul, she was certainly attractive, but at forty-one, a year older than Pam, the qualities that endeared Dana to him had little to do with the typical male yen for youthful sensuality. She was his soul mate—the completion of him in a way Pam could never in a million years hope to be.

And Paul would never leave Pam in the dust. She was a good and honest woman. He'd done his job by her in the past and intended to provide for her future. Her face with its simple, almost boring features materialized in his thoughts. He'd thought her pretty once—and though she'd lost the lithe and willowy appeal of her youth, he supposed she was still attractive in a maternal sort of way.

When it came right down to it, Paul made a mistake marrying Pam all those years ago. He'd been captivated by her girl-next-door looks that very first day he met her. At the time he craved her innocent stability and simplicity. He actually believed it was enough to get him through a lifetime. But, as he now could see so clearly, the affection he felt for Pam was a poor counterfeit for the love that simply never grew. She had been a good homemaker and mother, but the passion he had wanted from their union never materialized.

In part, Paul blamed her small-town background, which in the beginning had been part of her appeal. But as sincerely as he tried to emancipate her from the homespun roots, Pam's folksy approach to life was simply too inbred to make room for the spark of excitement he longed for in a wife.

Paul had all but convinced himself that love was only an illusion, something no one really had. Like every man he knew, he'd had opportunities for affairs—women who promised him everything. But all their smooth talk and beauty ever did was make him more sure than ever that what the world termed love was little more than a fleeting sexual chemistry.

Until he met Dana.

Everything about her was a wonder to him, from her shoulder-length dark hair and big brown eyes to the way she thought the same way as he did about almost everything. She was strong and confident and yet feminine—could hold her own in a roomful of suits but was still able to curl up in his arms in front of a fire.

For the first time in his life, Paul found himself singing along to the corny love songs on the radio. Hard as it was to believe, he tingled every time he anticipated seeing her again—even if it was at a meeting at church or over lunch at some out-of-the-way restaurant. Even now, almost six years later, his feelings for Dana were a mystical motivator that left him weak-kneed and willing to throw his life away.

"Do you think other people have this? This explosive camaraderie? This intensity?" he often asked Dana.

The hardest part of their relationship had always been that

she was more keen to the guilt of it all than he—especially when they broke down and allowed a more sexual element to enter in. Mostly, they'd been able to hold to the lines that Dana had drawn. Paul had learned that holding his own passion in check was the best way to assuage her doubt. That and calling her attention back to their miraculous love.

Whenever he did that, she'd consider his words for a long while, and then her eyes would light up. And she would smile and run her fingers through his hair and say, "If we were the only ones in the world who knew this sort of love, it would be a pretty miserable planet, wouldn't it? If I didn't love you with everything I am, I could never do this. You know that, don't you?"

The more intense things got between him and Dana, the more Paul was convinced that God put them together for a reason: Did the Creator of the universe want him to endure a loveless marriage when he had finally found the one woman he was meant to have? He'd been naive and hurried when he married Pam. But he was wiser now and still young enough to enjoy the rest of his life with this sophisticated woman who completed him as Pam never had.

And now there was this great new job as well.

He'd always had headhunters after him, offering him interviews with other financial organizations. But when, out of the blue, Liberty Financial in Los Angeles began to pursue him for its vice president, Paul was convinced God was presenting him with an out. Almost as if it were a fleece, he first turned Liberty Financial down. But the board had such limitless faith in Paul's abilities that they had come back twice, nearly doubling the original salary they'd offered to lure him away from Lifetime Savings and Loan. It was enough to turn any man's head! And especially a man who'd overcome as many obstacles as Paul had in his climb to the top.

Paul blinked at a set of too-bright headlights coming toward him and focused for the moment on the freeway signs. He imagined his new life, what it was going to be like to start all over again with another career challenge, another chance at happiness, another woman. One who excited him and inspired him and shared his world.

Angie, of course, was the one thorn in all of this. If it hadn't been for her, Paul might have left Pam years ago. But he held in there because he knew what divorce could do to a child. He couldn't have brought himself to do anything to destroy Angie. She was a wonderful girl—a lot like him in many ways. Pam was mainly to thank for the way Angie turned out, though.

And Angie would always have Pam. Soon she'd have college, too. Paul remembered what that was like. All that freedom and opportunity and self-involvement. Enough to erase every bad memory life held. College had been the best time of his life! Paul could hardly imagine Angie would look back long enough to worry much about him and Pam. His daughter might even be relieved to escape from the tension at home. If there was one thing he knew about Angie, it was that she hated confrontation as much as he did.

Though they'd never discussed it, it was clear to him that Angie sensed how it was between him and Pam—that she disliked the strain, the falseness, the lack of affection, the disinterest. He'd read accusation on her face many times. She blamed him. And why not? As far as she was concerned, the problems in the marriage *were* his fault. What did she know of incompatibility? Just maybe with her dad out of the picture, things would be less stressful for Angie. He'd rather she be happy. Out of sight, out of mind, like they said.

Someday, if she wanted, maybe the two of them could forge a stronger relationship. An adult relationship of peers.

Paul exited the freeway and made his way down the darkened streets. He couldn't worry about it now. It would all work out. Pam might have a few weeks, months maybe, of hard times. But she would eventually come to the same conclusion: The two of them were just better off without each other. There was so little between them as it was. Pam would be so much happier without the farce. Maybe some day, she would even thank him for not prolonging their agony longer than he had already. Then, maybe, for Angie's sake, they could even be friends. That's all they should have been in the first place.

Yes. Eventually, it would all be just fine.

He turned onto the last dark street and stopped in front of Dana's immaculate town home, the one with the Sold sign in front. Paul could see her silhouette through the sheer curtain, waiting for him. As he walked up the steps, the door opened and she stepped out, carrying a garment bag and a makeup case. A large suitcase was behind her.

"Hi." She tipped forward to kiss him as he reached for the bag. Her eyes were burdened with questions.

"It went surprisingly well," he said. "Ready, angel?"

Dana pulled the door behind her and looked directly into Paul's eyes, the fleeting trace of guilt gone now. "Oh, Paul…I've been ready for years."

Paul dropped her bags and pulled Dana into his arms, breathing in the fruity scent of her hair.

Finally. *Finally*, he was free.

Three

PAMELA LAY IN A ball on the bed and felt the light change around her, saw the first golds of dawn paint the wood floor, the hot light of noon flood across its planks, the quieter glow of sunset ease in. Her first sunset without Paul in nearly twenty-one years.

Other than that, she thought nothing except that it was essential for her not to move. She needed to contain the pain. As in labor, she breathed and huffed, but she kept stock-still until everything in her numbed.

At some point, she crawled into the shower and turned the faucet to scalding and let it drain over her as she sat on the floor, its heat searing her upturned face until the water turned lukewarm and finally cold. Though on the surface, she didn't even feel the difference, deep down, the assault of the extreme was what made her think again.

Hazy memories of their beginnings crept into her consciousness uninvited—memories she hadn't revisited in ages. The tall stranger slipping into the pew in front of her at Riverside

Assembly, immaculately dressed in a dark suit and tie, carrying himself much more confidently than any of her small-town boyfriends.

Pamela never had been able to remember the first words Paul said to her after the service, only that he'd been entirely gracious and polite. However, when Pamela confessed to Starla some months later that she had fallen in love, Starla called Paul "cocky and self-centered from the first," citing how critical he had been of the service.

But Pamela had no doubt Paul was the one God had for her because it was a fluke that Paul even showed up at Riverside that morning. He was supposed to have met someone for breakfast at the Perkins down the street and the guy never showed up. Guilt over missing his own service across town brought Paul through the doors of Riverside Assembly of God.

Guilt. And where was that for Paul now?

Pamela wrapped an oversize bath towel around her and went to lie on her bed, burrowing under the covers to ease away the chill that had crept through her wet body. She closed her eyes at the thoughts of their whirlwind courtship: From almost the first date, everything was about building a life together. Paul swept her off her feet with trips to the theater, museums, world-class restaurants, all the Minneapolis hot spots. When he wasn't at work—or Pamela at school—they were together.

Pamela had always believed Paul placed such importance in his future—in establishing a family of his own—so that he might push away all the sadness of losing his parents, most recently his father. After his father died during his senior year of high school, Paul moved away from LA to attend the University of Minnesota.

When he and Pamela met, he'd been two years out of school and was working as a loan officer for Lifetime Savings and Loan, feverishly intent upon working his way to the top.

Paul never said much about his family (nor did Pamela push for more), though it was evident how deeply he admired his deceased parents. All she knew was that his father had been an English professor at UCLA, and his mom died when he was a child. His father—entirely devoted to her—never remarried but raised Paul on his own, doing all he could to keep the memory of his wife alive.

"We're getting married, Pam," he told her on the seven-month anniversary of their first date and slipped a simple diamond solitaire ring on her finger. And then, in his typical down-to-business style, he moved them into marriage and their first home. At first, Pamela dropped only a few of her classes at the University of Minnesota, but within a year she gave up the idea of a degree altogether in order to assist her husband in his climb up the corporate banking ladder.

By the time they were married, Paul was already a member of the Rotary Club, and he soon joined one or two other prestigious service organizations. He did all he could to cement his reputation around town as a charitable, popular sort. It was all part of the game, and as skillfully as Paul played, his entrée into the corporate high life came quickly. He coached Pamela along, encouraging her to dress the part and learn the ways of the wives of the men he aspired to be.

Right before she turned twenty-one, Pamela discovered she was pregnant. As wrapped up as she was with decorating the house and the baby's room, she hardly noticed the pattern that was developing. But then, it was a familiar design in their circle of friends. Husband worked; Wife cared for home and child(ren). Husband had evening outside commitments (meetings, dinners). Wife had daytime outside commitments (meetings, luncheons, lessons, school activities) so she could be home for Husband when he came home for dinner.

And it had worked well for them, hadn't it? Wasn't their life exactly what Paul had always wanted? Where had she gone wrong? Just a few days ago, her family had been intact and life was perfect—and now it was as if Pamela had never known joy. Getting through one day until it bled into another was now her only concern. And as each hour passed, her emotions circled from explosive anger to drawn-out periods of such sheer pain that she cowered in a corner of the room like a beaten animal.

At first, there were intervals of madness—crazy, elated confidence that Paul would walk in at any moment. The notion that he'd deserted his life seemed so absurd, Pamela could only laugh and reason it away as a silly nightmare. He could *never* tarnish his reputation with something like this! Appearances were everything to Paul. What about Lifelines? What about their church? What of all the people around town who looked up to him?

Then there came moments when Pamela lay suspended in dreamlike consciousness, barely aware of her own body. Hunger blended with sleep, neither recognizable as a physical need. A dreamlike state usually followed the red, burning heat of anger— oblivion in the wake of explosion. And she would yearn for the simplest answer to the question: How could Paul do this to me?

An endless stream of questions followed: How could I have

not known? When did he stop loving me? How many women had this happened to—and how could I not have seen the signs? She'd read their stories in "It Happened To Me" columns in women's magazines, saw them on *Oprah,* spoke with them at parties. What turn of fate made this her story now?

How dare Paul throw it all away for some stupid affair! Adultery. The biggest 'thou shalt not.' The one always whispered about but rarely acknowledged.

She had always believed her husband was above such scandal for the simple fact that he cared too much what people thought. But now sickening memories came alive: silly smiles Dana and Paul bestowed upon each other that never quite made sense; phone calls at odd hours, Paul's voice gone all soft and gentle; Dana's omnipresence in their life.

Pamela cursed her naïveté and screamed her anguish to the empty house, unable to separate grief from rage. The impetuousness of his act convinced her that at any moment she'd hear the garage door…his car. That he would walk in, crying his repentance, begging forgiveness.

On Tuesday the phone rang, stopping just short of the machine pickup. Again it rang, disconnecting at Paul's "*Hel*-lo, you've reached the Thorntons…"

On the third attempt, Pamela sprang from her cocoon of blankets, flipped the ringer off, and shouted, "How dare you!" at the mechanical Paul. "How dare you leave me for…for her…that witch! I hate her! I hate you both!" She turned the volume to zero.

Hatred. It rang through her ears, burned her throat, and pierced her heart. Acrid, biting, evil *hate*—no lesser word could encompass her pain and hurt and anger. And if God heard her vindictiveness? Should she even care? What punishment could He mete out worse than this!

Late in the week she stopped sleeping in short exhausted bursts and finally conked out for four or five nighttime hours at a stretch. It still wasn't enough, though, for her waking was less certain—more dream than reality. On one of those bleary mornings, Pamela instinctively rolled toward Paul for warmth and realized he was already dressed and out the door. *Partially* realized. Before the thought was complete, truth slapped her awake.

She tossed the duvet aside and crossed the room to the dresser, the antique signature piece one of their decorators had recommended and Paul insisted they get. She picked up their sepia-toned wedding photo and brought it close to her face. This year's frame was an elaborate pewter. Last year's had been cherry wood. Why had she so painstakingly selected a pretty new frame for this one photo every year, an idea she picked up from *McCall's*? What difference now did it make that she'd resorted to stupid gimmicks to keep their wedding day fresh?

Pamela studied the faces before her, faces that were laughing into the camera, hardly owning the feminine one as her own. So young, so beautiful these two were. When had all that happiness dissolved? Paul had been her knight in shining armor, rescuing her from a life of simplicity, showering her with the promise of his future. She loved him. So much so that she'd lived her life to make him happy.

And he'd loved her once, too, hadn't he? When had it stopped? *Whatever happened to us!*

Looking back later, Pamela pinpointed that moment as a sort

of epiphany. It was the first time since she'd said "I do" that she honestly considered what there really was between them. The first time that she analyzed their history. And with each backward turn of the page, she began to understand what she had hidden from herself: The "us" had already been gone a long, long time.

I'm not sure anymore that Paul really loved me the way I do him. She shivered and crawled back into bed, drawing her covers tightly around her. *Not even in the very beginning...*

Four

ON THE FIFTH MORNING after Paul left, Pamela took her second shower and washed her hair. She even got dressed, but drew the line at shaving her legs or putting on makeup. Even to the mirror, she had no wish to announce that things were on the upswing. Then she flipped the ringer back on and turned up the volume on her answering machine.

The moment she took her hand away from the phone, it rang. She let the answering machine pick up, and as she listened, an acquaintance from church left a message that she was praying for her.

Praying for me? Why? What do you know?

Just then, Pamela remembered that Paul had told her that he and Dana had mailed a joint letter of resignation to the church for their involvement in Lifelines. *We told the truth*, he said, *to save you the embarrassment of having to do it.* His false humility had sickened her.

Especially now. By now, the whole of Hoyt Covenant was in the know and the shock waves would be rolling. How could she ever go back? No matter that it was Paul who left her. People could only guess at the details, and who knew what they assumed about her. She'd seen it happen before. The first time she walked into church, it would be as if a skunk had doused her with its putrid perfume. Sympathy would be offered, but at arm's length and with noses averted to stave off the smell.

When the mechanical voice of her machine announced, "You have eighteen messages," Pamela resigned herself to face the inquisition.

The first call on the machine was from their pastor, Reverend Jurgenson, the one Paul must have addressed the letter to. Reverend Jurgenson had been Paul's biggest supporter through the years, heralding her husband's achievements, getting him involved in his first service organizations, inadvertently fanning the flames of Paul's desire for recognition.

Reverend Jurgenson's wife, Sue, had been the nearest Pamela had ever come to a best friend at Hoyt. After Sue died of cancer ten years ago, Pamela treated everyone at church in a kindly but disconnected sort of way. She considered Liz Jenson a friend, but they rarely saw each other outside of social engagements as couples.

It hadn't been Pamela's nature to hold back. Growing up, she had known everyone and everyone knew her. But somehow she'd heeded the advice Paul himself clung religiously to: "Be careful not to get too chummy—it's not a good thing to be so open with everybody. Mystery appeals. It's more fun to just get involved with as many things as possible so that everyone can have a little bit of you. Keep 'em guessing, I always say!"

Reverend Jurgenson's message was dated Tuesday and was

simple and sincere. "Pamela. I'm so sorry. Paul's letter was pretty clear, and I guess there's not much I can say to ease your pain. Please call if you need to talk. I hesitate to say it, but I do believe this: God *will* get you through this."

The next call was from Liz. "Hi, it's Liz, honey. Reverend Jurgenson called us this morning and oh, boy. What do I say? I thought something was up with Paul Saturday night…Oh, honey, I'm so sorry for you. I'm sure you need time to think and pray. Please call, okay? I'm here. So is Harm. We'll be praying, Pamela."

And then, everyone and their mother left messages. Some were brief and thoughtful. Others were less than empathetic. One was from a woman who, in the midst of promising her support, implied that this predicament had come because of shortcomings in Pamela.

"I'll pray that God will bring forgiveness to you, that He will right what is wrong in your own life. Mostly that He will help you to forgive your husband so your marriage will be made whole again."

Pamela wanted to call and scream at her, but she knew the woman had no other way to justify why bad things happened to good people.

Other messages were more effective. One man even asked how he could contact Paul "to try to talk some sense into him."

Late in the day her machine picked up the gravelly voice of Tina Rohlersson, one of the few divorcées Hoyt Covenant had in its midst: "I know your pain, Pamela, and am praying for you. Don't feel like you have to call me back. I'd never expect it this soon. But I'm here if you need to vent."

Tina was a large, almost masculine woman in her midfifties

who always seemed so in control of her life. Her husband Ralph left her for a woman fifteen years younger—the wife of his business partner. The sordid tale made its whispered rounds at church and gained quite a few unverified details in each retelling. Tina somehow survived the gossip.

Despite Tina's strength, Pamela had always pitied her and did her best to chat with her on Sunday mornings. But never once in the past five years had Pamela gone past small talk and asked about Tina's emotional well-being.

Now, she desperately wished she could go back and do it all differently.

Pamela hit the Erase button one last time. The day had been little more than passing from moment to moment. But she'd made it somehow. And *now*, she thought with an exhalation of relief, it was finally dark enough to crawl upstairs and make an effort at sleep.

June 6

Dear Journal,

One week down, nine to go, and I'm lovin' it! I've finally gotten used to sharing one room with a family of four—even though I sometimes wake up with two little kids breathing on me, waiting for my eyes to pop open!

The family I'm staying with is well-to-do by village standards, but I'm sure the money they're getting from Hoyt to house me comes in handy. Their whole house isn't much bigger than my bedroom.

In a few days we start building the addition to Pastor Juarez's church. I'm looking forward to doing the construction, although it's really just concrete block with windows. Nothing like the work we did last summer in Appalachia. All this week, we've been teaching VBS—I've got first graders and there were twenty kids in my class the first day, twenty-eight the next, and today I counted thirty-two. But no complaints. They are as quiet as little mice—with me as the Pied Piper! It's a lot different from back home. These kids obviously really want to be here.

We are allowed to e-mail our family once a week from Pastor Juarez's office. When I got on-line this morning, there was an e-mail from Mom but nothing from Dad. The weird thing was that I sent the funniest e-card to his work address and it came back undeliverable. And I know it was the right address.

I know it's not possible, but part of me wondered if he just didn't like it and sent it back. I know he loves me, but I always get the idea he doesn't quite approve of me. And he was so weird at the airport. Stood off from everybody else. He's usually right in the center of things. I told myself it was because he was going to miss me, but that's not his deal. Mom was the basket case—but then, so was *everybody's* mom!

Five

JUDGING BY THE NUMBER of sentimental cards and notes spilling from Pamela's mailbox each day, the greeting card enterprise was a no-fail investment opportunity. *No one really knows what to say to me,* Pamela mused bitterly, *but sure enough, those greeting card people figured it out and wrote it all down with impeccable finesse.*

Just as she was running her letter opener under yet another flap, someone knocked on her door. More like thumped. And thumped…and thumped. Against her better judgment, Pamela rose from the couch with a handful of envelopes and cracked her door open to her first human contact in more than a week.

"Ya look like you've been hit by a Mack truck," Starla said, her nasally New York accent stronger than usual for the point she wanted to make. Dressed in white cotton capris and a magenta shirt, she put Pamela's hairy legs and stretched-out T-shirt to shame.

"Thanks." Pamela turned back inside and dropped the cards on her coffee table. "Want a good tip? Invest in Hallmark."

Starla planted her sunglasses in her black mane of hair. "Why didn't you call, Pammi?"

She shrugged her shoulders. "Didn't want to ruin your trip. How'd you find out?"

"Doesn't matter how I found out. Ah, Pammi." Starla groaned, walked into the darkened living room, and wrapped her arms around Pamela. "Honey, it shoulda been *you* to tell me this. You know I would have been on the first plane home! You shouldn't be going through this all by yourself."

Pamela pushed free of her friend and plopped down on one side of the sofa. "So who told you, Star?"

Starla opened all the blinds, and Pamela squinted as light assaulted her.

"Oh, honey, it was your Pastor Jurgenson. He called my hotel yesterday and gave me a whole lot more than an earful—"

"Reverend."

"'Scuse me?"

"It's *Reverend*, not Pastor. And for the record, I haven't talked to anyone. You think I can just pick up the phone and say, 'Guess what, girlfriend! My husband dumped me for another woman and moved to Los Angeles'?"

"Why not?" Starla was beside the couch, looking down at Pamela with a sort of maternal pity.

Pamela curled into a fetal position. "I was gonna tell you when you got back." She wound her fingers through her hair and looked at the end of a twisted lock, wondering why the recently highlighted blond suddenly looked so dull. Gray almost. "So, what did he tell you? Sit *down* why don't you. Stop hovering."

Starla seemed to consider the command.

"Starla, please sit. My neck hurts looking up at you. Especially in this blasted sunlight. How did he know where to get a hold of you?"

Only then did her friend lower her much heavier frame to the cushions on the other end. "From what your Reverend told me, you've cut yourself off from the world. Someone from your church suggested he call me...But how he found me is not the point. You *do* need me, and I'm here." Her expression softened, as did the harshness in her voice. "I'm so sorry, Pammi."

"Well, I'm glad it was you they called and not my mother."

"Ya have any coffee made?" Starla glanced around the atypically untidy room, lifting a well-groomed eyebrow at a mute Oprah on the giant screen across the room. "Don't answer that. I probably wouldn't drink it if ya did."

"I probably wouldn't remember how to make it anyway. Seems I've lost part of my brain."

Starla was up again and heading toward the kitchen.

"*Now* where are you going?" Pamela unwound her legs and spread across the couch. She pulled the blue fleece comforter up under her chin, more to cover up her hairy legs and dirty T-shirt than for warmth.

"Getting coffee."

"Thought you said you didn't want any."

"I didn't say that," Starla called from the kitchen. "Only that I wouldn't drink yours. No telling how long it mighta been in the pot."

Pamela heard a few cupboard doors slam, the bean grinder go

47

on and off, and water running. Starla came out not many moments later with a plate of cut-up apples, cheese, and some bagels she'd found in the back of the fridge. They were arranged in her usual Martha Stewart chic, a quality Pamela had always considered wasted on her friend's singleness. Suddenly, however, the fact that Starla was unmarried offered quite a bit of comfort.

"Forgot I had bagels."

"Lucky I found a few nonfuzzy ones! You're out of peanut butter, though. The protein would do you good. You can only live so long on SpaghettiOs and diet Coke. You probably haven't eaten anything decent for days. So eat. Then we'll talk. I'm gonna go siphon some Java from Mr. Coffee." She returned with two steaming mugs and planted one in Pamela's hands.

"I hate black coffee, you know that," Pamela protested.

"Tough. You need it today, honey. Besides, your cream is curdled and stinking up the fridge somethin' rotten."

Pamela sipped the bitter coffee, appreciating its warmth if not its flavor. Then she devoured the fruit and a bagel topped with cream cheese.

"Okay. What can you tell me, Pammi? I don't need gossip, but I do need enough to get a handle on what's happening here. First off, do you know who she is?"

"Do I *know* her? She's a friend! Sort of. Remember…" She could hardly say the name out loud. "Remember Dana Taylor?"

Starla's hand stalled as she lifted a bagel from the plate. "The woman who runs Lifelines with Paul?"

Pamela nodded, realizing she need say no more.

Lifelines—Hoyt Covenant's ministry to help single mothers with young children get off welfare and into decent-paying jobs—

had been Paul's brainchild. He orchestrated partnerships between the church and a number of peripheral organizations to provide food, short-term housing and day care, and job training.

"He was always so impressed by her," Pamela said. "That woman could do no wrong in his eyes."

"What is she again? Some sort of legal assistant or something?"

"She's a lawyer. And everything that goes with it. Liberal, outspoken, active, *pro*active…" Pamela was seething now. "When she first came on board Lifelines, everyone poured coins into her purse because she had them convinced she was out there, actually feeding the needy. But she's no different from Paul. They like the notoriety of the job, but they delegate the real work to everybody else."

Between bites, Pamela spilled the entire story about Paul and Dana, sparing no details. Her eyes remained dry, which was a comforting change. And somehow the interaction of caffeine, food, and Starla's no-nonsense way of dealing with life pulled Pamela up to the edge of the pit she had wallowed in for a week.

Enough, at least, to catch a speck of light.

"Well, ya can do two things," Starla said after hearing Pamela's grisly tale. "You can continue to hole up in this messy house, braid your leg hair, and let that gorgeous new blond go completely gray…or ya can put one foot in front of the other and start to walk again."

"Nice pat answer, Starla. Thanks." The sadness reached up again and snuffed out the light.

"Sometimes, pat answers are a place to start. And as horrible as all this is, I'm not here to coddle you—although I can do that fairly well when it's called for. There's a time for misery and a time for action. Be honest, honey: What other options do you have?" She looked expectantly at Pamela.

"I could fight it."

Starla pursed her lips. "Not an easy option."

"But I could, Star. What if—sure, they all say this shouldn't happen to Christians—but what if Paul's in midlife crisis or something? What if this is just a fling? She doesn't have a right to him! Maybe he'll get sick of her. We can still work it out. I love him enough to…to try."

"Oh, honey…" Starla looked at Pamela hard, as if weighing her words, then forged straight ahead. "Look, I'm not gonna say I told ya so, but Pammi, you know I've had my concerns about Paul from the get-go. Oh, I know he's a bigwig now and all…and he's maybe got a good side I just never was able to find. But to me he's always seemed so…oh, I don't know, so theatrical, put-on. Fake."

"That's not fair. He's just careful with his image. That's not wrong, is it? And what's that supposed to mean? *Put-on?*"

"Don't be so offended," Starla said. "Just listen to me. I kinda think he's," she wiggled her hand, "you know, that he's been floating along for years on doing all the right stuff, looking perfect, smiling at the right times, building his fortune. Forgive me, but the way it looks to me is that Paul puts more faith in his pretty little job description and expensive dark suits than he does in the Lord or in you. Until now, you've been a passenger in his sidecar."

"So now you're judging *me?* You're saying this is my fault?"

"No, Pammi, of course not."

"Then don't try to convince me I shouldn't feel like I've been totally stepped on and then tossed out like garbage! Because *you* don't like him, you think I should just smile and say, 'Thank you, Paul, for relieving me of your put-on Christianity and closet full of suits. Now I can be *truly* happy because I never really was before!' Good grief, Starla! You make it sound like I should be fine with this. That he can just leave me and…and get away with it!"

Starla shook her head sadly. "Fine? No. But unfortunately, he *can* get away with it. Legally, at least. Listen, I'm not saying what he's done is right. If he gives you a chance, I'd expect you to do everything you can to work it out. And pray for a miracle. But from what you've told me, he's gone. Taken what's-her-name with him and started over somewhere else. Are you prepared to hunt him down and try to change his mind? It may take that." Her eyes bored into Pamela's.

And Pamela stared right back, hating what her friend was saying. "Yes. If that's what I have to do."

"Pammi, I'm pretty sure he's been planning this a long time…" Starla's voice softened and pity coated her next words. "He was very disrespectful to you—not just now. He has been for a long time. Even in the beginning. I never liked the way that man just swooped in and took control of your life. And lately, it's been worse. Sometimes I got the idea the only reason he kept you around was to wash his underwear, cook his dinner, and raise his daughter. We should have read the writing on the wall. *I* should have for sure."

"Why you, Starla?"

Starla's lips tightened.

"What's *that* look for?"

"Okay…I ran into Paul and that woman downtown once. It was a while back."

"You never told me that!"

"I didn't think it was a big deal at the time. Although now I realize he fell all over himself to convince me they were waiting for people for some lunch meeting. Only it was obvious they'd already eaten. I'm sure it was a lie, now that I know better. They were already working on cheesecake." She lifted her brows meaningfully. "One piece, one fork."

Images of Paul sharing a fork with Dana materialized in Pamela's mind, and her eyes welled up with tears. "Only you would notice the cheesecake, Starla."

"Oh, I'm such an idiot. Pammi, honey, I'm so sorry. I shouldn't have mentioned that." She slid close to Pamela and put her generous arms around her, letting tears bleed all over the hot pink blouse. "He's just always rubbed me the wrong way. I'm sorry."

"No, I need to know those things, as much as it hurts. But it makes me sick, Starla. I can't eat…can't even sleep. I hate the nighttime even worse than the day. I wish I could just disappear off the face of the earth. And somehow I've got to tell Angie…not to mention my mother. What do I say? What am I going to *do!*" Pamela put her face in her hands.

"I thought about that the whole flight home. And I think I might be able to help with some of that. First of all, we need to get you out of here. And I know just the place. I wasn't planning to go until late next week—but now that I'm home early from that conference, maybe we'll head north today."

"What? You don't have to work?"

"It's Saturday."

"But next week?" asked Pamela.

"I'm on vacation as of this moment. You don't think I'm dishing out all that money to a new dentist for nothing, do you? The whole reason I hired him was to free up more of my summers for the cabin."

"I don't know, Star. I th—"

"So, this is the deal. Come with me. Today. You can spend the whole time in bed if you need to—as long as you let me keep an eye on you. And maybe you can drive up and see your mom when you're ready. You'll need to tell her sooner or later."

"Then it will be later. She's already in New Mexico tutoring those kids on the reservation."

"All right. Well, I could use the help opening my cabin. I haven't been up there yet this spring. How about it? We'll leave as soon as you get your stuff ready, and we'll be at Rabbit Lake before dark."

Pamela shook her head at the ridiculous notion of going north with Starla for any reason. Wasn't it the *last* place on earth she wanted to be? "I can't leave right now—"

"Why not? I thought you had all this time off anyway?"

"I do. It's just…"

"Come on, it'll be like the old days. You've got nothing holding ya here, Pammi." She stopped. "Have you heard from Angie?"

"She called last week and we e-mail. I didn't tell her anything, though. I can't yet. It would ruin her whole summer."

"I agree," Starla said. "Okay…Angie's fine for the moment. Ya have no work. And no legitimate excuse to stay locked away like Rapunzel. Me and you, girl? A whole week away? Come on…let's let down our hair!" She smiled her big-toothed let's-go-skinny-dip-in-the-lake smile—the one that always ended up getting them into trouble in the old days. And when had Pamela not fallen for it?

"Okay," she whispered, throwing off the blue coverlet and baring her hairy legs. "Let me pack."

Six

CHRISTMAS WAS THE only time Pamela journeyed back to her hometown, and it had been years since she had driven this way during warmer months. To say that Pamela and her mother weren't close would be true, but it was too harsh a statement, devoid of what they did share. They talked several times a month, and a few times a year, Joan made her way south to see her granddaughter. But that was pretty much the extent of it.

"I don't quite understand why you're still so into this weekend thing after all these years?" Pamela asked after she and Starla had been on the road awhile. "Seems to me you would have grown out of it by now."

"Northern Minnesota? Grown *out* of it? You mean like sucking your thumb or wetting the bed or something? Pammi, honey, that's never gonna happen to me. The north is in my blood. It's in yours, too. You just deny it."

She rolled her eyes. "Hah."

Soon after Pamela and Paul got married, Starla moved to California to attend dental school. When she graduated, she accepted a position with a Los Angeles clinic. It hadn't been until Angie's sophomore year of high school that Starla moved back to start her own practice. Since then, just about every summer weekend was spent up north at the little cabin she inherited from her uncle. Even when she lived in California, however, she made a point of vacationing at Rabbit Lake. And since her dad still lived in Lewisville, the trip served a double purpose.

"I guess it is pretty up here," Pamela admitted. "If you like the outdoor thing."

She tried to focus on the blur of trees racing past as they cruised north on Highway 169. But as soon as thoughts of her own life flooded back, the green turned dark and menacing and anxiety bubbled up inside, robbing her of air for a second or two.

"Pamela? You okay?"

"I...lost my breath," she panted, feeling a rush of light-headedness. "It's like..." She gasped again. "Like I just can't catch my breath."

Starla slowed the car to a stop on the side of the road and unlatched Pamela's belt. "Put your head down on your knees and try to breathe in and out slowly."

Pamela obeyed. *One, breathe in...Two, breathe out...*

"Little better?"

"Yeah," she said. "Felt like I was having a heart attack or something."

"I'm pretty sure it was a panic attack. I've had patients get them in my office. You want to get out and walk around a little?"

"No, I'm fine."

"Don't be too surprised if it happens again, Pammi. You've got a lot going on that would cause this type of anxiety." She pulled the car back onto the highway. "It would do you good to talk about it. Get it out in the open so it's not quite so frightening."

"I wouldn't say I'm frightened…at least I don't think so. I'm more angry and sad than I am scared."

"Maybe it doesn't have anything to do with Paul. We were talking more about going home and it's not that you go all that often. Could that be it?"

"No…"

But that was it, wasn't it? Not necessarily going home, but this independent traveling with a friend. Without the protective cover of my family. Of my own marriage.

Who was she now without her own daughter and husband to cling to?

"Why are you so dead set against northern Minnesota, Pammi?" Starla said. "You had a great childhood."

"I don't know, really. It's all just so boring—backward. People here have no clue what life is all about."

Starla glanced sideways. "Frankly, I think that's Paul speaking."

"And *I* think you're wrong. If I remember correctly, I wasn't the only one who wanted to run as far from home as possible all those years ago. You're the one who convinced me I needed to grow up. Not live in some small town all my life and never find out how good life can be."

"I never meant that you should run away and never go back, Pammi."

"I know, Star." She yawned. "Mind if I close my eyes a little. I've always been able to sleep in the car and I think a nap would do me good."

Pamela leaned against the window, her thoughts too jumbled to define. Starla was a big one for talking it out, and Pamela just couldn't sort it all out at the moment. As sunlight flickered across her eyelids, she sank into sleepy memories of previous trips to Rabbit Lake.

Although the two women were as close as sisters, Pamela had been to Starla's cabin only twice. The first time was shortly after Starla inherited it from her uncle—when she still lived in California. Pamela took a toddling Angie for a surprise visit on Grandma Joan's birthday, and detoured to Rabbit Lake on the way home.

Another time, when Angie was in second or third grade, Paul was back East at a business seminar, and mother and daughter headed north to join Starla for an extended vacation. Angie reveled in the freedom of lake life: swimming all day, eating what she pleased, staying up with the fireflies and loons, and sleeping in late, curled beside Pamela in the big bed up in the loft.

Even Pamela came close to falling in love with Northern Minnesota that week…close to letting go of her Paul-inspired stereotype of backwoods northerners who wouldn't know what fabric to use with what wallpaper. And if she had admitted it, part of her began to feel just a little guilty of robbing Angie of her heritage.

Pamela opened her eyes. Unfamiliar terrain passed by the window. "Where are we?"

Starla smiled. "About an hour from Rabbit Lake. Sleep well?"

"Mm-hmmm. This is a different way than we usually take to Lewisville. Prettier."

"It's gotten a little urban for my liking," said Starla. "Used to be either farmland or woods."

As Starla's black Saab closed in on the little highway towns, strip malls and SuperAmerica gas stations peppered the prairies. The stark, block-style buildings took up land where once cows and corn had staked claim. The closer they got to Lake Mille Lacs, however, the more rural it remained.

"Oh, I remember those!"

"Oh yes," Starla said with a smirk. "On our left, you will see the Rainbow Cottages. Freshly painted with the same vividly ugly paint the proprietors select year after year. Keep alert! Coming up is the scenic overlook at the Garrison Y—known around our state for its stupendous replica of the…uh…sunfish. Or maybe it's supposed to be a walleye."

Pamela laughed. "I have a picture of you, me, and Angie beside that thing. And that's the bait shop where we bought those awful leeches for Angie's fishing pole. Remember? I wouldn't touch them, and you insisted on teaching her to do it by herself. She was such a basket case she decided to use frozen corn instead!"

"Memories…like the corners of my mind…misty water-covered memories…" crooned Starla.

"Oh, please. If you're gonna sing, use the right words!"

In Crosby, Starla pulled into the Super Valu parking lot to get groceries. Pamela walked beside the cart like a little kid, grabbing the items she craved and throwing them in the basket.

"Thelma!" squealed Starla when they reached the checkout lane.

"Starla, darlin'! Welcome back! You're early this year...ain't ya? How 'bout this weather. Somethin' fine, ain't it? My tulips are up already, if ya can believe that. Seems ice was off the lake a month earlier. Gives things a better chance to get warm and all. But then, I never do keep track! Maybe it was that way last year, too. You stayin' awhile, it looks like?"

Pamela slipped Starla a twenty-dollar bill and quickly passed through the lane on the right, eluding introduction to the fifty-something clerk with turquoise eye shadow and bleached Aqua Net hair. The nonstop prattle of the woman unnerved her and reminded Pamela of every small-town grocery store she'd ever set foot in.

Not soon enough for Pamela they were back in the car, pulling onto the dirt road that wound around Rabbit Lake. Starla's cabin was way on the west side of the lake, almost straight across from where they'd left the highway.

She remembered the canopy of trees from before—a tunnel that on this day was all light and lime and yellow with the unfurling foliage of early spring. Almost overnight, Pamela knew, the green would grow dark and murky, barely letting summer's light touch the road below. Her photographer's eye was already framing, imagining a series of shots that unveiled the birth of spring light and the advent of summer shadow.

They rolled to a stop beside the cabin, and Pamela lifted her drive-stiffened legs to the ground and drew in a breath of the fresh lake air. "Isn't that incredible?"

They carried the bags in, and Pamela started to unpack groceries onto the countertop while Starla filled a cooler with ice.

"Don't worry about it," said Starla as Pamela started to wipe out the inside of the refrigerator. "Tomorrow, after a good spring cleaning, we'll stock the fridge and cupboards. Just put everything on the counter—except for what needs to be chilled. We'll stick those in the cooler for now. I need to go outside and turn on the propane so we can cook. I'll start the grill for the burgers, too. Be back!"

61

"I'll get everything started," said Pamela. "I'm absolutely famished."

Starla came back with an armload of wood and kindling, then set about opening all the windows to let in the outside air. "Need to get a fire going to get rid of all this stale air. It's like this every spring. Plus it gives me a chance to enjoy my fireplace. How's dinner coming?"

"Just fine. Burgers and bakers are just about done. Need to do the salad yet. It feels so good to cook," she said, setting the corn to boil. "Best I've done lately is zap a bowl of SpaghettiOs. Hope my timing isn't too off!"

It wasn't until Pamela took the first bite of her hamburger that she was struck with the irony of the meal they had chosen: Paul, who publicly prided himself on his healthful diet, privately craved beef and potatoes. And no meal pleased him more than hamburgers and French fries drenched in ketchup. It had always been the family joke.

The night before Angie left for Mexico, in fact, Pamela had made hamburgers. The odd thing was (she had thought it odd even then, before she knew what was to happen) that Paul kissed her on the cheek as she put the plate in front of him. Pamela couldn't remember the last time he'd offered such a spontaneous sign of affection.

The last supper. "Judas kiss…"

"What was that?" Starla asked.

Pamela's eyes teared up and she could barely chew. She looked down at her plate.

"What's wrong, honey? Ya look like you've swallowed a bug or something!"

"Oh. It's nothing, really." She took another bite of hamburger, but Starla's stare-down demanded an answer. "Really, Star, let it go. It's a stupid thing to get all emotional over."

"Tell me."

So she did—and afterward rolled her eyes. "I'm starting to think it's the little stuff that's going to hurt the most. Like why did he kiss me and smile? He *knew* what he was about to do! That kind of stuff rarely ever happened as it was. Kisses? Smiles? I keep trying to remember the good times—and it's weird, but the things that come to mind are scenes from photographs I've taken. You know, pictures from summer vacations when Angie was younger—Christmas morning—church picnics. Why can't I remember anything but those? Is it possible that that's all there was?"

Starla shook her head and smiled sadly. "There were more, Pammi. There had to be. You just see the world in pictures— you're a photographer. It's only natural that you'd remember those times best. Especially since you took most of the shots yourself."

"You think Paul remembers the good times? Maybe I should send him some of our photo albums. You would think he'd want to have something to remind him what Angie looked like as a baby...the places we took her. We did *go* a lot of places, you know. Long summer drives cross-country..." Pamela knew she'd begun babbling, that there was little rhyme or reason to what came out of her mouth.

"The three of us were always doing stuff together when she was little. Never Paul and I alone, though. That's why I was so excited for this trip to Europe I've been planning. He just agreed to it to get me to stop asking, I'll bet. Do you know we almost *never* went out to dinner alone after we got married? Not even on our anniversary? If Angie wasn't along, we always had at least one other couple with us—even the first year. I remember them, too. Bill and Mary Blessing. Her dad was running for congress that year and it's all she talked about. I couldn't stand her. But Paul thought she was the greatest thing since hamburger buns."

She stopped and looked at Starla. "I think maybe Paul just didn't want to be alone with me. Maybe he worried I had nothing worthwhile to say...maybe I bored him."

"Oh, Pammi, you were never the problem. That man's self-worth is all wrapped up in the impression he can make. Or the names he can drop. He's always trying to prove himself."

"And when I *did* talk, he always interrupted me and changed the subject. He wasn't like that in the beginning. He used to admire me, I think. You know something else I can't get off my mind? Last Saturday night I took him out for his birthday. Liz and Harm Jenson were along. When we got to our table, Harm held the chair out for Liz. And when we left, he slid the chair out from underneath her. A gentleman. And they held hands when we walked across the parking lot, Star! Every once in a while during dinner, he'd touch her arm—or she'd put her hand on his. I can't remember if Paul's ever done any of that for me."

Pamela stared down at her hands gripping the edge of her plate, and tears clouded her vision. Why had Paul been so inconsiderate to her? And why had she never called him on it? She knew Starla wanted to. Numerous times. When she moved back to Minneapolis to establish her own dental practice, Starla had commented right off the bat about the manipulative little things Paul did to keep Pamela at arm's length.

"I know the way Paul treated me bugged you," Pamela said. "Thank you for not pushing me about that, though. You don't know how close I came to talking to you about it a few months ago. All his white lies and meanness…It was definitely getting worse. I should have put more stock in it."

"I know, Pammi," whispered Starla. "Those things *always* got to me. I think that's part of the reason Paul always hated me so much. He knew I saw through it."

"You really dislike him, don't you?"

"No." Starla's smile was gentle. "I think I *used* to dislike him. But the more I've watched him and have seen why he does the things he does, the more I realize I pity him. I wish I would've spoken my mind all those years ago. Maybe I could have saved you."

Pamela shook her head and a tear rolled down her cheek. "Saved me? No…I loved him, Star. I would have married him just the same. He has so many good traits, too, which is why I fell in love with him so fast in the beginning."

Star looked a little dubious. "But maybe my hesitations would have slowed you down. Can I get ya anything else? 'Nother burger, more corn?" said Starla finally, rising to help herself to another cob of corn.

"Didn't you say you weren't going to coddle me? I'm fine, Starla. Really. Stop worrying."

It felt strange to be doted on. Usually *she* was the one in charge of things, making sure everything was done just so. Being out of her element was something Pamela managed to avoid. But the discomfort melted quickly this time, maybe because other than her job, there wasn't much normal left to cling to.

In a weird sort of way, she felt unencumbered—which could be good as long as she ignored the pain tearing through her heart.

"It's okay to let people help, ya know, Pammi," Starla said.

"I didn't realize it showed so much."

"It does."

"I guess it's just that being Paul's wife had a lot of responsibility attached to it. I feel a little like I've been fired. I can't imagine that I'll still fit into a world of couples and families—it scares me. What am I going to do? And with Angie gone, too, who am I supposed to be now if it isn't a mother…and it isn't a wife? My 'little photography hobby,' as Paul always called it, is a job, not a life. And church? My goodness! I don't know when I'll ever be able to face my friends there. Not to mention my mom. I couldn't bear her pity."

"Maybe for a few weeks you could take a break from church?" Starla tucked a heavy lock of black hair behind her ear so it wouldn't get doused in the butter dripping from her corn.

"What would people say? I don't want them thinking I'm running away." Pamela was nearly in tears again now.

"Go somewhere else for a week or two. Be anonymous. Give yourself more of a chance to sort things out. I'll be here most weekends, but maybe you could try my church."

Pamela shook her head sadly. "Yeah, maybe. Frankly, I'm glad I don't have to deal with it this week. I can't imagine what it's going to be like to sit alone in our pew for the first time—" Pamela choked back a sob.

"It's all right, Pammi. Take your time. I think we forget that sometimes God can be found in the most unexpected places. I often wonder if He'd rather skip out on some of our church services Himself."

They finished up dinner, cleaned up the mess, and by then, Pamela was so tired she was dying to just go to bed. The loft room upstairs, with its attached bathroom, was a large, slant-ceilinged space under the eaves. A wrought iron bed lounged beneath the long window that ran along the wall. The only other furniture was a pine dresser with a little oval mirror hanging over it and a cane rocker draped with a handmade afghan, similar to the ones Pamela's mom crocheted. The double bed was piled with pillows atop an overstuffed, brightly patterned comforter.

"It's not the most private room," said Starla, tossing the throw pillows to a cobwebby corner, "but it's got the best view of the lake!"

Pamela looked over the iron railing into the living room below, and then out the big glass window ahead and remembered that, in the light of day, she would be able to see across the whole lake from her bed.

Starla, four inches taller than Pamela's five foot five, bent awkwardly at her shoulders to avoid banging her head on the low slant of the roof. The floor creaked loudly as she walked around the bed and pulled back the blankets. "And besides, I'm just too much woman to call it my own!"

The two friends hugged good night, and after Starla climbed down the steps, Pamela put on a nightshirt, turned off the bedside lamp, and clambered into the tall bed like a child, pulling the thick, wintry-smelling blankets over her head so only her nose and one eye peeped out.

Somewhere on the lake the sad voice of a loon called, and Pamela wondered if it had a mate or if she was alone, too. The fading essence of winter mingled with the scent of lake she'd breathed earlier, and now she lay, ever so quietly, wondering how many minutes she had left before pain would overtake the freshness. When would sadness seep in through the cracks in her psyche and scare sleep away once again?

But none stole into that three-sided room in the lakeside cabin. For the first time in a week, sleep came quickly and usurped all chances sorrow may have had.

Seven

DANA SLEPT SOUNDLY in the crook of Paul's arm, still except for the occasional flutter of an eyelid. With his eyes, he traced her features, then glanced around the darkened bedroom of the home Dana had chosen and purchased for them months before. Silhouettes of unpacked boxes lined the naked walls like an unfamiliar skyline. The windows, too, were bare except for simple shades letting in slivers of moonlight along their perimeters. Dana's face was the only thing in this place he knew— and with her beside him, the alien surroundings were almost comforting.

When he accepted the job at Liberty, Paul couldn't help but wonder if being back in Southern California would douse him with memories and affect his present in any uncomfortable way. But unlike Minneapolis, where everyone in business eventually knew everyone, LA was sprawling with anonymity, and he guessed his two worlds would never collide.

The home he and Dana lived in was only three communities removed from where he had grown up, and yet it was over an hour's drive and a planet away. Though it would be nearly impossible to reconnect with anyone from his past, he wished that he'd kept in contact with one or two of his old friends from Central Avenue Presbyterian. It would have been interesting to see how life had molded the people who had, in many ways, been his inspiration.

The clock ticked away the night. Paul hadn't slept all week. Not that it mattered. Mostly, the sleeplessness was born of a happy excitement—the child waiting expectantly to board the roller coaster. Paul still couldn't believe that Dana belonged to him now and that they were poised on the edge of a whole new life.

Tonight though, his sleeplessness was tainted with something else: Dana had begun to doubt her ability to forever live with what she tongue in cheek referred to as "being a home wrecker." Though most times Dana forged right ahead—loving him and giving everything of herself to him—there had been extended periods when she pulled into herself and away from him.

The emotional separations had become a pattern that Paul learned to wait out, especially since she always came back seemingly more in love with him than ever before. *Once you leave Pam, it will get better,* she predicted. She could let go of the secrecy, start over in a new place, live without the albatross of guilt.

Though she'd not said a word, Paul had seen it in her face the previous morning, noticed it in her lack of motivation and coolness toward him when they'd come home from work. And he knew that if he didn't draw her out, get her to talk, things would only get worse. She needed that, and Paul was willing to do it for her. Over take-out Chinese at their kitchen table, Paul asked the familiar question, lacing it with the empathetic tone of voice he reserved for this subject: "Ready to talk about it, angel?"

Dana ceased scavenging with chopsticks in the little white box for the last bit of fried rice and looked up, her eyes big. "It's that obvious?"

"We're finally together…this is everything we've worked toward."

She shook her head and briefly closed her eyes. "I know. And I *should* be happy now. I will be, don't worry. This is what I asked for. It's not an…an affair anymore. Well, not in the strictest sense of the word." Her eyes were sad. Almost apologetic. "I guess I just didn't expect it to still feel so troubling. It's Pamela. I just can't stop thinking about her."

Paul cringed. "Don't. Please? You *know* my marriage was over long ago. You know I never loved her. Pam's gonna get through this."

"But I've watched her. She loves you, Paul. In a different, more dependent way than I do, but she does love you." Dana looked away, her voice fading to a near whisper. "And she must absolutely *hate* me."

"It doesn't matter, Dana. You have to stop thinking about her. I'll make sure she's fine. What you have to remember is that I don't love her. Nor do I dislike her. I want the best for her. But what you and I have is so far beyond that. There's no way I can continue to live without the type of connection we share. I never believed such a thing like this was even possible!"

Hadn't they gone through this a thousand times already? He and Dana were soul mates. They were *meant* to be together. In his heart, he'd been married to her for years now. More married than he ever felt to Pam.

Paul turned Dana's chin back toward him and smiled. "Hang in there for me, won't you, angel? Everything will be right once we get married. I love you, Dana. I need for us to be together."

"I know, Paul. Marriage will be that final step for me. I'm sorry."

Paul reached for her hand. "You don't have to apologize. I just don't like hearing the indecision in your voice. I really believe God put us together. And I think you believe that too, or we would never have gone this far with our relationship. Right?"

She nodded. "I don't get it, but yes. But then..." Dana looked down as another cloud passed across her eyes. "Do you know I haven't prayed—not really—for years. Other than go to church, I haven't really done much to pursue any sort of real connection with God. I used to have such a strong sense of His presence in my life, but I'm not so sure I know that feeling at all anymore."

"Now you're starting to sound like Pam...all this talk of feeling God. God isn't a feeling, Dana. I think our understanding of God changes throughout our lives. Maybe when you were younger, less practical, you needed that kind of feeling more."

Dana shook her head. Paul could read pain in her eyes. "Most of the time I make myself believe what you just said—and I'm satisfied. I can even buy that whole 'I'm in charge of my own destiny' thing, you know." She rolled her eyes. "But no, I disagree with you. Deep down I think we *always* need God. I've become too independent. Too self-reliant. And lately I keep thinking about all those Old Testament stories. The wrath of God and all that. I know you don't like me to say it, but we both know what we did was...questionable. What if God doesn't bless our marriage?"

Paul pushed aside his meal, slid his chair around the table, nearer to hers, and ran a hand down the side of her face. "I think you're worrying about something you don't need to fret about. But think about what you just said—Old Testament. God doesn't work like that anymore. Fire and brimstone and all that."

Dana remained quiet and Paul watched the thoughts cross her face. Then she nodded and encircled his neck with her arms. "Maybe you're right."

"Maybe?" he teased, feeling the mood lighten.

She grinned. "Yes, Paul, you're right. You're *always* right."

"And don't you forget it! Tell you what. I'll call my attorney tomorrow. Make sure he's doing everything he can to speed this divorce along. If I know you and your need for closure, a spring wedding will help. I *know* it. This weekend we need to find a church, maybe even start looking into another thing we can do together like Lifelines."

"It's not church I need, Paul. And I've got too much on my plate to get involved in some ministry right away. In fact, I think I'd prefer to stay away from church for a while. I felt like such a hypocrite at Hoyt those final few months."

"Soon then?"

Paul saw the beginnings of a smile. "Yes."

He smiled back. "Okay. You know what's best for yourself. But for the record…as far as I'm concerned, *you* are the best thing in the world for me."

Eight

PAMELA CREPT FROM the cabin with her camera, figuring the fresh smell of the coffee she'd started perking would eventually awaken Starla. Until then, Pamela was content to search for the loon she'd heard just before falling asleep.

With camera in hand, Pamela felt more secure, almost as if she had purpose again. Paul had always downplayed her photography. But now, she was more thankful than ever that she had insisted, way back in the beginning of their marriage, that she keep working part-time.

During her first month at the University of Minnesota, Pamela had been hired by a photography studio to do routine office assistance, but more and more often the owner called upon her for professional assistance. He had quickly discovered that Pamela had an eye for lighting and a knack of framing subjects in unusual and artistic ways. Not wanting to waste natural talent, he took her on as his trainee.

"If you're not going to stay on at the university, you should think about applying at the Minneapolis Art Academy," he said shortly after Pamela and Paul were married. "You have something special I'd hate to see wasted."

Pamela only smiled. "I don't need a degree in art to take pictures. My life is with my husband now."

When Angie was older, Pamela left the studio to freelance for the magazine she still worked for now: *Twin Cities at a Glance Magazine*. For the most part, *TCM* catered to tourists, though it had a strong reputation among residents as well because of its restaurant and entertainment reviews. As much as she enjoyed her job, Pamela often wished she could find a way to use her camera in a less commercial way. Her most creative work almost always happened outside of work—shots of Angie were among her best. Other opportunities came along, too, such as weddings or baby portraits for friends. And when Hoyt started Lifelines, Pamela took pictures for the brochure. She visited the women and their children in the shelters and befriended them, nearly overcome at times by the sheer longing she saw in their faces. They never minded being photographed, the children especially, shabby and somehow ancient, begging for acceptance…for love.

But this…Pamela sighed at the beauty all around her. This was the type of photography that thrilled her most.

The morning sun was warm, its reflection on the still lake almost as real as the sun itself. Pamela approached the reeds bordering Starla's property, searching for the loon. She skipped a stone four, five, six times across the smooth water, watching as the circles bumped together, then dissipated. Further out, a bird dipped to the water's surface with a loud "awww," then swooped up sharply, a fish flapping frenetically in its beak. She lifted her camera at the call, ready for a second fatal meeting of bird and fish, hoping she'd catch it before the fish was swallowed.

The shutter clicked. She was lucky!

Somewhere around the bend, a child hollered to a sibling that breakfast was ready. A ghost motor sputtered alive and propelled its boat into the lake to where Pamela finally spotted it, cutting through water toward the reeds to her north. She waited until the driver of the boat dropped anchor and sank his line, then she focused and shot, framing him against the tall foliage springing from the marshy banks behind him.

Hearing a slight rustling, Pamela wandered deeper into the tall grass to her right, toward a neighbor's dock. And there she was—perched just at the edge of the water, barely concealed by thin reeds. Pamela froze upon seeing her and then backed away. Still, the red eye blinked in alarm.

Her back was a perfect black-and-white checkerboard bleeding into polka-dot wings. Her breast—snow white. At first the bird's head also appeared black, but when a slight movement caught the sun, Pamela saw that it shined a lustrous iridescent purple. Around the loon's neck was a necklace of black-and-white stripes, an accessory that completed her spectacular appeal.

Pamela inched closer, as soundlessly as possible. Even so, the loon emitted a high-pitched cluck—more like "kwuk." Pamela froze again, and from the weeds swam another loon, flapping its wings menacingly at Pamela, yodeling a bit as if to beat home his point. Pamela knew enough to retreat from this mate come to protect.

Just as she made her way back toward Starla's, the cabin door banged, and Pamela turned to see her friend, cloaked in a vivid red kimono and matching flip-flops, ambling down the slope to the water's edge, carrying two mugs of the steaming coffee Pamela had started.

"I added sugar and cream for ya this time."

"What a pal. Thanks."

They stared across the lake, comfortable with the morning peace, the warmth of the sun at their backs.

"Get any good pictures?" Starla asked after a while.

Pamela nodded and sipped at the coffee. "Some great ones, I think. And I found the loon and her mate and snapped a few of them before they scared me away. Did you hear her last night?"

She nodded. "Haunting, huh? I love to watch them, but I don't know as much as I'd like to about ducks…loons…any of the water birds around here. I've always wondered if they mate for life—I sometimes think it's the same pair I see every year. I keep promising myself to buy a book."

Pamela stifled a laugh. Starla was always saying stuff like that. Whenever she tasted a particularly good cheesecake or heard a great song on the radio, it was always: 'I'm gonna track down that recipe' or 'Gotta get myself that tape!' To Pamela's knowledge, her friend never acted on the impulse.

"Don't bother. I'll buy one for you," Pamela teased.

"Oh, good."

"Remember the loons when I was here with Angie? Their yodeling and wailing sounded more like a coyote than a bird. Scared me to death!"

"That's right! You disappeared with your camera early that morning as well, didn't you?"

"I thought something was wrong with them," Pamela said.

She recalled how she found the mother loon, anchored to the

nest. That time, strange clicking sounds came from the bird's throat.

"And she kept moving her head around and staring at the feathers of her breast. I thought she was sick. Until I got a glimpse of the eggs. They were hatching! All that noise from the night before was pure and simple maternal excitement." Pamela smiled at the memory.

"I always wished you could have come back the next week," said Starla. "Right at the edge of my dock, that mother bird was floating with two chicks on her back, tucked into the feathers under her wing. It was the sweetest thing I ever saw. Though watching the little ones learn to fish is pretty neat, too."

Starla described how one parent would babysit while the other dove for small fish or insects, dangling the prey in its beak and letting the chicks take turns racing forward with webbed feet to devour the meal.

Pamela smiled. "I'm glad I found her. I thought she sounded close last night. Almost as if she were right outside my window."

"Everything sounds close out here, Pammi, especially at night. We could sit out on the deck and do no more than whisper, and that guy fishing out there would hear every word."

"So I guess we can't tell any secrets, huh?"

"Why not? Folks here wouldn't give two hoots about our petty gossip and intrigue. It's all about being good neighbors and being there during the crunch times—like when I need a cup of sugar or something."

Pamela laughed "Sugar is a crisis?"

"Of course! But seriously, all of us cabin folk are here for one reason: to get away from the hassles of the city and get back to what really matters. That's why I wanted to bring you here with me."

"And right now all that matters is that I'm *starving*. What's for breakfast?"

The two women headed back to the cabin and whipped up a heart-unfriendly meal of bacon, eggs, and biscuits with tons of butter. Usually, Pamela was careful about what she ate. Mostly for Paul's sake. But who was there to please but herself now?

After breakfast, Starla exchanged her red robe for shorts and a sweatshirt embroidered with a mosquito, Minnesota's state "bird," and joined Pamela on the deck overlooking the lake. And they finished off the pot of coffee before rousing themselves for the big spring clean.

Pamela took claim of the kitchen and the windows, while Starla worked on the bedrooms. Then they both descended to the basement utility area, which was the worst project of all. They took plenty of breaks, sitting out on the deck each time with coffee, fruit, cookies, and other snacks. By the end of the day, they were both bushed—but the cabin sparkled.

"This place has really come around, Star. I remember when you first got it…"

"The only luxury I had was a toilet that flushed! Uncle Burt came here to fish and that's about it. I don't think Auntie Clair ever stepped foot in the place."

"You blame her? You know, this would make a great spread for *Midwest Living* or some other vacation-home publication."

"Send 'em over. I'd love to show it off. You're the one with connections, honey!"

"Hmmm…not a bad idea."

The living room was filled with beautiful pine furniture,

artfully combined with smaller antique pieces. Northern motif quilts draped the overstuffed sofa near Starla's huge stone fireplace. She'd commissioned a local artist to paint a slightly impressionistic woodsy scene across one wall, and the others were bathed in a warm coffee color.

Two bedrooms were on the main floor, one a hunter's paradise with its bearskin rugs and scratchy Indian blanket wall hangings. The other, Starla's room, had a simpler Americana theme done all in red, white, and blue with antique toys and dolls accenting the empty spaces. It was a grown-up version of a child's room.

Pamela loved the loft area best. When she lay in the iron bed, she could see across the lake through the wall of windows overlooking the deck. It was like living in an Ansel Adams print. Pine trees cut into the frame on either side, and river birches composed the entire foreground and sloped down to a clearing by the water.

Before dinner, and after a shower to wash off the grime of the day, Pamela called home for messages. The first was from Jim, her editor at work, who must have called right after she left yesterday afternoon. "I know you're still on vacation next week, and I don't want to bug you. But here's the scoop. I'm short staffed. Any chance you might do a quickie shoot for me Tuesday or Wednesday? You'll like it and I wanted to give you first chance at it. It's a golf course shot for that tournament in September. You can probably nail it in half a day. Call me."

The next was from Liz—"Haven't heard from you and wanted to be sure you're okay. I'm going to stop this week and check up on you, so call me if you can."

After that, a few tail end prayer chain recipients. Then another from Tina Rohlersson. "Just checking on you," she said. "And wanted to let you know that I help to facilitate a support group that meets at Century Baptist once a month. Most of us have been in the same boat as you. We'd love to have you join us. Just know I'm praying for you daily."

And the last—Pamela's stomach lurched—was from Paul. "Call me, Pam. It's important."

She scribbled down the number he left and sank to the floor, breathing deeply, fighting the waves of panic and pain that threatened to tow her under again.

Could he have changed his mind?

The phone dangled from its wall cradle. Starla walked over and hung it up and sat beside Pamela on the floor.

Pamela shivered. She could picture herself in Starla's kitchen when she was in high school. She'd dropped the phone then, too—after her mother called, frantically panting out the news that her dad was en route to the hospital in an ambulance. That it wasn't likely that he would make it. While her best friend's arms were around her all those years ago, Pamela's father fought for his last breath. The brain aneurysm took his life before he ever reached the emergency room.

"Paul?" Starla asked, bringing her back.

"Uh-huh." She picked at a splotch of dried food on the floor.

"And?"

"He wants me to call. Says it's important."

"Want some privacy?"

"No," she said to the floor.

Starla pulled Pamela's chin up, looked at her. Saw through her. "You think he's reconsidering, don't ya?"

Pamela didn't say anything. But yes, she hoped that it was all just a terrible mistake, a crazy and quick midlife crisis. And that he wanted their life back. She'd even move to Los Angeles if that's what he wanted.

She stood up and dialed the number before Starla disappointed her right to hope. Paul's clipped "Hel-lo. Paul here," greeted her before the third ring.

"Paul. It's me."

"Pam. Finally! I've been trying to get a hold of you for days! Where have you *been?*"

"I'm at Starla's place. Up north. Do you…I mean, listen, I'm sick to my stomach over this. Do you…why did you want me to call?"

"I should have thought of that. Good to hear you're with Starla, but listen. I needed to let you know that things are moving fast on this end. And since we didn't get a chance to talk about it, I wanted to warn you about the papers you'll be getting in the mail. I know how you can get about legal stuff. But it's not going to be complicated at all. I've spoken to an attorney and—"

"What?" Her head spun. *Already?*

"I've retained an attorney for the divorce, Pam," Paul said with more deliberation. "He's sending the initial paperwork in the next week or so. Everything will be quite simple since we're splitting everything pretty much right down the center, fair and square. He's a good guy. Go ahead and call him if you have any questions. But for now, all you'll need to do is sign the papers when they come and send them back. All this first round of stuff does is get the divorce action started."

"But…" *Are you really this heartless?*

"Oh, and be careful about what you spend right now so nothing gets too confused. So far, I've left all our accounts open, but it would be best if you just write checks off the joint account and only use the Chase Visa. I'll send you a list of what we have so you'll have an idea of what the settlement will add up to. Don't worry, though; you'll be just fine."

He sounded almost pleased with himself.

"And I did say you could have the house, of course. There's plenty of equity if you ever want to sell."

Sell our home? Pamela fell back against the wall, salty tears stinging her face. Why should she expect anything different this time—he'd always been quick on the start when he had a plan. Almost as if he were afraid someone would steal it. A child with a cookie. But how many times had she had to clean up the crumbs?

"What about Angie?" she asked.

"What about her? I've got college tuition already planned for—"

"I don't mean that. I mean, what about *her*? You've already moved to California and filed for divorce. Have you even thought about what you'll say to your daughter?"

Paul was silent. And then: "I would think that should be something you do. The two of you are so close. And telling a kid something like that over the phone is hardly a good idea."

"Maybe you should come home when she gets back in August."

"No. That's impossible."

Pamela exhaled the bitterness. "Why are you doing this, Paul?"

"We talked about it already."

"Did we?"

"Pam? You're not going to contest this divorce, are you? All it will do is waste money. Minnesota is a no-fault state. I'll get this either way."

She'd heard the word *contest* a thousand times on the soaps, but what did it really mean? She already *did* contest this divorce.

"You're not, are you?" he demanded when she didn't answer. "Pamela?"

She walked toward the circle of people at church. Paul stood among them, Dana's smiling face beside his. She inched in beside her husband, not daring to go on the side where Dana stood. And still Paul subtly turned his body away, toward Dana. Always toward Dana.

"Are you going to answer me?"

"I heard you, Paul. You know, when I listened to your message just now, I thought maybe you realized what a fool you're being...that you called to say you wanted to come home and work things out. What about 'until death do us part'? What about 'what God has joined together, let no one pull apart'? How can the two of you live with yourselves! How can you do this to me, after I've been there by your side all these years! Someday you're gonna wake up and be sorry that all you ever cared about was yourself! And then it will be too late!"

"Don't do this, Pam," Paul said, enunciating each word. "I told you already, that's not going to happen. I'm *not* coming back." He paused. "According to my attorney, we can get the divorce finalized in less than a year as long as you're not con—"

Paul jerked the phone back as soon as Pam slammed it down, clenching his teeth in frustration. Why did she always have to be so self-righteous!

Until death do us part. Good grief, is that all she had? Did anyone but Pam still take that stuff literally? Her small-town, *Leave It to Beaver* expectations caused the death that parted them! Every time things didn't quite turn out as perfect as she wanted, she laid all the blame on him. As long as her life flowed smoothly, she was happy as a clam and left him alone. It was only when he screwed up that things went sour. Or when they had to spend more than a few hours at a time in each other's presence.

"Honey?" said Dana, coming from around the corner toting a cumbersome box. Her hair was tied back with a bandanna and she had dirt on her chin. "Who was that? Everything all right?"

Paul swallowed to get rid of the distaste. "Yeah. Fine. It was Pam. She…she just ticks me off, that's all. I was only trying to give her a heads up, and she laid into me. What else is new. I should've just let her deal with the divorce papers by herself."

Dana set the box down and came over to where Paul was sitting on the couch—the only foot of space not heaped with unpacked junk. "You have to remember *she's* not the one who wants this divorce."

"Why do you care so much? She's living in a dream world, Dana."

"Even so…"

"So she has a right to vent. I just panicked a little because she seems to think I might want to get back together with her. How can she still think we have a chance? Our marriage has been dead for a hundred years!"

"Paul, think about it. You've barely been gone a week. You've been working on the divorce for a few months already and it's been in your mind for years—but it was just sprung on Pamela last week. Try to see it through her eyes."

"Through *her* eyes? Honestly, I don't get it. I don't understand why she thinks she loves me. Why in the world would a woman want to hang on to someone who doesn't care about her? I stopped pretending years ago."

"You said it yourself. She's in a dream world, so to speak. Maybe routine and contentment has been enough for her," Dana said gently. "Maybe she thinks that *is* love. Either way, she hardly expected this. Don't push her so fast."

"You want me to slow things down? I thought—"

"You want to rush it all because you're worried I'm losing it," Dana said. "I'll be okay, Paul. Just give Pamela a little more time."

"How did you get so wise?" He smiled and reached up to pull Dana into his lap.

"I'm an attorney, remember?"

"Ughh!" Paul shot her a teasing look, and Dana punched him. "I just figured the quicker this moves forward, the less it's going to hurt her in the long run. But maybe you're right. I'll tell Bill to wait a few weeks to drop the paperwork in the mail. Pam's never been a quick decision maker. And she's not all that bright around legal stuff."

Dana leaned in and kissed Paul deeply. "Slow is fine. Just don't get the idea that I *want* this to draw out forever and ever. The sooner I have you all to myself, the better."

Nine

"I WAS MARRIED to him for twenty years, Starla, and he wants to undo it all in five minutes. He says he doesn't love me? What about commitment? He has himself convinced that his little infatuation with…with *her* is going to last forever. And all it is is lust. That's about as plain to me as the nose on your face! We've got twenty years of life between us. What does she have? A few stolen moments with someone else's husband!"

Pamela sat cross-legged on the floor, cradling a cup of tea Starla had slipped into her hands sometime after she'd slammed down the telephone. She inhaled the steam, letting warmth seep into her hands as if it could melt all the confusion and hurt away. Starla stole a pillow from the couch and spread out next to her, listening to Pamela's complaints and pleas about Paul.

"I can't believe how fast he's trying to get rid of me. That hurts more than just about anything else." Pamela sniffed. "He's going to cut me out of his life in record time!"

"Maybe you need to prepare yourself a little more legally."

"Oh, Star…please."

"No, no. Pammi, listen to me, at least. I realize it's the last thing you want to consider, but you said it yourself, this is going fast. You should at least think about retaining an attorney. I know a very good one. Maybe you should meet with her."

"Paul's already got one for us," Pamela's voice was empty of all, save defeat.

"*For himself.* You need one of your own, Pammi."

"Why should I pay money to some lawyer to tell me I'll be provided for sufficiently?"

"Because I'm not so sure you should trust Paul."

Pam turned her head toward her friend. "As generous as he's always been with everyone, there's no way he'd cheat me, Starla. I'm sure of that."

Starla lifted an eyebrow. "I don't mean to be cruel, but what would you call this thing he has going with Dana?"

Pamela drew her lips into a line. "Point taken."

"It's up to you, Pammi. But this lady is a patient of mine, and she's good at what she does. You could at least go see her."

Ten

THE NEXT MORNING, Starla had errands in town and invited Pamela to join her, but Pamela wasn't in the mood to see people and needed to return a few phone calls. She first left a message on Liz and Harm's machine, then called her boss at *TCM* and summarized (without launching into tears again) what had happened.

Then, to chase away the reminder of yesterday's pain, Pamela selected Arthur Miller's *Death of a Salesman* from one of the shelves in the cabin and pulled a chaise to a sunny spot on the deck. She immersed herself in its pedantic plot, but there were so many similarities between the antagonist and her husband that after an hour, she tossed the book aside and fell asleep in the sun.

"Ya in there, Pammi?" Starla called out much later, her voice rousing Pamela from sleep. "Can ya help me unload?"

"I'm coming!" Pamela shrugged off the drowsiness and headed down the deck stairs, toward the back of the cabin. She stopped short at the sight of Starla's car. Geraniums and vinca vine, begonias, impatiens and other flowering plants overflowed the trunk of the Saab, and a box of gardening supplies filled the passenger seat.

"Where in the *world* do you intend to plant all this?"

"This here? My window boxes and the beds beside the house. This isn't the half of what I bought, though. First thing in the morning, a delivery truck's dropping the shrubs and perennials I ordered. I buy a few new things every year, always on the weekend I open my cabin up. It's a tradition. This year, I went all out, and I'm putting you to work!"

Pamela's eyes flew open. "I don't know the first thing about gardening or landscaping."

Starla grinned. "Doesn't matter. All I need's your muscles!"

The two women sweated under the sun all week, cultivating the hard dirt just up the hill from the lake, breaking up chunks of clay and mixing in compost and fertilizer so the land would accept the new plants. Feeling the perspiration roll down her face and tickle her back, Pamela was tempted to jump into the frigid lake to cool off.

Though it had been years since she'd dug her nails into the earth, Pamela didn't mind it a bit. In fact, dirty fingernails aside, she wondered if she'd missed out on something primal. Something valuable. Paul had trusted no one but landscape professionals with their lawn. He hadn't even mowed the yard himself.

Day followed day—a succession of clear, early spring gold and light. And sometimes, for a moment or two, Pamela forgot she was a wounded, betrayed woman. The relentless, life-sapping bleeding began to slow.

At Starla's suggestion, Pamela started a journal. In it she

recorded all her rantings about Paul, the mad course of her emotion. She and Starla also fell into a routine of talking over a cup of hot chocolate by the fire before bed.

"One minute I have hope that God will spare our marriage. The next I want to just pull the covers up and die. Right now, though...all I know is that I'm scared," she confessed to Starla on their final evening together. "Actually, *terrified* would be the better word. I've never been alone before. Even when I first moved to Minneapolis, I had you."

Starla cocked her head to one side and considered Pamela through squinted eyes. "I have an idea you're talking *single* more than you're talking *alone.*"

"Yeah, maybe I am."

"I've always been single, but I've never minded it. Maybe you should talk to your mom about that one. I'd venture to say she'd have loads of advice on being single again."

"I doubt it," Pamela said. "There was hardly even a chink in her armor when my dad died. But I was devastated. Dad was my hero—the kindest, most loving father any girl could hope to have. Every once in a while she caught me crying in my room and there was this look in her eye...."

"What kind of look?"

"Maybe pity...but more like intolerance for tears. She thought I was an emotional weakling."

"She *said* that?"

"No. It was just that obvious. And ever since then, I've been out to prove myself to her. Prove that I'm strong. Make a good life for myself. That's why Paul was so great. I know there were things about Paul that she struggled with, but she loved his confidence and professionalism right from the start. And I know she admires us. And now I've blown that, too."

"*You've* blown nothing! She'll never think that, Pammi. She'll be sad for you."

"Exactly. And I just can't bear her pity."

94

"So you're just going to go on as if nothing happened and hope she never finds out?"

"Of course not, Starla. I'll tell her. Just not until I'm stronger."

"Just don't wait too long."

Pamela stared into the dying embers of their last fire and scrunched her cheeks to loosen the dried tears. "Thank you for this week, Star," she whispered after a while. "You've helped me see that I *can* do this. None of it's going to be easy, but at least I have more confidence that I can get through the hard days to come."

"I know you will, honey. You're welcome up here anytime, ya know. I'm here every weekend from here on in. And I'm just a phone call away at home."

"You and I haven't had so much time together since college! You're *so* good for me, Star…but I can't expect you to come every time I need someone. You rescued me during this first miserable week, and it's given me the desire to go on. But this isn't the real world." Pamela peered out the dark window and then turned back to her friend. "Somehow I've got to face the music now."

"That part may not be all that different from the way it was— you were always complaining how Paul was never around."

"That doesn't change the fact that I miss him…miss our daily routines. Miss the thought of slowing down, growing old together. Maybe that's what makes me so depressed…he doesn't care enough to stick it out with me. And maybe more than that, he's choosing to do it with someone else."

"Rejection?"

"Yeah, I guess. Paul *was* God's will for my life, Starla. Still is, as far as I'm concerned. He's being too quick to throw it all out the window. I will never stop believing that love is primarily a commitment. That's what lasts after the flames die down."

95

Starla nodded solemnly and squeezed Pamela's hand. "I think there's a bit more to it than just that. But I do know one thing— that man has absolutely no idea what he's giving up in you, Pammi. I love you."

"I won't stop asking for God to bring him back. I won't stop hoping. You know that, right, Star?"

Pamela read pity in her friend's eyes, but the words came back to her gently. "You wouldn't be you if you did."

June 12

Dear Journal,

Two down, eight to go.

We started building this week—what a dirty job! If it weren't for the swimming hole we walk to every night after work, I'd never get clean. For one thing, there isn't a tub where I'm staying. Or a bathroom. There's an outhouse and this hoselike thing and a curtain rigged up outside for showers—but we aren't allowed to take them every day. And when I finally do get a shower, news spreads like wildfire and all the kids in town show up to watch. The whole team has the same problem. It's a joke now. And we've learned to wear our bathing suits!

I like it here, but I think I'm more the inner city missions type. I miss Lifelines. I've been thinking about that a lot lately. I've done these missions things with church since before I can remember. But of them all, working with Lifelines was the best, especially when Mom, Dad, and I were working together that first year. Maybe that's why it was so much fun. We were actually hanging out together and liking it. Usually when the three of us try and do stuff together, it never turns out. We end up giving each other the silent treatment.

I just read over what I wrote and it sounds like we have a bad family life. Really, it's not horrible or anything. I mean, we've got a great house and my parents don't really fight. Mostly it's just that Dad isn't around all that much, and when he is, there's this sort of tension between him and my mom. And I feel sorry for my mom because Dad's kinda rude to her sometimes—like he ignores her when she's talking or says things to her he wouldn't dare say to anyone else. It makes me so uncomfortable that I pretty much disappear.

Being down here makes me think a lot about life and spiritual things and all. My mom and I can really talk about this stuff. But lately I've wondered where my dad stands with the Lord. He's into church and all that, but he never talks about his faith—the inside faith. I'm not sure he really knows what it means to "walk with Christ," as our youth pastor puts it. I wish I could ask him about it, but there's no way. He'd think I was judging him or something and he'd be all weird to me. I miss him though. I sure wish he'd e-mail me.

I miss Mom even more. This is the first time I've been away from home for a whole summer. And it's fun and all, but what makes it hard is that I leave for college right away when I get home. Everything is changing so fast, and as excited as I am, I'm also a little scared. But then, I guess it's all a part of growing up.

Eleven

SOMEHOW—SHAKING hand and all—Pamela got the key in her lock Sunday afternoon. The door floated open on a current—and memories flooded in like ghosts.

There, through the window, was the shadowy form of Angie on the backyard swing set, the ancient, discolored equipment suddenly brand-new in Pamela's mind's eye. She could hear Paul's whistle as she stepped into the entryway, his heavy step following her through the garage door to the kitchen.

And smell him…oh, she could *smell* him. That musky-sweet scent he favored still lingered in the hallway and clung to the family room easy chair. But it was strongest in the closet where he'd always put his briefcase and trench coat first thing when he got home. More than anything else, the cologne was nearly Pamela's undoing.

But she refused to cry. Not now…not yet…

Pamela surveyed the mess her living quarters had become and wondered how she could not have noticed it last week. Newspapers and envelopes littered the floor under the mail slot.

And a SpaghettiOs-stained bowl was on the coffee table next to the empty cups she and Starla had used, greenish black fuzz growing at the bottom of one. Not to mention the dots of mold peppering the rock-hard bagels and cream cheese. At some point, Pamela had stacked three empty diet Coke cans near the TV. Neatly—if not consciously.

In the bedroom, the knit dress Pamela had worn to Paul's birthday dinner was crumpled on the floor. Underwear and hose and sweats were scattered all over. And in the bathroom, specks of water spotted the mirror, and green toothpaste was a cementlike squiggle all the way to the faucet.

The whole scene was disgusting. It reminded Pamela of the silent battle she faced daily: snatching Paul's dirty underwear from the floor or bedroom chair, picking hair out of the shower drain, retrieving his used mugs from wherever he'd left them. In the things that mattered to him, Paul was a picture of order. But when it came to their home, he was a hurricane. Funny how little any of that mattered now.

Pamela finally let loose the tears she'd bottled up all day and cried herself to sleep.

Monday morning she pulled back the blinds and made herself breakfast, then set to work tidying up the house. It didn't take much, though, before she plopped down on the couch in front of the TV.

On Tuesday, she took a shower and blow-dried her hair— lighter again with all the time she spent in the sun at Starla's—and applied the first shades of makeup her face had seen in two weeks. Then she cleaned as she had never cleaned before.

On Wednesday, Pamela went back to work.

Her editor at *Twin Cities at a Glance Magazine*, Jim Jarvis, had known her forever. And though Pamela had always held back from developing relationships with her other coworkers, Jim was a friend. He gave her exactly what she needed her first day back: a mindless shoot at a new Italian restaurant. No forethought. No creativity. Pretty much point and shoot.

The entire job was simple enough to do on her own, without any extra lighting or setup technicians to have to converse with all day long. The solitude was a blessing.

When she'd bagged her last few shots, she pulled the rolls of film she'd taken at Starla's cabin from her case and developed them alongside the pictures for *TCM*. As the colors and shapes materialized in their chemical bath, Pamela couldn't help but smile at the contrast: The photo of the early morning fisherman floated beside a candlelit picture of *Rigatoni al Porcini*. Ignoring the other magazine prints, she clipped the lake shot on the overhead line to dry, then feasted her eyes on the interior pictures of Starla's cabin, a menacing red-eyed loon, the rain rushing across the water toward a hazy sunset, a neighbor's dock reaching into Rabbit Lake.

Pamela massaged her temples. Where did it come from, this homesick feeling that suddenly was so overwhelming? Northern Minnesota was far too rustic and unfashionable for her liking these days—a place to escape from, not to! The people she'd grown up with were far too unrefined with their boxy '70s ramblers or run-down farmhouses carelessly decorated—ugly, even. Pamela loved the city and its well-heeled citizens, ready-to-go wallpaper stores, and restaurants that served more than deep-fried walleye.

So why this overpowering urge to go north again?

Starla would be pleased...not that Pamela intended to tell her. She called every night just to make sure Pamela was okay. And as honest as the conversations were, Pamela's odd longings for the north were locked away and protected.

But on Friday afternoon, when Starla uttered the familiar *you could join me at the cabin again this weekend, you know,* Pamela faltered just a bit. It would be so easy to go...

"No," she said a second too late. And though Starla must have heard her momentary doubt, Pamela rushed on. "I...I need to do this on my own for a while first. You can't be my savior, Starla. But thanks anyway."

But with nothing to do all weekend, "doing it on her own" proved useless. She puttered around the house, considering, then rejecting, the option of packing up Angie's bedroom. Finally she sat down at her computer, typed in the keyword "divorce," and surfed the net. In the end, Pamela ended up in a chat room with a woman whose husband left her for another woman three years before.

When Pamela asked how divorce proceedings had gone, the woman wrote: STILL PENDING. Her not-quite-ex-husband promised her right at the start an agreed-upon fortune, a fair settlement in light of their financial position. Like Pamela (whose username was "PamT"), "Flowerlady5" had opposed the divorce. Despite the ugly circumstances, she wanted to work things out. She loved her husband.

But, she wrote, things changed.

PamT: What things?

Flowerlady5: Let's just say Brad got greedy. And mean.

PamT: He decided not to be fair?

Flowerlady5: In the beginning, he promised I'd get support of at least sixty grand a year plus a nice chunk of our retirement and investments. It was far more than I needed since our kids are grown. He had a few business problems after that—nothing big, but he got scared. I felt sorry for him, so I agreed to less. Didn't consult an attorney until later and when we fought for more, the ante dropped again. I'll be lucky if I get thirty now.

PamT: Thousand? A year? He can do that?

Flowerlady5: Not legally, but he's learned the tricks. I should have retained a lawyer right away, before he started hiding stuff. But I lived with Brad for thirty years. I thought I knew him. We've been in court ten times already over different parts of all this and we've barely begun. If my lawyer can't turn this around somehow, I'm going to have to find a way to bring in some money on my own. I was a housewife for all our marriage. Never went to college. Never even had a part-time job. Not a happy picture. You have a lawyer?

PamT: No. But it's different with us. My husband would never do that to me.

Flowerlady5: Trust me. We all said that. Get an attorney ASAP. The best one you can find—and don't worry about the cost. You're still married; your husband will foot the bill.

Before she logged out, Pamela ordered six books on divorce from Amazon.com, determined that she would at least read up on the legal process. If only there were some way to win Paul back and avoid all the upheaval. It was all so overwhelming!

What, really, did Pamela know about how much they had, except that it was a lot? Of course she maintained her own account with the money she earned from *TCM*. But keeping track of the rest of their finances was Paul's domain. He was the banker, after all. Far better equipped than she to handle their investments and other business matters.

For Pamela, it had always been so easy: write the checks, do the shopping, clean the house, cook the meals. Their cars were paid for. And she was sure the house was nearly paid off. But as to retirement accounts, investments, and insurance policies, Pamela was embarrassed to admit, she knew next to nothing.

Suddenly, she was terrified. What if Paul kept up this mad pursuit of his as Starla predicted he'd do? What if he *did* turn the table on her and got selfish all of a sudden? Maybe it wouldn't be that bad an idea to at least talk to Starla's attorney friend. Make sure everything was kosher.

After all, Paul had cheated her once already. He could easily do it again.

July 8

Dear Journal,

Five down, four to go.

Mom sent a care package today and it was great! Weirdest thing
was that she put in a package of Oreos instead of the incredible
chocolate chip monster cookies she always makes. I don't think my
mother has *ever* gotten store-bought cookies! I love Oreos. It's just
that it was so not my mom. But I guess she's big into her job, now
that she doesn't have me around to slow her down. Truthfully, I like
that she's too busy to bake. I was starting to worry a little that she'd
miss me way too much this fall. Especially since Dad's never home.

Mom and Starla spent some time at Rabbit Lake a few weeks
ago—she sent along some of the pictures. Talk about nostalgia! I'll
never forget the time she, Starla, and I spent a week there. I hardly
wanted to leave, but even back then I could tell Mom was having a
hard time being there. She's got this thing about being up north,
close to Gram's. I know they love each other and all, but we never
go visit Gram except at Christmas. And it's too bad, because I love it
up north. Dad hates it even worse than Mom. I must be a genetic
mutant. I mean, I love the city…but I wouldn't complain if they had
raised me up north.

We went shopping at a little village about an hour from here
this week. I can't believe how much stuff I got! I got pretty good at
bargaining and bought enough to take back as souvenirs—and to
give to the kids I live with. My Spanish has improved so much in a
month that I could even tell when I was being schmoozed by the
vendors! Dad would have been proud.

So far, I like teaching Bible school better than building. I love watching the kids' eyes when something I've been trying to explain finally sinks in. I've been thinking that maybe I could major in education. I think I'd be a really good teacher.

Twelve

PAUL DUTIFULLY OPENED the hymnal to the Apostles' Creed, but he spoke the words without even a downward glance at the book in his hands. "I believe in God the Father Almighty, maker of heaven and earth. And in Jesus Christ, His only begotten Son, our Lord…"

He didn't need the book; the words fell from his lips the way they always had. And it felt so right to speak them again. Familiar even, despite the modern glass and steel sanctuary so different from Hoyt's dark oak and stained glass. The feel of this congregation, however, was more like the church he'd attended all those years ago in Los Angeles.

This was Paul's second visit to Church of Zion, and he was certain it was everything he wanted in a church—large, important, strong community involvement. A place to belong. As of yet, none of the people around him knew anything about him. Not beyond the smiling, good-morning handshakes they had exchanged at the minister's mandate only minutes before. But they would.

Ever since he left Hoyt, Sundays had been uncomfortably empty. But it wasn't the sermon he missed. Or the music or the liturgy. Mostly it was the satisfaction that he was doing his duty. What Paul craved more than anything was to be needed. He was itching to dig in and work so that he could regain some of the respect he'd sacrificed back in Minneapolis. His involvement would be even better here, though. Bigger and more meaningful because of the strata of people who called this congregation their own. It was a place to connect professionally and a community in which he could grow.

"I can't wait till you see this place, Dana! You gotta come with me next week."

But Dana stared at him with a look that bordered on pain. "Why is it so important for you to go to church right now, Paul?"

"I've always gone. It's just something I have to do."

"Maybe it's comforting to you, but I need time to work through some of this emotion by myself first. I can't just sit there and listen to a sermon that would only make me feel more guilty than I already do."

Paul was quiet a moment. "What I don't get is why this whole depression thing you get is so much worse now than it was when we had to hide our relationship. To me, it seems like it would be easier now that we're trying to make it right."

Dana's eyes clouded over and she paused for a long while before answering. "It should be, but it's not. Not yet. In Minneapolis I think I was caught up in the thrill of our romance—and for the most part I kept all the guilt at bay. Maybe I hid it from you and even from myself. Now that I've actually ruined a marriage—"

"You didn't ruin a marriage."

"Now that we've chosen to be together, I live in fear that everything will change. That somehow I'm going to lose you. As divine punishment or something. A consequence, I guess."

"There's no way you're going to lose me," Paul said.

Dana was quiet.

"You aren't. I promise you that."

"I hope not," Dana said softly. "Oh, Paul…I certainly hope not."

Thirteen

THE HOLDING PATTERN Pamela entered was strange comfort—work, work, work, and sleep. Outside of the people at work, Starla was the only one she spoke with. But even to her, Pamela didn't confess the worst: That there were times—especially those lonely nights when she woke up and couldn't fall back to sleep—when nothing seemed worth it anymore. Her life seemed a mere blip in the scheme of the world. A blip that could be erased by the bottle of pills in the nightstand beside her.

The only thing that stopped her hand from popping the cap was Angie. When she focused on her daughter, Pamela found strength to turn the radio on—to seek companionship in the voice of the nighttime announcer and the soft music that came before dawn. Sometimes she begged God to make Paul realize his mistake and then fell asleep dreaming that he had returned. Other times sweet images of making up swam through her head.

Though she told no one, that dream kept her putting one foot in front of another.

And then one afternoon, two months almost to the day that

Paul had left, Pamela received an imposing packet in the mail. Inside was the summons he had warned her of, alerting her that her husband had indeed filed for divorce. All the document needed was her signature as proof that she'd received this official notification of his intent to leave.

She dragged her eyes back to the top of the first page. Listed as the cause for the divorce was "an irretrievable breakdown of marriage."

Isn't it I who should decide that? What does Paul have against me...other than he thinks he doesn't love me?

Or did the court consider that irretrievable? Maybe the county court should add a new line to the list of reasons for divorce: Loss of love. Was something as subjective as 'falling out of love' reason enough to void a twenty-one-year marriage?

It wasn't sadness or loneliness that scared sleep away that night, but anger. What little rest Pamela caught was sacrificed to violent nightmares of shouting, of cursing, and of payback.

All the next day Pamela's wrath grew, and it was all she could do to speak kindly to the lighting technician and stylist assisting her with the shoot. Mostly she avoided conversation altogether for a few days.

Doesn't God want me to be happy! she yelled inside her head, not daring to speak such words aloud. *Is He closing His ears to my prayers?*

She finally called Starla. "Hey. It's me. Got a minute?"

"More than a minute, honey. What's up?"

"I'm losing it, Star! And it's about all I can do not to rip someone's head off! I got the paperwork for this divorce Paul is so gung ho about pursuing."

"Oh, honey…"

"And it was stuck in between the *Hoyt Herald* and my *Good Housekeeping*! All three wrapped up with a little rubber band. Didn't have to look twice to realize what it was. I swear he planned it that way! Probably thought it would cushion the blow!"

113

"Pammi…"

"And would you believe our twenty-first wedding anniversary is in two weeks? Paul's timing is absolutely impeccable. I don't get it, Starla. How can God let Paul go through with his plans? All I do is pray these days! The Bible says He hates divorce. Why would He let this happen! It just doesn't make sense. And it's not fair!"

"I don't have the answers you're asking for, Pammi. God doesn't always make sense. I don't get it either. But He does love you."

She smirked. "Nice sort of love this is."

"This isn't completely about God, Pammi. Paul was the unfaithful one."

"You know, Starla, people who've never been through a situation like this are *hardly* qualified to give advice."

And then, for the first time since high school, Pamela hung up on Starla. At first, she thought it was worth it. She was right, wasn't she? Starla didn't really know what she was talking about.

Pamela nursed her anger in the darkening living room, staring out the bay window. The lights blinked on in the Anderson's house across the street—first in the living room, then the kitchen, then somewhere deeper in the house, perhaps the hallway. And finally in an upstairs bedroom. Two shadows merged and then moved as one from the window. The master bedroom, Pamela thought.

In a while, one lonely streetlight shimmered on and surged off again—groaning, it seemed, toward full illumination. Could she wish on a lamppost as she'd done all those years ago with the first star in her northern sky? Once the other lights came on, however, flickering up and down her street, Pamela abandoned the thought.

After a while, she reached for the phone, then leaned back again, too embarrassed at her juvenile reaction to call back right now.

In the end, Pamela's bitterness turned to quiet weeping. She wept for all she and Paul had been and for all they would never be. And then her grief gave way to great bursts of sobbing, the type of breath-catching cry she hadn't had since grade school. Finally she wiped the tears from her cheeks and turned the lights off and crawled upstairs to bed, drugged by her agony into a restless sleep.

Fourteen

LEFT ALONE FOR a moment, Pamela looked around at the elegant office and wondered why she had ever listened to Starla or heeded the advice of Flowerlady5. She wished she could blink her eyes and just disappear...avoid the embarrassment of walking out on a bad decision.

But Sharon Stouffer knew her entire life story now. Had seen her cry. Pamela felt like a fool staying, a worse one for wanting to escape.

If ever there was a stereotypical attorney's office, this was it: imposing and at the same time comforting. Mahogany was everywhere—on the wall-to-wall bookshelves, the desk and its return, the upholstered captain's chairs flanking the floor-to-ceiling windows. Every other space was clothed in scarlet, from the mottled carpet to the Victorian-era wallpaper. And though Pamela wasn't partial to red decor, she had to admit Sharon Stouffer's office was exquisite.

She closed her eyes and remembered the last time she and Paul had been in an attorney's office. Dana had been along. She had referred them to an associate of hers regarding some legal matters in establishing Lifelines. Pamela had felt like a fifth wheel that day and wondered why Paul ever invited her along. Dana, of course, was in the know legally, and Paul held his own. Pamela said not a word and felt like a fool as the other two shot questions back and forth and quickly worked toward a solution.

The door opened and Sharon, a stunning silver-haired woman in her fifties, returned. "I'm sorry for the interruption, Pamela. But tell me now. Other than these—" she indicated the summons, a check register, and the meager supply of financial records Pamela had been able to compile—"you have nothing else that could help us establish net worth? Tax returns, account statements…"

Pamela shook her head, humiliated by her lack of knowledge but unable to spit out that she had changed her mind and wanted to leave. "He must have moved them from the house a long time ago. There was a filing cabinet…"

"Don't worry, your situation is hardly atypical. We'll be able to subpoena the rest. If you'd like me to proceed, that is."

"Well…what exactly would happen if I decide to…to retain you? I mean, what good would it do me since Paul is…oh, I don't know. I'm completely at a loss here. I'm sorry."

"It's okay, Pamela. I understand how hard this is for you. Let me explain the process to you at least." Sharon leaned forward in the antique swivel chair at her desk and tapped a pen on the notepad in front of her. "Basically, it's my job to protect you. Since Paul has filed, we'll go ahead and sign these documents. Then subpoena your financial records for the discovery process. You know you are entitled to half of everything?"

"Yes. And he's giving me the house on top of that."

"That certainly sounds fair. But many times I find that what one person deems 50 percent is not exactly the case. That's what discovery is for. We want to be sure you come out with what you deserve. Especially since you've been a homemaker for twenty years. At his insistence. Oh, that's another thing. Whatever you do, be sure you don't minimize your lifestyle and expenses right now. Spend what you need—live the same, or even a little above, what you normally would do. And keep detailed records. It will help in the settlement decision. Don't use this time to try to be thrifty."

117

"That's not what Paul told me." Pamela's stomach was queasy with confusion and the dogmatic way Sharon rattled off the facts. "And I can't imagine we'll need to do that discovery, or whatever you called it. He's sending me a list of everything we have. Maybe it's best that I just go along with what he suggests."

Sharon raised her eyebrows and stilled the tapping motion of the pen. "A *list*. And he wants you to agree to it, I'll bet. Tell me something. Did he also say you could contact the attorney he retained if you have questions?"

Pamela's eyes widened. "Yes."

Sharon's expression hardened. "Usually when this happens— and believe me, it does all the time—there's something to hide. Your husband doesn't *want* you to retain your own attorney, Pamela. Mostly because he knows it will be costly—I won't deny that's a valid concern. You're probably looking at a five-thousand-dollar attorney bill. And that's if Paul's fairly decent. By compiling this list and encouraging you to contact *his* attorney, he's trying to show a generous front. That way, no dangerous questions are asked." Sharon's eyes bored into Pamela's. "You must understand that I'm telling you this based on countless other cases—not just to earn myself a pretty sum of money should you desire to retain my services. And incidentally, my record on hunches is unbeaten."

Pamela pressed her heels into the floor, tightening the muscles of her thighs. Her fingers dug into her palms and her teeth were clenched. Even breathing was put on hold.

"Basically, Pamela, there's nothing new under the sun. Your husband wants to look all shiny and clean and generous, but I'd bet my bottom dollar that he's just trying to keep more for himself. That he's got plenty tucked away somewhere you'd never think to look. Money that he's earned and believes he's entitled to keep. Regardless of what he's done to you. I think you owe it to yourself to make *sure* he's being fair."

Pamela released the balled-up fists. Her voice was quiet. "I don't want to fight. You don't know him…he'd *hate* me for this. I just can't bear to cause him—"

"Pamela." Again, Sharon caught Pamela's gaze and held it firmly. But her voice was softer now. "I hear more in your voice than an opposition to fighting your husband for *money*. I've laid out the basic facts for you. But you need to consider all I said against this: If you still love your husband, fight for him until you are *sure* he doesn't want to stay married. Don't sit back and wait for him to come to you. He won't. Go to him. Find out for yourself if there's still a chance. And if you still need me after that, come back and I'll help you."

An exhausting array of emotions stormed in and out of Pamela's days after her consultation with Sharon Stouffer. She rarely had time to consider one before the next came to usurp its place. She had hoped to be in a better place emotionally when her daughter came home from Mexico, but barring Paul's immediate return, Pamela was starting to believe emotional recuperation was pie in the sky.

And as for Sharon's advice to hunt Paul down? The fear of rejection was too powerful.

If Paul ever found out Pamela had met with an attorney, he'd be furious. The consultation alone cost her $250, which she paid for from her own account. There would be no more checks to Sharon. She knew that much at least. Whatever Paul offered—fair or not—would have to be fine.

July 29

Dear Journal,

Almost home free.

Bible school got over a week ago. We're just putting the final touches on the church. And I was sick for the last two days. It's not the greatest place to be sick…can't lay around and watch soaps all day. Can't even really lay around.

I have to admit, I'm so ready to go home. I need my bed, I need a real shower, I need McDonald's, and I need my mom. And in spite of the fact that he's not written me once, I even miss Dad. I don't care how busy Mom claims he is, it bugs me that he couldn't find time to write.

He's always like this when I'm gone. The out of sight, out of mind thing. It's like he totally forgets he has a daughter. Mom says it's not that at all, though she never has offered a better explanation. Sometimes I get sick of hearing her blind defense of him. I'd do it differently, that's for sure. And if I ever get married, I *swear* I will *never* marry a man like my dad. *Never*.

Okay. I'm grumpy. But I guess I'm just horribly homesick. I'd do anything for more time at home before I leave for Belton.

Fifteen

"I *KNEW THIS* was too good to be true." Pamela was already running late, and now this?

"I'm sorry, Pamela," Jim said, "but this isn't negotiable. I promise you he's not going to direct your shots. Just let the guy tag along. Talk to him if you want. Blow him off if you want. But this is his baby, and if he wants to watch you work, we let him."

"Just because he's your friend…" she mumbled under her breath. "This is not the way I work, Jim. You know that. Writers always think they know it all."

"Come on, Pamela. He's not gonna cramp your style. The holiday issue is the biggest one of the year, and you know Chad's article is great. You told me so yourself."

When Jim had assigned her to photograph Christmas traditions of those who owned the century-old homes in one of Minneapolis's most prestigious neighborhoods, Pamela could have kissed him. But now she wanted to spit! Chad Freeman had grown up in one of the mansions around Lake Harriet, the beloved city lake she was heading to today. Two novels he'd written in his earlier years had gained national acclaim, though lately, his literary endeavors were mostly limited to regional poetry and short stories.

"It *is* a great idea, but I don't need his input. He's already done his job; can't you let me do mine? Alone?"

"Not this time, Pamela. I've got to go. And you're late. We'll talk later."

When Pamela finally pulled up in front of a brick mansion overlooking the lake, she was prepared (as much as possible) for a long day dodging the advice of the rich-boy poet she'd read about in the newspapers. He had arrived before her and was leaning against his car—a middle-aged man in a relatively tame sedan, as opposed to the ritzy sports car she'd anticipated— chatting with the lighting assistant. Much to Pamela's surprise, Chad was quick to open her door for her and introduce himself.

"Thanks so much for letting me join you," he said with a grin. "I promise I'll just watch. I gave Jim my word that I wouldn't disturb you in the least. He's pretty impressed with your work, it seems."

"Oh. Well…that's nice to hear."

Chad had changed a bit from the publicity pictures she'd seen of him: He was older than she thought he was—somewhere between forty-five and fifty. His formerly conservative, dark hair had grown long and a bit gray and was tied back with a black strip of leather. On him the look was both masculine and approachable

"And I do appreciate your consideration. I have to admit,

though, I'm not usually so late to a shoot," she said. "So if you'll excuse me, I think I'd better head right up and introduce myself to Mrs. McPherson."

With her lighting assistant in tow, Pamela knocked on the door, which was opened almost immediately by an elderly woman. "Mrs. McPherson?" she asked politely, holding out a hand in greeting. "I'm Pamela Thornton from *Twin Cities At A Glance Magazine* and—"

"Oh…my, my, my. You're not gonna bring all that stuff in, are you? It'll *ruin* my floors!" Pamela read panic in the woman's eyes as they anchored on the metal equipment cart at the bottom of the steps.

Chad heard the comment and rushed to Pamela's aid, taking the woman's papery hand in his own. "Oh, not all at once, Mrs. McPherson. We'll just take what we need." He smiled toward Pamela. "You've met Pamela, I see? She's a *wonderful* photographer. I'll bet you can't wait to see the incredible pictures she takes of your home. She'll make you a star! By the way, I'm Chad—Mortie and Ruby's son. Remember me?"

"Chad Freeman? Why, that's right! I wouldn't have known you at all! All that hair! How *is* your mother, dear? We were so sorry to hear about the Alzheimer's."

"She's healthy and in wonderful hands at Cathedral Heights. And that's an encouragement. Thank you for your concern." He released her hand. "Tell you what—why don't you show us where we can put our shoes. And before we bring any cameras and lights in, I'd love a tour of this spectacular home!" He turned to Pamela with a wink. "Now, I've seen this palace a few times before, but something tells me we're in for an amazing treat today."

Maude McPherson smiled. "Oh, I'd *love* to show you my home. And don't worry about your shoes, really—it's nice and dry outside now, isn't it?"

And then, as soon as Pamela and Chad completed the tour—and Chad flirted his way into Mrs. McPherson's favors—the equipment came right in without any problem at all.

By noon the next day, Pamela had to admit she was glad Chad was a part of the shoot. Not only did he woo and charm the homeowners—most of them wealthy, elderly widows who would have griped at her left and right not to get dust on their Persian rugs—he bewitched Pamela as well with anecdotes his parents had passed down to him of Minneapolis in its earlier days and stories from his own life. He'd visited nearly every country in the world in his pursuit of the consummate writing haven.

"Believe it or not, though, my favorite is a little coffee shop on Lyndale Avenue and Lake Street in Minneapolis. I take my laptop to this spot by the window and write to my heart's content. Too bad the place closes at midnight."

"After all the remarkable places you've been?" Pamela asked.

"The people are so eclectic. They inspire me."

Most surprising of all, not once had Chad interrupted her shots with a single bit of advice. Somehow in the midst of compliments such as *You got it, Pamela! That's exactly how I've foreseen it,* or *I have no doubt you have the most creative viewpoint of any photographer I've ever worked with,* he extracted from her the story of her life—her northern Minnesota upbringing; the divorce she was so desperate to avoid; the up and down cycle of her emotions; and her apprehension about Angie's homecoming.

"Your husband's the one who stands to lose," he said at one point. "I've never found anyone I love enough to spend a lifetime with—but I definitely believe that's the way it should be. My mother is in a nursing home for Alzheimer's patients, but Dad goes every day to see her. He's totally devoted to her. Your husband may think a simple divorce will free him from your marriage, but the legal process isn't what really defines or disentangles a relationship. At least not for you. Your heart does that. And I'll bet it's no easy task to tell your heart that it's over after this long."

Pamela pulled her eye away from her viewfinder and smiled sadly. "It isn't. At least for *me*. Paul seems to have walked away unscathed."

"Oh, you can be sure he'll have a price of his own to pay."

"You have *no* clue how badly I wish that would happen! I think that if he and that…that woman— I lay awake at night dreaming up ways to get back at them. I want them to feel the pain I live with at their expense." Pamela looked down again, embarrassed for revealing her bitterness to this near stranger. "I'm sorry, Chad. That was uncalled for."

He winked. "No problem. I can't tell you how often I've been told I'm in the wrong profession. Being a talk show host might not be bad. I have a unique ability to draw out the best in people!"

"And the worst?" She smiled an awkward response.

"You were just being honest, Pamela."

Pamela felt his eyes on her often after that—and toward the end of their final day together, she gave up the remaining bit of reserve that usually kept her from connecting with people she worked with. Something deep inside responded to his friendliness and the warmth of his glance.

Pamela had to admit it felt good to be with a man, to be so obviously appreciated and to converse so easily. Deep down she understood that his admiration had just as much to do with her as a woman as it did with her profession.

When they parted, Chad took Pamela's hand in his. "You are a very talented, very beautiful woman, Pamela. You need to know that. Don't let your ex-husband destroy any of that."

She had tears in her eyes. "I won't. Thank you."

He was silent for a moment, his hand warm around hers. "I've really enjoyed these past few days. I'm just a little disappointed they went by so quickly. I hope, for your sake, that your marriage works out…but if things don't go as you hope," he grinned, almost shyly, "could I call you? Sometime later…down the line?"

Pamela couldn't help but laugh. "A date?"

Chad grinned again. "Or a simple cup of coffee?"

"Well…I don't know…"

Chad threw an arm over her shoulder and squeezed. "Don't worry. It won't be until you're ready."

Sixteen

MINNEAPOLIS–ST. PAUL International Airport had been under construction for as long as Pamela could remember, making for horrendous traffic problems and parking nightmares. She'd accounted for all of this, but even so, according to the overhead monitor in the terminal, Angie's flight had already arrived.

Pamela took the escalator down to the baggage area and immediately spotted Todd, one of the Hoyt mission team members, wrestling a bag from the carousel. She watched, amused, as the nonathletic Todd dropped a bag to the ground and pushed his horn-rimmed glasses higher up on his nose before picking up the cumbersome duffel and lugging it off to the side.

Pamela craned her head to find Angie. She was harder to spot—a mere drop in a sea of other Minnesota blondes. But there she was, chatting with the other kids, standing near her huge duffel, her backpack slung over one shoulder.

Pamela hurried over and wrapped her arms around Angie, who was a good three inches taller than Pamela. "My goodness! You grew!"

"Mom!" Angie grinned and pointed to the bright yellow platform tennis shoes that added at least two inches to her height. "Like 'em? I did the whole bargaining thing and got an awesome deal."

"Do I like them? Hmmm. Do I have to answer that?"

"Oh, Mom! Aren't they great?"

Pamela's glance took in the whole of Angie, all tan and blonder than ever. She wore a pair of baggy denim jeans, frayed at the bottom, and an ugly striped, scoop neck T-shirt that reminded Pamela of the worst of the '70s. Angie was the spitting image of Pamela as a girl, but today there was something of Paul in her, around the eyes maybe. The thought was mildly discomfiting and Pamela shook it off.

"The shoes aren't my favorite, no. But I will admit they *are* you. And you're way past my influence in the wardrobe department!"

"Don't worry, Mrs. T.," said Todd, grimacing at Angie's shoes. "I hate 'em too!"

Angie slugged him on the shoulder. "That's because you have no taste." Then she hugged him. "Oh, Todd, summer went so fast. I'm gonna miss you!"

"We gonna get together before you leave for Belton? I don't take off until the very last week of August."

"Definitely. Call me?"

Angie swapped good-byes and hugs with the other kids she'd spent the summer with and leaned to pick up her duffel. Pamela grabbed another bag and started to head toward the checkout.

"Man, it seems weird to be home," someone said.

"See you all Sunday!" called Angie. "Don't forget your guitar, Matt! Hasta luego!"

"What's on Sunday?" asked Pamela, linking her arm in Angie's as they made their way past the man checking tags on the luggage and on toward the doors leading out.

"Um…church?" answered Angie, glancing at Pamela.

Pamela nodded but said nothing, for her stomach had, without warning, launched itself into her throat.

"We're supposed to get up and talk about our trip a little—and we thought it would be great to sing some of the Spanish songs we learned." Angie leaned forward to readjust a strap digging into her shoulder. "I thought maybe Dad would be out here circling the airport so you wouldn't have to park."

Pamela's smile was awkward at best. "We'll have to hike. Sorry."

"You in the ramp or the side lot?"

"The ramp. We've got to lug this stuff a ways…sorry."

They trekked to Pamela's car, chatting all the way—or rather Angie chatted while Pamela listened. After throwing her bags in the trunk, Angie hopped into the front seat and continued to gush about the incredible time she had, how poor but unbelievably generous the people of Mexico were, how hard she had worked, and how wonderful it would be to take a real shower again!

"And I have a ton of pictures. And souvenirs for you guys. Maybe we can stop off at Dad's office? I can run in real quick and say hi?"

"I don't think he's around today."

When am I going to tell her?

"That's okay," Angie said. "I can't wait to get home and get unpacked. That plane ride was horrible and I'm starving! Did I tell you about the kid we called Tortilla Boy?"

Not just yet. Don't steal away the vibrancy.

130

But every second that Pamela smiled or laughed seemed a mockery in light of the heaviness in her heart.

"Angie…"

"Yeah?"

"Oh, honey." She licked her lips and started again. "Angie, there's something I need to tell you. Your father…the reason he didn't e-mail…Dad left, Angie. He's moved to Los Angeles."

"What?" Pamela felt Angie's stare and turned to look briefly into her eyes. "You're serious, aren't you?"

"He says he wants a divorce. And…" Her eyes welled up with tears she had prayed would not flow today. "And he thinks he's going to marry Dana Taylor."

"No way!"

Pamela spilled the rest, sparing few details.

For too many moments, Angie was deathly quiet. Only the muffled sounds of the highway filled the car. Pamela longed to turn the radio on to absorb the silence and make words unnecessary. She could feel the anger, see the tension at the corners of Angie's mouth.

"What an *incredible* hypocrite," Angie said finally. "He thinks he can tell people what to do and how to do it—pretend like he's got it all together. And then he just walks away?"

"I know, honey…I know."

"He wanted everyone to think he was the *man*. His reputation was so important that even every little thing *I* did had to be perfect. He couldn't handle losing face. No way, no how."

Pamela had no clue how to respond.

"Los Angeles, huh? Oh, sure. That's probably the only way he can handle it. Disappear from his adoring public."

"I never thought of that," Pamela said, more to herself than to Angie. "Facing everyone here would have been impossible for him."

"You know what's weird, Mom?" Angie's voice was quieter now. "So many of my friends at school have divorced parents. There was something nice about people knowing I wasn't from a broken family. But Dad was never around. We weren't really any different from anybody else. We just fooled ourselves."

Pamela reached over for Angie's hand. "I'm so sorry, honey. I should have tried to—"

"Don't, Mom." Her voice was thick from holding on to tears too long. "I'm glad he's gone! I hated the way he cut you down all the time. I hated that it was so miserable whenever he was home…" She stopped, took a shaky breath. "And I hated how nice he was to Dana all the time."

Pamela stared straight ahead, gripping the steering wheel too tightly. "What?"

"I think I knew." Angie's voice was an embarrassed whisper spoken to the window. "About him and Dana. I've seen them."

"Seen them, Angie?"

"I've seen them at places together and stuff."

"Like in restaurants?"

She nodded. "And the grocery store. And once in the mall. I was sick to my stomach for weeks."

"And you never told me?" Pamela's own stomach was all in a bunch. Had she been the only one in the dark?

"It wasn't anything I knew for certain—and I was scared to say something because all I really had were suspicions. Sure, they were shopping…but they worked together. Ran a homeless ministry. I don't know. I thought…well, if I had been sure, I would've said something. I should have! Man! What a *jerk!*"

"Angela Marie!"

"It's a little late to respect him, don't you think, Mom? I've pretended at it for years and am glad I don't have to anymore. I'm sorry you're hurting. I can't imagine what it must be like to find this out. The thing is, I *hated* the way Dad was sometimes. Especially to you. But it's not like I could say or do anything about it. I'm just a kid."

Angie's eyes penetrated Pamela's silence. Then, in a gentler voice, she said: "Oh, Mom…I wish I'd been here for you."

Wiping away her tears, Pamela reached across again and laid her hand on Angie's knee. And Angie covered it with her own. "Oh, Angie, it's best you weren't. I needed time alone with all this first. And *you* have a life to live."

"It's okay, Mom. I want to be there for you."

"No," Pamela said firmly, with more strength than she really had. "Do *not* assume responsibility for this. I appreciate your support, Angie, but I've got Starla. And I have a responsibility toward *you*. I want to listen to you and…and if you need someone else to talk to, someone professional, we'll find that too. Okay?"

"Okay," she answered softly, wiping moisture from her cheeks. "But…I'll be fine eventually. I really will, Mom. I'm pretty used to him not being around. And I hardly think I'll miss him at school! You're the one this is going to hurt the most."

"The thing I worry the most about is how this will affect your relationships with boys. When you get married, I don't want—"

"Mom, stop! Getting married is just about the last thing I want to do!"

133

The car was silent for a few minutes.

"So, does he want to talk to me, Mom?"

"It doesn't seem so, honey. He thought it best that I be the one to break the news."

"Someday, he'll need to talk, Mom. And I'll be ready."

The maturity of the statement filled Pamela with melancholy. She pulled into the driveway, turned off the car, and reached over and took Angie in her arms. "I love you, honey. And in his own way, I know Dad does, too."

"It's done," Pamela said into the phone when Starla picked up on the other end. She'd spoken to her friend early that morning, mainly to apologize for hanging up on her the last time they'd talked. "I told her, Star."

"What time is it?" Starla said. A bit groggily, Pamela realized.

"Oh! Were you asleep? I'm sorry." She looked at the clock on the stove. Midnight. "Oh, man! I had no idea it was this late! I'm so sorry…"

"Don't worry about it. I just nodded off. So? How'd it go?"

Pamela exhaled deeply, finally feeling the lateness push down upon her. "Okay and horrible. A weird combination of the two." She summarized the conversation she'd had with her daughter, relaying her concern over Angie's ability to emotionally withdraw so easily from her father. "She'll have to deal with it in her own time. I can't push her. But I just hate to see her hurt. The worst for me is trying to be strong—to show a good front for her sake. I'm so afraid she'll try to assume responsibility for my pain."

134

"Don't be your mother, Pammi."

"What's *that* supposed to mean?"

"Think about it. *You* may not think this, but I have a strong hunch that when your dad died, your mom wanted more than anything else in the world to protect you—to keep you going forward with your life. Including not letting you see her fall apart."

Pamela closed her eyes and shook her head. "No—this is different, Star. I have no problem admitting my pain to Angie. My mother was cold. And strong. She didn't need me. She never has. That's just her way."

"Well, either way, just don't be so afraid to show your emotion. It's rough on Angie now, but I have an idea she'll work it out much faster than you will. She's a great kid. I've always known that. Ya did a good job with that one."

"I did, didn't I? I wish we had more than two weeks left together."

"I know. It's gotta be tough. And I've been thinking—you're going to need something to look forward to when she leaves. Why not come to Rabbit Lake for Labor Day weekend? You've said no all summer, but I'd sure love the company for the long weekend."

Pamela sighed. "Okay. I'll think about it. My mom gets back from New Mexico the end of next week…and the responsible part of me says I should go see her."

"Thata girl! Kill two birds with one stone."

"I said I'd *think* about it."

"Think all you want, Pammi...but I won't take no for an answer." She laughed.

"Starla?"

"Yes..."

"Go to bed. You get pushy when you're sleep deprived!"

August 7

Dear Journal,

There's *no way* I'm gonna sleep tonight. And I desperately need to. I am *so* beat! But right now, I don't know if I should cry or beat up my pillow or scream.

Did I know this was coming? It sure felt like it. I mean, in a way the whole scene in the car with Mom today was like a dream. Whenever I saw my dad with Dana (which was more than just once), deep down I did kinda wonder if something was up. I just couldn't let myself think about it. It felt icky. Kinda like *I* was the one doing something wrong.

But now it makes complete sense. That and the fact that Dad was always heading off somewhere with Dana for Lifelines business. I'd never have said this out loud, but sometimes it even bugged me that Mom let him go. Sure, Lifelines was important, but it didn't require nearly as much time as Dad put into it. He ran the program—everyone else worked it. And it wasn't his full-time job.

And Dana? She was *way* too nice to me, always asking me stupid questions about my volleyball games and stuff. Like she cared! Except for Starla, none of Mom and Dad's other friends ever gave me birthday cards. Dana not only did that, but she put money in the envelope. Dad always made some stupid comment about how thoughtful she was. But I *knew* she was just kissing up to him.

I'm so mad right now I could punch a hole in the wall or do something else totally unreasonable! But I need to keep it together for Mom. She's pretty much losing it. Not that she's telling me much. She looks like some sort of cancer patient, though. I saw that as soon as she walked up to me in the airport. And old? She looks practically as old as Gram!

I have to be honest. I wanted so badly to be home. But now I wish I could just disappear. If only I had some assurance that Mom would be okay without me, I'd leave tomorrow for school and start my own life. I don't want to think about any of this. I just want to pretend nothing ever happened. It's all just way too much to take.

Seventeen

"So...WHICH TUX did you decide on?" Dana asked. She had a silk garment bag slung over her shoulder. Paul was at the kitchen table, packing up his laptop.

"The double-breasted," he said. "It's a bit more formal. What about you?"

"The black dress. With the antique earrings you bought me a few years ago."

The two of them had gone shopping for Dana's dress together and had actually ended up with two. "Good, I like that one best anyway."

"Why didn't you say something before?"

He smiled. "Because I thought you really wanted the purple one."

A fleeting memory of Pam crossed his mind. *Do you like my new dress? I thought of you when I picked it out.* He couldn't even remember its color now or if he gave her the approval she constantly sought from him.

"I *hate* the purple one! I only bought it because I thought you liked it!"

He laughed and pulled her into his arms. "Do you have any idea how anxious I am to show you off?"

"Oh, please…"

"Really, Dana. This grand opening tonight is really a big deal. You'll get to meet Phil and everyone else at the bank, and anyone who's anybody in LA will be there. I only wish I'd been on this project from the start. It would've been a phenomenal experience to rub shoulders with all the people who've got their fingers in that little pie. Just wait till you see it. Lanesborough is out of this world."

"Wow! You weren't kidding," Dana muttered two hours later when they'd relinquished their car to a valet and made their way inside Lanesborough Park and Towers, the elite condominium complex/indoor park in downtown LA that Paul's bank had financed.

Paul had toured the complex earlier in the week, but his daytime visit had none of the romance of what awaited them that evening. He escorted Dana down the fragrant wood-chip path through imported greenery and flora to the center of the park where other visitors strolled, admiring the building. The trees overhead were adorned with minuscule white bulbs, and other lights were buried in the ground foliage. The glass dome twenty stories above was more sky than ceiling, a convincing touch that took away all feel of being inside a city high-rise.

"Look up," Paul said, indicating the decks encircling the park from the fourth floor on up. Each resident had a bird's-eye view of the water falling over cliffs, fish swimming in ponds, and lush greenery.

The couple made their way into an open pavilion, past the dance floor where a jazz combo was just setting up, to the table where Phil Cooper, Liberty's president, sat with a striking blonde conversing with another guest. She looked no older than thirty.

"Hello, Phil," Paul said, holding out his hand. "This place is even more phenomenal at night, isn't it? I'd like you to meet Dana."

Phil took Dana's hand in his own. "What a pleasure! I've heard so much about you. I guess it's about time I finally got to meet you." He turned his head to the blonde at the table. "Julia, honey, come join me a minute. This is Paul Thornton and—"

"And you must be his wife," Julia interrupted with a smile, standing to join the group and offering her hand to Dana. Paul felt Dana stiffen at Julia's mistake. "Phil thinks your husband is the best thing since sliced bread."

Paul laughed. "This is Dana, Julia. Only hope I can live up to the compliment."

"You're an attorney I hear?" asked Phil.

"I'm with Patterson, Jacobs, and Cray, yes," she said.

"Good firm," said Phil. "So tell me…what do you think of Los Angeles? Little different from the Midwest, I'll bet?"

"Well, I grew up not too far from here, so it's a bit of a homecoming for me," Paul said, relieved to see a smile return to Dana's face. "I think I can speak for Dana, though, when I say we've thoroughly enjoyed making LA our own. So much to see and do. Talk about night life! Still haven't hit the tourist hot spots though. I promised to take Dana up to the J. Paul Getty Museum one of these days."

"Don't forget to make reservations," Phil said. "Not that I've been there myself—I've just heard you can't get in without them. Sometimes I fear we long-time residents don't enjoy this city nearly as much as we should. I've lived most of my life within twenty miles of here, and it's almost embarrassing to admit, but I think the last time I did any sightseeing was when I was fourteen or fifteen years old. If I'd have had children, maybe I would've made more of an effort."

"Kids are definitely a good excuse. I took my daughter to Disneyland and the *Queen Mary* and all the museums in town when she was around nine or ten." Paul had thought so little of Angie in the past three months that he was surprised at the easy way he brought her into the conversation.

"A daughter? You have other children, too?" Julia asked, looking at Dana.

"Just Angie," Paul said quickly. "And she's all grown up now...starting her first year of college this fall." *Next week,* he thought.

"Isn't that Richard Goodhue?" Paul asked, indicating a portly man chatting with a few other people across the dance floor. To Dana he whispered, "Goodhue was the mastermind behind Lanesborough."

"Sure is," Phil said. "You haven't met then?"

"Not yet."

"Man's a visionary. You oughta hear what he's got in mind now! Huge project out in Long Beach. Will put this to shame. I wouldn't doubt that's what he's after Mayor Lewis for—that's him beside Richard. Like an introduction?"

Paul smiled. "Love one." *The mayor of Long Beach.*

Paul placed a hand across Dana's shoulder, and they followed Phil and Julia toward Goodhue and the mayor. "Richard…Mayor Lewis? Wonderful night. Absolutely phenomenal. I'd like you to meet Liberty's new vice president…"

Just as they were being introduced, a *Los Angeles Times* photographer asked them to gather close for a picture, and everyone circled the mayor and turned toward the camera.

The entire evening was more of the same: a string of networking and social chitchat. And intensely heady and satisfying for Paul.

"What a night!" he sighed happily when he and Dana finally got home at two in the morning.

"I've never met so many people in my life!" Dana tossed her heels into the closet and sank to the bed to massage her toes.

"Have to admit I was a bit nervous about making a good impression. Not only on them, but on you."

"On me? Why would that concern you, Paul? I love you— and the whole night was wonderful." Dana's eyes darkened a bit. "I do feel a little guilty letting Julia and everyone else think I'm your wife, though."

Paul kissed the top of her head, smiling to hear her refer to herself that way. "You're way too sensitive about that, angel. We're basically man and wife anyway. And we're getting married this spring."

"Hopefully," said Dana. "But sometimes I think it would feel more right if we didn't live together."

"Is that what you want?"

"Oh, Paul…not really. It's just that—"

"Good. Because if you think anybody there tonight really paid a bit of attention to our living arrangements or marital status, you are gravely mistaken. What they don't know won't matter two bits in the long run."

"It's not about them. It's more about the way *I* feel."

"Then come here and let me make you feel better," Paul said, reaching for her and running his fingers over her face. "Dana, I love you so much. You know that, right? You know that I have never felt more married…more committed in my whole life?"

He leaned forward and kissed her gently, then pulled her into his arms.

"You looked absolutely phenomenal tonight, by the way."

The next morning, Paul got up before Dana so he could attend the early service at Church of Zion before meeting her at their favorite café for brunch. He grabbed the paper off the front step and routinely paged through, seeking the business page. But he stopped short at the front page of the Metro section.

There, right alongside the feature article about Lanesborough Park and Towers Grand Opening, the *Los Angeles Times* featured the photo of him and Dana, standing with Richard Goodhue, Mayor Lewis, and Phil and Julia. The caption identified them as "Vice President of Liberty National, Paul Thornton, and wife, Dana, partner with Patterson, Jacobs, and Cray."

Paul was tempted to dispose of the newspaper on his way to church. Instead, he buried the Metro section in the other sections and hoped Dana waited until later this afternoon to read the paper. She was sure to hear about the picture at work on Monday anyway.

She'd get over it. It was good publicity, right? It couldn't be all that bad.

Eighteen

PAMELA DROWNED HER nerves in a cup of coffee loaded with cream and sugar and grabbed the car keys from the hook by the door. She leaned against the back doorjamb, waiting for her daughter to come down from her bedroom. In all of Angie's eighteen years, there had been no more than three or four Sundays their family had missed going to church. And as of this moment, her daughter still had no clue that Pamela had skipped the entire summer.

It wasn't that Pamela had avoided telling her. It was just that Angie had enough to deal with. Every day she'd gone the gamut of emotion—from anger to sadness to frustration to tolerance. There was no way to compress the healing process, but at least Angie was talking freely and thus far, showed no signs of the type of depression that could ruin her college experience. Her vision seemed clear.

"Let's go, Angie—we're going to be late," Pamela called, heading to the car. Angie was quickly at the back door, pulling it closed behind her.

"It seems weird not having Dad drive us to church, doesn't it?"

"Very." Pamela looked sideways and breathed in deeply. She remembered clearly the last time the three of them had driven to church, the weekend before Angie left for Mexico. "Sundays have been the hardest for me. It's the one thing we all did together. I've...I've not been back yet, Angie."

"Back to church? You're kidding!"

Pamela turned away and blinked away the tears. "It's just been too hard for me, all alone and all. Not going just kind of happened."

"All summer?"

"I couldn't, Angie. I was so embarrassed, I couldn't bear to face anyone. My life at Hoyt was so wrapped around you and Dad, and with you gone—and him—I couldn't bring myself to walk through the doors. I couldn't deal with the questions—the pity. I thought it might get easier after a few weeks, but the opposite ended up happening."

"I'll bet you feel *really* weird going today, then," said Angie.

"My hands are shaking." She offered a tentative smile. "I should probably have skipped the coffee."

"It's different for me, I guess. Church is like home. Comfortable. I feel good there. And I want to see my friends and all." She paused and Pamela smiled in spite of herself. "Hey, I know...instead of staying with the group, I'll come sit with you as soon as our Mexico presentation is done. How's that?"

"I'd really like that, honey. Thank you."

"No problem. I need it, too, I think. I'm only here for two Sundays anyway. I guess you and I should just stick together for now."

Pamela made it through the service, but that was the easy part. Afterward, a crowd assembled around her, welcoming her back. Their smiles were knowing and their hugs sympathetic. And thankfully, all the questions were Paul-less inquiries: Did Angie have fun in Mexico—they certainly did a nice job this morning, didn't they? When are you leaving to take her to Belton? Did you sign up for the women's dinner in September yet? Liz tells us you're working more with the magazine these days…

And there were a few promises for invitations to dinner and one to brunch after the service, which she politely declined.

Liz met up with her as Pamela headed downstairs to get coffee. "I'm so glad you're back, Pamela. We've missed you so much. I didn't know whether or not I should have stopped by, or…"

"It's okay, Liz."

"And I didn't want to keep bugging you with phone calls. It seemed like you wanted to be left alone."

"Really, Liz, I'm fine. I've had a lot going on."

"Harm and I would love to take you out for dinner one of these days."

"How about if I give you a call?"

"Hi, Mrs. Thornton," said the young mom serving coffee at the pass-through window of the church kitchen. A baby was asleep in the sling around her neck.

"Congratulations on your baby, Christy." Pamela smiled and reached for a cup of coffee. "A boy?"

"Yes," beamed the girl, turning so Pamela could better admire his swollen, pimpled face. "Brandon David. He's three weeks old today, aren't you, pumpkin. Mommy's beautiful baby." She ran a finger under his chin. "Can you wake up, pumpkin? Open your little eyes?"

Pamela could hardly think of another generic thing to say, so she just smiled, reached for another sugar cube, and wandered among the conversation circles, searching for a group she might mingle with.

She felt like a stranger. The familiar burgundy carpet of the fellowship hall seemed suddenly gaudy and unwelcoming. And the noisy din of the room no longer comforted, but alienated. Even the coffee she sipped from her Styrofoam cup was bitter. But then again, it always had been pretty rotten stuff.

"Did someone organize meals for Betsy Boeddinger? She had a girl, I hear," one woman was saying. "Somehow, I missed the sign-up sheet."

"What was up with the microphone this morning? It was buzzing like crazy all during the sermon. Thought I was gonna scream!"

"You know, I sure hope the committee is planning the women's event for before Thanksgiving this year," said someone on her right. "December gets so busy."

Pamela had a crazy urge to dump her coffee on the floor and run from the mundane conversation and petty concerns of these church people. And though most everyone she passed offered a friendly greeting, it seemed trite. Insincere. As much as she wanted to be ignored, she was also frustrated by the lack of concern everyone had for Paul's betrayal. Here she stood, cheated and deserted by her husband, and no one even blinked an eye! Inside, behind her polite smile, Pamela screamed, *Aren't they going*

to express some outrage? Paul left with Dana Taylor, for Pete's sake!
One of our own!

And then Tina Rohlersson was beside her, rescuing her. "Stand with me," she whispered. "I'll help get you through. This was the hardest day for me, too."

151

Pamela thought back to all those times she had avoided the *d* word around Tina—and the clouds cleared. Maybe the truth was that these people *did* care. They just had no clue what to say. And when it came right down to it, nothing anyone said would make a bit of difference anyway.

August 15

Dear Journal,

I have to say, these have been the hardest days of my life.

I feel like I'm the mom and Mom is…well, Mom's just not herself. And of course I understand, but it's still hard. When I get home from doing stuff with my friends, I hear her crying in her room—it's so horrible sounding. Like a whimpering puppy. And she keeps this pile of books on divorce on the table and is constantly asking me if she can read stuff out loud to me—passages that she says are *just* like Dad or *just* like her. I'm sad for her and all, but I get a little tired of hearing it. I guess the books must help her feel normal or something. But I think it's kinda weird. She practically lives in those books.

I know I should be praying day in and day out for God to bring Mom and Dad back together. But sometimes I wonder if Mom might someday be happier without Dad around. I mean, he wasn't the greatest to her. Like Terri's dad. I love hanging out at her house. Her dad is so sweet—and the coolest Christian. Terri told me that ever since she was little, he prays with her and her brother every day. And I love watching the way he is toward Terri's mom. You can just see they love each other. I always wished my mom could have that.

For as long as I can remember, Mom's been trying too hard to make it seem like our family was perfect. Especially when I had friends come over. Sometimes I get this idea Mom really didn't know we had problems. That she thought we were normal. Other times, it seemed as if she was wearing a mask. A smile that wasn't really a smile. I've always known she wasn't as happy as she made everyone think she was. How could she be, with the way Dad was?

I told my friends about all this, and they let me cry awhile. And it felt good. I don't like to cry in front of Mom. She just gets weepy all over again.

153

August 16

Dear Journal,

   This afternoon, some guy called for Mom. Usually when the phone rings, it's for me or someone from work calling for Mom. She was in the shower, so I took a message. He told me to tell her, "Chad called about getting together." When I told Mom, she actually smiled.

   Hmmm. What's up with that?

Nineteen

"LOOK AT THIS! It's from Melinda Henshaw!" Angie said, dropping a pile of mail on the kitchen table and tearing open an envelope.

"Do I know her?" Pamela asked.

"She's the girl who's gonna be my roommate at Belton. I thought about writing her; I just never did. But she wrote me. How nice! Listen to this—"

The phone rang and Pamela reached for it. "Hello, Thornton residence."

She was greeted by muffled air.

"Hello?" Pamela repeated.

"Mrs. Thornton?" A woman's voice.

"Yes…"

And then a click. It was the fourth time in a week the same thing had happened. The second time the woman called—and it had been the same voice—she'd asked for Paul. Some numbers she'd learned to screen out using Caller ID. This one came up "unavailable."

"Who was that?"

"Wrong number...I guess. So what's Melinda have to say?"

"Not all that much—but she does want to talk before I leave. Isn't that cool? Mostly she's wondering if I have a decent stereo or if she should bring hers. And she wants to know what other stuff I'm bringing. That way we won't crowd our room up with all kinds of extra stuff. She sounds really nice, though! I'm gonna go try and call her now. Is that okay?"

Angie was so excited, Pamela could hardly resist a smile. "Of course!"

Pamela sorted through the remaining mail and came across an envelope addressed in Dana's familiar flowery script. Pamela immediately sliced her opener through it and pulled out a typed, one-page sheet titled "The Thornton Estate." It was the list Paul had mentioned earlier in the summer.

How dare he let that woman take care of his personal business!

On the top half was a brief summary of all their assets, ranging from bank accounts, investments, and insurance policies to their cars and Pamela's higher-end jewelry, including the newer, diamond-encrusted wedding ring Paul had given her on their ten-year anniversary to replace the simple solitaire and band she'd worn until then.

On the bottom of the paper was an itemized list, adapted from the above items, of what Paul proposed to sign over to Pamela—the smaller of the two savings accounts, one of the insurance policies, her car and jewelry, and a few of the investment accounts which, as noted in parentheses, would turn over monthly dividends that alone would be more than enough for her to live on.

Base amount, not including annual interest: $2.2 million was typed at the very bottom of that column. And beside it Paul had printed: "The house and everything in it is yours. Last appraised value: $425,000. There's not much left on the mortgage, so I'll pay it off before the divorce is final."

Below that, he'd scribbled in a different-colored ink: "Don't worry about Angie's tuition. I committed to that long ago and I won't let her down. I'll be in touch."

The whole thing felt so cold, so black-and-white. Nothing of Paul was evident on this sheet of paper she held in her hands—save, of course, his scribbled notes about the house and Angie. And just the faintest hint of musk.

"O dear Lord…what am I supposed to do with *this?*" Pamela wondered out loud. Her stomach was rumbling and she felt hot.

"With what, Mom?"

"Oh…" She looked up and saw her daughter coming from the kitchen. "It's nothing. Did you get through to Melinda?"

"First tell me what bug just bit *you.*"

Pamela got up and hurriedly stuffed the paper in the desk drawer across the room.

"No. Don't do that! It's from Dad, right?" Angie went to the desk and pulled the paper from the drawer, scanning it before Pamela had a chance to grab it away.

"That's not your business, Angie! Please…"

"So. This is it, huh?" She plopped down on the couch and scanned the list. "Just draw a line down the center and call it even? Except of course for the house. Yours. And look here. Gee, he's washing his hands of me, too. Pay my college tuition to get me off his back."

"That's not his intent. Stop. Please?"

"Why, Mom? So I don't put it all in black and white for you? Dad thinks life is a Kit Kat bar that he can just split between the two of you! Can't you see that!"

Pamela shook her head and leaned against the desk. "I don't know, honey. I don't know anything anymore. Anyway, what can I do about it?"

"Look, Mom. Your marriage has always been off-limits to me, which is fine. Maybe you're doing all you can do. I guess it's not my business what you do. But *I'm* not part of the assets he can just distribute."

"Honey, he's just trying to be—"

"Mo-om! Listen to yourself! How can you defend him? He's never really cared about me. Not now. Not when I was a kid. Oh sure, he came to my games every once in a while or whatever. But don't you think I knew he did it because he *had* to? You *wanted* to be there for me. There's a big difference between desire and obligation."

Pamela shook her head sadly. "I'm sorry, honey."

"Stop *saying* that! I'm not blaming you. Just don't try to pretend it's okay. You always did that."

"I did not pretend," Pamela said, stronger now. "Angie, I did the best I could with your father. You need to know that. I loved him. I loved him very much."

"Yeah, with some sort of blind loyalty."

"Angela, you're out of bounds now!"

Angie sighed. "Okay, I'm sorry. I just can't relate to your kind of self-sacrificing love. I can't remember the last time Dad was affectionate to you…or acted like he loved you. It was always you doing the loving."

"He used to be different. Really. I remember one time when I was sick—*really* sick—when I was pregnant with you. Nothing but an A&W Mama Burger and a root beer float would calm my nausea. The only A&W franchise was over half an hour away. Dad was in the middle of a big project, but when I mentioned how badly I craved one of those floats, he stopped what he was doing and drove out to get me one. Of course, it was completely melted by the time he got back…

"And there was the time he planned a surprise party for my thirtieth birthday. I felt like a queen for the day. He even paid for some of my family from up north to stay at the downtown Hyatt."

"I remember that." Angie smiled and the tiniest bit of tension left her face. Pamela gave up her perch at the desk and joined her daughter on the sofa.

"And I'll never forget how he cried when you were born. All those tears running down his face at the mere sight of you. He adored you! And I used to love watching him hold you when he got home from work—nothing was more beautiful than the look on his face when he said hello to his baby girl. When you got a bit older, he melted whenever you'd run up to him with your arms open wide, begging to be swooped up to the ceiling."

Pamela moved closer to Angie and put her arms around her. "It wasn't always bad, honey. You'll have to take my word on that one. I'm angry, too. And so hurt I can hardly see straight some days. I fooled myself a lot about my marriage. Our family life. Especially during these past few years. But please understand that my love for your dad goes way back. I can't just disconnect it, no matter how simple it may look from the outside. And there's no doubt he loved you very much. It's just so complicated. Don't throw it all out. Please?"

"Oh, Mom…" Angie's tears were falling now. "It's so much easier for me to hate him—to forget about him. I know it's not right. I love him, too; that's why it's just so hard."

"Love is why this all hurts so much, Angie. Mostly because our love for him just wasn't enough."

The final days before Pamela and Angie left for Illinois breezed by in a rush of packing, saying good-bye to friends, organizing, and last-minute shopping. And then, all too quickly, the day of Angie's departure was here. The night before, the two of them had loaded Angie's little car to the gills with boxes and bedding, clothes and toiletries. Nearly her entire bedroom, in fact, was stuffed into the Saturn Paul had bought for Angie's seventeenth birthday.

At four-thirty in the morning, before the sun was even up, Angie backed her car out of the driveway. Holding to Interstate 94, the little car wound its way east through the familiar sections of Minneapolis and St. Paul. When it carried Pamela and Angie across the St. Croix River into Wisconsin, the sun had finally edged up over the horizon. A comfortable quiet reigned supreme during those early hours, and Pamela couldn't help but stare lazily at her daughter as she drove—trying to find her little girl in the confident young woman beside her.

She had expected the trip would be their one last chance to talk about the divorce, especially since the past week had been too busy to do much more than prepare. But, nearly as soon as she raised the topic, Angie shut it down.

"Mom, if you're doing this whole talking-it-out bit for me, let's not anymore, okay? I'm handling it. And right now, I want to focus on what's coming. I'm so excited I can hardly stand it, and I want to stay that way. Can we leave Dad alone?"

For the remainder of the drive they talked about everything else except Paul and the imminent divorce. And then, in what seemed a blink of an eye, the two of them were immersed in the unmistakable high of new and old students descending upon the campus of Belton University. Pamela and her daughter made their way to Angie's dorm, a beautiful brick building that seemed almost Ivy League, met her roommate and a few of the other girls on the floor, and unloaded the car.

Hours later—after Pamela had done all she could to ensure Angie's adjustment—mother and daughter stood by the taxi that would take Pamela to the airport. They had planned for this quick departure, and though the energy and excitement of being at school had brought Angie bravely thus far, now—in front of the cabbie—she finally broke down.

For this last moment, she reverted to Pamela's little girl again.

"Oh, Mom…" Angie said, finding no embarrassment at all in falling into her mother's arms. "I *already* miss you. How am I going to do this without you?"

Pamela wiped away her own tears and held Angela's face between her hands. "Don't even ask the question, honey, because you just will. You will because you are ready. And because you need to. It's a whole new world for you, now. You're all grown up."

"Are you…are you going to be all right, Mom? You know…without me?"

Pamela breathed in deeply, feigning strength for Angie's sake. "Angela Marie Thornton, I *promise* you I will be okay."

"I love you so much, Mom."

"Oh, honey…I love you more than life itself."

Pamela opened her eyes when the cabin pressure and airspeed changed. Below her the multitudinous lights of Minneapolis twinkled their welcome. She closed her eyes in disgust. Home. The last place on earth she wanted to be.

There was no way she was going to be all right.

Her cheeks felt stiff where the tears had dried before she'd dozed off. Luckily the seat beside her was empty and no one witnessed her pain. Oh, sure, Angie would be home for Thanksgiving, Christmas, and other holidays over the next few years. But her little girl was gone forever.

Did Paul have any clue what it felt like to be so alone? Everyone but her had a life. Every book she'd read on divorce promised things would get better…even Starla said stuff like that.

But no kind word or bit of professional advice would erase her desire to just stay on the plane and never go home.

August 31

Dear Journal,

I love college! I love college! I love college! Sure, it's only been a few days, and I haven't started classes yet, but living in the dorms is like one big slumber party. I don't remember ever being so happy in my life.

The only thing that bugs me is that when I wake up in the morning, before I'm completely awake, I have this weird sense of sadness. It takes me a nanosecond to figure it out. My parents are getting *divorced*. Other than that little bit, I'm surprised at how little I find myself thinking about it. There's a part of me that feels guilty about wanting to escape it all.

My check for tuition came in the mail today. From Dad. And when I saw it, all I could think of was that list he sent Mom—me on one side, the house on the other. He put his new phone number on the note and said he'd call soon so we could "talk."

Great. I live in fear of the phone ringing now. What are we supposed to talk about? I don't *want* to hear his side of it. I don't *want* him to explain how he feels. I don't *want* to have to tell him how lousy I think this whole thing is.

But I also don't want to tell him I think Mom's going to be happier without him in the long run. That will give him the idea I approve of what he's done. And I don't! What am I doing? I don't want to think about this!

Okay. Readjust.

Melinda. She's great. She's from a town in Illinois called Rockford, has long red hair, and is just about as tall as I am. We have the same taste in clothes—so our wardrobes just doubled! She's got a boyfriend at Belton—a guy she met at the camp she worked at all summer. His family lives near Chicago, so she often goes to his house on Sundays. So far, nothing about her bugs me. But then, we're a lot alike.

164

I got all the classes I wanted: Art Appreciation, Old Testament History, Philosophy, and Composition. I'm also taking Bowling, believe it or not! Poor Melinda ended up with almost nothing she needed—and she's still on the waiting list for one she absolutely has to have this semester. She's already declared nursing as her major so her courses are pretty set in stone.

Classes start Monday. Labor Day. I guess they figure we might as well labor. Hah.

Twenty

EARLY FRIDAY AFTERNOON, Pamela tucked a small bag in the backseat of her car and set off for Starla's cabin. It had been a tough week for her learning to live without Angie all over again. And though she was looking forward to going north, to being with Starla, she was also apprehensive about seeing her mother.

Joan had called Wednesday night to let Pamela know she was home safe, and as casually as possible Pamela told her mom she would be in Lewisville Monday morning.

"Just for a day? Why not come for the weekend? Or…is something wrong? Is it Angie being gone? You never come home, Pammi, are you all right?"

She sighed. "I'm fine, Mom. Starla invited me to her cabin on Rabbit Lake for the weekend. And I just thought it would be good for you and me to get together since I'll be up that way."

"Didn't you just start working full-time?"

"Yes…"

"And you can take a day off? Maybe you should wait until—"

"It's Labor Day, Mom. Listen, if you'd rather I not come—"

"That's ridiculous. I don't see enough of you as it is."

That's the way it always was with her mother, Pamela thought now as she drove. Go one way, and she made you feel you should be heading another. Head that way and Joan turned it all around again!

Ahead of her, a car stopped for a traffic light. The man driving leaned over and kissed the woman beside him. And just that quick, Pamela was angry, a red-hot jealous anger that had nothing to do with the kissing couple. Paul had never once kissed her passionately in the car, or anywhere else for that matter. At least, not for a very long time.

Had he ever really wanted her like that? Or had Pamela just fit his bill for a wife? She floored the pedal to pass the obnoxious lovers. Why did everyone else but her have a partner?

After a while, Pamela turned on the radio and tried to forget. Finally, the soothing music began to thread its way through the disarray to calm her shattered emotions. She was closing in on Lake Mille Lacs—the ugly strip malls were far behind. Lush green land rolled from one knoll to the next, and a deer bounded across the two-lane highway a quarter mile ahead. The pressure in her head melted away as mile after mile of lake raced by the window.

Surprisingly, for a holiday weekend, traffic was quite bearable. Pamela would have expected more of a rush of city folk to enjoy these final days of summer. As clear as the roads were this evening, Pamela made it to Rabbit Lake in record time, even braving a stop at the Super Valu for a half gallon of mocha chip ice cream and the ingredients for chocolate chip cookies.

Pamela's tires crunching the dirt road announced her arrival, and Starla came outside to greet her and accept the offering of ice cream. "Ya musta read my mind!"

"Oh, no. It had little to do with you, Starla. I thought I'd die if I didn't get some decent chocolate into my system!" Pamela followed her friend into the cabin, feeling a rush of gratitude at having this other life to escape to right now.

167

An evening chill drifted from the lake as the sun began to dip toward the horizon. "You too warm for a fire?" Starla asked later, after the two of them prepared and devoured a homemade pizza.

"I'm always cold; you know me. I was just gonna start coffee."

Starla donned her red kimono and laid the fire while Pamela pulled a sweatshirt over her tank top and men's pajama bottoms and took her spot on the couch with a mug of coffee.

"Okay, Pammi. I've been saving this little bit of news all night." Starla plopped down on the chair next to the couch. "Guess who called me yesterday? I'll give you a hint. He's a very old—as in auld lang syne, not age—acquaintance of ours. A musician."

"I've never known any musicians."

She grinned over the rim of her cup. "Someone we knew in high school...played guitar...long stringy hair..."

"I haven't got a clue, Star."

"Ken Turner."

"Who?"

"Ken. Ken Turner! You remember..."

"Oh!" Pamela laughed out loud at the picture the name conjured: greasy hair, round face, intense eyes, scrawny legs. "How could I forget the Tiny Tim of Lewisville High! He called *you?* Why on earth?"

"His sister, Tracy, is a patient of mine. She was about four grades ahead of us, but we figured out a few months ago that we sort of knew each other. Turns out Ken lives on Sunset Lake, which is only about fifteen miles from here. Anyway, Tracy told him I have a cabin up here, and he called to see if I knew anybody who was looking for a place. He's a Realtor, sort of. Sounds like he just started." Starla stretched her legs in front of her and leaned against the front of the chair.

"Unless he's really changed, he hardly strikes me as the Realtor type." Pamela lifted her coffee mug to her face and let the steam mottle her skin. "Did you happen to ask if he still writes those spooky songs and plays the ukulele?"

"He played guitar, ya weirdo!"

Starla laughed at Pamela's reminder of the high school talent show when Ken had impersonated Tiny Tim's "Tiptoe Through the Tulips" with such fervor, they had all been a little stunned. Stunned and nervous. Ken had been different from everyone else at a time when different just wasn't okay.

"You know, that's one person I might have gone to a twenty-year reunion just to get a peek at."

"Pammi! Listen to yourself! You sound like you're still in junior high. And I'll bet there's not a bit of Tiny Tim left in him anymore. Men always get better with age, lucky dogs. Didn't ya think Ken was kind of cute, in a different sort of way?"

"Cute? No, not in *any* sort of way! He was *weird*, Starla."

"Better watch your p's and q's. He's a Christian now."

"He told you that?"

"Sort of just came out in the conversation."

"Well, that's an about-face. He was pretty much of a heathen, smoking pot all the time, dressing scary, not to mention all the other stuff he probably did. I can't imagine him…normal."

"*Normal*, Pammi? By that I take it you mean business suits and ties?"

"Well, you said he sells real estate."

Starla rolled her eyes. "All I know is that I'm gonna drive over tomorrow morning and take a look at the cabin he's selling. He's having quite a time finding a buyer, and I have a patient who may just bite."

"I'll come along."

"Really?"

"Sure. He's probably safe. You know, selling real estate and all."

"Oh, I forgot to mention he only does that part-time. The rest of the time he writes music. Christian music. I get the idea he kind of fell into the real estate thing by accident."

"Pays the bills, I'll bet." Pamela pictured a forty-year-old Ken, cross-legged on a beach, strumming a guitar, receding hair stringy and hanging down his back. And singing his own rendition of "They Will Know We Are Christians."

"Actually he's done rather well in the music industry. His songs are performed by some bigwigs in the industry."

"Oh?" Pamela looked at her sideways. "Really?"

The dying fire needed attention, and while Starla stoked it, Pamela headed to the kitchen to mix cookie batter. "This stuff may be deadly to my body, but it sure is a great fix."

"To missing Angie?" Starla called from the living room.

"Yeah. The plane ride was horrible, Star. And yet as much as I miss her, I'm glad for her, too. She loves it so far. That's what makes it bearable for me."

"Remember how great those first few weeks of school were for us? I thought I'd died and gone to heaven!"

Starla joined her in the kitchen, and they leaned against the counter, ate half the batter, and baked the meager remains, reminiscing the whole time about the good old days.

"You know, I was thinking…" Pamela said after a while. "I've really put on weight since college. I know that bugged Paul. And if there were other things I could have changed…"

"Pamela! Don't you start doing that. I mean, when your husband chooses another woman over you, it's pretty normal to ask yourself what's wrong. But in this case, I don't think even Paul could say it had much to do with you. I mean look at you! You're *not* overweight. You're beautiful, Pammi! Plus, you're talented and smart and…"

Starla grabbed a still-hot cookie and dropped a broken portion in her mouth. "Heh meh try te blem some—" she swallowed—"to pick apart some personal attribute of yours, but was that really the issue? Your marital problems went far deeper than that, Pammi."

"I know all that, Starla. Sometimes the thoughts just drive me crazy, that's all. And then I start obsessing about a body overhaul!"

Starla laughed. "Complete with electrolysis and liposuction? Let's go, girl! Make the appointment! I could use a little nip and tuck myself!" She poked her finger at the girth beneath her kimono, then reached over to hug her friend. "This isn't about the way you look, honey. Really."

"I know that, Star. It's just hard sometimes. Having Angie

home kept the thoughts at bay. I'm just glad I have to get up and go to work every day again now. I think I'd go crazy if I didn't have that."

"My prediction is that you're going to thrive on the chance to really explore your talent."

"Jim's been giving me great projects all summer. I get so into what I do that the days just fly by. It's the weekends that get me. I *hate* Sundays."

"Have you considered going back to church again?"

"No. Not yet. And *not* Hoyt. I handled it the two weeks I went with Angie because I had to. But I'm done there."

"Okay, then…"

"Everyone there knows I built my entire life around a man who dumped me. I didn't finish school because Paul told me to quit. I didn't seriously pursue my career because he wanted me at home. I kept his social calendar, entertained his business associates. I even dressed the way he wanted me to! Standing there in that fellowship hall, all I could think was what was going through all those people's minds when they looked at me. And I felt like a fool."

Starla closed her eyes and nodded. "I'm sorry, Pammi."

"It's not anyone's fault, Star. I'm just not ready to throw myself into a place where I won't have the same life anymore. Sometimes I'm not even sure it was ever my life to begin with. Does that make sense?"

"Very much so. If it's any encouragement, I never thought it was either. You made yourself over to fit into Paul's world." She reached for another cookie.

Pamela bent to take the last sheet from the oven, quiet for a few moments while she considered Starla's words. "Can I tell you something?"

"Sure."

"Promise you won't say I told you so?"

"Of course not."

"Okay. I resisted coming back to your cabin all summer, but this is the only place I feel whole. Myself. You know that? It's like everything back in Minneapolis just stays put. I come here with nothing but me and I can think more clearly. Sometimes I wish I could stay here forever."

"It's an escape. That's why I've always loved it so much, too." Starla smiled gently and looked toward the deck. "Ya know, why don't you take a walk out on the dock? Heaven is so close on nights like these, I sometimes think I can touch the face of God. Looks like there's even enough moonlight to see by. Most often, it's so dark you can't find the ground!"

"It's practically freezing!"

"Oh, get off it, Pammi. It's at least sixty degrees. Go on, get outta here. I'll do up these dishes and maybe have just one more little cookie."

Pamela sat on the end of the dock for a very long time that night. At first she fought the urge to go back inside and hunker down under the quilts on her bed. Instead, she wrapped herself in the itchy Indian blanket Starla sent out and watched the water. A loon drifted by, stopping to stare, and when Pamela didn't move, it swam away, disinterested. She could hear it call across the lake a while later and was surprised to hear another answer, closer by. Goose bumps skittered up and down her arms at the characteristic warble of their throats.

Other than the loons, she thought how emptied of sound the air seemed...deathly quiet. But soon she realized it wasn't quiet at all. Pamela was simply used to the clamor of the city—the honking, electric buzz, airplanes, voices. Now, she began to pick up on the music of the lake, and as her awareness grew, so did the cacophony of sounds. Then, slowly, the discord blended in perfect harmony.

A firefly buzzed near her ear and blinked as it passed. The lake lapped rhythmically at the sandy shore. A squawk of a distant bird, a barking dog. And someone way around the bend was talking quietly. So quietly, Pamela couldn't make out words, only the cadence of a human voice.

What was that Starla had said about touching the face of God? Pamela certainly was aware of His presence. And for the first time in a very long while, she felt the urge to talk to Him. "It's been so long, Lord...and I can't help but wonder if You even hear me these days."

And after that first broken phrase, she just started talking out loud, sharing with Him all her disjointed, disorganized thoughts, even her anger. Pamela sensed Him listening. She could almost feel His arms around her. And if she had been cold, now she was warm, even when the breeze blew against her face.

She let the peace of the lake leak into her soul and calm her. The battle still raged. But as He did every time she asked, God came near to Pamela and comforted her with His presence.

Starla was asleep when Pamela wandered inside, and she

went immediately to the loft. She closed her eyes, and when she next opened them, it was to the bright sun beating down upon her through the window above her bed. She felt cleansed and renewed—the first unbroken sleep she'd had since she'd last been north.

Twenty-One

NOT IN A MILLION years would Pamela have guessed the dusty-haired, sinewy man who opened his door to their knock was the same Ken Turner she and Starla once knew from Lewisville High School.

Pamela went dry in the mouth and displaced all etiquette—an amazing feat in itself considering her religious adherence to Miss Manners. But she could barely drag her eyes away from his face, and wouldn't have at all except Starla interrupted her staring with a boisterous, "Boy, it's great to finally see ya again, Ken!"

Pamela smiled weakly, "Hi, Ken. It is…it's been such a long time." Her eyes were glued to the scarred flesh covering the left side of his face from forehead to neck, a disfigurement she just wasn't prepared for.

Ken touched his face and smiled. His voice was surprisingly gentle—not deep, but laced with a bit of a raspy air. "Changed a bit since high school, haven't I? I've come to almost look forward to the reaction."

It took Pamela an embarrassed moment to realize Ken was addressing her shock.

"I used to only show my good side." He turned to model. "Still quite handsome, don't you think? But not only did I get an incredible kink in my neck, I realized it only delayed the inevitable. People need to stare or they'll never get over it."

Without the burn, Ken would have been easy to look at—fair-yet-outdoorsy complexion, soft blue eyes and long lashes, high cheekbones. Set off as they were by his thick, light brown hair, his features had a definite Nordic appeal. How sad to be ruined by such a thing, thought Pamela.

"Look at all that gorgeous hair, would ya! I bet Pamela a Big Mac you'd be bald as an eagle by now!" Starla said.

Pamela envied her friend's quick wit and brassy attitude that never failed to set people at ease. "She didn't really."

Ken laughed. "Rogaine does wonders! Man, it really is great to see you! You two haven't changed a bit."

"I beg your pardon! I've grown up at least three sizes since high school," said Starla.

"Excuse me for not noticing," Ken teased back, his eyes resting on Pamela's. "You *both* look amazing. Exactly how I would have expected."

"Thank you, Ken. You're definitely good for my ego," Pamela said.

He still looked more musician than Realtor—an image that may have been encouraged by the scar. And though his baggy jeans shorts and black T-shirt were not the Coldwell Banker attire sported around Minneapolis, it suited him. Angie would like this guy, Pamela thought.

"Would you ladies like to take a peek at the cabin? That's it. Right through there." Ken pointed toward the grove of birch and pine trees that bordered his property. "The former owners, the Millers, were good friends of mine, and I helped keep the place in shape whenever they weren't here. When they decided to retire to Florida, they put the cabin on the market. It's a wonderful little place—*little* being the operative word. And there is no reason it won't sell to the right buyer. Everyone in the market for a cabin just seems to need more space—or less charm."

"*Less* charm?" Pamela asked.

"You'll see what I mean. It's only the size of a fishing cabin, but about as far from that as you could imagine. But the way it sits on the hill, you can't really add on, so it doesn't appeal to the vacation home set either."

"So what do your friends want for it?" Starla asked.

"Sixty-seven thousand. Considering what the Millers put into it, it's sad, really. But they need to get rid of the place by October at the latest. So, I'm really counting on those friends you told me about, Starla."

He winked. If you could call it a wink. It was more of a facial flinch, since Ken's scar drew the skin so tightly around his left eye that only a sliver of eyeball showed. Pamela suddenly hoped Starla's patient would buy the cabin. For Ken's sake.

"Shall we head on over?"

He led the two women through the thick grove of trees, out to a clearing. Pamela froze as they came through the shadows—awestruck by the prettiness of the little cabin standing off in the sun to their right. It was a pale Victorian pink, which would have been insulting on any other building, but was exactly what this place called for. The trim was all blue and white, including the carved window boxes overflowing with pink geraniums. Pamela just wanted to stare…to take it all in.

The house reminded her of a gingerbread house she and Angie had created some long-ago Christmas. The hill sloped gently toward the lake, broken now and again by a huge pine or birch tree. A set of wooden stairs led down to a long dock jutting out into Sunset Lake, which glimmered in diamondlike patterns of sun. A ring of waterweeds and lilies grew thickly at its edge, thinned back around the beach area. Behind the cabin, but not close enough to cast a shadow, was a thick forest of native northern trees. Pamela's chest constricted with the beauty of it all.

Pamela saw the cabin fringed by the fiery hues of fall and then pictured it wrapped snugly in a blanket of snow, frost streaking the windowpanes. The wanting was almost more than she could take.

"I'll bet it's absolutely enchanting in autumn," she said.

Pamela was even more enamored when she stepped foot in the sunny whitewashed porch the back door opened to. Though it had the look of a porch, the room was really part sitting room, part dining room, and overflowed with white wicker furniture.

"This is like a dollhouse!" Pamela exclaimed.

Starla smiled. "Darling, isn't it?"

Ken ushered them through the door and down a narrow hallway. On the left was a tiny, green-tiled bathroom, and on the right, the hallway opened to the kitchen. Hardwood floors and pine cabinets graced the space, which was not much bigger than the bathroom.

The wood floors, interrupted only here and there by faded

rag rugs, continued into the cozy living room. On the far outside wall was a stone fireplace, flanked by two comfy armchairs. Opposite them was an overstuffed blue and white gingham sofa, and an old chest sat in front of the couch, doubling as a coffee table.

The only bedroom was up the steps, accented in the palest of blues with bold navies splashed here and there. Its furniture was dark oak—a captain's chest at the foot of the bed and a weathered dresser and mirror to the side. There was the feeling of being at sea when you walked into the room. Peaceful and serene.

And that serenity reached right into Pamela's soul and wound itself around her resistance. Try as she might to release the notion that she and the cabin belonged together, she could not ease it from her mind. While Ken and Starla chatted outside afterward, weighing the pros and cons the cabin might have for Starla's patient, Pamela remained silent. Finally, when she and Starla headed back to Rabbit Lake, Pamela said, "What would you say if I told you I'd like to buy that cabin?"

Starla swung her head around so quickly, Pamela was worried she'd lose control of the wheel. "You can't be serious, Pammi?"

"I don't know…I'm probably way too emotional right now to even think of such a thing. But part of me wants you to tell those friends of yours to take a hike—the place is mine!"

"But you're not really the cabin type. And I thought you hated the north."

"I thought I did, too. But it's weird…You know what I told you last night? About how I feel better here than I do anywhere else? I can even sleep straight through the night here, Star. And I don't need the radio on! Do you know the last time I've been able to fall asleep without noise of some sort? When I was here in May."

"That's not a reason to buy a cabin."

"Not by itself, it isn't. But to me, it's one of the biggies—at least it is when you consider the meaning behind it. I feel at peace here, and if it can help me sort through stuff, why not? I love it, Star. Sure, winter's coming and I obviously wouldn't get much use out of a cabin until summer. But what else am I going to do with my weekends next summer? And Angie would love it."

"You don't have to buy your own place to get away, Pammi. You two can come with me any weekend you want."

"Yeah, you're probably right. And Paul would kill me. The last thing he said when we talked was to be careful how I spend money. Sixty-some thousand dollars isn't exactly careful."

"That's an understatement."

They drove in silence for a bit, and then Pamela started back in, "But would I ever again find such a deal? Ken said the Millers are having a horrible time selling the place 'cause it's so small— and didn't he say they wanted to get rid of the furniture, too? Starla, it's like it was made for me—size and all. What if I took out my own mortgage? I could more than qualify on what I'll make working full-time. All I'd have to take out of our joint account is the down payment. What do they usually ask? Twenty percent?"

Starla looked a little nervous. "He'd *kill* you."

"Yeah."

"But you're really considering this, aren't you?"

Pamela grinned just short of sheepishly. "I think so, Starla."

"Well…just for the record, I think your apprehension is right. You definitely need to think about this, Pammi. You're under a lot of pressure right now, and fast decisions like this are…well, they're not always smart. And I'm not just saying this because of Paul's little warning. Don't get me wrong. I'd love for this to work out for you—but it's a big responsibility."

"What if I just went ahead and did what I wanted anyway?"

Starla laughed and rolled her eyes. "I'd have to say that's a trait I haven't seen since high school—and in your case it's even a little bit refreshing. Used to be that once you got a bee in your bonnet, no one could talk you out of it."

Starla paused—and Pamela knew she'd scored a point.

"Okay, Pammi, at least do this. We'll call Ken and tell him you're considering buying the cabin. It's not going to sell overnight. Talk to your bank, and if you still want to proceed when you get all the facts, offer the Millers sixty thousand and see if they bite. I have a suspicion they'll counter with not much more than that just to get it off their hands."

Pamela beamed at her friend. "Thank you, Star. I can't explain it right now…but this feels so right to me."

Starla shook her head. "I still can't believe you're actually considering this. But—shoot me later—I'll do what I can to help. I've never been afraid to eat my words. Who knows, it might be a great thing for you and Angie!"

Twenty-Two

"YOU WANT TO buy a *what?*"

Pamela's mother was shocked. But then again, with not even a "Hello, glad to see ya, Mom," it was to be expected. The very first thing Pamela said after she'd hugged her mom was, "Guess what? I think I'm going to buy a cabin near Crosby."

In less than twenty-four hours, her seed of an idea had grown into a full-fledged plan. By midnight, she'd convinced Starla she wasn't crazy, citing not only the emotional escape but also the investment benefits such a purchase might offer.

Now, seated at Joan's kitchen table with her hands wrapped around a mug of coffee, Pamela described the cottage in glowing detail.

"What does Paul think of all this?" Joan asked. "I can't imagine he'll want to come north every summer weekend."

Pamela stared at her mother and pursed her lips. "No, I can't imagine that he will."

And with as much control as she could muster, she explained all that had happened over the summer. Her mother listened quietly, tears glossing her eyes. Finally, Joan reached across the table and took Pamela's hands in her own. "You've been dealing with all this by *yourself?*" she whispered. "Why didn't you call me."

"In New Mexico? I couldn't spill something this big over the phone."

"But it's been *three months*. How did you do it? Angie wasn't even there."

"How did I handle it? Alone. The same way you did, Mom. When Dad died?"

Joan blinked and a vacant look crossed her face—until understanding dawned. "But there wasn't anyone else, Pammi. My parents were long gone. You were a child! I couldn't exactly fall apart in front of you, now, could I?"

"I was a year and a half younger than Angie, Mom. Why *couldn't* you have cried with me? You were so cold."

"Cold? I was devastated, Pammi! I loved your father more than life itself. You and your father were everything to me. When he died, I still had to make a life for us. I had to be strong for you. Do you know I didn't sleep more than three or four hours a night for over a year—not unbroken sleep, at least. The bed...it just felt so empty. Sometimes, my throat ached all day long from holding back the sobs. And there were times all I could do was sit here, in his chair at the table, and hold the newspaper like he once did...just so I could wrap myself around his memory." She sniffed back the tears. "Do you really think I felt *nothing* when he died?"

Pamela looked around the kitchen—sunny and bright, but its vinyl flooring still a tilelike pattern of avocado green, accented with decades-old gold appliances. An archive of '70s decor. For so long, Joan's lack of taste embarrassed Pamela. How many times had she offered to hire a decorator to refurbish the little house for her mother, only to be turned down time and again?

Now she saw that all her mother's treasured memories of Pamela's father, and of Pamela as a child, were packaged in harvest gold and avocado green. Pamela shook her head in disbelief. Of course her mother had been devastated. Why had she allowed a child's interpretation of grief color her view of Joan all these years?

"I'm so sorry, Mom. You've just always been so strong, so capable, so independent—*much* more so than me. I was the weak one. All my life I've wanted to prove I could be just as strong as you."

"And that's why you didn't call me about Paul right away?"

"Partly. Words didn't come all that easily at first. They still don't. But really, I wanted to tell you in person, Mom." Pamela's heart constricted at the sorrow, the empathy she saw in her mother's eyes. Not pity. "And I know how much you respected my marriage."

Joan sighed. "I respected *you*. Pammi. The choices you made were the best you knew to make. But if truth be told, I have always been concerned about your marriage."

Pamela stared at her mother. "What?"

Joan pursed her lips. "He was so different from you—nothing like the man I had always pictured you marrying. A man more like your father, perhaps. Someone who could see into your soul and draw you out. You see the world in such a beautiful way, Pammi—you're an artist. Sometimes I was concerned that Paul repressed that in you."

"You never said anything."

"What right did I have? He was good to you, took care of you...he loved the Lord. You and I—well, we're different, Pammi. I thought maybe my opinions about the man you needed were all based on my own preferences."

"And we drifted apart after Dad died, so you probably wouldn't have even felt comfortable bringing it up," Pamela said.

"Maybe. I often think you and I might have grown closer through the years if circumstances had been different. Not that Paul is all to blame. Some of it is just us. We both value our independence—and that's okay. I see the same thing in Angie. Only, you two are much closer than you and I ever were. Hold to that, honey. Don't ever let it go."

Pamela nodded, tearful at the melancholy of her mother's statement.

Joan moved closer and put an arm around Pamela. "Oh, Pammi, I wish I could make this all go away for you. I'm so, so sorry. How's Angie taking all this?"

"We had some good, long talks before she left. And judging by this first week at Belton, being away is probably the best thing for her. She doesn't bring Paul up all that much with me right now, other than to ask if *I'm* doing all right. I think she's slightly removed from the pain—or maybe she's forcing herself to be— which for now might be okay. But then, I do realize this divorce isn't really about her. She deserves to be free of as much of it as she can."

Joan smiled. "She sure does. I remember feeling that way about you once upon a time. As much as I missed you, part of me was glad you could get away and start your own life, grow away from the pain. What about church? I can't imagine that's been easy for you."

"It hasn't. I feel like a sore thumb. All those families and couples."

"I know exactly what you mean. It's hard to be alone after all those years. And as much as your old couple friends want to include you at first, after a while they just kind of forget. It's not that they are purposely neglectful or anything...it just sort of happens. It took me years to find my Ladies."

Pamela considered the four women Joan called her "Ladies," an odd assortment of widows from different walks of life: a sixty-eight-year-old Spanish Catholic; a fiftyish spitfire of a waitress; a soft-spoken woman in her late fifties; and a sixty-four-year-old who had survived four husbands. As different as they were, the women enjoyed going to the movies, playing cards, and going out to eat together once a week or more.

"I'm going to pray that happens for you. There has to be one of those divorce support groups down there in the Cities."

"I'm not ready for a group yet, Mom. Besides, I have Starla," Pamela whispered.

"But it would be so good to spend time with people who can understand your emotions. Please don't hide yourself away, Pammi."

"I'm not. I'm working, remember?"

"Thank the Lord for that. It's good to immerse yourself in something meaningful. But you need a bit more than just that. So tell me about this cabin...can you really afford it right now? You're making decisions pretty fast. Are you selling that big house of yours, getting an apartment or something?"

"No, Mom, I don't need to. And I don't want to change things all that much yet. Not until Angie adjusts a little more and I know for sure...well, until things settle down. I know it sounds crazy, but don't worry. I'm working full-time now and make plenty to support myself. And if Paul keeps on with this—the law says I get 50 percent of what he and I had. And he's giving me the house on top of all that."

"Oh? Well, that's something. Have you talked to him?"

"Only once." She could hardly keep the longing from her voice.

"You're still hoping he'll change his mind, aren't you, Pammi?"

"Yes." She paused. "I'm convinced he's just having a midlife crisis—and I can get through that. I *really* can. It's not like Paul to act this irrationally. If I just give him time to work it all through, and not nag at him, maybe he'll see what he's throwing away. And if he doesn't..."

"I'm worried you're setting yourself up for more hurt, Pammi. Maybe you should see a counselor. Get some more advice?"

"I may do that at some point. But Starla's been a good listener. I think being up north with her, away from home, has done me a lot of good. That's another reason I really like the idea of buying the little cottage on Sunset Lake. There's something so tranquil...I don't know...it's like I deal with stuff better when I'm there. With all the memories and pressures back home, I've had a hard time connecting with God. I know place shouldn't matter, but it comes easier to me there. Does that make sense at all?"

"It does, Pammi. It does. Maybe not everyone feels it like that, but to me the Lord seems nearer when I'm out in the open. I think it's not Him nearer, though; it's me. I let go of the rest of life, get it off my mind easier. And when I take hold of it again, I see more clearly. You've been running from home so long, it's no wonder God led you back when you most needed it. And maybe you can finally be who you are. Not who Paul or I or anyone else wants you to be."

189

Twenty-Three

PAUL LOOKED UP the number in his Palm, condemning his sweaty palms and the butterflies in his stomach. The stress was almost more than he could tolerate. *This is my daughter, for Pete's sake!*

"You're not divorcing Angie," Dana kept telling him each time he put off contacting his daughter. "Call her! The first time will be hardest, but at least get those lines of communication open again."

But 'again' implied communication in the past. And Paul had never discussed with Dana how stilted things were between him and Angie. The girl had been so much easier to show love to when she was small and everything he said or did inspired smiles and belly laughs. In recent years, Paul had been clueless as to what Angie wanted of him. Even in the best of times, they seemed to butt heads and freeze each other out. He'd given her a car, provided wonderful opportunities for her through school and church, gave her plenty of spending money. *And now, a private college education completely paid for? What I would have given for something like that.*

Paul reached for the phone and dialed. "Angela Thornton's room please," he said to the sweet-voiced operator on the other end. Dare he hope she was out?

The operator connected him, but it wasn't Angie who answered. "May I speak with Angela Thornton, please? Or maybe just leave a message?"

"Just a minute." The girl barely covered the mouthpiece. "Yo, Angie! Pho-one!"

It seemed an eternity before his daughter came on the line. "Hello?"

"Angie, it's Dad." His heart pounded as the silence wore on. "Hello? You there?"

"Yeah," she finally said, "I'm here." She paused again. "I'm just not sure what I'm supposed to say to you."

"Are you doing all right…at college, I mean?"

"I'm fine."

"That's great, honey. I'll bet you had a great summer in Mexico, huh?" Paul massaged his temples.

"Yep. Best experience of my life."

"You like your classes?"

"Just started them this week. But yeah, I think I'll like them fine."

"And your roommate? What's she like?"

"She's great."

"Get the check I sent?"

"Yeah, I did. I mailed the financial office receipt back to you yesterday."

"Okay. Well…thanks. I'm glad to hear everything's going

well." Angie was silent, and Paul felt her judgment of him eke through the phone lines. "Well, call if you need anything at all. You have my new number, right?"

"You sent it with the check. Not that I'll need it…."

"Okay. Guess I deserved that. But," he paused, searching for words that would summarize what he felt, "you've always made me proud, Angie. You know that, right? You know I love you regardless of…of everything going on."

"Yeah. That's what you've always said."

"I mean it, honey. None of this has anything to do with you."

"Yeah…I know." He thought he could hear a quaver in her voice. "But…I'd really better run. Bye, Dad."

"Have a good day…" But Angie had already hung up the phone.

At least she talked to me. Paul stretched backward in the recliner. He opted to not turn on the lights, though the room had darkened as the sun went down. He closed his eyes. *Push the negative thoughts away. The call is over. Think positive.*

And there really was so much good happening in his life. Liberty National was proving to be the best career move he could have made. A few of his proposals had been integrated by the board and already Paul was making points with his management staff. His only complaint was finding—and keeping—capable financial officers.

Another good thing: Dana would be home early tonight. And early was rare. He'd tried to take the opportunity on nights like these to do special things with her. Court her, so to speak. And despite the gloom that still colored a good number of her days, the two of them had managed to find a great deal of happiness together. And for the first time in as long as he could remember, Paul was at peace with his world.

"Honey?" Dana called. "You home?"

"In here."

Her heels clicked across the tiled entryway and she rounded the corner to the great room. She wore a new burnt-orange business suit that lit her face with a warm glow. She was obviously in a pleasant mood today. "Why are you sitting here in the dark?" Dana asked, flicking on the overhead light.

"Just daydreaming. How was work?"

"Busy but good." Paul watched as she slipped her shoes off and reached up under her skirt to roll the thigh-high nylons down her legs. "I need to get out of this tight suit, and then shall we go out for dinner? I'm not really up to cooking tonight."

"Sure. Mexican or Italian?"

"How about McDonald's?" Dana grinned, filing through the mail she'd dropped on the table beside him. "A Big Mac is all I've thought about all day. Oh. Here. This looks official."

Paul accepted the package from Dana and opened it, scanning its contents briefly before handing it to her. "What's a Notice of Judicial Officer Assignment?"

"Not a big deal," she said. "It's just telling you who your court referee is. Oh, Steve McKensie. I've met him. Nice guy. He's the moderator you've been assigned for family court back in Minneapolis. Nothing you need to do really until the settlement hearing date is assigned. That'll probably take a while. My guess is after Thanksgiving sometime."

"How long after that until the divorce is final?"

Dana's face brightened. "Depending on the judge's caseload, you'll be free a few months after that. March for sure. And there might be a way to pull some strings."

"I'm *so* glad to see you smile." Paul pulled her to his knees and massaged her shoulders as she opened the remaining mail. "You think Pam got a copy?"

"I'm sure she did…hmmm…" Dana pointed to the handwritten address on the envelope she was opening: Mrs. Paul Thornton. A red X crossed out the word *Mrs*.

"Paul," said Dana as she rose and handed him the contents of the envelope. Her face was pale. "Look…"

It was the photo of them that had appeared in the *Los Angeles Times*. Someone had scrawled the words YOU NO BETTER THAN HIM! in red letters across Paul's face. He flipped the clipping over, but there was nothing written on the back.

"Give me the envelope." His voice was brusque.

Dana handed it to him, and Paul turned away so she couldn't read the panic on his face. Inside there was nothing, and other than the mark through the *Mrs.*, the outside of the envelope offered no other clue. And then the weight of thirty years came crashing down on him, and it was all he could do to conceal his reaction.

She's still here!

"Paul?"

It had to be her, even though the private investigator had found no trace that she was still alive.

"Paul, what is it?"

He turned to face Dana with a practiced smile. "Nothing, I'm sure. I guess I don't know what to make of this, but I'm sure it's nothing to get too upset about."

"Nor should we just let it go," Dana said. "Let me show it to Cal Delaney at work. He used to be a police detective. It's a little threatening, and this *is* LA. Do you know how many psychos there are out there? Murderers. Stalkers out for some sort of revenge. I see them in court every day."

"Come on, Dana. Murder? This is only a news clipping. We'll keep our eyes open, but don't get all uptight about it. Anonymous letters are usually sent by cowards. They rarely do anything more than threaten."

Dana looked dubious. "If you say so. But for the record, I don't like it at all. You better believe that if anything else comes, I'm gonna talk to Cal."

"Okay, okay…"

"What do you think it means? 'You no better than him'? *Who* are you no better than?"

"Good question."

September 6

Dear Journal,

Dad called today. It was horrible. He acted like nothing had changed. Part of me wanted to lay into him—but the other half wanted to punish him with my silence. And now I feel guilty because I was so cold. Why is that? After everything he did, why do *I* feel bad? I just can't talk to him about anything real.

I've got an essay on Descartes for philosophy due next Tuesday. I couldn't even get through the first sentence of the article on him! I don't think I have a philosophical bone in my body. I've only had that class two times so far, but I think it could break me.

Twenty-Four

"I CAN'T BELIEVE I did this all on my own," Pamela said to Starla when they met for dinner to celebrate her purchase of the cabin on Sunset Lake. They'd not seen each other since Labor Day weekend, and Pamela was proud that she'd refrained from calling her friend every night for a change. "Shouldn't I feel guilty or something?"

Starla laughed. "Not unless you forget to pay your mortgage."

"Hah! It's great to have something to focus on—to look forward to. The only thing I regret is that by the time it's really mine, I won't get many weekends warm enough to enjoy it."

"Why not? That cabin is winterized. You have any clue what a deal you got? Your roof is sound, the well is full, and Ken gave you that septic system certification, right?"

Pamela looked up from her food, embarrassed. "I didn't even realize I had a septic system or that it was something that needed certification."

"You'll learn as you go. I'll help, don't worry. Just know you're making out like a bandit in this deal. I'd be embarrassed to tell you how much money I dropped into my cabin the first five years!"

"I should be terrified at the added responsibility. But I'm not at all."

"Good."

"Even my mom didn't think I was crazy. She understood completely. You were right about her, by the way. Losing my dad *was* hard on her. A lot more so than I believed."

"You think things might be different between the two of you now?"

"If you mean will we spend more time together, then I'm not sure. That's never been our way. What will change is the way I see my mom. She's not cold or completely unconcerned, the way I've always thought she was. I probably won't be so afraid to be honest with her about the hard things. Eventually, that may bring more intimacy between us, but I don't think we'll ever be as close as Angie and I are."

"That's probably okay," said Starla.

"Yeah, it's a lot of work to cultivate the type of relationship that Angie and I share. That you and I share. Maybe if my mom and I lived next door it would be different. I'd work harder to build a friendship with her." She shrugged. "Anyway, I think she and I understand that about each other better now. It's enough."

"With that, and your job of course, and now the cabin…things seem to be looking up a bit. I'm glad."

Pamela sighed. "In some ways, I guess you're right. I didn't tell you this, but I got this thing in the mail Thursday from Paul's attorney. Nothing too important, but I didn't freak out about it. I'm not sure what the difference was this time. But I was okay."

Neither woman said anything for a bit, and then Pamela continued. "For lack of a better word…I feel like I'm coping. The nights are still lonely, but at least my days are filled."

"Speaking of nights, would you be interested in going to that new Julia Roberts movie with me? It's supposed to be a great chick flick!"

"Love to!" Pamela said. "Tomorrow night work? Or Saturday?"

"I won't be around much this weekend. I was thinking Monday maybe?"

"You're going to the cabin?"

"Well, actually…I have…" Starla inhaled and looked directly at Pamela. "Okay. There's something I need to tell you."

"I've *really* come to hate that phrase, Starla. What's going on?"

Her face looked like a child who had gotten caught with her hand in the cookie jar. "Well…I've met someone."

The revelation struck with such force, Pamela wasn't sure what to say. And a whole spectrum of feelings churned around in the pause that grew between them. Jealousy. Loneliness. A large amount of honest happiness for Starla. She deserved this, of course.

"When did this happen?" Pamela finally asked.

"Last month. The week Angie got home."

"*That* long ago? Why didn't you say something? We've had plenty of opportunity to talk."

"There wasn't anything to tell at first. And you weren't in any shape to hear even the basics. I guess I could've said something at the cabin, but I thought it would be better to wait. I wanted that weekend to be about you, not me."

"I appreciate your sensitivity, but really, you don't have to pussyfoot around me, Starla," said Pamela, feeling a bit annoyed.

"Yeah I did." Starla's voice was gentle and carried no trace of anything but compassion.

"Well, don't anymore," Pamela responded more brusquely than she intended. "I gather things are going well?"

Starla's smile was tentative. "Yeah…better than I ever dreamed. His name is Adam Strom. He's a patient at the clinic—not my patient of course, but that's how I met him. We just kind of hit it off. He's funny and kind and sweet and treats me like I'm the only woman alive."

"So, what does he do for a living?"

"He's in banking."

"You're kidding."

"No. But not the financial end like Paul. Adam's the head of marketing for a teachers' credit union in St. Paul. And guess what else?"

"What?" said Pamela.

"His background is Jewish—like mine! It's like God just dropped us in each other's paths, Pammi. He attends a messianic Jewish temple, just like the one we went to in New York." The dreamy look was back. "I really like this guy, Pammi. Everything about him. My dad will be thrilled if…"

"If anything comes of this relationship?"

"Yes…and something tells me it might, Pammi. I've never clicked with a guy as much as I do with Adam. And he feels the same way."

"Do me a favor then, okay? Don't keep it from me anymore.

I won't deny it hurts that you have someone and I don't. But this is part of life and you're my best friend, Starla. I *am* happy for you."

"Thank you, Pammi." Starla smiled. "That means a lot to me."

Now, even Starla has someone.

The solitude was unbearable that night. And the urge to call Paul undeniable. How many times over the past few months had Pamela picked up the phone only to put it down again? Tonight, though, she needed to hear his voice, to feel his presence if just for a moment. Maybe this time, he would sense the loneliness in her voice and it would inspire him to try again. Maybe he'd even tell her to rip up that cold sheet of paper he'd titled "The Thornton Estate," along with all the other legal paperwork she was accumulating, and say "Let's put this behind us and start over."

Without even trying to talk herself out of it, Pamela found Paul's number and dialed. She'd been patient, waiting for God and time to work their miracles of change on him. She needed to know what chance they still might have.

"Hello?"

Dana.

The mere sound of *that woman's* voice deflated Pamela's spontaneity, and it took every bit of control she had not to slam the phone down.

"May I speak to Paul?"

"Just a minute, please."

Oh, brother. As if she didn't recognize my voice.

"Paul here."

"It's me, Paul. I...uh..." *What was it she wanted to say?* "I...well, I guess I just wanted to ask you about this stuff I got in the mail last week."

"Pam? Oh. Well. How are you?"

"How do expect me to be, Paul?"

"Okay, well never mind that then." His laugh was awkward, nervous, the laugh she'd heard him use countless times to minimize stress. "What stuff are you referring to?"

"The notice of legal—"

"Oh, that. Don't worry about it. It's nothing. Dana says it's just to inform us of the moderator who's been assigned to our case when it goes to court. I can't imagine he'll be needed all that much...since we're in agreement over the settlement and all. Right? Anything else?"

Dana says? Did Paul have any idea how badly it hurt to have him defer to Dana just now! Had he no remorse?

"No. That's all..."

"By the way, did Angie tell you we had a nice little chat?"

"Good. This hasn't exactly been easy for her."

"Sure sounds like she loves school. I'm glad we could do this for her, aren't you?"

"Paul, don't. You're acting like nothing has changed between us. I don't want this divorce, okay? I never have. Angie isn't happy about it either—so don't make it sound like your decision has had no affect on her life. You have *no* idea how far reaching the consequences of your actions will be."

Her stomach hurt, and Pamela could hear Paul breathing on

the other end, but he said nothing. She wanted to strike back, hurt him as badly as he'd hurt her.

"By the way, I bought a cabin this week."

"You *what?* You're kidding, right?" His voice had turned hard—none of the schmooze was left.

"No, I'm not. It's close to Starla's place and—"

"No! You can't do that, Pam! I told you in no uncertain terms to watch your expenses until the divorce is final! You have *no* right to spend my money right now!"

"I most certainly can, because it's a done deal! I'm taking out a mortgage and have written a five-thousand-dollar check from my own account for earnest money. And at the closing, I intend to pay the balance of the down payment from *our* account. But don't worry. It'll barely be a dent in *your* money. Certainly a lot less than what you've spent on rent. Or did *she* buy a house for you?"

"That's none of your business."

"Then my cabin is none of yours."

"We'll see about that, won't we? Be careful, Pam. That's all I'll say. Be very, very careful, or you will find yourself not quite as comfortable as you thought you were going to be."

Pamela slammed down the phone and pressed her hands to her thighs to still the shaking.

Twenty-Five

HAWTHORNE, CALIFORNIA. Ugliest city he'd ever seen.

Paul could spit at the airport from where he stood looking at the dilapidated apartment building that housed the woman who threatened all over again to destroy his life. Of necessity, he'd kept tabs on her through the years, but then her trail just stopped. Paul assumed she was dead—and even the investigator he'd hired came to the same conclusion. But unfortunately, Luanne was very much alive.

Paul crossed the street and spiraled his way up the concrete and wrought iron steps to the fourth floor and around to the back side of the building. Number 422 was a corner unit in the efficiency apartments—overlooking the dead grass and garbage wasteland between here and the airport.

The rubber-backed drapes were drawn, as they probably always were. But he had no doubt what the room held. It would be a furnished apartment—the twenty-year-old orange-and-brown plaid that always came with buildings such as this. Luanne would have a TV, an empty gin bottle on the coffee table, a worn old afghan, an ashtray overflowing with butts, and dirty bowls left over from who knew how many days' meals.

It was a scene forever burned into his memory.

Get it over with, he told himself as he knocked. *Deep breath.*

Three times he knocked, but the only response he got was an elderly woman poking her head through the curtains of the apartment next door and staring as he passed, her wary eyes following him all the way down the balcony to the steps.

I'll be back, Luanne. You aren't going to ruin my life just because he ruined yours!

October 1

Dear Journal,

I'm so excited! I'm seriously considering going on this inner city mission project over January term. We got these flyers about it the other day and it looks a little like Lifelines, only I'd actually get to live in downtown Chicago in a rooming house. We can choose what area we want to help with, but I already know I want to tutor grade school kids. That way if I do major in education, like I think I'm gonna do, I'd get credit for it. I have to raise twelve hundred dollars in support, but I know Gram would help. And Mom. And probably Dad, if I got up the courage to ask.

I told Mom and she thought it was something I should check into. We talk every Sunday—though sometimes I kinda wish it wouldn't be so often. Ever since that first time Dad called and I kept it from her, she keeps asking if I've heard from him. So then I made the mistake of telling her the next time—and she fell apart! Wanted to know what he said about his job, if he asked about her, if he seems unhappy…

I *hate* this "being in the middle" thing!

The hard thing for me is that I can tell Dad's trying really hard to connect with me. More than he ever did before. And part of me wants to just let go and talk to him. But the other part, the part that wants to be mean to him for Mom's sake, wants to yell at him and tell him what a jerk he is.

I'm going to drop philosophy and take it again next semester with a different prof. I'd rather try again than fail a class—and so far, with two Cs on papers and a D on my first test, I'm doomed.

Melinda and I drove into Chicago last Saturday and rollerbladed along Lake Shore Drive, right next to Lake Michigan. The leaves are starting to change and the weather was all cool and crisp. It was so awesome!

On Sunday, I went along with her and her boyfriend, Jeff, to Willow Creek Church and then to his house for dinner afterward. The best part was that I met Jeff's brother Jason. He's a senior at Northwestern University and is going to med school next year. He's one of the coolest guys I ever met. I'm not holding my breath, but I have an idea he's gonna ask me out.

Twenty-Six

THE DOORBELL RANG just as Pamela slashed a tube of lipstick across her lips. She ignored it since she was already late to her downtown photo shoot.

The bell sounded again. Who'd be here at this time of the day? It was hardly light yet!

Pamela ran downstairs and opened the door to an FTD deliveryman holding a large purple plastic bag. "Flowers for Pamela Thornton."

"Oh! Well, thank you."

Paul? Pamela carried the bag inside and knelt on the living room floor to unwrap it. Inside was a bouquet of more than a dozen roses—a faded antique peach, tinged with a vibrant pink.

"Who in the world!" A purple envelope was buried in the stems.

May I buy you dinner next Wednesday night? I have a proposition for you. A very professional one, I assure you.
Chad Freeman

Pamela dropped the note on the floor and picked up the roses, inhaling their rich, sensual aroma. When was the last time *anyone* had sent her flowers?

What would Starla say about this? They planned to meet for lunch today, which was a welcome thing since Pamela was seeing less and less of her friend these days, immersed as she was in Adam.

A dinner date. No, not a date. And if she were legitimately single, would she date? How strange it would be, if it ever came to that, to share her life with someone else. Pamela cringed and wondered now if she'd *ever* be ready for another relationship.

Pamela scratched her left ring finger with her thumbnail—as of yesterday, the ring was off again. She'd taken it off in the beginning and put it back on again in the past few weeks. Today's pasty band of skin was a stark reminder of her up again, down again hope.

Was she supposed to call Chad with her answer? No…he had initiated. He'd call.

She glanced at her watch. *Ughhh. A half hour late.* Pamela quickly filled a vase with water, placed the roses in the vase, and set the arrangement on her kitchen table.

When she got to the office, her phone was ringing. "This is Pamela Thornton," she answered just before her voice mail kicked in.

"Did I catch you on the run? You sound out of breath."

"I'm sorry?"

"Pamela, this Chad."

"Oh, hi! I just got here. Running really late. I was supposed to have been at my shoot already." She laughed. "But I guess I could put a *little* blame for that on you. Thank you for the beautiful roses!"

"You're welcome! Hope I didn't get you in trouble—I paid the florist an arm and a leg to make sure they delivered them before work. So? Dinner Wednesday okay?"

"I...well..."

He laughed. "Breathe easy, Pamela. I have a very legitimate business proposal to discuss with you."

"Care to enlighten me now?"

"Only if you say no to dinner."

Pamela relaxed at the casual timbre in his voice. "You're not planning to make this easy for me, are you?"

"I aim to please. I won't make this uncomfortable for you. Don't think of it as a date, okay?"

"I appreciate that. Even if my husband and I were...well, I guess I just need time to think the whole dating thing through. But if you're serious about this being a business dinner...I don't see how I can refuse." She took a breath. "So, okay. Yes. I'll go. You have me curious now."

"Great! I'll respect your wishes. Have you ever been to Bella's?"

Pamela must have been quiet too long because Chad said, "Not your favorite, I take it?"

"I love it. But so does my husband...it's one of his favorite places. We went there the night he..."

"Then we'll go to that new place downtown—heard of the Mad Hatter? It's South American cuisine and supposed to be excellent. And since it only opened last weekend, there's certain to be no memories lurking in the corners."

"Thanks, Chad. I'd enjoy that."

"And by the way…bring your portfolio."

"My photos? Come on, Chad, tell me what you've got up your sleeve!"

He laughed. "Not until Wednesday. Have a good day!"

Pamela hurried off to the Metrodome. The Minnesota Twins hoped to garner more support for baseball next season by offering free pregame activities in the plaza outside the arena. *TCM* was running a feature on it in next month's issue. Pamela's assistants had been there since seven, and by the time she arrived at eight-thirty, the setup was all done perfectly, per the art director's mock-ups. Luckily, all that was required of Pamela on this job was to snap the photos.

She was done a little after noon and walked the two blocks to the coffee shop where she had arranged to meet Starla for lunch. She found a cozy armchair and, after ordering coffee, settled in with the newspaper to wait for her friend. Halfway through an article in the *Star Tribune*, Pamela noticed her reflection in the mirrored wall across from her. If she hadn't recognized her own scoop neck white T-shirt and faded Levi's, she wouldn't have known herself.

At some point during the past months, Pamela had let go of the conservative way she'd always dressed. Her hair, overgrown as it had become, was pinned up with clips in a messy style that made her younger…no…softer, perhaps. And the effect wasn't bad at all, Pamela had to admit.

If only Paul could see her now. She resembled again, in many ways, the girl he'd fallen in love with all those years ago. She no longer felt matronly—didn't act or think ten years older than she was. Partly it was her job. Pamela was thriving from the energy her career had doused her with.

Emotionally and spiritually, something was different as well. She was coming alive again. In recent weeks, Pamela's commitment to the Lord had been growing outside the limited box she had for so long confined it to. Church attendance was still not a priority. She had lost her heart for the traditional trappings of Christianity she'd embraced since childhood. In its place, however, was a deeper, more constant communion with the Lord—one that spoke of relationship, not of duty.

"Hey, you! How's the coffee today?" Starla, tailed by a waitress, reached down to sample the coffee from Pamela's cup. "Uggh! Bitter. Even with all that cream you poured in. Maybe I could have some iced tea? And then we'll be ready to order."

"Hi, Star." Pamela smiled, awed as ever by Starla's commanding personality. "Saved you a chair."

"Thanks." She sank into the cushions and peered across at Pamela. "You look terrific, ya know that?"

"Thanks. It's the job. But you, my dear friend, look beautiful, too. I'll bet Adam has a lot to do with that. I couldn't help but notice the amazing connection you two have. It was…refreshing."

She'd finally met Adam, and as uncomfortable as it had been to see Starla's and Adam's enjoyment of each other, she understood it completely.

With his thick hair and black beard, Adam reminded her of a burly black bear. He was a jovial guy—strong enough to hold his own with Starla and big enough to dwarf her. There was no competition to outdo each other, however, as she had seen with other boisterous couples. The two complemented each other perfectly. The best thing—and the hardest—for Pamela to witness was the respect Adam awarded Starla. That was something she'd never had with Paul.

The waitress arrived with Starla's tea and took their order.

Starla doctored it up with Sweet'N Low and sipped at it while Pamela told her about Angie's plans to work in downtown Chicago during January. "She'll probably be hitting you up for support," said Pamela.

"Not a problem there. Angie knows she can always come to me for that sort of thing. I've made kind of a big decision, by the way. I think I'm going to join Temple Jeshua."

"I wondered how soon that might happen."

"Have you ever been someplace and even the very first time you go, you just feel in your bones that it's right? That you're exactly where you belong?"

"Oh, yes."

"That's what it was for me, Pammi. I don't remember very much of the church we attended in New York, but I loved being there. And my dad has always missed it. Even if nothing ever pans out with Adam—which I can't imagine, by the way—even then, I *belong* in that church. It's like going home."

Pamela waited to respond while the waitress placed their plates in front of them. "Sometimes you can be away from something your whole life," Pamela mused, "and never realize how much you miss it. And then it just clicks."

Starla nodded, her mouth full of tea.

"That's exactly how the cabin on Sunset Lake feels to me. I know it's not the same thing as finding a church, but to me, it's going home. Or maybe it just symbolizes that I'm going back to being who I was supposed to be. My mom saw that—said something about how I can stop trying to please everyone else now."

"I've been telling you that for years."

"I know, Star. But it didn't sink in until now. I feel like I've turned a corner somehow—and I think it's partly because of the cabin. I hate the whole idea of what's happened to our family…but I can hardly wait for next weekend to get here so I can move in!"

Starla grinned. "Far be it from me to deny that you seem happier these days. By the way, I'll be in Lewisville with my dad Friday night and part of the day Saturday. You want some help getting set up?"

"Truthfully?" Pamela screwed up her expression. "I'd *kind* of like to do it myself. It's such a big step for me that I want to savor it. But you could drive over for dinner Friday night."

"That'd be great, Pammi. I know exactly what you're saying. There's nothing like making a place your own. Call me when you get in and we'll decide a time. Ya know something? It totally slipped my mind to ask what Angie had to say about all this."

"About the cabin?"

"Was she thrilled or what!"

"Well…" Pamela bit her lip. "Actually, I haven't said anything yet. And I'm not going to until she comes home for Thanksgiving. I'm thinking about maybe the two of us spending the holiday weekend up there. But…" She poured the remaining cream from the little pitcher into her cup and stirred in some sugar. "I did tell Paul."

"You didn't!" Starla's eyes were wide. "You told him about the cabin?"

"He would have found out anyway. He wasn't all that happy about it."

"And that surprised you? What did he say?"

Pamela popped a potato chip into her mouth. "Oh, he flew off the handle and said something about not giving me everything he promised. But I decided I wouldn't allow myself to get too worried. According to what I've heard, he has no choice."

Starla put her fork down. "Honey, you need to go back and visit Sharon. I think it's time to put her to work protecting what's yours."

Pamela sighed deeply and shook her head. "Every time I hear that, it bothers me. Actually, it disgusts me. If I were to do that, I'd feel like a money-grubbing monster, Starla. And frankly, the idea of hiring an attorney to force Paul's compliance horrifies me. It's against everything I am. Don't you realize that?"

"But what if he's serious? He could do something totally sneaky. And you *deserve* that money. He's the one who discouraged you from working all those years, who asked you to stay home and be his little maid."

"No. Not just him, Starla. I made that decision, too. I wanted to be available to him and to Angie. I wouldn't have done it if it wasn't what I wanted to do."

"But you need enough to live on."

"*Enough* is the operative word, Star. Yes, I need *enough* to live on. But even if he gave me *less* than 50 percent, do you have any idea how much that is? A lot. With what I make now, I could support myself if I had to. Anything he gives me is icing on the cake…savings for Angie and my future…emergency funds."

Starla shook her head. "It just seems so wrong to let him off all that easily, that's all."

"I know you're just trying to help—and I appreciate that. But I'm still hoping this is just a horrible nightmare. That something's gonna shake him up and he'll come home." Pamela saw Starla roll her eyes. "I know. I know how you feel about that. But I can't stop praying for that. However…if he *doesn't* realize what a mistake he's making and I *were* to retain Sharon Stouffer, I just know how he'd react. It would be far worse for me! He hates to waste money. And hiring another attorney is a huge expense."

"Whatever you decide. But you *do* know that Paul doesn't have any right at all to be upset about your cabin. Especially since all he had to shell out was seven thousand measly bucks."

"He'll eventually figure that all out. Really. I know him. The more I think about it, the more I'm sure he just overreacted. I think it's just the idea of my not consulting him first that got him so mad."

"I suppose you know best," Starla said. "I don't like it, though. Just for the record."

Twenty-Seven

AUTUMN.

Pamela had always considered the word as graceful as the season it named. She seldom chose its less refined synonym. And yet, perhaps *fall* was the better description: Once summer ended, the season of changing leaves and crisp weather began—and then fell away.

The closer Pamela got to Sunset Lake, the more apparent this became. Two or three times, she pulled to the side of the road to photograph autumn's waning shock of fire. Blood red sumac lined the highways, and behind it, giant ferns were tipped with a dry reddish brown, curling wherever the green had slipped away.

The further north Pamela drove, the more trees had dropped their leaves. The sky remained a nearly fraudulent blue—as if an artist had mixed all his blues and whites and greens and purples together to shock with color before his landscape froze to the boring, steely hues of winter.

As it did each time, Lake Mille Lacs surprised Pamela with grandeur just as she rounded a bend in Highway 169. Its edges were mirrors reflecting not only the sky, but also the yellowed trees along its banks. Pamela stopped to nab it on film, centering the shoreline between sky and water in a study of symmetry. Mirror image.

A child and his father stood on a dilapidated, rotting dock precariously planted in the water. Pamela snapped their picture, a striking contrast against the endless lake. Man versus nature.

She finally made her way down the dirt road, past Ken's home, and stopped on the gravel of her own driveway. Before she did anything else, she pulled out her camera to record this, her first day at Sunset Lake, on film. A flock of geese in an overhead V interrupted the quiet afternoon. They passed quickly, honking until they were long out of sight. Pamela spotted a loon fishing way offshore; another popped up from the depths to join him seconds later. A few dry, brown leaves floated near her own beach.

Small things. But to Pamela, each was a sign of welcome. And she smiled her thanks.

Once she'd unlocked the door of the cabin and carried in the few boxes she'd brought from home, the sense of welcome grew even deeper. The Miller's left-behind furniture could have been chosen by Pamela, it suited her taste so well. She wandered happily around the rooms, thinking of a photograph she could frame for that wall, a painting she had that might look good on this one. And what about that ugly old ship-in-a-bottle she'd packed away in the attic years ago? It might have resurrected life in her loft bedroom. And maybe a framed map or antique shipping chart?

Downstairs, she unpacked and tucked away the kitchen items, towels, and sheets she had brought along. And then she organized the groceries in cabinets and peeked into nooks she was itching to become familiar with. After she'd completed those few chores, she stood out on the deck and watched a neighbor around the bend ease his boat beside a dock.

She saw the loons again floating near Ken's dock. It thrilled her to think that maybe they'd return next summer—that she could witness for herself the birth of the chicks. As she watched, they raced across the water, gathered speed, and then gracefully lifted off. Pamela suspected that sometime within the next few weeks, the loons would begin their journey to the warmer south.

After a while, Pamela went back inside and made the promised call to Lewisville.

"I'm here, Star," she said. "I'm actually here."

"So, how's it feel?"

"Amazing."

"You definitely picked a good weekend. Can you believe how warm it is—especially after that cold snap we had last week?"

"Indian summer." Pamela sighed happily. "Are we still on for dinner? I'm cooking."

"Wouldn't miss it. Can I bring something?"

"No, I brought groceries from home. Tons more than I can eat in a weekend. Just get here as soon as you can."

"I'll be there in under an hour."

Then, almost as if she had willed Starla to her door, someone was knocking.

"Well, hi there!" Pamela smiled when she opened the porch door to Ken.

"I've come to officially welcome you to Sunset Lake." He grinned, lifting a large, wrapped box from where it sat behind him on the ground. And then, conspiratorially: "This is supposed to be good for business. Most Realtors give stuff like a tin of cookies or bottle of wine or something. But...I don't know. This seemed more appropriate."

"You didn't have to," Pamela said as she ushered him through the screen door, trying not to laugh at his package covered with big purple Barney figures. Her eyes went right to his scar, but already it seemed less odious.

"You like the paper?"

"Do I have to answer that?" she said, now laughing outright. "Don't tell me...it was left over from..."

"Oh, no! No leftovers for you. I bought it special. Come on, open it!"

Pamela carried the box to the table and was surprised to uncover a portable CD player. "Wow. Thanks!" she said. The gift definitely outshone a tin of factory-made butter cookies.

"And I confess...I'm not really a Barney fan. It was either that or wedding bells."

"In that case, Barney is best. And the CD player is wonderful!"

Ken suddenly looked a little shy. "The Millers took their stereo, and you probably don't have an extra one lying around the house in Minneapolis. Music is so nice to have up here...since there isn't TV. At least the Millers never had one, and I wasn't sure if you—"

"It's wonderful, Ken. Very thoughtful, actually. Boy! I hadn't even thought about TV, but I guess I probably won't bring one up either. I can't imagine reception is all that great anyway."

"It's not. Unless you get cable."

"Hey, Starla's driving in from Lewisville for dinner. Would you like to join us? It's a celebration you should be a part of since you're partly responsible for—" she swept her arm across the porch—"this lovely abode of mine that landed you such a hefty commission!"

"After you finagled nearly ten grand off the price, there wasn't much *hefty* left! I'd say you *owe* me dinner." When Ken laughed, his left eye disappeared into scar tissue. He put a hand on the back of her shoulder and smiled. "Can I contribute to the menu? I baked earlier today."

The ease with which Ken touched her and moved into her personal space was something Pamela would have to get used to. Not that she disliked it. Starla was just the only other touchy-feely person she knew.

"I'd like that. Dessert was something I never planned for anyway."

"Okay, then, I'll be back when I see Starla's car. And…" he looked sheepishly down at his striped scrubs, "I'll dress for dinner."

"Don't bother. I'm a fan of comfort these days."

Left to herself, Pamela pulled the chicken breasts from their Styrofoam containers and poured a bottle of marinade on top of them in a big Ziploc bag. Then she prepared the accompaniments— wild rice, a spinach salad, a sun-dried tomato bread she'd picked up from the bakery. Usually not big on entertaining, she relished the preparation today, this first time in her new kitchen.

Starla and Ken showed up simultaneously, laughing at a shared joke, and let themselves into the porch. Listening to them, Pamela couldn't help but wonder if Starla might be attracted to Ken if Adam weren't in the picture.

"Hey, you two! Come in here, why don't you," called Pamela. "I'm slaving away at the stove and could use some company."

Ken entered first, in Dockers and a golf shirt. "*This*, my dear Pamela—" he placed a beautiful platter on the countertop—"is the dessert I promised."

Pamela lifted the edge of the tinfoil. "Mmmm. Did you see this, Starla?"

"Cheesecake! A man after my own heart," said Starla, squeezing Ken in a playful hug. "But then you do owe me for getting us old friends back together."

"Old friends, huh?"

Starla raised an eyebrow at his sarcasm.

"Need I remind you that neither of you two lovely ladies ever gave me the time of day. Not that you were alone. I have no qualms in admitting that I was the single most avoided kid in the school."

"For the record, I liked you fine back at Lewisville High. You were just a little…" Pamela searched for the right word.

"Weird?" Starla volunteered.

Ken tried to suppress a smile.

"No, just different," Pamela concluded. "Most musicians are."

"Thanks, but I prefer *weird*," Ken said. "Has less conservative connotations. I never did care much about what people thought of me. Still don't. Weird suits me. And maybe it does go with the territory. That whole creative genius thing and all."

"Oh, my. The man's humble, too," Starla said.

"I hear you've done some things professionally with your creative genius," Pamela said.

Ken nodded. "There's a CD of some of my stuff in the box

with your new stereo, if you want to listen."

"You record, too?"

"Not for public consumption. Mostly I compose."

Pamela went to the living room to plug in the CD player. In a few seconds, Ken's voice wafted through the room in a vaguely familiar song. She looked at Ken, seated on the other end of the sofa from Starla. "I've heard this on the radio! *You* wrote it?"

Ken nodded.

"Wow. I had no idea…" She caught Starla's eye and could easily read the I-told-you-so look her friend was sending her way—but Pamela stuck out her tongue and went back to the kitchen. "You could have said something, Star."

"I did. He's one of the best composers in the industry. Or so I hear. Your sister mentioned your name is a hot ticket around Nashville these days."

Ken was quiet, as if the sudden fanfare made him feel awkward. "I just write what God gives me. It's what I do, but I'm glad it's making an impact."

The three chatted a bit through his music, giving Pamela time to finish up all the dinner preparations she insisted on doing herself.

"This is great stuff," Starla said. "I've never really listened to much Christian pop, but I'm impressed. I should pick up a few more CDs."

Pamela laughed. "And if you forget—as you've been known to do—I'll buy you some for your birthday."

On the recording, Ken's voice was throaty and deep and even raspy on occasion, but it was what his songs called for. Pamela recognized one or two more numbers from the radio, but she thought Ken's own renditions were filled with such integrity and poignancy that, in comparison, those other, more trained voices did little justice to his songs.

She was stirring the wild rice when Ken came to stand near her. "Can I set the table?" he asked, opening exactly the right cabinet and counting out the dishes as Pamela nodded. He headed to the porch and returned for the silver and glassware just as the CD finished.

"That was beautiful, Ken," Pamela said. "Thank you for sharing it with us."

"That's what it's all about, Pamela."

The night was one of the most enjoyable Pamela had spent in months. Starla dramatized abominable tales of high school in the seventies—and Pamela or Ken corrected the details when she exaggerated too much. All three roared at the pure stupidity of their escapades. When Starla begged a reprise of the Tiny Tim routine, Ken ran home for his guitar and put his all into "Tiptoe Through the Tulips." His performance was even cornier than Pamela remembered.

"No wonder Pammi thought you were weird!" Starla said.

"And to think the man wears it as a badge of honor!" Pamela hooted across to Starla, who was laughing so hard her face was purple.

"Even you two beauty queens have to admit I turned out kinda nice," said Ken, cocking his head to one side just like a mongrel puppy Pamela's mom had once rescued.

The conversation buzzed until after midnight, when Starla

opened her mouth in a yawn so wide, her jaw popped and water streamed from her eyes. "I gotta get outa here or I'll never make it home," she said, slapping herself to stay awake for the twenty-minute drive.

When she'd gone, Ken helped clear away the dessert plates and coffee cups. And then Pamela walked outside with him, following him as far as the grove.

"I can't begin to tell you how good this cabin is for me, Ken. I feel like a new person. Already! I have hope and it's like the sadness is…"

"I'm glad to have helped." He put out a hand to slow her step. "I know you've gone through some hard times. Starla told me a little. But you're right—Sunset Lake has healing capabilities, Pamela. I think that's why God gave it to you."

"You have experience in that area?"

"I was hurting once, too. Unbearably so. And God used this place in my life…just like He's doing for you."

"You think sometime you might tell me about yourself? Those yesterdays that caused you so much pain?"

Ken was so quiet, Pamela thought she had offended him. But when they stopped at the edge of the trees between their cabins, he turned to look at the sky and then down at her. She was surprised to see a tear scoot down the shiny, pitted surface of Ken's burn.

"I believe I may actually be able to do that." He smiled, then, and swiped his fingers across his half-closed eye.

Pamela wrapped her arms around herself to contain the shivers that skittered across her skin. Her sweatshirt seemed threadbare against the chill of the evening.

"Well…" she said slowly. "I guess I'd better head back. Thanks again, Ken…for everything."

"And thank *you* for a fun evening. It's going to be great having you for a neighbor, Pamela. Good night." He kicked his legs up in a funny little cha-cha, the goofiness back again. She giggled after his retreating back.

Instead of going inside as she intended, Pamela detoured down to the lake. Suddenly she wanted to experience the water at night. The stars were out—pricks of light in an otherwise black world. This must be the deepest dark Starla had described, she mused. The light on the deck gleamed a faint circle of light toward the lake, barely enough to keep her from tripping.over shadows. But Pamela made her way to the edge of the lake and sat down. A fish jumped to her left, startling the quiet. She smiled.

Life could be *so* good.

A loon called from the weeds between her dock and Ken's. Another answered from overhead, his sound protective and reassuring. And then Pamela heard the splash when he landed on the phantom lake somewhere in front of her and moved toward shore. She heard their hunkering down in the weeds, their cries not yet quiet.

Pamela dared to envision her entire family here—she and Angie and Paul. The way it was supposed to be. And she was buoyed by the image. *Thank you, Lord, for all that You will do.*

Finally, Pamela wandered back to the cabin and lugged Ken's gift and his CD upstairs into the loft, beside her bed. She played it quietly, listening more intently this time to the words as she lay in the pitch-black northern night. Ken sang of peace—and of letting God take the sadness away. And he sang of joy.

Pamela fell asleep as his raspy voice breathed hope into her dreams, and she smiled at the promises Ken claimed for himself, knowing God would be true to her, too. Hadn't she already felt, in fact, the gift of hope?

231

Twenty-Eight

THE NEXT DAY, Pamela put on jeans and a sweatshirt and went to explore the two acres of land behind her cabin. She walked a little way into the woods and then came back to check out the shed, the garage, and even an old outhouse, a neat little building hidden among the trees.

She found the garage nearly as neat and clean as the house itself. The Millers left behind a push lawn mower, a big beach rake, a little trimmer, and numerous gardening tools. Two garden hoses snaked over a hook on the wall, and she'd already spotted another attached to the spigot at the front of the cabin.

The shed adjacent to the garage was loaded with more beach equipment: the wooden platforms from the dock the Millers had dismantled, lawn chairs, deflated rafts, a net that looked like it might be for water volleyball. And in the back against the wall— Pamela could hardly believe it!—was a two-person paddleboat. She felt as if she'd hit pay dirt.

It was heavy, but she managed to drag and push it all the way down the hill to the lake.

Sunset Lake was small, Pamela realized a while later as she paddled around the bend, back toward her house and Ken's. In little under an hour, she'd explored nearly half of it and intended to make her way around to the other side as well. She was heading slowly past Ken's house, admiring it from the lake side, when he came outside and waved to her.

"Want some company?" he called.

"My legs sure do! This is the best workout I've had in ages!"

She paddled the boat up to his dock, which, unlike most of the docks on the lake, was still in the water. She held out a hand, and Ken climbed in.

"So I take it you already went around the bend that way." He pointed behind him.

"Yep—and now I want to see the other side. By the way, does our road go all the way around the lake?"

"No, it stops at the farm. Actually, the guy's a dairy farmer and he owns a good portion of the land around this lake. As soon as we get past your other neighbors there, you'll see his pastureland begin. Miles and miles of it."

"Really? I thought it was going to be more lake homes."

"Nope. His property borders nearly half of the shore of Sunset Lake, which is a good thing. We only hope he never sells off his land. More vacation homes would kill the lake—all those extra powerboat wakes lapping away at our shoreline. Plus the farm adds character. Sometimes, early in the morning before they get milked, you can hear his cows mooing. It's really a pretty sound."

"Do they sing with the loons?"

He laughed. "That would be an interesting duet, wouldn't it? Loony Cow Tunes, we could call it. I should work up the lyrics."

"Oh, please…" Pamela rolled her eyes and smiled in spite of herself.

As they pedaled past the neighbors, Ken called to one of them out working in her yard, and she returned the greeting. Then they reached the farmer's land and followed the shoreline around.

"So, you like working for a tourist magazine?"

"I do. But honestly, if I could make a living at it, I'd prefer taking pictures of less commercial stuff. You should have seen me on the drive up—I stopped every twenty minutes or so. Couldn't get enough of the trees. I should've brought my camera along. Those cows up there would be great subjects."

The pastoral scene ahead reminded her of the calendars her mom used to hang on the bulletin board next to dental appointment cards and dry cleaning receipts.

"Photography sounds a little like writing music. You paint pictures with your camera, interpreting your subjects by how you frame them. I do the same: I combine notes and words to form musical pictures of the way I see life."

"I never thought of it like that. But you're right, of course. All creative people do that, don't they? Writers, painters, photographers, musicians. Photography seems so much simpler, though. I see something, I determine the best angles and adjust my lenses and lighting. And I shoot. I imagine it takes a lot more foresight to figure out lyrics and notes and all?"

"Actually, I can't say I really plan any of it," Ken said. "When I sit down at the piano or with my guitar, it's because something has been beating in my head to come out and be written down. It's interesting how the style of what I write changes every so often. It comes in blocks. In the early years, I wrote mostly chorus-type songs for large group worship—now, it's all solo material. I don't know why that is. Maybe…" He looked a bit confused.

"Maybe what?" Pamela stopped pedaling and turned slightly to look at Ken, who had also stilled his legs. They floated toward a group of geese wading in the weeds offshore.

"Years ago, before I wrote Christian music, I lost my wife and little boy. I struggled with such intense depression, I nearly didn't make it. When it started to get better, I relied on the Psalms to get me through. And the Psalms made up the majority of my first attempts at writing for the Christian market. David's words, as universally comforting as they are, tend to lend themselves to congregational music." He started pumping again.

In her heart Pamela agreed with him about the Psalms. Recently, they filled her prayer journal. She knew God had given the verses to her as comfort for her situation—just as they apparently had been to Ken.

"I'm glad you've found your niche," she said.

"Know something funny about that?"

"What?"

"I never was a fan of contemporary Christian music. Pretty hypocritical, eh?"

"I don't know…maybe not. Maybe you just have the inside scoop on it. I worked with a gal once who wrote for Harlequin romance on the side. Swore she would never read one! Not that I blame her."

Ken laughed. "Don't know if I like that analogy, but maybe that's it. It's worlds better than it was when I first got started, but Christian composers—me included—still need to make their own way in the world. So often, Christians copy the world's successes and hope it works for them. I have a strong belief that Christian artists need to step out on their own, develop their own style, be excellent in what God asks. I try to do that, and if I succeed, the glory is God's."

"That might be why you've done so well," Pamela said. "You're a fresh voice."

"That's what I hope for. Although I admit, it's certainly a lot easier to latch on to a trend that works." He took a deep breath and groaned. "My legs are about to fall off. Want to head back?"

They steered the paddleboat toward Ken's dock, and as he climbed out he said, "Like to join me for a cup of coffee?"

"Love to." Pamela accepted his hand as she rose from the boat.

Time seemed a nonentity up north. Coffee stretched into late afternoon and then into the dinner hour, and Ken invited her to share the meal with him. If it weren't for the chilly darkness that eventually encroached upon them as they sat out on Ken's deck, Pamela would have had no clue how many hours she'd spent talking with her neighbor that day. Earlier, rather than let the chill force them inside, Ken had brought out two blankets for them to wrap themselves in.

"Look at those stars," he whispered, as if seeing them for the first time.

Pamela craned her neck, trying to take it all in. "Why is it that they are so much brighter here, even closer looking, than they are in the city?"

"Neon saps their energy—steals it right away."

"Really?"

"Oh, I don't know." He laughed, still looking at the stars. "It's just something my wife always said."

"Your wife. Tell me about her. And you had a son?"

Pamela watched Ken's face as he looked up again, quiet for a long moment.

"My son wasn't even a year old when he died of SIDS—crib death." His voice was soft and full of sadness. "Elise and I had been married two years—she was a miracle to me, helped me change my life around. She led me to the Lord. A month after Sean died, Elise was diagnosed with leukemia. It was horrible…it took her over a year to die." He stopped for a moment, and when he spoke again, the raspiness Pamela had heard in his music was there now, more than ever. "It's been twenty years and I still miss her."

Pamela's throat was thick with emotion as she reached over and put her hand on top of his. There were no more words between them.

In an odd way, she relished the experience of accepting into herself someone else's grief. Occasionally she could hear the lap of the lake against the shore when the breeze picked up. But still they sat, feeling no pressure to speak or even to look over at the other.

After a while, Ken gently squeezed her hand, wiped the tears off his cheek, and slowly stood up. "Thank you, Pamela. Your silence was the most understanding thing anyone has ever said. I haven't talked to anyone, except Elise's mom and dad of course, about my wife and little boy for years…it's hard, even now. But for some reason, I needed you to know."

"I'm glad you told me," Pamela said. She got up and hugged

his shoulders gently. Then she walked to the front steps leading down from the deck and made her way through the little birch grove. But the whole way back, Pamela felt Ken's eyes follow her, seeing her safely home.

She tiptoed through the darkened cabin, got ready for bed, and slipped Ken's CD in the player. She drifted toward sleep, the sound of a loon echoing into her consciousness from somewhere way across the water. Yodeling, it seemed. And then a sort of wailing from another loon, closer in to shore. Back and forth the calls went. A concert of the night.

Twenty-Nine

LATE SUNDAY AFTERNOON, as was her routine at home, Pamela dialed Angie's number. It was something she looked forward to all week—she'd call every day if only Angie would let her!

The day had warmed up to nearly seventy degrees—warm enough in the sun to sit outside on the deck with the cordless phone. With the sun glittering on the water and the crisp scent of autumn in the air, it was difficult not to tell Angie she was calling from Sunset Lake. But Pamela was determined to surprise her daughter with a trip to the cabin for Thanksgiving.

"Hey, Angie!"

"Mom! I tried calling you all *day* yesterday! And you don't have your cell phone on, either."

"What's wrong?" Pamela was suddenly frightened by the panic in her daughter's voice.

"Nothings *wro-ong*. At least it wasn't until I couldn't reach you, and then I got all panicked. It's not like you to just disappear like this!"

"Slow down, Angie, and tell—"

"I was planning to go to Willow Creek with Melinda again and I knew you'd be calling today and so I thought I'd call you yesterday. So then when I couldn't get a hold of you, I got worried. Starla's gone too—I even tried her cabin. I finally called Dad thinking maybe he might have a clue—"

"*Dad?*"

"I know, I know. But he *did* know where you are." Pamela could hear accusation in her voice. "Did you *really* buy a cabin, Mom?"

Pamela groaned. "Your father told you. I wanted to surprise you."

"He thinks you're losing it—and boy, Mom, this *is* pretty spontaneous."

"I'm not losing it, Angie. You know me better than that. This is exactly why I wanted to wait until Thanksgiving to tell you— to *show* you I'm not crazy. I didn't think springing it on you over the phone was a good plan—and once you see it, I know you'll love this place as much as I do."

"But Mom…"

"No, Angie, listen. So many things have happened lately— good things—and a lot of it is tied up in my buying this cabin. Dad doesn't understand. In fact, he's absolutely furious with me. But that's just because he isn't in control. I can assure you, this is definitely the right thing for me."

"Since when do you even *like* northern Minnesota? Neither you nor Dad ever had anything good to say about it…not even when I begged to spend more time up there with Gram. None of this makes sense to me."

"Things change, Angie."

Pamela went on to explain a little of what she'd so recently discovered about herself, including how she'd unknowingly altered so much of her true self to fit into Paul's world. "And I misunderstood Gram, too. I thought she didn't care. Some of my running away from here had to do with that as well. Basically, honey, I avoided coming home for all the wrong reasons."

243

"I've heard people do weird stuff when they're in a crisis….like spend a lot of money…go off the deep end."

"Did your father say that?"

"Sort of. But I do know it's true. And Dad seemed so concerned."

"Angie, listen. Your dad is *mad,* not *concerned.* I used a small amount of money from our joint account and that's what's bothering him. But I'm paying for the rest of it myself. And I *can* afford it. He shouldn't have pulled you into all this. Trust me…this is a good thing. And you'll love it here, Angie. Remember how much fun you had at Starla's cabin when you were little?"

She was quiet for a moment. "Yeah. Best vacation I ever had. I have to admit, I always wished for a cabin after that."

Pamela laughed. "Your father could *never* have handled it. Owning a cabin forces you to slow down. And that's foreign to him."

"I wish he could have been different." Angie's pause was so silent, so complete, that Pamela wondered if the connection had been broken. But then: "You know, I *definitely* don't want him back like he is now. But if I could have a perfect world, I would wish Dad to be different. I wish he'd sit down and talk with us about important stuff—you know—stuff like you and I talk about. Our feelings, our dreams, what makes us mad, what makes us totally excited. And we'd all head up to that new cabin of yours, Mom, and not look at the clock once!"

Pamela smiled. She and Angie hadn't had such a meaningful conversation since before she'd left for Belton. "Me too, Angie. I'd do anything for that. Even now, angry as I am…and hurt…I *still* believe Dad and I could make our marriage work if he would just give it a chance."

Angie didn't answer, and the silence became awkward.

"Angie?"

"Yeah, I'm here."

"What is it, honey?"

"You'd want him back even if he *wasn't* different? If he was the same old Dad?"

"If he'd be willing to work on our marriage—"

"The Bible permits divorce in the case of adultery, Mom. I've read that. Dad's never going to change. He left you for another woman, and you have the option to just let him go, you know— and *that* would be in God's will too, right? It seems so much simpler without him. Do you actually miss him?"

"Not when I focus on the rotten parts. And on what he did to me. But there are other times when I miss him so bad that—"

"But is it *him* you miss or just being married? Because I miss having a father—but I can't say I miss Dad. Not the way he was."

"I don't know, honey. But regardless of how I feel, I'm not sure giving up that easily is what God wants me to do, either."

"I know it sounds mixed up, Mom—and really, more than anything, I do hope that Dad will change…like you want him to.

But I guess it's just that I want him to do it by himself—far away from us. Maybe I want to see proof of real change before I welcome him with open arms." Her voice dropped to a sorrow-filled whisper. "I just don't want him to keep hurting us…you…"

Pamela stared at a house across the lake and let Angie's words settle themselves upon her heart.

"Honey…maybe it's not really a matter of *want*." Pamela breathed deeply, hoping she still had the maternal ability to soothe her daughter. "I don't *want* to have your dad come back to me, only to look at him and know that he's been involved with another woman. But part of me knows I have to keep praying for reconciliation. And if that happens, I trust that God will do something to ease the horrible thoughts I have. That he will make us like new again. And yes, I do agree with you—in some ways my life is much simpler without him. It surprises me how much so. So praying this way isn't what I always feel like doing." Pamela closed her eyes and shook her head, thinking again of the enormity of what she continually asked of God. "But I think it's what I have to do. Does that make sense to you?"

"Yeah," Angie said on the other end. Her voice reflected little hope, however.

"Angie, this is the first time since August that we've been able to talk about your dad and you haven't shut me down. For a while, I just thought it was too soon, but I'm starting to worry about how this is affecting you. Maybe if you can't talk to me about it, you could talk to someone else. I'm sure we could get in touch with a good counselor there—"

"I'm fine, Mom. Really. It's not what you think. It's not as if I obsess over this every day at school…I don't. I love it here and am so happy with my life. The only time I get this stressed out is when…well…"

"When I bring it up?"

"Yeah. Or when Dad calls."

"I'm sorry. I vowed to myself I wouldn't lay the heavy stuff on you, honey."

"I understand, Mom. And I know I've got to deal with this someday. I can't avoid it forever. I'm just not there yet, okay?"

"Okay," Pamela whispered. "I trust you, honey."

By five o'clock, Pamela's overnight bag and the cooler with all the leftover food was in the car.

"Leaving so soon?" Ken called from the grove, just as Pamela was locking up. He'd been gone most of day, she knew, first to church and then to see friends.

"Seeing that I won't get home till after seven, I'd say I held out long enough!" Pamela smiled as Ken closed the distance between them. "But I'll be back sometime Friday afternoon. I've got to pack in as many weekends as I can before winter hits, you know."

"I've got something for you to listen to on the way home." Ken held out a cassette tape.

Pamela turned it over and looked for a label, but the tape was blank.

"It's a dubbed copy of some of those early songs I told you about yesterday. The ones I wrote when my wife died. I tried to kill myself…and the gas can exploded in my face before I could finish the job. There was a piano in the psych ward I got checked into, and I don't even remember playing or singing half the stuff

I did. But one of the nurses kept a tape recorder going. When I left, she gave me the tapes she'd made—and later, I rerecorded the songs. It was God's way of giving me strength to go on."

Pamela's eyes welled up at the thought of what Ken was sharing. "I hardly know what to say…"

"I thought maybe you might be encouraged by them." He glanced at the car. "Looks like your coach awaits." He swept his hand gallantly toward Pamela's car, and she paraded down the course he indicated and buckled herself behind the wheel.

She smiled. "Thank you, Ken. See ya Friday!"

Thirty

HOME IMPROVEMENT was one area Paul and Dana completely disagreed about. Not that their tastes were incompatible. Mostly it was because Dana insisted upon doing much of it, including the painting, herself—claimed she couldn't justify hiring someone for the few hours it took to paint a room. And Paul, wanting their home to be perfect in every way, preferred to hire a decorator rather than sweat over a job that would look amateurish at best when it was finished.

But, sacrificing better judgment, he gave in to Dana.

They had been working all night on the worst room of all— the family room—a modern disaster of angles and soffits and high beams. Worse yet, Dana had gotten creative and set to work on a faux finish. He'd pointed out a few problems along the way, hoping he could at least provide an objective eye. But by the time she was a quarter of the way through, it looked horrible. And that was putting it mildly.

In Paul's mind, it was as if she'd set a kindergartner to work with finger paints. He watched her for a moment more, trying to find the beauty in her faux painting with its clumps of green here and there, no consistency to any of it.

"Is it supposed to be that…I don't know…mottled-looking?"

Dana turned from her perch on the ladder, her eyes icy. "Okay, that's it. The little comments you've been making all night…you need to stop, okay? All you do is criticize! I already *told* you it's supposed to look this way. Twice! I've done this before, Paul. And hiring someone isn't going to make it look any different. Wait until it dries."

Paul shut up, not wanting the tension to escalate. He was stressed out enough as it was with the threat of Luanne hanging over him. He'd gone back to her apartment two more times, including this morning's visit, to no avail. Right now though, the thing that troubled him most was the distance he felt growing between him and Dana. It was as if something had stolen in and taken away their happiness.

"I'm just not—" Just then the phone rang, and Paul reached for the cordless a few feet away, ever so glad he'd been saved further argument. "Hel-lo. Paul here."

"Poor Pauly ain't had much luck, has he?"

Paul turned and walked into the kitchen. "You and I need to talk," he hissed.

She laughed. "I must have had you real worried to get ya back here trying to pay me a call three times!"

Paul took a deep breath. "It's been a long time, Luanne. Maybe I just wanted to make sure you're doing all right."

"After thirty years? I'm not stupid. Time's way past for that, Pauly. My guess is you got my letter and needed to be sure *you're* doing all right. That it? I got you scared?"

"Not much of a letter."

"Picture's worth a thousand words, ain't that what they say? Sure said what I needed it to, didn't it? It's true. You know it. You *ain't* no different than him. I *know* that girl you married all them years back ain't the woman in the picture. Don't you think that I ain't kept tabs on you all these years? You may've washed your hands of me, but I been watching you, waiting to see if you would turn out bad as him. Almost thought you had it beat, didn't you? Almost wiped me away like chalk on a blackboard."

"What do you want, Luanne?" Paul ran a shaky hand through his hair.

She cackled. "Oh, I don't want nothing you can give me, Pauly. But you better believe I got something for *you*. You need to know once and for all that you're no better than the dirt you sprung from. All these years pretending to be someone special."

Paul could hear the ladder creaking, Dana easing herself down. She'd be in the kitchen in seconds.

"Listen," he whispered. "I gotta go. When can we talk? We have to finish this."

Again that awful laugh. "Hah! I really got ya, don't I? I get home nine-thirty most nights. I'll wait." And with that she hung up.

"Who was that?" Dana asked, rounding the corner as Paul clicked the phone off. Her voice was abrupt and devoid of gentleness.

"Just…Pamela. She was all bent out of shape again. You know her."

"What's going on this time?"

"Ah…I guess it's the settlement hearing. It's been set for right after Thanksgiving."

"*I* didn't know that."

"I forgot to mention it." He opened the fridge for a Coke and looked back at her. "December third."

Dana looked at him as if she was about to say something, then tightened her lips and shook her head and started to walk away.

"Dana? Hang on. I'm sorry…"

"Never mind. There's nothing you can do about it anyway, Paul."

"Do about what?"

She sat down in one of the chairs by the kitchen table and started picking at the splotches of green paint on her forearms. "Okay. Honestly?" Her eyes searched Paul's, and when he didn't answer, she continued. "I just don't know if I can take this much longer."

"I was wrong about the paint, and I just learned of the hearing a few days ago. You should be happy it's all coming to an end."

"That's not it, Paul."

"So what is it this time? Me? Your job? What's got you so uptight now? What on earth is so bad?"

"What's so bad? Let's see—the guilt, Pamela, Angie. But you know what the worst of it is? God! I can't keep running from Him, Paul! I've been running for almost six years now, and I just can't do it anymore!"

"Slow down, Dana." Paul sat in the chair next to her and tried to make his voice as soothing as possible. "Can't do what?"

"I don't *know*. Sometimes this whole thing seems so hopeless. And you're just happy-go-lucky. But inside, I feel like I'm drowning."

"Calm down, angel…everything's going to be—"

"No! Stop it! I can never say anything to you about how I really feel because all you want is for me to snap out of it. Oh, you do it nicely, with your smiles and your positive spin. But really, Paul, guilt is hardly something I can snap out of! I think I just need to be alone. I need time to think about this…or…or…never mind!"

253

She hurried upstairs and slammed the bedroom door. Paul stood there trying to figure out what had just happened, then finally he went into the family room and gathered up the painting equipment. After he'd washed all the brushes and rollers and wrapped up the paint cloths, he collapsed on the couch.

His thoughts were a jumble of apprehension over Luanne and Dana. Dana, he could probably reason with…get her to see the light of day. She just needed some time to refocus. But Luanne? That woman could bring every bit of his life crashing down on his head. All it would take was one little phone call to anybody who knew him.

Dana loved him for *what* he was now. *Who* he was. And where he came from. That included the lies he'd told about his 'family.' If the truth came out, who would he be in Dana's eyes now?

The clock ticked away an hour, then two. Still he didn't move.

And then, from behind him: "Paul. I'm sorry. This is so hard for me, but we need to talk."

He looked up. Blue moons lay beneath her eyes and grayish strands of hair sprang from her formerly immaculate dark waves. What was happening to Dana and how had he missed it before?

He shook his head slowly, willing his frustration away. "There's more?"

Dana went over to the couch across from him and sat down. "I can't do this—swing from one extreme to the other. It just isn't me. *You* can't do this. I think—" she blinked away a tear—"I think you should move out for a while, Paul. Give me time to think and to deal with this by myself."

Move out?

"Don't look at me like that. Please…you must have felt it coming."

"I can't believe you're doing this to us." Paul said, feeling like she'd just punched him in the stomach.

"I'm not saying it's over. I just need time. Alone. And so do you, Paul. I could be wrong, but I think you've buried your own guilt so deep you're convinced it's not there. Or you think going to church every Sunday purges you somehow. My guilt is all on the surface making me miserable. I can't sleep. I've got headaches all the time. And I've got to do something about it. I *need* to get some help."

Paul stared across the room toward the window just to the right of Dana, struggling to remain in control. "We could go together. And still be married by spring."

She pushed a hand through her hair and sighed. "I used to think getting married would solve everything. I love you with every ounce of my being, Paul, but that isn't the answer. It's like putting a Band-Aid on a head wound. I'm starting to see that now."

"I don't get this. We're so good together!"

"Yes, but we've got stuff we need to take care of first. You need to talk to Pam. You have to do something about this strain between you and Angie. I know you and Pam had a rotten marriage…but you made a commitment to her. And for the life of me, I can't figure a way out of it anymore."

"You're saying I should go back to her? Are you crazy!"

Tears trailed down Dana's cheeks. "No, that's not what I'm saying. Oh, Paul, I don't know…I just need time to think. To pray. To figure out what God wants of me. I still love you, Paul. The one thing I know for sure is that I need for us to stop living together right now. Maybe in a few weeks we can start spending time together. But I don't know yet. I need to get better first. Physically and mentally. I'm falling apart!"

"All right." He hung his head. For the first time in as long as he could remember, he was speechless.

"You'll leave tonight?"

Paul nodded.

"I know you don't quite get this, but it's—"

But Paul had already walked away, blocking his ears to the rest of her words.

Thirty-One

PAMELA MANEUVERED her large black folder through the revolving door, bending it slightly to fit. Even in the enclosed space she could feel the Latin beat. And when she came through the door, she was bombarded by the mariachi and guitars and brilliant colors of the Mad Hatter. Though it was gray and raining outside, a tropical and intoxicating energy buzzed about the high-ceilinged restaurant.

"Chad Freeman," she answered when the hostess asked for her party.

"This way, please."

With the portfolio pinned under her arm, Pamela followed the hostess through the indoor rain forest to the table where Chad was already seated.

"Glad to see you didn't chicken out," he said, rising to seat Pamela. "Interesting place, huh?"

"I'll say. Though I feel a little out of season in long sleeves!" She smiled her thanks, remembering how Paul had never performed such simple niceties for her.

"I've heard the food is pretty authentic—especially the seafood."

Pamela tucked her folder between her chair and the adobe wall beside them. "I'm dying to know why you wanted to see my portfolio. I feel like I'm on a job interview!"

"Maybe…" Chad grinned and mimed a zipper closing his lips. "But not a word until we order!"

And he was as good as his word, for small talk was their only fare until the waiter departed with their order locked firmly in his memory. And then Chad said: "Okay. Here's the deal: I'd like you to consider working with me on book about northcentral Minnesota—a coffee-table book, I'd guess you'd call it. My poems. Your photographs. I hear via the *TCM* grapevine that you recently purchased a cabin near Crosby and that you originally hail from the area—Brainerd, wasn't it?"

"Are you serious, Chad?" Pamela's eyes were wide. "Work with you on one of your books? I'm a nobody. You could get a top-notch photographer—"

"I can't tell you how many of those top-notch photographers I've interviewed in the past four months. But after working with you on that Christmas project for *TCM*, I know you've got something the rest of them don't. And of course when Jim told me about your background, it cinched it. I've already written the poems and contracted with a publisher for this book. All I need is a photographer."

"Wow. I don't know what to say."

"A simple yes would be nice. But there are a few things to consider. Is your cabin winterized?"

Pamela crinkled her brow in confusion. "Yes, but why?"

"My work is a collection of seasonal poetry on the beauties of the north—a good many of them are about winter. It would be easier for you just to stay up there when you're working rather than to drive back and forth. And I'd like to have everything to my publisher by this time next year at the latest, so one winter is about all you'd have to work on it. Originally I'd hoped to be done by July…but unless something in your current collection would suit my summer and fall selections, that will be impossible."

259

"I might actually have a few that would work," Pamela said. "But…are you sure about this? You haven't even seen any of my work. Other than the Lake Harriet homes we—"

"Jim has shown me everything you've done for *TCM*. I've seen enough to know your style—and I already know we work well together. Sometimes that's all that matters. But I did ask to see your portfolio. I hope you brought more than just hotels and restaurants."

Pamela laughed and lugged her leather case up to the table. "Oh, plenty. Those are hardly my most exciting subjects!"

Chad started to sort through the pictures she offered. His eyes anchored on the shots she'd taken for the Lifelines brochure Hoyt Covenant had put out, and he said not a word for many moments. Pamela's hand jittered slightly as she sipped from her glass. When had her work ever been examined so critically?

"These are absolutely captivating," he whispered. "I can almost read the story in their faces. Did you take this at your cabin?" he asked of the early spring shot of a fisherman.

"Not on Sunset…but nearby. A good friend of mine owns a place on Rabbit Lake."

"Ah. Crosby. I know the lake," he murmured. "Simply beautiful."

Pamela wasn't sure if his description was of Rabbit Lake or her photographs.

Through the remainder of Chad's viewing, Pamela remained mute and did all she could to ignore his dissection of her shots. His looking was peppered with phrases such as: 'ah yes' and 'nice interpretation,' and 'very sharp.' Every once in a while, he'd say, 'mmmm,' and Pamela wondered if it was praise or criticism. Finally, Chad pushed away from the table and reached for his water.

"Well, I have to say, you are better than I even dreamed you would be. I have brought along a copy of my manuscript—you might want to read my poems before you make your decision. You can take it home with you." He leaned down beside him for the black binder he'd laid on the floor, then pushed it, open, across the table to Pamela. "As you'll see, it's all arranged by season. Not that they are explicitly seasonal in their message…I think you'll understand when you read them. I originally allowed for this winter, spring, summer, and fall in a photography schedule. But if you'll let us use some of what you just showed me, we're ahead of schedule, and that can only be to our benefit."

"But…you've seen enough to know? I mean…this is it? You really want me to work with you?"

"Haven't I already made that clear? I knew that before I even saw these photographs, my dear Pamela. What I'm concerned about is if you can swing it without a full-time job for awhile."

"Not work? I don't think—"

"That's why I asked about your cabin. With the amount of photography you'll need to complete over the winter and spring,

I'm not sure you'd be able to handle your regular forty hours a week. This is a different sort of job, but it is a job."

"I just don't know if I could manage it…or what Jim would say."

"Could you work out some sort of a minimized work schedule with him? I told him very little, but he is aware of how badly I want you to work with me, and I think he'll be willing to negotiate. As far as finances go, we'll get a sizable advance to start out with. That should help a bit. My books have always sold well, and I expect the total proceeds will more than make up for the difference in your lost income over the next six months, only you'll have to hang in there until the book is on the market for the rest of it. But that may be asking too much? I don't know what your financial picture is."

"I can't believe this. Why me?" Pamela asked, trying to keep from smiling.

"Why not you? You're a very sensitive photographer, Pamela. I've spoken with a dozen others…have seen their work." Chad ran a hand through his hair, which was unbound tonight and nearly touching his shoulders. He shook his head. "Yours is the first that moves me. And for this project, I'm certain I'll find nothing like it. Anywhere."

The waiter and an assistant came to the table and placed large plates of food in front of them and refilled their beverages, asking if there was anything else they needed. When they backed away from the table and left them alone again, Chad said: "Do you like poetry, Pamela?"

Pamela took a bite of her salmon while she considered her response. "I like poetry I can understand. I don't like to search endlessly for meaning in archaic language and unfamiliar metaphors. I hated English lit in high school. Remember how teachers used to make you write a one-page synopsis of what you thought the poet was trying to get across? I couldn't find literary analogy if you paid me! It was the only class I nearly failed."

Chad tossed his head back and laughed. Pamela felt a pleasant tension well up in the pit of her belly as she watched him. She wasn't the only woman in the restaurant who was looking at him, either. Paul, handsome as he was, had nothing of Chad's sensual appeal.

"Believe it or not, I never got more than a C in any high school English class I ever took," Chad said. "I hated that stuff, too. But I have no doubt your soul will connect with my poetry. I say exactly what I mean. The way you do with your photographs. We think the same."

He tore a piece of bread from the loaf in front of them and buttered it. "Like I explained earlier, this book is a done deal, publishing-wise. Read my poems—let me know. You *are* the best, though. And if you say no, I'll probably can the whole project."

Pamela laughed. "Chad, you are quite persuasive. You've brought me an opportunity I can hardly refuse. I'm not sure I even need to read your poems to know our work will mesh. I have to confess, I picked up one of your books after we worked together. You're very good."

"Thank you." His eyes were penetrating.

"This is a lot to think about. My job…Paul…I'm not so sure he would…" She stopped just short of voicing her questions about whether her husband would approve of this arrangement. What did it matter any more?

"I understand."

"No," said Pamela, shaking her head. "It's just that today I had a letter from my husband's attorney. Our settlement hearing date is scheduled for right after Thanksgiving. Everything in my life seems to be happening so fast…that's all. What happens if when I get started, you decide you don't like my work? These are my best. What if this is as good as it gets?"

"You forget I've seen you in action. I've seen you create beauty from the sterility of houses! And by the way, I'm working on another book right now, too. A novel. So, if you decide to take this one on, you're going to be pretty much on your own. I'll be in Spain until Thanksgiving."

"Spain?"

"My brother's wife is from Madrid. Her family has a vacation home I use when I need to get away by myself."

"You want me to send the photos to you as I complete them?"

"No, that can wait until I get back. After you've gone through the poems, we'll brainstorm a bit. And we can talk on the phone whenever you need to. But I trust you."

"Okay, Chad. I'll do it."

He reached over and took her hand, holding it gently across the table, his thumb caressing the side of her wrist. "You'll never be sorry you said yes."

For a moment, Pamela left her hand in his, transfixed by his eyes and the promise they held. Something deep inside of her stirred at his touch. Then, she eased her fingers from his. "I don't doubt that for an instant."

"Now, I'm in need of dessert and a cup of coffee," he said. "Although champagne might be more apropos!"

Thirty-Two

IN ONLY A WEEK, the trees that sheltered the cabins encircling Sunset Lake had relinquished a good portion of their leaves to the dirt road, which was now a crunchy carpet of yellow. When Pamela passed Ken's house and pulled into her driveway, she could see for the first time another neighbor's place, way off, down the road a piece. Everything was harsh and too bright without the shadowy fullness of leaves. And in a way, the barrenness ushered in a sort of melancholy.

But the photographer in Pamela couldn't help but see beauty as well. And as she had the previous week, before she even unloaded the car, Pamela reached for her camera bag and loaded a roll of film into her Leica. She snapped pictures of the half-clothed branches, the lake with its skim coat of rotting leaves, and the golden road she'd come in on. Then she rewound the first roll and popped another in, walking down to the water's edge to capture more lake country on film.

By the time Pamela pulled her overnight bag from the backseat, the sun was already quite low in the sky. She hoisted the bag on her shoulder and kicked through the piles of dry leaves, hardly able to even see the walkway leading to her cabin.

"I didn't think you'd ever stop!" said a voice behind her.

"Hi!" Pamela smiled, turning to greet Ken. "I know. I'm a little obsessed, but I don't want to waste a minute of autumn. I feel like if I blink, it's going to be gone."

"You're sure fun to watch. I had no idea it could take so long to push the shutter button on a camera. All that focusing and repositioning you do! I'd love to see the finished product when you're done."

She laughed. "Then you will. So, how long were you watching me?"

"For a while. I heard you drive up. Actually I came to see if you wanted to share dinner with me. I've got plenty and hoped maybe I might save you from cooking since it's so late."

"You are a godsend! Let me get settled and open a few windows and I'll be right over."

Twenty minutes later, Ken opened his front door to Pamela. "Come on in," he said. "How's it feel to be a regular?"

"Two weekends makes me a regular?"

"Well…two weekends with the promise of all next summer." He smiled in his lopsided way.

"It feels great. I only wish I would've discovered this place earlier, when it was warmer! What a difference from last weekend. It almost smells like snow." She playacted a shiver. "So, are you gonna let me come in or make me stand here and freeze all night?"

"Oh! Sorry." He stood aside as Pamela walked inside. She glanced around again at the neatness of this big open room she'd seen last weekend. "Did you have a good week?"

"Actually, it was *wonderful!* I have a new job."

"What? You quit the magazine?"

"No, but I may be dropping my hours down significantly. Have you ever heard of Chad Freeman?"

"The writer? Sure have. I have a book of his poems somewhere around here, I think. Why?"

Pamela told Ken about the book she'd agreed to do with Chad. "It's a remarkable opportunity. And I can hardly believe I'm going to make money taking the type of pictures I've loved taking all my life."

"I've not read either of his novels, but his heart is clearly evident in his poetry. I can't tell if he's a Christian, but he seems to have a lot of wisdom," said Ken, touching upon a subject Pamela wondered at herself. "I imagine you'll really enjoy this partnership."

"That's another reason I was so intent on getting those pictures earlier this evening. Business. As much of a pleasure as it was."

"I didn't offer you the official tour last weekend, did I?" Ken said. "Would you like to see the rest of my home? It isn't anything phenomenal…and it isn't decorated as nicely as your place. But…I built it all myself."

"Really? Meaning you put up the framing, the walls, roof…"

He nodded. "All of it. I had help with the heaviest stuff and I hired an electrician and a plumber, but most everything you see was done with my own two hands. I worked every summer in high school for a building contractor, so I kind of knew what I was doing."

"Wow. I didn't think it was possible to really do this type of thing all alone."

Where Pamela's cabin was all comfy clutter, Ken's was spacious and open, free of pictures or knickknacks save a rustic painting of an old barn above the fireplace.

The centerpiece of the living room was his cherished grand piano, which was in front of the bay window overlooking the deck.

Ken led her down the hall on the side of the house to the room he called his studio. The disarray and clutter was a shock after the empty neatness of the other rooms.

Pamela saw four or five guitars, some standing, others hanging from hooks; another piano, this one sized for a studio; a drum set; an electric keyboard; a computer with more attachments than she'd ever seen; a trumpet; several recorders; and a high table with a few harmonicas lying on its black felt cloth. And there were sheets and anthologies of music all over the place—some lying on the floor or propped on stands, some flowing over onto the equipment, a few with pencils upon them, obviously in the middle of being written.

Ken also owned a complicated assortment of sound equipment and a large board with tons of dials and switches that he said was for recording and mixing. He did a lot of introductory recording right here in this room, had even designed the walls and ceilings for the best acoustics, he explained proudly.

"It may look like a colossal mess," he said, hands thrust deep in the pockets of his jeans, "but I know exactly where every little thing is."

"The basement is a walk-out," Ken mentioned as they

returned to the living area and he poured Pamela a large goblet of iced tea. They stood on opposite sides of his kitchen peninsula. "You probably noticed that from the lake last weekend."

"Is it finished?"

"No…I don't really need it except for storage. It is heated, though."

"I'm glad my cabin is winterized. Starla's isn't, so she doesn't come up all that often past Labor Day. I get the idea she kinda enjoys pining away all winter for her summers at Rabbit Lake."

"How about you? Planning to be around much this winter?" asked Ken.

"I wasn't at first, but now with this book thing, I'll be here quite a bit. I need to work on rigging up a darkroom. And I'm planning to bring my daughter up here Thanksgiving weekend." She looked absently into her glass, thinking of what she'd allowed herself to dream for the holidays—Paul, Angie, and she spending a snowy, magical Christmas here at Sunset Lake. "I'd hoped that maybe for the holidays…I keep praying that God will restore my marriage."

"And you're losing hope?"

"I feel, in some ways, like I'm just holding my breath." Pamela leaned forward on her elbows and looked dejectedly across the countertop at Ken. "I got notice of our settlement hearing in the mail this week. It kind of deflated my prayer life."

"I'm sorry, Pamela," Ken said gently.

"Yeah. So am I." She dipped her finger in the tea and circled it slowly around the lip of the crystal goblet, concentrating on the low-pitched whine crescendoing into the room.

"You've been expecting God to force Paul's hand because you prayed for it?"

She looked back at Ken. "No…yes…I don't know, Ken. It seems so impossible to think that Paul and I could ever be melded back together the way things are now. But can you imagine what it would say about God's greatness if He accomplished such a thing? Talk about miracles."

Ken walked to the stove and put on two oven mitts, then pulled a casserole pan out of the oven. "Lasagna okay?"

"Sounds wonderful!"

"Don't be too impressed. It's the only really decent thing I can cook. I'm a pro at desserts and I can bake an average loaf of bread—" he pointed to the sourdough cooling on the counter— "but real food eludes me."

"That's the opposite of me. I love to bake cookies, but other than that, I hate baking. I get frustrated because nothing ever looks as perfect as I want it to. I always have such great ideas—but the real thing falls so far short of that it's pitiful."

They sat down at the table and Ken asked if he could say the blessing. Pamela bowed her head in response. "Heavenly Father, thanks for tonight, for the food that we've not had to struggle unduly for, for our beautiful lake and homes, and for this new friendship You've given us. Help us to obey You and love You even when it's hard. Amen."

He served her a piece of lasagna, and she helped herself to salad and bread.

"So, do you think it's wrong for me to just give up? Stop praying for Paul to come back? Sometimes I don't see what good it does."

"I wasn't saying that you should stop praying," Ken said. "What I was getting to is that when He answers prayer, God doesn't always do it our way, even when it seems like what we're asking for is what He would desire. That's the hardest part. I've been through the wringer and back, but all I know for certain is that God is in control and He asks us to love Him, to have faith in Him, to rest in Him. The hard part is figuring out how to do that—it's an up and down battle. It's up to you to decide if you can have that faith in His plan for your life, even if He allows your marriage to disintegrate. Just like he allowed my wife and little boy to die."

Pamela rolled Ken's words around in her head. How easy it would be if she could blindly accept it all…how easy and how incredibly impossible!

The cabin was quiet except for the jazz playing softly from speakers behind them and the clink of flatware on stoneware. Pamela's eyes wandered to the bay window, and she saw that though Ken's outdoor light cast a splotch of luminescence into the air, the deck below it seemed to drop off into nothingness. That's kind of how she felt: Every once in a while, things looked amazingly clear. And then it was as if she were being asked to jump off into thin air.

"This is really delicious, Ken," Pamela finally said.

"Thanks. Too bad I don't have anything else in my repertoire to top this. I maybe should have started slow—bratwurst or something grilled—and built up to a bang."

Pamela smiled. She felt no pressure to fill the quiet with empty chatter and appreciated that every once in a while he would let something about himself float into the space between them, as gently and subdued as a leaf falling from a branch. And in return, Pamela offered a leaf from her own tree. By the end of dinner, they had a neat pile before them—little pieces of themselves they offered companionably to each other.

She thought again about her marriage, about Paul and how little she'd actually learned of him over the years. He would never have sat and talked to her like this. Not even when they were first getting to know each other. This give and take was something Pamela had always craved.

"...blueberry pie?" Ken was saying.

"What? I'm sorry. I was out there for a minute!"

Ken laughed. "I asked if you'd like some blueberry pie. Coffee is already made. Why don't you grab a cup and go find a place to sit in the living room. I'll cut the pie."

Pamela went to the peninsula and poured herself a cup of coffee from the air pot, then added a healthy dose of cream and sugar and sank into one of the big chairs by the fire.

Ken came and sat on one corner of the couch, putting her pie and his on the small table between them. He looked over the piano, out the window. "Nice night. But you're right...there's a sense of snow. The end of October is early for much more than a few flurries, but you never know this far north."

Pamela picked up her plate and took a bite. "So, do you get lonely here by yourself all winter?" she asked.

"Oh...sometimes, I guess. I've gotten used to it. I always was a loner. Even when I was married, Elise and I spent our time with only each other. This place suits me. And I know she would have loved it."

"What was she like, Ken?"

"Free-spirited and kind. Everyone loved her. She smiled all the time—not the kind of smile that's put on for social reasons. It came from inside her, almost like she couldn't keep the corners of her lips from arching up. Elise really knew the Lord. When Sean died, she cried of course—and lived in that horrible grief for so long. But even in her tears, there was something special—not a smile, but something like it. A heart smile, maybe. She never lost her faith, her love. Not even when she suffered so from the leukemia. Oh, she yelled at God—told Him she was angry at all the pain she'd had in life. She yelled good and hard for a while. But then she was just quiet. After a while, her body wasted away and only her eyes held life. The pain was horrible, so bad the morphine didn't even cut it after a while. And she finally just prayed God would take her. And He did."

273

"And you wanted to go along with her, didn't you?"

"That's exactly what I wanted. I was furious with God. I wanted answers. But the answers never came. I still don't have them. Won't until heaven. He wants me here still."

He raised a hand and absently ran it down the scar on the side of his face. From where Pamela sat, on the other side, Ken's chiseled face was perfect. Handsome, even. The way it would have been if the explosion hadn't disfigured him. He turned then, and she saw all of him—and accepted him completely, scar and all. Had she ever met anyone who, by sharing himself, called up the questions in her own soul as this man did?

"Why do you still have faith in God? After all you've been through?"

"Because I love Him. In the midst of all the suffering, He has shown Himself to me. He comforted me. I know it doesn't make much sense, but that's the best I can say. I have faith because it is the *only* thing I can do."

The stars in the pinpricked canopy that hung over the lake spoke to Pamela of a huge God, much bigger than her problems. And hadn't He shown that He cared enough about her to surprise her with joy? That thought alone should be enough to keep her going forward, shouldn't it? Pamela knew that small as her measure of faith was, it was still there...somewhere beneath all the questions and hurt that so often told her that faith amounted to nothing at all.

October 28

Dear Journal,

I was pretty surprised at my midterm grades. All Bs and one A, but that's in bowling so it doesn't really count much. I like school and all, but mostly, I'm looking forward to January and going to Chicago.

I called Gram this week to see if she would want to support me for the Chicago trip, thinking she'd send a couple hundred to get me started. But she sent me a check this week for the full twelve hundred dollars! I could hardly believe it! I was planning to call Dad and hit him up for some cash, but now I won't have to at all. Actually I haven't heard from him lately, which is weird because for a while there he was leaving messages every few days.

My social life is…what can I say…amazing! I've gone out with Jason three times now, not counting church on Sundays. Melanie and I go to Willow Creek most Sundays now to see the guys. This other guy, Sam, asked me out today—absolutely gorgeous—but I said no. Not that Jason and I are an item, but just in case. Jason isn't cute like Sam; he's tall (and a little skinny) and fairly serious—although he's got a great wit. I think he's good-looking, but Melanie calls him "educated looking," whatever that means. Maybe it's the glasses. Or maybe it's just the med school look.

I was pretty blown away at Willow Creek church last week. Mom has this friend at her cabin—Ken—who writes Christian music. I didn't think much of it when she told me, but on Sunday *two* of the songs we sang had his name on them! So it turns out that Mom knows a famous musician! I get to meet him, too, since she's taking me to the cabin for Thanksgiving.

I kind of like the idea of not staying home this year for Thanksgiving. Too many memories. Usually Gram comes down and we get this big turkey and all—but the last few years, I kinda felt like we were just going through the actions. Putting on a happy show for Gram's sake. It was so hard to find things to talk about, so they all ganged up on me—and it's pretty hard to be the center of attention all the time.

I changed my mind about this whole cabin deal. Mom did a good thing buying that place. She talks more about that now than she does about Dad. What a relief.

October 29

Dear Journal,

What is it with my mom and famous men? Now it's Chad Freeman—this guy who hired her to do photography for his book. I had a consultation with my composition prof about my research paper and happened to ask if she knew who he was. Well, Tildy was pretty impressed—apparently she's read all of Freeman's books. Turns out he's a well-known writer. Go figure!

Dad called yesterday. I didn't talk to him, but he left a message that if I needed him, I should call his cell phone number because he will be out of town for a while. Part of me wants to call and rub it in about how well Mom is doing—her cabin, this whole book thing, and all. I especially wanted to emphasize the part about "without you around." But whenever I bring up her name on the phone, I feel like he pulls down a screen. He puts on this fakey voice and says stuff about how all he wants is for her to be happy because he knows this divorce is the best thing for both of them.

Thirty-Three

"MOM?"

"Angie! This is a nice surprise in the middle of the week!" Pamela put down the camera she was peering through and held the cell phone to her ear, stomping to warm herself in the frigid air. She still had at least fifteen minutes to wait before the sun dipped below the horizon and cast its gold pink light behind the Metrodome. "Everything okay?"

"Yeah…but I just found out something kinda strange. Has Dad called you at all?"

"What? No…why?"

"Well, I called to remind him that next semester's tuition is due, and Dana answered, which was awkward enough. But get this. She was acting all weird when I asked what time Dad would be home. I've had the hardest time reaching him."

"You don't have a cell phone number?" Pamela asked, watching the sun sink, hoping she wouldn't miss her shot. "Or couldn't you try him at work?"

"I don't have his work number. And I only get his voice mail when I call his cell. So just a little bit ago I called the house. And Dana acted all weird when I said I couldn't reach Dad, and finally she just came right out and told me that Dad is living at a *hotel!* She didn't give details, but I have the number. And she sounded pretty stressed. I think they split up, Mom!"

"Seriously? Oh, Angie…" Pamela frantically motioned to her lighting tech that she needed more time. "Oh, Lord! You *are* serious aren't you? Angie, hang on a minute, okay?"

Pamela covered the mouthpiece. "Gordie! I have to take this call. There's no way I can finish the shoot tonight."

"You're crazy! We've got it all set up! Look at the lighting, it's—"

"I'm sorry. This can't wait." She turned her back on the lighting tech and his assistant and went back to her phone call.

"Okay, start over. What *exactly* did Dana say, Angie?"

"Just that she and Dad had some decisions to make and that it was best that they not be together right now. That Dad moved into a hotel. But it was the *way* she said it…all depressed and toneless."

"*Good,*" Pamela muttered. "I'm sorry. You don't need to hear that."

"And she started trying to apologize to me for Dad—and for her—but it's like, you know, she just stopped after that. It was really weird."

"Can I have the number of the hotel? And his cell phone number? I don't think I ever got his new one."

"*You're* gonna call him?" Angie's voice was laced with doubt. "Are you sure you should? I mean, maybe you should wait for him to call you. If that's what he's going to do."

Pamela closed her eyes and thought about the suggestion. "No. I'm *definitely* going to call him. Regardless of what happens, your father and I need to talk."

Thirty-Four

"YOU GONNA COME in and sit or just stand there and gawk?"

Paul followed her in and sat in the blue vinyl recliner near the door, somewhat taken off guard by Luanne's living room. Though her decor was cheap and out of style, it wasn't the collection of rental rejects he had expected. A floral-patterned sofa hugged the far wall and a decent print hung above it. Other than the print, the walls were bare.

The placed reeked of smoke and stale cigarettes, their butts filling an ashtray on the end table beside him. And he was right on the money about the gin bottle. It sat between them on the oak coffee table—a half-filled glass beside it on a coaster. The last time Paul had seen her, Luanne had been two-thirds of the way through another bottle of gin. The sight of her, wasted and all alone in that long-ago apartment, was something he'd never been able to scour from his memory.

"What do you want, Luanne?"

"Good to see ya, Pauly. Life's been treating you well, I see. Handsome, you turned out to be."

"Luanne. Get to the point."

"Nice little family in the Midwest. Nice little love nest out here in sun country."

"Stop it. I came to hear what you want, not to discuss my life. Say what you want to say so I can get out of here." Paul did all he could to keep the rage from his voice.

"I called your house in Minneapolis."

"What! You—"

"Called about six or seven times, just to hear her voice. See if I could hear how bad she was feeling over you. Even asked for you once or twice before hangin' up, just to see."

"You talked to Pam? Why are you playing these games? You already knew I was living in LA! You're insane, Luanne"

"Me? Insane?" She lit a Marlboro and inhaled deeply, blowing it straight toward Paul. "I didn't want to get all chummy or nothin'. Just wanted to see what I could find out from her voice. I know these things ya know, Pauly. And I could feel it in her. The betrayal. The loneliness you gave her. That rage that creeps up when you're not paying attention. It was all there. You just walked off and dumped her. You're just like him."

"I am *nothing* like Les. And what I have chosen to do with my life is none of your business."

Paul clenched his teeth and stared across the coffee table into Luanne's pale gray eyes—their hue almost identical to the wiry hair that hung in uneven strands across her shoulders. It had once been a beautiful, almost silvery blond. As a boy he'd always wanted to run his fingers through Luanne's hair.

"You still doing your Sunday thing? I thought church-goin' people were against cheats like you." She got up and moved the ashtray from near Paul to the table in front of her, then refilled her gin glass.

"Leave Pam alone, Luanne. She's fine. She will be well provided for and—"

"Ah…provided for. Is *that* all you think I wanted from him? *Money?*" A flicker of something hateful passed across the gray eyes. "Even if he had it to give, do you think *that* would have taken away all the pain of what your father did to me? When your mama died, I accepted you as my own. Loved you and your daddy with all my heart. I was happy for the first time in my life."

How could you have been happy? He treated you like a live-in maid!

For all the romantic stories he'd told about how his father kept the memory of his mother alive, the "college professor" raising an infant son on his own, Paul knew absolutely nothing of his mother. He'd never even seen a picture of her. And when she died, Les Thornton, stuck as he was with a week-old baby, knew he had to get married again.

Luanne had been a waitress at the greasy spoon down the street, pretty enough to catch Les's eye, if not his heart. And he was a janitor at the local high school—simple in his pursuits, boring, and nothing special to look at. He worked all night, slept most of the day. And somehow, in between changing diapers and cooking and picking up after Paul's father, Luanne waited tables. The two of them went out Saturday nights and came home laughing and singing and smelling of booze.

That was the whole of their miserable life.

As he grew older, Paul was pretty much on his own. He rarely saw his dad, and the less he needed Luanne, the less time he spent at home. If she had been happy in their shabby, two-bedroom apartment, Paul would never have guessed it. At least Les was not a violent or angry man—and perhaps for Luanne, that had been enough.

Paul, on the other hand, filled his life with academics, friends, and activities at Central Avenue Presbyterian in downtown Los Angeles each Sunday morning and evening. He'd attended the church since he was six, when his dad had put him on the church-operated bus each week in order to catch a few more hours of sleep after a late night of drinking. Not one of his friends—most of whom were from very wealthy families—ever had a clue he was from the ghettos of Torrance. They'd been back and forth to Europe more often than they had visited Torrance or City of Industry. His friends owned vacation villas in the mountains. They had beautiful clothes and great cars. And in all of it, they were happy to invite Paul along. He watched and learned and participated as much as he could, but he yearned for more.

And evidently his father did, too.

When Paul was a junior in high school, Luanne made a surprise trip home during her lunch hour to treat Les to a steak and baked potato from the restaurant. Only she found him still in bed. And he wasn't alone. From what little Paul ever understood of the situation, his dad had been involved with the woman from his work for over a year. And she wasn't just any woman. She was Vicki Hilkes, Paul's English teacher. Luanne begged and pleaded for her husband to stay—but Les had found something in Vicki that Luanne could never give him. A sense of worth.

"How can you do this to me?" Luanne had yelled as Les's Ford pickup drove off down the street. She was on her knees in the road, screaming and cursing after them as traffic dodged her. "How can you leave me after all the years I gave you! I hate you! I hate you both!"

Paul could remember shrinking down below the window of the pickup truck to avoid the stares of their neighbors.

They drove straight to Vicki's four-bedroom home in Manhattan Beach and never looked back. It was a dream come true for Paul. His father was a different man around Vicki—more talkative, never drunk, far more involved in life. And Paul had fewer qualms about letting his church friends pick him up or drop him off at home. Life was still less than what he aspired to, but it was finally acceptable.

Paul never once missed Luanne—wouldn't even have thought about her except for the worried conversations he overheard between his dad and Vicki regarding Luanne's unwillingness to sign the divorce papers Les had served on her.

And then, six months into his new life, the bottom dropped out. Paul got off the school bus and saw an ambulance parked in front of the house. When he reached the door, he could see Les lying motionless on a gurney and Vicki sobbing in the arms of one of the EMTs. Les Thornton had suffered a massive heart attack and died before anyone could resuscitate him.

Luanne left frantic phone messages, pleading for Paul to come "home" where she could take care of him. But he had no desire to return to the dingy apartment in the city—even for the few months he had left until graduation. Though his relationship with Vicki was little more than that of a landlady and tenant, she was supportive of his goal to attend college and extremely helpful in locating the financial aid he needed. As far as Paul was concerned, that was far more than his stepmother had ever done for him.

Paul looked across at Luanne, who was humped over, lighting her fourth cigarette. Her skin was pasty and blue-veined, her eyes hollow and sharp with hatred. She couldn't have been much older than sixty-five, though she looked eighty. Was it possible that Pam could turn this vengeful? The thought disturbed him more than just a little.

"This is about Les, not about me. And you need to leave Pam alone," he said.

"But I can't leave her alone. You don't get it, do you, Pauly? I intend to do everything I can to *help* her. Free her of her burden, so to speak."

Luanne lifted a photo album from beneath the coffee table, reached between its pages, and held up the newspaper clipping of Paul and Dana. A look of pure hatred crossed her face. "This one here even looks like your daddy's little Vicki a bit, don't she? And take a look at *you*. Never did look much like Les, but you sure 'nough got his disposition, didn't ya? We just needed to wait long enough to know for sure. Think that would make it easier on your wife? Knowing betrayal's in your blood?"

She was paging through the book on her lap, and Paul could see that it was filled with memorabilia of him—photos from his childhood and clippings, articles, and other odd things from the years since he'd lost contact with her. The most recent, evidently, was the picture of him and Dana. Paul shivered, though it was nearly eighty degrees outside.

"How did you…"

She cackled. "I'm a pro at finding information, Pauly. I have quite a collection here. You oughta see it. Keeping up with you has helped me stay focused."

"On what? Revenge?" Paul closed his eyes and asked the question burning in the back of his mind. "Why do you blame me for what my father did?"

"Oh, I don't blame you for what *he* did. *You* walked out on me, too."

"Luanne, I was just a kid!"

"You don't think you owed me? Oh, you didn't grow inside me, but you were my *baby* just the same as if you had. I gave you the best years of my life! And then you just up and left. Went right alongside him to his little whore's house!" Luanne pressed her Marlboro into the ashtray and drained the last of her gin. "Even after he died, you wanted nothing to do with me…treated me like I was dirt. And what's worse, you humiliated me, Pauly. I won't ever forgive you for that. Not ever!"

Paul didn't want to remember that part. It had been the worst day of his life. Right after high school graduation, Luanne showed up at Central Avenue Presbyterian. She walked right into the Sunday school room where he was talking to a few of his friends. He almost didn't recognize her, she'd lost so much weight. Her hair had turned brittle, and her face was all puffy and red. Where once Paul had considered her pretty, Luanne had turned ugly over the past year.

Paul did his best to stay invisible within his group of friends. But Luanne spotted him.

"You don't belong in that whore's house any more!" she had

said loud enough for everyone in the room to hear. "Come home where you belong."

"Are you insane, woman?" Paul said and then looked around the room with an awkward laugh.

"It's time to come home…"

He grabbed her arm and pulled her away from the circle and toward the door—hissing in her ear to be quiet, then saying for everyone else's benefit. "I'm going to take her to the office. See if they can get her some help. She's obviously sick."

Paul had been able to steer clear of Luanne after that—though he did let her know through a letter that he had enrolled at the University of Minnesota and had no intentions of returning to California. But she had obviously kept tabs on him. Silently. Stealthily. And with a mind to destroy him when the opportunity arose.

"What do you want, Luanne?"

"Maybe you should just go back to your wife and set things right with her the way your daddy never did with me…Make amends for the past. Then maybe I'll stop."

Paul clenched his teeth. "I am *not* Les, Luanne. And you need to let this crazy notion of yours go."

She smiled. "Do I? What if I wrote a letter. Told your wife, your *real* wife, what you and your daddy did to me. Told her you ain't no bigwig son of Professor Lester like you've pretended to be all these years, but just the son of a go-nowhere janitor. That you made up a story to impress everyone. I gather she hates you pretty bad right now anyways. My guess is that she'd probably want to share my letter with other people. Say…that gal you're with. Or that little girl of yours. Or maybe them people you work with."

"Don't do this, Luanne," Paul said, struggling to keep a begging tone from his voice. "You don't need to do this, you know. It won't do you any good."

"Oh, Pauly…you have no idea how much good it's gonna do me."

"I was just a kid who wanted a chance to *be* someone. I wanted a life. Don't you see that? I never thought of it as hurting *you*."

"Just like you never thought about what running off with some other gal would do to your wife?" Her eyes were chips of ice. "Men *don't* think. All you see is yourselves. And…it's already done, by the way."

"What is?"

Luanne reached back into the thick book on the coffee table and pulled out two sheets of paper—photocopies. "I mailed it tonight."

"To Pam? You sent her a letter! Are you crazy!" Paul could feel his heart hammering in his chest. "Why are you so hell-bent on ruining me! You didn't even give me a chance to talk this out!"

Luanne's calm was eerie. She got up and opened the door. "I gave you almost thirty years. It's too late now. But by putting your future in your wife's hands, I guess I gave myself a little present. I never had a chance to get back at Les. Watching what happens to you will surely be the next best thing."

Paul got out of his chair. If the neighbor lady hadn't walked by at that moment, he would have strangled Luanne. "You'll pay for this," he hissed under his breath. And then he stormed out the door.

Thirty-Five

PAUL'S CELL PHONE started ringing just as he stuck the key card in its slot. He pushed the door open and reached for the phone. "Hel-lo, Paul here," he said, expecting his travel agent with the Minneapolis flight information he'd called about on his way back from Torrance.

"Paul? It's me."

"Pam? How—"

"Did you and Dana break up?"

He exhaled a puff of air. "Where did you hear that?"

"Did you, Paul?"

"Well…to be honest, I was going to call you in the morning. I'm trying to get a flight out so I can come home for a few days." Pam was so silent on the other end he wondered if perhaps the connection had broken. "If that's okay with you, I mean. It's a little short notice—"

"No! I mean, yes, I would like that."

"Okay, then. I'll call you as soon as I have the flight information. Thanks, Pam."

For a few minutes after he hung up, Paul stood by the window looking out over the Los Angeles skyline. If only it had been Dana way back then, instead of Pam. He'd have told the truth right from the start. All the lies he'd made up seemed so childish now. Now the truth had to be kept from coming out. And he was furious with Luanne for making him go to such extremes to cover his tracks.

Paul wished he could call and tell Dana how badly he missed her. Maybe suggest they get together for a bite to eat when he got back from Minneapolis. But the one time he had called, she made it clear that she wouldn't even *talk* to him until after Thanksgiving. She'd even suggested again that he call Pam.

"Talk to her," she had urged.

"What about?" he asked.

"I don't know. That's up to you. But I think you need to clear the air."

Maybe she was right. Perhaps flying home to meet with Pam wasn't such a bad idea at all. He turned from the window and grabbed his key card. Right now, he needed to get out of this claustrophobic room—and the hotel restaurant had become a familiar haven these days. There he could at least chat with the night waitress. She was a nice girl. Reminded him a little of Angie.

Maybe he'd even go sit in the lounge after dinner. The jazz combo was decent, and a drink or two always took the edge off his boredom. Not to mention his stress.

Thirty-Six

"You'll never believe it, Star!"

"What?"

"He's coming home!" Pamela shouted into the phone. "Paul's coming home!"

"You're kidding."

"No, I'm not! He's flying in tomorrow sometime. Can you even *believe* this? Just when I was about to give up, God's finally answering my prayer, Starla!"

"Did he *tell* you he wants to work things out?"

"No...but he and Dana aren't together anymore. He's living in a hotel. What else could he want? He was so...so *nice*, Star. It was completely unlike him! You should've heard his voice."

"But he didn't say anything specific?"

"*Specific?* Don't do this, Star. Please?" Pamela hung her head and massaged her temples. "Do you realize you've *never* encouraged me to reconcile with Paul? Why can't you, of all people, believe this is God's hand at work!"

"Oh, Pammi…"

"Why is that? I barely see you these days as it is. And then when I do, you're so negative. Why can't you just hope for the best for me, instead of look for the bad in everything?"

Starla inhaled deeply. "I just know Paul. If he wanted to reconcile, or was even leaning that way, then why wouldn't he just come right out and say it?"

Pamela said nothing.

"Granted, this may be a step in the right direction. I just don't want to see you hurt, honey. That's all there is to it. Paul doesn't love you. His entire heart would have to change—"

"I think that's *exactly* what's happening," Pamela said.

"Okay, I'll be the first one to kiss that man's feet if I'm wrong. I want it to work out for you, honey. But I want it to be different this time. *Better*. I want you to know what it means to be loved by a man. Really loved, Pammi."

"I just want him back, Starla," she whispered. "I need him more than you could possibly know."

Thirty-Seven

PAUL WASN'T ABLE to get out of LA until a day later than he'd planned. And then his flight was delayed until after midnight. Pamela had checked the airline's arrival information since eight, and finally decided it was best to wait until morning to call his hotel in Minneapolis.

But come nine A.M., Pamela punched in the number to Paul's room extension, hoping he was awake. Her stomach was in tatters.

"Paul here," he said on the first ring.

"Good morning. You made it in, I see?"

"Not until two this morning. Talk about a miserable flight."

"I was thinking maybe we could have breakfast. If you're up to it."

"Sounds good. An hour from now okay?"

"How about Perkins?" she offered.

"I was thinking it would be nice to see the house…I could stop and pick something up on my way over. Caramel rolls from Byerly's maybe?"

"Sure. Whatever you'd like. I'll put the coffee on. And Paul?"

"Yeah?"

"I'm looking forward to seeing you." He didn't respond immediately. "I mean…it's been a while. I've done a lot of thinking and…well, it's gonna be hard, but we'll manage. Right? It's good for us to talk."

"Yeah, I agree. See you in a little bit."

She was reaching for the mugs at the back of the cabinet when she spotted him through the kitchen window, getting out of the rental car he'd parked in the driveway. It was such a familiar sight that Pamela's heart skipped a beat.

"Hi." She smiled, opening the back door for him.

Paul's face had acquired a few more wrinkles over the past six months—or it might have been the taut expression on his face. She couldn't tell. His hair was definitely saltier.

"Hi." His eyes swept down her jean-clad figure. He handed her a bakery bag. "You look good, Pam."

"Thanks." She slipped a thick ceramic mug into his hands—black coffee, the way he liked it. "I had to search for this. I packed it away when you left."

"Still think it's the best cup in the world." He grinned. "Haven't found another like it."

"So…um…it was a bad flight, huh?"

"Plane was two hours late. Some problem with the wind flaps," said Paul, sitting down in his old chair by the kitchen table. "You seem to be doing well."

"I am." Pamela placed two plates of pastry on the table, choosing the spot across the table from him. She told of her book deal with Chad—and of how much her new cabin was coming to play in all that.

"It's been good for me, Paul. I'd love for you to see it…it's beautiful!"

"Good for you," was all he finally said as she refilled his mug for the third time. "And the book sounds nice. Looks like your little hobby is finally beginning to pay off."

"Little *hobby?* Do you have any idea how big a start this could be for me, Paul?" She reached across and touched her husband's hand. "No. I don't want to do this. I don't want to bicker. You came here to talk to me, right? How about if we talk…"

He pulled his hand from her to scratch the side of his nose. "You're right, Pam. I'm sorry. This is nice, isn't it? Just sitting here drinking a cup of coffee. I don't remember the last time I did that without my computer or paperwork in front of me. How about if we go sit in the family room. Much more comfortable than these hard old chairs."

"I second the motion," Pamela said, following him to the other room and taking a seat on the couch.

He stopped at the hall table where she'd arranged a number of framed photographs—most he'd seen before, some brand-new. Then pushing aside a pile of unopened mail, Paul leaned against the table to study a shot of Angie Pamela had snapped at Belton.

"Nice picture," he said, turning the frame toward Pamela. "She looks so grown-up—reminds me of you when we first met."

Pamela smiled, warmed by the bittersweet burst of nostalgia

Paul inspired. "I took it by the dorms. Angie was so happy. And I was so…so *without* her. I still miss her so much. Did she get a hold of you by the way?"

"I need to call her. She's left a few messages about tuition." Paul picked his coffee cup up off the little table and went to sit in one of the wing-back chairs. "I was thinking that maybe I'd fly to Chicago around the holidays. Or…how long does she have off for Thanksgiving break?"

"She has to be back in school Monday morning. Why?"

"Oh, I was just thinking I could spend some time with her when I fly back for the settlement hearing. I could come Saturday—"

"The settlement hearing?"

"Tuesday? Right after the holiday weekend…"

"But! I thought…I thought that you came here to work things out. You're not with Dana anymore…"

Paul stared across at her, his eyes wide. "Oh…No, Pam. No. You don't get it. I still intend to go through with this divorce," he said softly and not unkindly. "I just thought it would be good to…well, to touch base beforehand."

"But…but you came here to see me."

"It seemed like the time for us to talk might be right. To try and put the past behind us. You can't honestly think that I would stop the divorce proceedings, Pam. After all this? Is that really why you thought I was coming out here?"

She stared into her coffee cup to avoid the mockery she knew would be in Paul's eyes. "I don't know exactly *what* I believed."

The tears were flowing now and she knew how much Paul hated that. Sometimes he'd reacted to her tears in anger; more often it just flustered him and he escaped. "Could you excuse me for just a bit? I...I just need a moment."

Pamela escaped to the bathroom and placed a cold rag over her face for a minute. Then she walked back out into the family room.

Paul had moved back toward the hall table again, was looking down at her pictures. He turned toward her when she entered the room. "Look, Pam. I should go. I can see this was a mistake. I wanted to touch base with you, yes. I thought we could talk about Angie...and maybe I hoped you would see things differently by now. And we could find a way to be friends. I don't want to be cruel, but we should never have gotten married in the first place. I don't love you and I can't live like this anymore. It's all been a lie."

"A lie? Is that what you think we had? I thought it was commitment. And memories. And *love*! We had something once, Paul. I *know* we did. You're the one who's wrong there."

"Believe what you want."

He turned to leave, but Pamela grabbed his elbow. "Don't. Not yet. You owe me this chance to say my piece."

His eyes were hardened now, but he leaned against the table. After a bit he asked: "What do you want from me?"

Pamela closed her eyes and considered his question. "I'm not sure now. Maybe I want to hear you say that you're sorry—"

"I *am* sorry."

"Oh? Not sorry enough to try to work it out, though. What *are* you actually sorry for, Paul?" Her sadness had been almost completely replaced by anger now.

"I'm sorry that things between us didn't work out."

"They *could* have. We could have gotten help. Made it better than ever before, Paul. Do you know that?"

Paul shook his head and then, to her great humiliation, he laughed—a bitter, scornful little laugh. "Oh, *right*, Pam. Don't you get it? I don't *love* you. You expect some counselor can teach me that? You were a good mother and homemaker…and I respect you. I like you, even. But that's all there is. And I finally have realized that's not enough for a marriage. Listen, I really don't feel the need to go through this all over again."

"Go through it *again*? Oh, thanks, Paul. In case you don't remember, we never *did* go through it. You didn't give us a chance! You left one half hour—do you hear me—*one half hour* after dropping your little bomb. And we haven't talked since. Unless you count those brief little phone conversations we've had."

"That was what you wanted."

"Excuse me?"

"The half hour the night I left. I planned to stay until morning. You're the one who told me to leave."

Pamela's eyes flew open. "I can't believe you even *said* that. You expected me to sleep in the same house with you, knowing what you had done! What you were *about* to do?"

"Pamela, we have nothing more to discuss. Our divorce will be final in a few months, and as soon as it's final, I'm…I'm marrying Dana. I wish you the best; you're a good person. I suggest you get on with your life."

Dana. There it was—the name she'd tried to push out of her thoughts for all these months. *Marrying Dana.* Pamela kept silent, breathing, willing Paul to disappear and at the same time, desperate to keep him there. Desperate for another chance to put it all back together. Was she a glutton for punishment?

"I thought maybe whatever you felt for that…that woman had worn off."

"I never said that. We haven't broken up, Pamela. We just need time to consider our future together. And Dana thinks…we *both* think it's better to be apart for a bit to do that. But it isn't your business, Pam."

"Do you love her? Do you!"

Paul was silent—but his eyes bored into Pamela's.

"And what about your relationship with God, Paul?"

She watched the muscle at his jaw tighten, then release. "That's *my* business. But one thing I do know is this: God doesn't want me to be trapped in a loveless marriage. I had it all wrong before—God isn't a cruel overseer who forces us to keep doing things we don't like. He's a force for good. For peace. I'm finally free of all that guilt that was heaped on me before by people like you…like Reverend Jurgenson…like your precious Starla."

Pamela shook her head. "Free? After you've ripped apart our family? I doubt it."

"Maybe you can't forgive me, but God has. And that's what counts the most."

"Okay, Paul," Pamela dug her nails into the palms of her hands. She took a deep breath and loosened her grip. "I can see debating this with you is pointless."

"Can I go now? Or is there something else you feel the need to talk about?"

Pamela narrowed her eyes. "What about Angie?"

"What about her? I've tried to talk to her. I'm not the one

who's barred that door, you know. And I'll *keep* trying. She's my daughter. Good-bye, Pam. I guess I'll see you in a month."

Every muscle in her body tensed as he turned away from her and walked out the door. But oddly, as she watched him back his luxury rental car out of her driveway, Pamela felt her anger ebb away. And as it did, a strange sorrow began to fill its place.

Paul was right about one thing. She couldn't force him to love her.

Thirty-Eight

PAUL HAD SIX miserable hours left to kill in Minneapolis before his flight left. The morning he'd spent with Pamela made it all the worse, but being back in Minnesota was a far tougher pill to swallow than he had expected. Memories of happier times washed over him—alienating him from the city he'd once loved. And it was harder still with this forced separation between him and Dana.

At least he'd accomplished his mission—he still had his pride. Luanne's letter was tucked in his pocket.

So, Pamela, it's in your hands now. I waited most my life to pay back the pain them two men caused me. One's dead, sure. But the other keeps on with it. Now with you knowing the truth, we can get back at him. You're my best hope. Maybe he'll learn this time.

Despite all the trouble he'd gone through to purloin the letter, he realized he might have acted out of panic. Pam probably wouldn't have responded as Luanne had hoped for. Sure, she might have found a way to inform Dana, knowing how much that would hurt him. But letting the information out to a wider audience was beneath Pam's dignity.

306   Paul reached in his briefcase and turned his cell phone on. The message indicator came on, and when he checked, he saw that Angie had called. He tried his daughter's room at Belton, but she wasn't there. But when he gave his name, the girl who answered volunteered to find her, telling Paul to try back in fifteen minutes.

"I got your message to call," he said when she picked up the phone twenty minutes later. "I did send out your tuition check. Is everything else okay, honey?"

"I've been trying to reach you all week." Her voice was deadpan.

"I'm sorry…things have been so busy lately—"

"I hear you went home."

Home. Paul cringed at her word choice. "Yes. I'm still here, actually. My flight doesn't leave until this evening."

"I just talked to her," she said.

"Oh. Well…is she doing all right?"

Angie's silence hung thickly. Then: "You really care?"

"Of *course* I care, Angie. I was married to her for a long time. You don't just completely stop caring."

"Oh really? You sure have a funny way of showing it."

"Angie, this is hard enough as it is—"

"No. Stop. I've been thinking—maybe it's not been hard *enough* on you."

Paul clamped his mouth shut and listened as Angie spouted

off all the reasons his involvement with Dana was wrong, how cruel he'd been to her mother, how little responsibility he'd taken in rearing Angie, his emotional indifference to her, and on and on. It was little more than he expected—and yet in hearing it, he felt the anger of self-defense percolating inside him.

"Angie, do you really want me to stay married to your mom even though I don't love her?"

"I'd expect you to at least go to counseling."

"Why is that everyone's answer? Counselors can't create love where there is none, Angie. I wish I could make this all better for you—but you'll just have to accept the fact that not everything will always have a happy ending for you. I thought you might understand that part a little better now—but obviously you still have some growing up to do."

"Great. Resort to belittling me. So tell me, how would *growing up* make a difference, Dad?"

"Because you'll know that things aren't always so black-and-white. I love Dana, Angie. I've never known *anything* like this before."

"Oh, sure. You say that now. What about in ten years—or will you just fall out of love with her then, too?"

"Angie, Dana is perfect for me in a way your mother never was. I messed up twenty-one years ago, okay? And staying with your mom now would be the worst thing I could ever do. Not just for me, but for both of us."

"What about the Lord, Dad? You're leaving Him completely out of the picture."

"I'm not going to say that God and I don't have a lot of things to work out, Angie. But that's between Him and me. I have no doubt I'll have consequences to pay—but this is a decision I've made because of what I know to be true. Your mother is a good person. I want the best for her—*I'm* just not it."

"No kidding," Angie said.

"None of this means I don't love you, Angie. That hasn't changed. In fact, I'd like for us to try to see each other…maybe I can fly out there and we can sit down to talk. Try to work on salvaging something between us. I'll call you back when you've had more chance to digest this."

"Sure. Whatever."

"I love you, Angie."

A labored pause hung between them. Finally she said quietly, "I love you too, Dad."

And when the connection was broken, his eyes were moist.

November 15

Dear Journal,

I'm so psyched! Melinda *finally* decided to go on the Chicago trip with me. She's been holding out because her class schedule for next semester got so messed up and she hoped one of her required classes would be offered during the January term. But it's not, and she can at least get nursing credit for this trip, so it's worth it.

The best thing is that we'll be able to room together, which should be an interesting experience in itself. We have to share a tiny dorm at a women's rooming house with two other girls—just like some of the Lifelines locations. This one is right downtown in a not-so-great neighborhood. It's all part of the environment though—much more my thing than Mexico, I think.

I'm can't wait to see Mom's cabin at Thanksgiving. And to meet Ken. And see Gram! It's all I can think about. Well…mostly. I think about Jason an awful lot, too. He's swamped during the week with his premed program, but we're spending nearly every weekend evening together now. He's the coolest—and I really like the fact that he's going to be a doctor. It'll be hard to be away from him over Thanksgiving—but as everyone says, the coming back part will be wonderful!

Dad called again yesterday. Since he went back to Minnesota, he's been trying so hard to connect with me—he's even sent me stuff. Not just money, but flowers and cards and little thoughtful things like articles he's read. I didn't think he had it in him.

And he really tries to get me to talk when he calls. Like he cares about my life. Why didn't he do that before? Maybe he's changing. I'm scared, but part of me wants to believe it.

He's still not back with Dana. I asked—and it was pretty awkward. From what little he said, he's definitely not too happy about it. When I told Mom, she said something about it being fair play that he was as miserable as he made her.

I told her I didn't think that was very nice. But she doesn't like it when I say anything even halfway supportive of Dad. I hear it in her voice—which is like a rubber band. When she's in a good mood, it's all loose and happy. When she's stressed, her voice gets all tight and chippy.

And lately she's got this kind of mantra that's her answer for everything: "If he's so different, then he'll stop this divorce." I just don't get her sometimes. She's got a better life now than she ever did with him. And she still wants him back? Go figure.

I mean, I know that God wants marriage to be permanent. I've been really praying about it a lot lately. I even prayed that God would work a miracle with them. But the only thing that's completely clear to me is that my dad was miserable. And so was my mom—only she tried to tell herself for years that she wasn't.

I don't doubt God can still change things and use all this for some really intense lesson about His power or something. It just seems more and more obvious to me that He's not going to. And I don't get it at all.

Some of my friends say that I should break contact with my dad completely because he's living in disobedience. But that just doesn't feel right to me. Would Jesus have done that? I don't think so at all. Shouldn't I start trying to at least find a way to *like* my dad?

Thirty-Nine

JUST AS CHAD had predicted, Jim was more than just a little bit amenable to Pamela's reduction of hours. They worked out an arrangement similar in many ways to the one she'd had when Angie was in high school. Two, three days a week at the most—and now she got her pick of assignments.

Usually she spent Monday and Tuesday on a shoot, and on Wednesday morning she left for the cabin. By then, Pamela had already set her thoughts to the framing and plotting of shots she intended to capture over the next few days. A certain buzz of excitement coursed through her at the idea that these pictures would be published—not in some regional tourist magazine, but in a book that would bring tremendous exposure to her work.

If Pamela were completely honest, she'd admit she was driven by the nervousness of "what if." What if Chad didn't like what she'd done? What if he had to get someone else and start all over again? The worry served as a positive force, however, and did nothing to dull her creativity. In fact, Pamela's eyes interpreted everything differently these days.

Even the dreary November landscape was worthy of capturing on film. In past years, Pamela dreaded the gray weeks before the holidays; the dullness sapped her energy. The trees she especially loathed—their naked, angry branches lifted skyward, rudely demanding a blanket of snow. Now Chad's poetry washed her formerly dismal viewpoint with a clean perspective. Instead of ugly, the landscape outside her little cabin window became ethereal.

All became brilliant fodder for her study in black-and-white photography: days so cold and clear that the sun hung low over the lake, and its light, instead of pouring down from its summer high, shot out like silver spray paint. The water, with brittle patches of ice lining the shore, shimmered black beneath all that silver. The snow with flakes so enormous, almost artificial, they were like the white paper cutouts Angie used to tape on their windows.

She told Chad about her progress each time they spoke on the phone, and he seemed as enthused as she with the photos she described. And though Pamela offered to send copies of what she'd done so far to his Spanish hideaway, where he was working on the first draft of his novel, he insisted that he trusted her to do what she did best.

So, precariously armed with his faith in her, Pamela pushed creativity to its limits. For one of Chad's selections—a lonely poem about a child waiting for summer—Pamela drove an hour to Pequot Lakes to photograph Starla's niece, whom she had talked into modeling for her. Sarah was almost eleven, caught in that ungainly stage between childhood and adolescence. To Pamela, it was a magical age—elusive and enviable—a final moment of leftover girl.

She took pictures of Sarah on the lonely swing set behind the girl's home. Long brown hair blew across her face, catching on the matted fake fur collar of her red jacket. Barely a hint of a smile played in eyes that looked not quite straight at the camera. Earlier, Pamela had asked Sarah where she went to be alone.

She pointed out the window. *Out there.*

As beautiful as the portrait was, Pamela suspected Sarah would probably hate it for the childishness it revealed—and detest it all the more for hinting so obliquely at the young woman she was growing to be. Once Sarah got older, Pamela suspected she would cherish the photo, as would her parents. For the beauty of the portrait was not in the clothing or the background or even in a beautiful smile. It was, rather, in the honesty of a fleeting moment captured.

Ken (guaranteed the anonymity of shadows and backlight) posed for her as well. The result was a profile of him standing on his deck, looking toward the cool winter sun setting over Sunset Lake. His dark hair was ruffled by the wind, his expression contemplative.

For Pamela, the back and forth days of fall and early winter had fused her life to Ken's in a way she'd never expected. She was often surprised at how alike they were. Soul mates, Angie would have called it when she was younger. Most evenings, often after a shared dinner, they lingered late into the night to discuss the deeper things of their lives, including Pamela's feelings about Paul and the divorce. If there was one thing he helped her to see, it was that she had come to a turning point in her feelings toward Paul: The anger still surged and boiled under the surface, but Pamela had finally accepted the inevitable end of her marriage.

In the back of her mind, she couldn't help but wonder if Ken had become a substitute best friend, since Starla was drifting from Pamela in the gradual manner of women in love. The two still talked on the phone, of course. But face-to-face time was hard to carve out of their busy weeks—not only because of Adam, but also because of Pamela's own hectic work life. Pamela had little doubt that over time, their intimacy would find its balance again. After all, her relationship with Starla had weathered Pamela's marriage and half a nation's distance.

In the meantime, she was strangely content.

One Saturday, Pamela woke to rain beating overhead, inches from her face. The roof slanted down over the head of her bed, magnifying the sound, and the downpour surrounded her wakening like an endless round of applause. But she didn't want to hear it. So, she rolled over and slept again, knowing she had no real need to crawl from under the cocoon of blankets this cold, wet morning.

Finally, at eleven o'clock, Pamela turned up the furnace to chase the chill out of the air and took a shower. She sat, wet headed, in front of the French doors, wrapped in a blanket, and nursed a bowl of oatmeal as she watched sheets of water pelt across the lake. When the downpour finally let up and began to mix with wintry sleet, she picked a book off the shelf and hunkered down for a day of reading.

The rain was still dripping when she woke up early Sunday morning—and outside everything was muddy and dank. On a lark, Pamela called her mother. She hadn't gone to church since August and had been feeling more than just a little homesick for a worship service.

315

"Glad I caught you," Pamela looked out the window. "I was thinking about joining you for church this morning."

"I'd love it, Pammi! Meet me there?"

When she pulled into the parking lot, she couldn't help but be drawn in by the familiar quaintness of her home church. It was something from a Norman Rockwell painting—a small whitewashed box with a tall steeple and stained glass windows. And the grandma types milling about the entryway in their wool coats and disposable plastic rain hats completed the picture. Truthfully, it would have been easy to fall back into her old habit of judging this northern congregation as parochial. But something new had clicked in. A respect for simplicity.

Pamela found Joan (already seated in the weathered pew her mother had always chosen) and slid in next to her as a number of familiar faces turned to smile or touch her shoulder in welcome. She felt their eyes upon her during the entire service. And as she and her mother made their way out, Pamela held many a warm, wrinkled hand in hers, caught the joy shining in their eyes, and heard their sincerity—saw evidence of their love for the Lord. How had she missed all this before? Whatever made her believe these northern people were dull and boring?

Pamela followed her mom's immaculate old green Cutlass to a little café in town for brunch. Sitting across from Joan, whose plate overflowed with the Lumberjack Special, Pamela said, "It was good to be back, Mom."

Joan smiled, but all she said was, "Nice sermon, wasn't it?"

"It was rather appropriate. Especially that part about not trying to write the endings to our own stories...that God is the author of our lives. You know what I was thinking about?"

"What, honey?"

"Something Ken said to me a while back about how I was hoping to force God's hand. I didn't quite get it at the time, but I think Ken might have been right. It doesn't make sense that a Christian would choose to end their marriage, considering what the Bible says. So, every time I prayed for Paul to come back, I truly believed God had no choice but to let that happen. My *words* would be the instrument of change."

"You wanted to write the ending?"

"Yes, and I think I'm seeing now that *God* is the one who holds the authority to do that. For some reason, He's allowing this divorce, and I think I need to grasp on to the fact that He knows best. No matter what the result is."

"Or however long it takes to understand His reasons?"

Pamela nodded.

"That's a pretty powerful thing to come to terms with, Pammi."

"Especially when my marriage is about to be flushed down the toilet. I think I can *accept* God's will...I'm just not sure I can ever forgive Paul."

Joan's eyes were soft with sympathy. "It's got to be hard to be this close to the end, Pammi. I've suggested this before, but have you thought any more about trying to find some sort of Christian support group for divorced people—folks that would know exactly what you're going through?"

"I don't know, Mom…"

"It couldn't hurt, Pammi. Every single one of those people has gone through what you're now going through."

"This sounds so petty, Mom, but I hate the idea of being labeled a divorcée."

Joan reached across and laid her hand on top of Pamela's. "I can only imagine how hard that is…but maybe it's time to swallow your pride. Don't make the same mistakes I did. You don't have to walk through this on your own. There are people who can help."

"I know."

"Angie seems to be doing well," Joan said.

The waitress returned with fresh coffee, and when she left Pamela took a few bites of her omelette.

"She's getting so excited for her Chicago trip. Every time I get her on the phone, that's the only thing she can talk about! Thank you so much for helping her with the expenses. You didn't have to do all that."

"I wanted to. And it's a great opportunity."

"Yes, I agree." Pamela paused. "Can I ask you a question, though?"

"Sure."

"Angie *could* have spent the entire month of January at home. Do you think she's doing this to escape? I wonder if she might have even done that in the past. Ever since junior high she's signed up for every little missions trip she could."

Joan shook her head. "No, I don't think that's the reason,

Pammi. Not intentionally, at least. I think Angie just has a natural gift for helping people and a driving need to use it. Sure, there's probably a part of her that's running. But I'm not so sure I'd analyze that if I were you. She's not hurting herself."

"You're right. You know I'm taking her to the cabin over Thanksgiving weekend? I was wondering if you would join us on Thursday for dinner?"

"You sure you want to do that? You could just come my way."

Pamela grinned. "I won't mind it at all. Actually, I was thinking about having a few more people, too. Ken and Starla, and her dad. And I'm hoping Adam can join us as well. It might be fun to start a new tradition, don't you think?"

The two women finished brunch and paid the bill. When they parted ways outside the door, they were doused once again with the wet chilliness in the air. By the time she got back to Sunset Lake, Pamela was crawling with goose bumps and could hardly shake them off.

Over the lake, the sky hung low—a wet, gray blanket slowly soaking up more moisture to dump later in the day. And though yesterday's rain was mixed with only a little snow, she suspected today's precipitation would be all white.

Even the inside of the cabin was moist and cool and thick from being shut up against yesterday's storm. She packed her overnight bag and cooler and started back to the Cities.

Forty

"Sɪᴛ sᴛɪʟʟ! You're making *me* nervous!"

"It's your fault, Chad!" Pamela teased and continued to pace back and forth. Chad was hunched over the light table, examining the slides she'd provided him of her photographs.

"It would have been much easier on me if you'd at least have let me send you a few examples," she said.

"Didn't I say I trusted you?" Chad balanced his magnifying ring atop the slides and turned toward Pamela. "Besides, the burden of trouble will be on me if I can't use these. Not you. Just to put you at ease, though…they're everything I expected them to be. If not better."

"Really?"

"Really. Relax, Pamela! Do you want something to drink?"

"How about water." She was grinning from ear to ear.

"Sparkling, to match your mood?"

"Tap is fine if you have some ice, thanks." She walked happily away from the drafting table and went to the window. Chad's town home was on the twenty-second floor of a downtown building. "What a view! I'll bet I can see my house from here."

"Probably could if you knew exactly where to look. I love living this high above the world. Smack-dab in the middle of downtown. To me, it's pure heaven." Chad put a cold glass in her hands and stood beside her, looking out. "So....do you have plans tomorrow?"

"I'm working. My boss is a slave driver. Has this book deadline he *insists* on meeting."

"Ah, but he means tomorrow *night*. And if I know this wonderful boss of yours as well as I think I do, I'm certain he'd also insist that you take some time off and maybe—"

"Excuse me, but did you notice how many winter pictures we still need? A *lot*. I'm leaving in the morning for Rabbit Lake. It snowed up there last night."

"And there's certain to be much more a few days from now."

He reached up and brushed a hair from her cheek and held her gaze. And though she sensed it coming, Pamela shivered at the contact.

"Would you like some company?" he said. "I could drive up—we could do the town."

Pamela stifled a giggle. "Which one? Brainerd?"

"There's got to be something to do."

"You're way too good to me, do you know that?" She'd already told him about Paul's little trip to Minneapolis and her stress over the upcoming hearing. "To be completely honest, my cabin is a haven. Not that I don't intend to share it with my friends—"

"But you need some time by yourself this weekend?" he finished quietly.

Pamela nodded. "Yes. But maybe…" She was going to suggest that they go out for dinner sometime between Thanksgiving and Christmas. "Oh…never mind."

"You're ready, aren't you?" Chad asked, ever so softly.

His eyes probed hers, and Pamela felt a pleasant tension in her belly. Then, without taking his gaze from hers, Chad reached for her glass and set it on the table beside them. "Someday, not so far from today…" He slowly pulled her into his arms and brushed her lips—a question to which Pamela nodded yes. He bent again, this time covering her lips in a deep kiss.

Chad drew Pamela closer, their kiss growing passionate and more demanding. Other than quick, hurried kisses in high school, she had never been intimate with a man other than Paul. Had never wanted to, really. This time, however, the temptation to throw caution to the winds took her by surprise. Mostly, because she considered herself far beyond this kind of ardor. Pamela's hands fluttered up and down Chad's back, aching to press further, to feel more. His groan stopped her, rooted her again in the reality of what was happening between them.

And ever so slightly, Pamela pulled away.

"Can I see you, Pamela?"

"I think so…I just don't know when, exactly." Her eyes begged his understanding. She couldn't remember if she'd ever been so stirred by chemistry. It erased all thoughts of Paul from her head. Maybe Chad was just what she needed…maybe…

"All right. I'll be waiting," he whispered, running a finger down her cheek, across her lips, to the hollow of her throat. His smile was understanding, and at the same time it conveyed disappointment.

Pamela pondered their relationship during the drive to the lake the following morning. As little time as she had spent with Chad, Pamela felt she knew him intimately through his poetry—he was romantic and sensitive, perceptive and charming. And just below the surface, a current of independence gurgled and boiled, threatening to explode. This wildness both terrified and enticed her.

Pamela wanted to jump in with her eyes closed. She wanted to experience the type of reckless romance she'd never known before. Her hunger to be touched, to be cared for, had reached the point of starvation. And the idea of salving her loneliness with Chad brought such relief she could almost wrap it around her like a fur coat.

And yet, something—be it her unresolved marital status, her moral convictions, or a deeper thing as yet undefined—*something* held her back.

Forty-One

PAUL WAS LATE. So late he had to park in the overflow lot behind church. The organ thumped its prelude as he hurried up the steps to the front doors. But as soon as he stepped inside, he stopped dead. Standing just to the left of the library entrance, waiting for him, stood Dana. She cradled a Bible in her hands—something he'd never seen her do before—and even from across the room he read nervousness in her expression.

"Hi," she said as he approached her. "Mind if I sit with you?"

"I can't believe it." Paul's heart was full. This was where he'd wanted her to be for months—the one place he knew could bring them together again.

"I wanted to come to church with you and then go somewhere and…talk."

"Nothing would be better."

Paul knew better than to say much more right now. It was best to let the situation lead him. During the entire service she clung to his hand, tears pouring down her face. Her Bible was open on her lap and every so often she paged through and focused on some passage she'd found. He'd been embarrassed by her emotion, but at the same time, he knew that Dana had to get through this in her own way.

And if it brought her back to him…

As they stood to leave, a lady touched Dana on her shoulder. Her eyes were young though her thin, papery skin revealed her age. "Thank you for sharing your tears, dear. Whatever it is you seek, don't give up until you've found it."

"This is my first time back to church in…in months," Dana told her, wiping the mascara from under her eyes.

"I'm so glad you've come back then, dear. God bless you." She smiled and turned to walk away.

Paul led Dana to his car and unlocked the door for her, squatting beside her for a moment to be sure she was all right. "Let's pick yours up later, okay?" She nodded. "Where would you like to go? Should we hit Eggstra, Eggstra for old time's sake?"

"Would you mind driving to the beach? Down toward Laguna maybe? I need space."

"If you're sure…" He paused, willing her to change her mind. But she said nothing. "Then that's where we'll go."

The drive down the coast was awkwardly empty of conversation, and it reminded him of the old days with Pamela. Every so often, a look of pain crossed Dana's features. "Are you okay?" he finally asked.

She turned to him with watery eyes gone soft and emotional. "Yeah," she whispered. "I am."

He smiled then. "I was surprised to see you there this morning. Thank you for coming, Dana."

Paul could feel Dana's eyes on his face. She said nothing for a bit and then, "I can see why you like it there. At that church, I mean."

"I think you might too, if you give it a chance." Paul looked sideways. "Dana? You were pretty clear you didn't want to make any decisions until after Thanksgiving. But with you showing up today, I was hoping maybe you'd changed your mind. Have you?"

She closed her eyes and leaned her head back against the seat. She took a deep breath and looked toward the sea. "Angie called for you at the house—"

"I know that."

"No, she called again last week. Your cell phone was off and she thought you were back home. She mentioned you flew back to talk to Pamela."

Paul glanced at her. "Yes."

"Are you still pursuing this divorce?"

"Of *course*. The settlement hearing is a week from Tuesday."

"Then I want to go with you to Minneapolis, Paul."

He pulled off the road, into an ocean overlook. He turned to face Dana, his heart beating a bit faster. "You still want us to be together?"

"I want us to date, to get to know each other in the right way."

"Date? Like high school?"

Dana nodded. "And nothing physical. I'm drawing strict lines. I don't want you to move back in until after we get married."

"After all we've been to each other, why are you putting us in this box? I don't get it."

"This is about the closest I can come to doing the right thing, Paul. Some people have told me the *real* right thing would be to leave you, entirely give up the idea of marrying you. Repent for all I've done and go my own way without ever seeing you again."

"That's crazy."

"No. Listen. As hard as I've tried to make myself leave you, I *can't*." Dana's eyes teared up again. "I've been studying the story of David and Bathsheba in the Bible. And despite their sin of adultery, God forgave them and allowed them to marry."

"And He'll do the same for us. I've already felt that He has."

"You're missing the point. God forgave them—but they still had tremendous consequences to pay. Like the death of their baby. And a war-torn kingdom. And serious bouts of depression for both of them. And—"

"But you don't need to impose consequences upon us, Dana. That's God's job."

"Is that what you think I'm doing? No, Paul. All I'm doing is proceeding the only way I can. You were never mine to have…and I wanted us so badly that I started taking for myself what only God had to give. As of this moment, you are still married. I'm going back to Minneapolis with you because I have a few people I need to see—and I want to be there for you if you need to talk, because I love you. But that's all I can be for you right now. A friend. I'm still confused…but I know God is going to lead me through all this somehow."

"I don't want to lose you."

Dana smiled through her tears. "I love you, Paul. And eventually I hope to marry you. But it's got to be done this way or I can't go through with it."

Forty-Two

"AND LORD," Pamela continued, the last one around the table to offer her prayer of Thanksgiving, "I thank You for the blessing of Sunset Lake, Angie's homecoming, my work, and all these wonderful friends gathered around my table. Thank You for walking with me through this difficult year—and seeing me to happier days. In Your name I pray, Amen."

"Amen," echoed the rest.

Adam, who sat between Starla and her father, looked at Pamela. "Would you mind if I offered a *berakhah*?" he asked with a smile—a shy, boyish one that seemed comically out of place for such a big man.

Pamela raised her eyebrows. "A what?"

"A berakhah," Starla said, "is one of the Hebrew prayers given for the blessing of food."

"Then by all means, go for it, Adam!" said Pamela. "I would be honored."

He pushed his large frame to a standing position, lifted his hands, palms upraised, and spread them wide above the table. He prayed first in Hebrew, then repeated it in English: "Blessed are You, Lord our God, King of the Universe, who brings forth bread from the earth. Blessed are You, Lord our God, King of the Universe, who creates the fruit of the tree and the fruit of the earth. Blessed are You, Lord our God, King of the Universe, by whose word all things come into being. Amen."

He opened his eyes and slowly lowered his arms, then sat down. The appreciative hush lasted another few seconds while Starla beamed at Adam—and Pamela was pretty sure she caught a flash of tears in Starla's dad's eyes.

"Okay, everyone, dig in!" Angie yelled.

Suddenly, a sea of hands reached for platters and bowls amidst a riot of convivial voices. Norman Rockwell would have been impressed! The number of people packed around Pamela's table or sitting on the wicker sofa with plates propped on their laps invigorated her. No one seemed to mind the crowd, gauging by the laughter and conversation filling the smallish back room of Pamela's northern home.

Adam and Ken really hit it off, and Joan and Starla's dad, Vernon, had a great time catching up on all the years since Pamela and Starla's high school graduation. They were practically neighbors, but only rarely ran into each other at Super Valu or whatnot. A few times during dinner, the two of them collaborated in frightful tales of their daughters' escapades, each telling the parts they knew best. Pamela laughed to hear their interpretation—Starla denied till she was blue in the face—and Adam hung on their every word, guffawing in great roars of laughter, eager to soak up all he could of Starla's girlhood.

Angie was totally taken with Ken, as Pamela had known she would be. He held his own with her inquisitive daughter and the two of them bantered back and forth, talking about music and other subjects they seemed to have in common. As Pamela watched them, she couldn't help but wonder if Angie would get along this well with Chad. And what she would think if things...well, if he and Pamela ever started dating.

In between getting to know Angie and Adam, Ken played host, trolleying between his place and Pamela's with delectable fare from his oven and refrigerator. Pamela's own little kitchen was ill-suited for a holiday crowd, so the turkey had roasted all morning in Ken's oven, as had the stuffing and the pies, which he'd volunteered to make. He carved the turkey, kept glasses filled with water and milk, and passed salads, rolls, and potatoes to the people on the couch whenever needed.

"Hey, Ken," Starla said at one point, "whose Thanksgiving dinner is this anyway? Yours or Pammi's!"

"I'm only a mercenary! She paid me for my culinary abilities, don't ya know?" Ken said.

But none of his help seemed out of place in the least. In fact, Pamela really couldn't have done it without him. Their eyes often met in friendly appreciation through the course of the day, whether at the table, over the traditional Thanksgiving game of Monopoly, or later, as they served dessert to overstuffed guests who miraculously found room to squeeze in "just a small piece, please" of pumpkin praline pie.

"Pammi! Don't tell me you baked a pie?" Joan teased. "Angie told me you completely gave up baking. And I felt so bad for her for all those Oreos you keep sending that *I* send her cookies now. *Home-baked* ones."

"Hey, now…I lead a very busy life these days." Pamela glared at her mother good-naturedly.

"Credit for the dessert actually goes to Adam," Starla said proudly. "Another male chef along the lines of Ken here, I do have to say."

As much as Pamela had come to enjoy the usual solitude of her northern getaway, she cherished more than ever the cheerful bustle of people filling her cabin that Thanksgiving Day. She had never been one to entertain before—in fact, even when, in Paul's business dealings, she had been obligated to entertain, Pamela had food catered in. Not that she minded the cooking all that much. Paul just wanted everything perfect. Far more perfect than Pamela could manage. More often than not, he suggested they take their guests out.

This was different, however. It pleased Pamela to share her life with the people around her—to cast her overwrought concern for having everything perfect out the window.

In the middle of dessert, Adam clinked his fork on a glass. "May I have your attention, please? I have an announcement to share with all of you." He turned to Starla, who was grinning from ear to ear.

"I am pleased to announce that just last evening, my darling Starla, with the approval of her dear father, agreed to become my wife!"

Pamela crossed to her friend and threw her arms around her. "Congratulations, Starla!"

"Will you be my maid of honor, Pammi?" Starla whispered.

Pamela wiped a tear from her eye and whispered back: "Of *course* I'll be your maid of honor."

"So let's hear the story. Details please! How did you propose, Adam?" yelled Angie, silencing the babble around the table. "Where's the wedding going to be? And have you set a date?"

"We're thinking we'll have the wedding sometime toward the end of summer," Starla said. "Maybe August. And we both agreed that the best place to have it would be at my cabin. I've always wanted an outdoor wedding."

Adam feigned disapproval. "Excuse me, darling, but I believe that the questions were posed to *me*."

"Oh, puh-leeze excuse me."

Adam turned his back to Starla. "To answer your question, Angie, my proposal turned out to be much less romantic than I'd planned. I asked her in Vernon's den." Everyone groaned. "My *intention* had been to make a bigger production of last night, but good old Star here," he thumbed over his shoulder, "walked in on us just as I was asking her father for her hand."

"Forty years old and the man still thinks he needs to get Dad's permission to marry me!"

Vernon grinned. "I wouldn't have it any other way, Starla. But I agree with Adam—you *were* a nosy one! She walked right in on us, and out-and-out demanded to know what poor Adam and I were discussing. And I tried to get rid of her. But you know Starla. Persistent. Just like her mother!"

"Oh…I wish your mother were alive to see you walk down the aisle," Joan said.

"I know." Starla's brown eyes went all velvety. "I miss her a lot right now. But after all these years, at least Dad will get a chance to see me greet my groom beneath the *huppah*."

"It's something I've hoped for since the day I first laid eyes on you," Vernon said.

"Someone care to tell us what a huppah is?" Angie said.

"Oh, honey, just wait until ya see it!" Starla said. "It's the best part of a Jewish wedding ceremony. It's this big, beautiful, canopylike thing the wedding party all stands under. It will be absolutely *dripping* with flowers."

Dripping with flowers.

It was the same phrase Starla had used to describe Hoyt Covenant when she and Pamela peeked at the sanctuary before Pamela's wedding. Paul had insisted that Pamela not look—it was to be his surprise since he was footing the bill for the entire thing. But neither she nor Starla could resist, and Starla's jaw dropped at the elaborate display of flowers and greenery.

"It's like it rained and God dropped every bloom right here in Minneapolis! It's dripping with flowers! And smell..." she inhaled. "Oh, it smells like heaven!"

Pamela had been speechless at the gift her soon-to-be husband had bestowed upon her. But now she couldn't help but wonder if Paul had made the sanctuary beautiful for her or for the important business acquaintances he had invited to share their day.

She shook the thoughts clear and concentrated once more on Starla, who was interrupted on occasion by Vernon and Adam, explaining the traditional elements they hoped to incorporate in their ceremony.

A curious blend of sadness and peace welled up inside Pamela at her friend's enthusiasm. Starla was getting married. And come Tuesday, Pamela's marriage would be one step away from complete dissolution.

Angie and Pamela headed home late Friday afternoon, primarily so Angie could spend a little time with her high school friends, who, like her, were home for the long weekend. But also, it was to continue one tradition the two of them looked forward to each Thanksgiving weekend: decorating their home for Christmas.

On Saturday, the two of them pulled out the box of branches and stems and put together the huge tree everyone always said looked so real. With the first Christmas music of the season blaring from the stereo, she and Angie put the lights up, twisted garlands round banisters, and displayed knickknacks by the hundreds in their traditional places on the shelves and walls of Pamela's home.

For once Pamela had little desire to bring Paul into their conversation. Angie would be gone by late Sunday afternoon, and only then would Pamela allow herself to mull over Tuesday's settlement hearing. And she intended to do it alone.

"Are you okay, Mom?" Angie asked as she stood back and surveyed their work.

Pamela raised her eyes from the string of lights she was trying to unravel. "Yeah, I am. Why do you ask?"

"It's only three days away…"

"I'll be all right, Angie. Really. Are you doing okay? We always talk about how I'm handling the divorce—but you're part of this family, too."

"I'm handling it."

"If this had to happen, I'm at least glad you have a life of your own—away from here where you don't have to deal with it every day."

"I appreciate that you don't bring it up so much every time we talk. It makes it easier for me to work my own things through with Dad. He's really trying."

Angie put down the garland she had been winding around the banister and crossed the room to the little table of framed photos. "You put out the family picture from last year's Christmas card, I see."

Pamela nodded and joined her, taking the photo in her hands. "I'm not sure why. It makes me sad. But now I can't seem to take it off the table."

Paul was smiling that big, toothy, Hollywood grin that practically swallowed his face. He'd been involved with Dana even then. Right when the photographer snapped the picture! Most likely he'd already had plans to leave.

"A while back Dad sent me a card with a fifty-dollar check in it—and he signed the card with both their names. I told him how bad it bothered me to see her name with his. And do you know, he doesn't even remember signing her name?"

"You believe that?"

"Yes."

Pamela shrugged her shoulders. "I think he did it purposely, Angie."

"No, Mom, that's my whole point. Dad's not intentionally cruel. He's just all wrapped up in this. And for me, his total ignorance might be why I can start trying to forgive him."

"That may be possible for you, Angie. But for me?..."

"It is different for me. I don't have to forgive Dad for betraying me. I just need to forgive him for being uninvolved when I needed him most. I heard somewhere that forgiveness means you give up your right to get even. I need to do that. Does that make sense?"

"All I know is that until your Dad sincerely apologizes to me for what he's done, I won't be able to forgive him. I could if we would get back together. But how can I now?"

"Mom, *please* listen. I'm not talking about *you*. I'm ready to rebuild a relationship with my dad. Can you let me do that?"

"Oh, honey…I'm sorry. Sometime I just can't see through my own frustration. I have to let you do that with your dad." Pamela set the family photo back on the table and pulled Angie into her arms. "It's not like I don't want you to be close to your dad. That's what I've wanted for you all your life. It's just that now, I'll not be a part of it."

"I know that, Mom."

"I can't imagine you'll ever get him to actually say he's sorry."

"I used to think that forgiveness on my part would require that," Angie said. "I'm not so sure now. On the plane flying home, I was trying to think of places in the Bible where forgiveness was offered to unrepentant people. I couldn't remember any. But what about that verse that says 'while I was *yet* a sinner, Christ died for me'? Christ died for me and forgave me before I even breathed one breath on this planet. He forgave me before I asked."

"But we still need to ask for His forgiveness."

"Yes. But when I did ask, it was already there. A done deal. Maybe that's what I need to work toward with Dad. Forgive him in my heart and hope that someday, finally, he'll see the light and ask for it. And I'll be able to tell him I already did that."

"You're not going to tell him that you're forgiving him?"

"I'm just going to work on *doing* it—thinking of him in a new light may be a better way of putting it. It's not like I'm going to get all buddy-buddy with him or anything right away. I can hardly imagine what that would be like."

Pamela looked at her daughter and was proud of her. And there was no doubt that Angie would be freer for her decision. Pamela only hoped she could be strong enough to support her…to keep her mouth closed from all the spiteful things she still wanted to spill about Paul.

Forty-Three

ON MONDAY MORNING, Pamela headed to the Mall of America to get a bit of her Christmas shopping done. Actually, the trip to the mall served two other purposes as well: Get her mind off Tuesday's settlement hearing and assuage her loneliness for Angie following such a wonderful holiday weekend. After a good three hours of traipsing from store to store, browsing and selecting gifts for Angie and a few others on her list, Pamela finally abandoned her mission.

Why in the world did I ever think shopping was fun?

Earlier, she'd spotted a coffee shop on one of the upper layers of the mall, and now she headed back there, practically salivating for a burst of caffeine. Pamela lugged her merchandise and an extra-large mocha to a table looking down on an open area where a teeming mass of shoppers scurried. She took a sip and closed her eyes a bit, relishing the warmth and aroma of her coffee.

A baby wailed loudly at a table near her, and Pamela turned to see what the problem was. Instead, her eyes landed on a woman a table beyond that—and her heart stopped.

Dana! And right beside her, of course, was Paul.

Pamela turned her body toward the railing, desperate to fly over it and disappear. But she couldn't resist the urge to look once more at the woman who had stolen her husband. As nonchalantly as possible, Pamela turned her head. Just as she did, the people at the table between them began to get up and leave, and Paul caught her eye.

"Pam," he said, with a nod in her direction. Dana's eyes snapped on her like a camera's autofocus.

"Hello, Paul." *Oh, the awkwardness!*

"Funny meeting you here."

"I was shopping. Obviously. Hello, Dana." *I should just get up and leave.*

"Hi, Pamela," Dana said.

Even the sound of the woman's voice grated on her nerves. Pamela tried to meet Paul's eyes. "Please tell me you're not intending to bring *her* along to the hearing?"

Paul barely raised his eyes.

"Oh, please, you mean to tell me you can't manage this all by yourself? You need her along to hold your hand?" Pamela slid her gaze to Dana, leaching strength from her obvious discomfort. "But then, you've been doing that for quite a while now, haven't you, Dana. Kind of *stole* that job from me, didn't you?"

"Pamela, please," Dana said quietly. "I….I'm sorry I hurt you."

"You're sorry! Then what are you *doing* here?"

"I don't think we should do this now. At some point we should all sit down and talk things through instead of living with this unresolved tension."

"*Tension?*" Pamela felt a growl building at the base of her throat and dug the fingernails of her left hand into her palm. "You don't have a clue what tension I've lived with! You're both too wrapped up in your own little world to see the pain you've caused me!"

"Pam, don't…" Paul said in a voice she hardly recognized for its silly, cowardly pitch.

"No. *You* don't." Pamela said slowly and straight into his eyes. "You may be marrying this…this—"

"Yes, Pamela, I am marrying Dana. I'm happier with her than I have ever been."

"How you can say that, Paul! Your union is outside of God's laws. How will you ever be happy?"

"I've heard enough. Let's go." Paul stood and began to gather their packages and move quickly from the table, indicating for Dana to follow him. Like a dog. Same inconsiderate man. At least that much hadn't changed.

And though Dana did rise and follow, she looked back once as Paul walked away. And Pamela could have sworn she saw tears in her eyes.

Pamela cradled her lukewarm mocha in her hands and stared at the table. Her own eyes filled with tears—and she felt an ugly, empty void bleed into every corner of her soul. She had a right to vent like this, didn't she? She was hurt. She was angry!

She felt the eyes of other customers on her and wondered how many people had witnessed the soap opera she and Dana and Paul had just enacted. And the longer she sat, the more sickened she became. It was almost as if all the wrath and vindictive words she had been so proud to have found minutes ago served no purpose at all.

Humiliated and humbled, she picked up her bags and walked out.

Forty-Four

THE COUNTY COURTHOUSE downtown was an ancient building created, presumably, to inspire awe. But to Pamela, who sat alone on a stone bench outside Room 322, its marble interior was a cold commentary on ages of misery. The halls echoed with the dissolution of families, the suffering of victims, the often emotionless fait accompli of myriad legal professionals.

Down the hall, the elevator door slid open, and Paul and his attorney walked out.

"Good morning, Mrs. Thornton."

Pamela nodded.

"Pam." Paul's eyes questioned whether or not she was going to be sticky.

"Paul," she said, then turned away.

The attorney ushered them into the miniature courtroom where the robed moderator sat at the front—papers spread before him, smiling to assuage the inevitable discomfort of silence. Pamela chose a seat at the thick oak table on the left side of the tiered semicircle of chairs, and Paul and his attorney sat together at the table on the other side.

"Can I offer coffee or tea to anyone this morning before we start?" the moderator asked.

Only the attorney helped himself to a cup.

Paul and Pamela skimmed the paperwork that was first explained, then put before each of them, in turn, to sign. There was no conversation—nor any dispute—save the necessary "yes, sir" and "no, sir" given to their moderator. The entire process lasted under an hour.

"When can I expect the final decree, sir?" Paul asked.

"It could be as little as a month. Just depends on the judge's caseload. When he, or she, reviews your documents and signs them, your divorce is final."

For the first time since they had entered the room, Pamela caught Paul's eyes.

"Are we *finished?*" she asked.

"Yes, Mrs. Thornton."

Pamela slid her gaze from Paul's face, stood up, and walked out of the room. Her eyes were dry, her sentiments all used up.

Forty-Five

KEN WAS HANGING a wreath on his door when Pamela's car crunched over the snow-crusted gravel between their homes late Tuesday afternoon. And, from the looks of her own door, he'd hung a big evergreen wreath for her as well. He came over to greet her as soon as her sedan idled to a stop.

"I hope you don't mind..." He swept his arm toward Pamela's door.

"Of course not! It's beautiful, thank you!"

"I wanted to put lights on one of your evergreens too before you got back. But then, last I heard, that wasn't going to be until Thursday or Friday."

"Jim didn't need me—and I figured I could use the time for my book. I've got a few more shots to get in before the big snow hits." She grimaced. "But truth be told? I needed to escape."

"Thought so. Things not go well with Paul, I take it?"

She screwed up her face and gave a thumb's down before she reached for the trunk button in her glove compartment.

"That bad, eh?" He lifted a box from her trunk and carried it through the door onto her porch. "I don't think I've stopped praying since you and Angie took off."

"Give me a few minutes. I'll unpack this junk and come over."

344

Ken handed Pamela a mug of hot chocolate as soon as she walked in, and she carried it to one of the big chairs by his fireplace. Humiliating as the experience was, she relayed the details of the mall confrontation. "I still think my feelings are justifiable, but the way I exploded like that—right in the middle of the coffee shop—that wasn't right. Sometimes it's so hard to be a Christian, you know that? The world can hate their spouses forever over stuff like this, but I'm expected to forgive. And *her?* How in the world can I ever forgive her? Even *thinking* about them together still cuts."

"And how did the hearing go?" Ken asked, coming from the kitchen. He moved the guitar propped in the chair opposite her to its stand next to the sofa and sat down.

"No surprises," Pamela said with almost no expression in her voice. "It was over in less than an hour. I left the courthouse, threw a few things together, and drove straight here. I haven't even talked to Starla yet. Left her a message that I was coming up here and just took off."

Ken propped his feet on the coffee table. "You're not falling apart, though. That's better than I would have thought."

Pamela shivered. "Just wait. Something's bound to happen now that the camel's back is officially broken. Maybe I'll have a nervous breakdown or something."

"You could plan one. Better make sure it's after Christmas though, or you'll miss out on more time with your daughter. She was great, by the way."

"She *adored* you. I think you're her new idol." Pamela smiled. "Don't be surprised if she sends you something to autograph. Angie was never one of those who plastered posters of rock stars on her wall—though she did have one of Mel Gibson on her ceiling for a while. Paul hated it—kept nagging at her to take it down before it peeled the paint off the ceiling."

"There's worse things a girl could do."

"Not in his opinion. Paul is the only meticulous slob I've ever known. God's the one who will have to deal with that man now, I guess. God and Dana." She slid from her chair and curled down to the floor and stretched her legs forward so her toes nearly skimmed the screen of the fireplace. "One thing I just don't get are the little comments Paul keeps making—both to me and to Angie—about how *happy and free* he is now. How can he be, when he's totally destroyed our family?"

"Maybe he really does feel that way. Paul's got everything he wants—all the creature comforts—which brings a sort of contentment."

"You should've seen him, though, Ken! He looks so old and worn out. He calls *that* freedom?"

"Remember, he believes that what he has now is better than what he had with you. But only God knows his heart."

"I will always hate hearing that, Ken."

"I know and I'm sorry. I'm sure it feels like a slap in the face."

Pamela considered what Ken said for a bit, then sighed. There were no tears—not even deep down. In a way, she felt as if she were narrating her story from the distance of years. "After Paul and I met earlier this month, I pretty much accepted the idea that our marriage was kaput. But today, I completely gave up the fight, Ken. I gave it *all* up."

He reached over and touched her hand, turning it so he could hold her fingers in his own. "You needed to, Pamela. All things considered, it was the only thing you could have done."

Forty-Six

THE WEEKS BEFORE Christmas—traditionally busy, rushed, and emotionally high—passed in a blur of insignificance. Pamela completed her pictures of the drab, early winter days, and was pretty much on hold with her photography until more snow fell. Jim was pleased to give her a few more hours during those days.

Pamela would have loved to spend some of her extra time with Starla. But even though Pamela knew that her friend tried hard to rein it in around her, Starla was focused on Adam and on planning her wedding. There were days, not many surprisingly, that Pamela just couldn't take it.

Not wanting to squelch Starla's joy, Pamela spontaneously picked up the phone and called Tina Rohlersson. As much as she'd pooh-poohed her mother, Pamela knew the time had come to connect with someone who'd been through a divorce.

Tina invited her to join her and Helena, another divorcée, for coffee that evening.

Pamela slid into the booth at Bakers Square across from Tina and Helena, and even before the conversation began, she knew she was doing the right thing.

"My husband married the other woman," Helena said after Pamela gave the two women a rundown of what happened Thanksgiving weekend. "Someone I've never met—and never want to. Bill had been unfaithful to me in the past, two times that I knew of, and I finally gave him an ultimatum. I just never thought he'd leave...Eight years ago. Eight years and it *still* hurts. But good has come, too. When my youngest graduated from high school, I went back and finished my degree—and God has blessed me with a great job and a surprisingly full life."

"Never in a million years did I think I would be divorced," Tina said. "To me, it just wasn't an option. I was willing to forgive it all if only my husband would come back. But he threw all that forgiveness right back in my face. Said he didn't want it. That he didn't love me anymore—that he'd met the love of his life."

"I can relate there," Pamela said. "I kept praying that God would bring Paul back. But our divorce isn't even final yet, and he's already planning his wedding. It's such an incredible rejection."

"It may feel like that, Pamela," said Tina, "but you did everything you could. You have to keep trying to remember that no amount of changing you could do would give him what he wanted. His leaving was not about you."

The three women shared more of their stories, and as her mother had hinted might happen, that's what lifted Pamela's spirits the most: discussing her pain with people who'd walked in her shoes. Helena wasn't quite as vocal as Tina, but her quiet acceptance was something Pamela valued. With both of them, she was able to unburden herself in a way she couldn't do even with Starla. Not that Starla wasn't sympathetic. She just couldn't be *empathetic*—and right now, that's what Pamela needed the most.

"It may not look that way now, but I promise you things will get better," said Helena.

Tina shook her head and smiled sadly. "Oh, I can't tell you how often I heard that phrase when I was going through my divorce. *Things will get better.* Inside, I cringed every time and sometimes even wanted to spit, it was so bad. After a while, I just tuned 'em all out and put a polite little grimace on my face. And now, I'm a hypocrite for saying it, but it *does* get better, Pamela. Not that it will ever go completely away. But give yourself time to let God heal your broken heart. Oh!" She covered her mouth. "There's another pat answer..."

Helena spoke of how God had used her divorce to bring problems in her own life to the forefront.

"I feel that, too," Pamela agreed. "Paul should never have walked out—but I see now that I really enabled our marriage to disintegrate over the years. His business always took precedence over building our lives together. And I hate to even admit this, but getting him up on that highest rung became *my* biggest goal. Deep down, I knew that wasn't really what mattered. What I wouldn't give to do things differently now."

"Ralph and I were like that too," Tina said. "His business was the most important thing in our lives, and wealth came to us rather painlessly. We became lethargic: in marriage and in our faith. We surrounded ourselves with people who encouraged our indolence."

Pamela closed her eyes for a moment. "I realize this whole recovery deal is a series of stages, but I keep going through them over and over again. Loneliness is the worst culprit of all—it goes away for a bit and then it hits hard again. I have good friends, and I've even been asked out by a man I work with. As cautious as I try to be, part of me wants to just jump at the opportunity to be with someone who likes me."

"I go back and forth on that one," Tina said. "Sometimes I'd say that becoming involved in another relationship might help your healing process—other times, I just think it might delay it. I've never met anybody who was interested in me, so I'm probably of little help there. Helena dates a bit, don't you?"

Helena smiled. "In a way. I have a very good friend who's a man. There's not much of a romantic feeling about us, but we spend a lot of lonely evenings together."

"Have you found a new church yet?" Tina asked.

"No," Pamela said. "And frankly, I'm even okay with that for a little while longer."

"Are you mad at God? I only ask because I went through that…it's pretty much part and parcel of this whole thing."

"I think I was for a while. But that doesn't have much to do with why I haven't been going to church. Ever since I was a young girl, I've adhered to that rigid rule of going to church every Sunday morning and Sunday evening. That rule and its little bylaw: Have a quiet time with the Lord each morning. When it comes right down to it, church and all the trappings lost quite a bit of meaning for me. I intend to start looking soon. It's just hard all alone."

"Church hunting all by myself is the whole reason I finally just stuck it out at Hoyt," said Tina.

"I can't do that. For too many reasons."

"I understand exactly. My house is what kept punching the memory buttons for me. I had to sell it and move on."

"Interesting," Pamela said. "My daughter just said something to me about 'rambling around alone in this big house.' I guess I never even thought about moving."

"We'd still love to have you join our support group," Helena said as they were leaving.

"I can't promise anything right now, but I'll keep the option open. I'll be back and forth between my cabin and Minneapolis quite a bit over the rest of the winter, but who knows? Maybe I'll pop in one of these evenings."

"Maybe New Year's Eve," Helena said as they reached their cars. "If you haven't got plans, we always have a party. It's one of the tougher holidays to be alone."

"I'll be alone, but I don't think I'll mind it. I'm heading north that morning. The novelty of my cabin still hasn't worn off! Thanks for taking the time to listen to me, ladies," Pamela said before she shut her car door. "Seeing how you two have survived has given me a little more oomph to keep on going."

Forty-Seven

IT SEEMED ALMOST unfair that Christmas ran so close to Thanksgiving. Pamela had finally gotten used to not seeing Angie for months. And *bam!* She was home twice in a four-week span. And then her daughter would be stolen away again for another eternity.

Because of the upcoming Chicago project, Angie had only eight days home—and every one of them was taken up with places to go and people to see. The morning she flew in, the two of them drove straight to Lewisville for the annual holiday gala. Joan and her four siblings held a standing reservation for the Hall, a boxy brick landmark that was a combination town meeting place, gym, auditorium, Lyons Club Pancake Breakfast/Spaghetti Supper emporium. It had been visited by generation upon generation of Lewisvillites and was a prominent part of Pamela's hometown memories.

Sometime before Thanksgiving, names for the famed Christmas gift exchange were drawn and distributed to all the relatives. The tradition, which had once been creative and full of meaning, lost its original intent somewhere along the years, most likely due to the mushrooming of Pamela's extended family.

At more recent gatherings, the gifts were chintzy and hurried. Without fail, Pamela received some corny little inspirational calendar or book or some tasteless knickknack. And Paul always ended up with black socks or gloves—or a cheap paperweight for his desk that got tossed before it ever came out of the box. Angie, on the other hand, had always been thrilled with the Barbie doll clothes or other simple toys, books, or CDs she received.

The food was the same homespun fare Pamela had known growing up—beef and wild rice casserole, baked bean and hamburger hot dish, tuna surprise, chicken spaghetti casserole, white bread and rolls, twenty kinds of Jell-O salad, and hundreds of desserts.

She smiled thinking of the timeworn tradition of it all. Every year, the adults sat in a circle of ancient metal folding chairs and chatted. The toddlers played in the center, and the older children tore around the gym, up and down the steps leading up to the stage, and in and out the doors—screaming and yelling and sweating until some noise-sensitive grandparent tottered out to silence them momentarily. The high schoolers stood in their own hushed, awkward little circles, no longer knowing what to say to cousins seen only once a year.

Always, Pamela tolerated—and secretly looked forward to—all this bedlam. But Paul gritted his teeth and escaped outside the first chance he got, preferring to walk an hour in the December cold rather than talk fishing and hunting with his country in-laws. She remembered how sorry she felt for him. But now, as she and Angie made their way through Lewisville and parked in front of the Hall, Pamela realized how misdirected her pity had been.

"It feels different for me this year," Angie said, staring at the familiar building. "But not because of Dad even. I feel kinda like I've passed through to the next stage. Like I should maybe sit in the folding chairs with the grown-ups this year!"

Pamela laughed. "That's funny. I've always thought of it like that too. Just wait until you get married. It's an even bigger deal then."

As soon as they entered the town hall, Angie joined a group of nearly adult cousins congregating near the oversize coffee urn. Pamela, greeted immediately by her own mother, was absorbed by family who were perhaps a little more attentive toward her than usual.

"You doing okay, Pammi?" Joan asked much later, after they'd made their way back to the little house Pamela had grown up in.

Angie had already headed upstairs to Pamela's old room to crash.

"I can't imagine that was all that easy this first year without Paul beside you."

"I'm fine, Mom. And frankly, not having Paul there wasn't the problem. You know what a stick-in-the-mud he always was at these things. I guess I just got weary of everyone asking me the same old questions. It brings it all back. And Uncle Ed kept pestering me about Paul."

"He's a little forgetful these days, honey."

"A *little*? He wanted to know when Paul was going to take him salmon fishing on Lake Superior again! Paul? *Fishing?*"

Joan laughed, then hid her smile behind her hand. "Oh, my…that was your cousin Jenny's husband who did that every year. He's quite the outdoorsman. A different breed altogether from Paul."

356

"Yeah, well…he followed me around half the night. Finally Aunt Gertie came and took him away."

"She knows how he can be. And she's completely sympathetic to your situation."

"And I appreciate everyone's sympathy, I do. But it's so hard."

"I know, Pammi. I went through the same thing when Dad died. Sometimes family events are the hardest to navigate."

"It was different for you though, Mom. At least you could be certain you hadn't done anything wrong—that people weren't wondering about what fault you had in it. Dad *died*. He didn't leave you. I'm the only one in that whole group of people whose marriage has failed."

"Honey…your ring may be off that finger, but you can bet your bonnet that you weren't the only one there with a failed marriage. But your point is valid. Death is easier by far. By far."

December 26

Dear Journal,

Mark this one down: Mom and I got through our first Christmas without Dad.

It was a little weird, and there were times when I wondered if it would all fall apart…especially on Christmas Eve. Usually the three of us all went to the candlelight service at Hoyt, and it's something that I've always loved—the music, the emotion, the dim lights. And there was something complete about sitting between Mom and Dad in the pew up in the balcony where we never sat except on Christmas Eve.

This year, Mom and I went to a little church down the street from us. I wanted to go to Hoyt, only I couldn't exactly tell Mom that and she never suggested it. She hasn't been back there since summer. It was her idea to try something different—"start a new tradition" was what she called it. But I didn't like it at all. Everyone at the church knew everyone else and I felt miserably alone in the midst of everyone else's holiday bliss.

At least Mom's and my little celebration afterward was nice. We opened presents, and she loved the necklace I gave her.

Really, the whole time was pretty okay as long as I avoided talk of Dad. I haven't told Mom yet, but he wants to fly out to see me while I'm in Chicago. I'll tell her tomorrow before I leave, I guess. It's not like I think my mom's gonna have a fit about it…I just know it'll be hard for her to hear. Sometimes I wonder if she's jealous of the fact that he's still sorta in my life.

Or maybe the hard part for her is that he wants to be in *my* life…not in hers.

I'm a little worried about what she'll do over New Year's Eve. She and Dad always went out on the town that night. It was a big deal to them. She told Gram she wants to spend it by herself up at Sunset Lake this year—go to some little church she spotted outside of Crosby. The thing is, I know Starla invited her to do something with her and Adam, and Mom turned them down. I just don't like the idea of her wallowing alone up there all by herself.

I miss Jason. But with him at Northwestern—only a few miles from where Melinda and I are gonna live—I'll probably see him more than ever. He's picking me up at the airport the thirtieth—and we'll spend New Year's Eve together. He's taking me to the top of the Sears Tower! Talk about romantic…

Forty-Eight

PAMELA FOLLOWED a group of people out of the cold, into the cozy front hall of the church. She was, of course, slightly uncomfortable being alone at a holiday service bursting with family cheer. But she got over it as soon as she entered the candlelit sanctuary, still festively adorned for Christmas. Candles, beribboned with gold, were mounted in the sills of each tall window. More were attached with holly and evergreen to the pews—and still others were held by the ushers. It was a silent, flickering sea of golden light and pine boughs, evocative of the solemn, ancient cathedrals she'd seen in European travelogues she'd watched on PBS.

A candle-carrying usher led Pamela to a bench occupied, thus far, only by one elderly couple. As she'd walked down the aisle, she took notice of the people: not only was the older crowd represented, but there were also many teenagers and young children. And though she hadn't been—until just this minute—aware that she was weighing the pros and cons of this little church, she had to admit, she liked the mix.

The couple next to her smiled warmly as she sat down.

"Welcome, dear," whispered the woman.

Pamela smiled and nodded and turned her head toward the front.

"Are you a visitor?"

Pamela turned to her again. "Yes. I have a cabin near here—noticed the sign out front and thought I'd attend this evening."

"How nice to have you stop by."

The lady's husband craned his head around his wife and said, "You'll have to come to regular service one of these Sundays."

"I think I might just do that."

The woman smiled again at Pamela. "Ah, but these special ones are always so beautiful."

A string trio commenced the first sweet notes of "Silent Night," and Pamela closed her eyes, glad to have one last reminder of Christmas, which had come and gone so quickly.

Just as the pastor planted himself behind the pulpit to give his greeting, Pamela felt a gentle tap on her thigh. She followed the woman's eyes toward someone down the row, past her husband. Ken sat beside him, beaming at Pamela. He whispered to the man and lady, who then whispered a little too loudly to Pamela— "You're a friend of Ken's! Why didn't you tell us?"

"I didn't know until now that you knew him," she said. "This is Ken's church?"

"Has been for years," she whispered.

Pamela smiled across the couple again at Ken and finally settled into the soft cushion of the pew to listen to the music and speaking and special readings. When the pastor rose to deliver his message, a peaceful quiet settled upon Pamela. The earlier discomfort of being alone in a crowd was gone.

At the conclusion of the service, Pamela offered an arm to the woman—who told her her name was Lucy—and walked up the aisle of the still-packed church toward the fellowship hall. Ken followed with Lucy's husband, Charles.

"Wasn't that exquisite," Lucy said. "I've always loved New Year's Eve services best of all."

"That's what you said about Christmas Eve," Charles said with a laugh.

"You're right! I think I must love them both the same then."

"It was beautiful," Pamela agreed.

"Will you join us for coffee the next time you come to church?" Charles asked.

"Charles—you must first find out if she'd *like* to come back," Lucy said.

Ken laughed. "He thought he'd tempt her with coffee first."

"Either way, I'd be honored," Pamela said.

"Why, look at this snow!" Lucy said. "Two inches must have fallen while we were in there!"

The foursome said their "Happy New Years," and once Ken had seen Charles and Lucy safely through the snowy parking lot to their car, he walked with Pamela to her own.

"I had no idea this was your church," she said.

"I know. And Charles and Lucy are my in-laws."

"I should have guessed."

"It's amazing that you're here, Pamela. I don't remember ever telling you its name. It's a God thing, don't you think? So…" He pushed up the sleeve of his coat to peek at his watch. "Have big plans tonight?"

"A good book by the fire count as big?"

"Nope. Why don't you come over to my place? I've got some leftover eggnog and plenty of firewood."

"I would love to."

Not only did Ken provide the eggnog, he also whipped up a batch of chocolate chip cookies, knowing Pamela's fetish for them. The two of them sat by the fire and talked of his church and the large role Ken played in its music ministry. The quality of the orchestration and vocal talent had impressed her—and even during the service Pamela had assumed there had to be some well-organized musician at work behind it all.

"Did you have a nice Christmas?" he asked later.

"Simple, but yes, it was quite nice. You?"

"Ditto. My sister in Minneapolis spent the holidays with her husband's family, so I celebrated Christmas Eve with Charles and Lucy and then, in memory of my dad, I went ice fishing on Christmas Day."

"A tradition, I assume?"

"My dad was an ice fishing fanatic. Since Christmas Day was one of the few days he had off, our family celebrated the whole schmiel on Christmas Eve so he could get up early to fish the next morning. We opened presents and had a big meal—always roast beef—and then went to bed. Once, a year or two after my sister moved to Minneapolis, my mom took me to church on Christmas morning. When we walked into church, I was scared to death—and maybe a little in awe of the formality, since it wasn't anything I'd ever seen before."

"How old were you?"

"Twelve."

"And that was the first time you were ever in a church?"

"As far as I can remember," Ken said. "Mom and Dad weren't churchgoers. I think my mom had some sort of a conversion experience in the hospital before she died, though. I remember thinking she'd gone off the deep end, talking about Jesus dying on the cross and coming back to life again. She scared me to death! I hadn't turned my life over to God then, obviously, but I'm pretty sure she'll be in heaven when I get there."

363

"And your dad?"

"Never. He died two years before Mom did. He was killed in a car accident, and she died of a fast-moving breast cancer. I wasn't close to either of them, which makes me sad now. I met my wife not long after that."

Both sets of eyes were on the fire, watching the flames lick furiously at the log Ken tossed in.

"When I was a little girl, we celebrated on both days—my mom and dad and I went to the Christmas Eve service at our church, then came home and ate popcorn and drank hot apple cider. Sometimes, Mom and I made popcorn balls. I got to open one present, usually a new pair of pajamas and some slippers my mom knitted. I don't know why I always got so excited about new jammies! Then on Christmas morning, I ran into their room at the crack of dawn and forced them to come downstairs. First, I looked in my stocking, where Dad always put a brand-new, hardcover book."

"I remember when he died."

Pamela lifted her gaze from the fire and looked at Ken in

surprise. "You do? I never talked about it. Not in school."

"I sat behind you in math that year. I had the weirdest urge to reach out and touch your hair."

She laughed. "You're kidding! My hair was always so long and stick-straight. I hated it!"

"It reminded me of doll's hair, and I wondered if it was soft like that." Pamela could almost swear Ken was blushing. "Anyway, when your dad died, you cried a lot in class. Softly. But I remember seeing you wipe tears away with a handkerchief when you didn't think anyone was watching."

Pamela stared at him a moment longer, and then looked back at the fire, remembering. "The handkerchief was my dad's. It was a tough year."

"I'll bet. He was a good man, wasn't he?"

"The best."

Other than joking reminders of their common past, Ken and Pamela had never really talked about their youth—and there was something gracious about sharing memories on a New Year's Eve so far removed from those good old, golden rule days. Gracious…and also restorative.

She had this image of Ken as a druggie musician—a loner nobody wanted to be around. The more Pamela listened to him reminisce, the more she realized how off-kilter that picture was. He was intense, that's all. And though he admitted that he had smoked a little pot, the whole drug addict aura surrounding him was mostly gossip.

"I had no problem at all with those rumors," he said. "In the early '70s, it was a cool image for a musician to have—especially since I aspired to open for bands like Pink Floyd or the Stones. I was a loner…but not because people avoided me. I was just that way."

"It fits your personality, I guess."

"I'm still no social butterfly. Did you know that I dated Susie Delacore for a year and a half?"

"You did not!"

"I did, really…through all of our junior year and half of our senior. But since we were on such opposite ends of the social spectrum, it started to get complicated. We never told a soul and spent a lot of time at her house—or going to the movies outside Brainerd. I didn't want anyone to know."

"Why not?"

"I was afraid it would ruin her reputation. I knew what people thought of me."

"That's really sad, Ken. Why did you break up?"

"I think we just decided we were too different after a while. I can't remember if I instigated it or if she did. I do remember feeling sad for a while, but it wasn't all that painful." He smiled. "Young love…"

"I dated everybody, I think."

"You did, I'll vouch for that!"

"Not like that. I never was in love with any of the guys I went out with. Never even thought I was. Life is easier that way!"

"Is it?" His eyes were suddenly serious.

"What?"

"Is life easier without being in love?"

"In a way…" she said carefully. "But that doesn't mean it's better. I think my life has fewer complications now. But maybe I'm just scared. I'd like to hope that when things are right in a marriage, those complications are part of the joy."

"They are." Ken's voice was soft and Pamela could tell he was far, far away.

The fire was flickering and fading, sending off weak sparks that flared only briefly before dying. Pamela watched it quietly and felt the air shift as Ken unfurled his legs and left the room. He came back momentarily and sat down beside her again, placing a small, gold-wrapped box on the floor in front of her.

"What's this?" Pamela asked.

"Open it and see."

She unwrapped the little box, a jewelry box. Inside was a delicate gold chain—with a filigreed snowflake hanging from it. Pamela held it up so it glimmered in the fire light as it turned. "It's absolutely beautiful, Ken. Thank you."

"It's a belated Christmas present. I have so few people to buy presents for these days—and when I saw this I just knew I wanted you to have it. Now you'll always remember your first winter at Sunset."

Pamela lay in bed that night, listening to the whisper of falling snow and thinking about the simple evening she'd just spent with Ken. Last year, as with every year before that, she and Paul had driven all over town because Paul insisted that they put in an appearance at every one of the six parties they had been invited to. They'd not gotten home until three in the morning, though Pamela had been bone tired and sick of socializing long before midnight.

Tonight had been one of the best New Year's Eves she could

remember. No champagne toasts or stuffed artichokes; no drunken, slobbery kisses from strangers; no incessant small talk or faces frozen in a seasonal smile. Pamela's heart thudded thankfulness for the uncomplicated relationship she shared with Ken. He was her friend.

True as that was, a few times over the past weeks Pamela had felt Ken's eyes more warmly upon her than even a very close friend's might be. And she couldn't exactly say it made her uncomfortable. She rather liked it. It was the same warmth she felt with Chad.

No. Nothing like Chad. With Chad she felt heat—self-conscious heat. With Ken she felt familiar and safe and understood…and he expected only the same of her.

Pamela yawned. *Why in the world am I reading into the simplicity of my relationship with Ken?* There was no pressure, no rush. None of that painful urgency to define her feelings and move ahead that was so much a part of her long-ago relationships with boys…men…with Paul.

It wasn't like that at all. For now, Pamela was content that she'd been blessed with the companionship of such a wonderful man.

Forty-Nine

In the morning, the ground was covered with six inches of new snow. The forecast warned of more by nightfall, which seemed likely given the thick, steely sky. Pamela looped her camera round her neck, put on warm clothes and cross-country skis, and crossed the frozen lake to the island.

Stalwart birds that braved the north left three-pronged prints along the edges of the island. She took pictures of the markings and tracked their feathered owners, pleased to find them still on the island and more than willing to pose, as long as she stayed back a ways. Pamela hashed her way to the center of the small preserve, and fell on her back in the snow to shoot through huge pines to the iron gray sky.

Pamela spent an hour or more on the island and then skied back to warm herself by the fire, sipping a cup of hot chocolate. The remainder of the day she spent in the darkroom she'd rigged a few weeks back, developing the photos she'd taken, immensely pleased at what came out.

When she layered the photos across the table for Ken's

perusal the next day, he said, "Pamela, these are phenomenal. I had absolutely no idea you were so good!"

"Gee, thanks. Just a so-so photographer, you assumed?"

"No! It's just…"

"Ken, I'm *kidding*. I think Chad will like them, don't you?"

370

"No doubt about that." Ken looked at her, a questioning expression on his face.

"What?" Pamela said.

"Is there anything between the two of you?"

"Me and Chad? No…well…he's become a good friend. And…" She thought of the kiss they'd shared and her face grew warm.

"Oh." Ken laughed. A bit awkwardly, Pamela couldn't help but notice. "Hey, you don't owe me an explanation. I'm sorry, Pamela."

"No. Listen, Chad's asked if he can call me when I'm ready. I'm just not so sure it will ever go much beyond friendship for me. I really respect him, but I don't think we're enough alike that I'd ever want to pursue anything serious. I just haven't gotten around to telling him that. Frankly, I'm flattered that a man like him would think of me in a romantic way."

"Don't belittle yourself, Pamela. You are a beautiful, creative, intelligent woman that *any* man would be proud to be with."

"Paul excluded?"

"He has no clue what he's giving up."

The promised storm was twenty-four hours late, but when it came, it threatened to hang around for days. Pamela was glad she had no need to return to the Cities yet.

Before she climbed the stairs to her loft bedroom, she stuck her head out the porch door to see how much snow had fallen the past few hours. The bone-chilling wind slammed the screen door hard against her and nearly knocked her over. In the thick and whirling flakes, she could barely make out the yellow glow of light over Ken's door.

Already the snow drifted deep against her little cabin and weighed heavily on the birch trees between the two homes. An unfamiliar wind screamed from the lake—wicked and old and cruel. Pamela could hear its call long after she burrowed deep beneath a down comforter and the extra blankets she'd tossed on her bed.

The storm raged all the next day. Power and phone lines were out from Garrison to Crosby, making the fireplace Pamela's only source of warmth. Ken shut down his house and spent the day at Pamela's, loading her fireplace with wood every hour. The two prepared coffee over the flames in an antique pot he dug out just for the occasion, and later he heated leftover stew in a cast-iron pan. Ma and Pa Ingalls would be proud, Pamela thought.

By nightfall, the power was still out—and snow was coming down hard again. The little transistor radio she kept on hand for emergencies forecast no end of this until late the next day. Pamela worried a little about the pipes, but Ken assured her it would require quite a few more days of no power and subzero weather for them to freeze. But she wasn't so sure. A chill was beginning to seep through hidden cracks and seams of her home, despite the warmth of the enormous fireplace.

Finally, Pamela pulled the blankets off the bed and brought

them to the hearth. "Will you stay?" she asked. There wasn't even a sense that what Pamela offered was anything other than the nighttime warmth of her home.

As was their custom, their talk went deep—deeper even for the lateness of the hour. "How's Angie doing in Chicago?" Ken asked as he threw another log into the fireplace.

"So far, so good. She's in her element, working in the city and all. She tells me Paul is flying out to see her sometime in the next week or two."

"Oh? That's a step in the right direction."

"But I don't *want* him there," she said too quickly. Then she shook her head in embarrassment. "I'm sorry. It's just hard. We should be visiting her *together*. I mean, Angie tells me she wants to try to talk to him. Work things through. She thinks the time is right…and has even gone so far as to say she thinks he's changing. I've been trying to get him to change for years! To slow down. To spend time with his daughter. Why is he doing it now? Angie says she's getting closer to forgiving him for what he's done. Do you think that's even possible to do for someone who doesn't ask, or even want, to be forgiven?"

"Of course."

"I don't think I do," she said. "If someone's not ready to change, what's the use in letting them off the hook?"

"I'm not so certain that's what forgiveness does. Put it this way…say your father is a child-beating alcoholic who forces you to run away from home when you're sixteen. You hate him for all the physical and emotional misery he's put you through. Years later, you finally get your own head together…let's say you become a Christian. You find out that you need to forgive him despite the wickedness and evil. You with me so far?"

Pamela nodded.

"After agonizing, once more, through all the stuff he's done, you come to the conclusion that with God's help, you're ready and willing to tell him you've forgiven him. Of course, you hope that he might have changed—not that you really think he has. But you've already made the decision. You go home, the first time in years, and find out he died five years before." He paused for a moment. "Now, I realize how simplistic this example is but...can you still forgive him?"

"Sure...he's dead."

"And how do you go about doing that?"

"Oh, I don't know. You just do. Maybe write it down, bury it on top of his grave. I read about someone who did that once. Maybe just say the words to an empty room...at least that's the first step. I guess the rest—the feeling part—would come more slowly."

"But he never said he was sorry, Pamela. And he never will."

Pamela was quiet.

"No...he never said he was sorry," she whispered.

"Could you write it down...or speak it to the empty room? Could you verbally begin the process and let God take you the rest of the way? He's good, you know." Ken smiled at her. "And faithful."

"I don't know, Ken. I just keep thinking of all Paul did and—"

"Maybe it's not something you can do yet." He reached for her hand and brought it to his lips. "I'll keep praying for you."

Pamela closed her eyes at the warmth of his touch, his kiss on her fingertips. Her heart fluttered a bit in a way that was oddly disconcerting. She opened her eyes to his darker ones. She could see the flames reflected in them, warming her with their intensity.

"You are very special to me, Ken. Do you know that?"

He stared at her for a minute longer—and Pamela was nearly certain he was going to kiss her. But he grinned his lopsided grin and pulled her close in a hug. "I sure do. And the feeling is entirely mutual."

Much, much later they fell asleep in front of the fire, cocooned in heaps of blankets. A few times, she roused herself just enough to toss a few logs in and stoke the coals. She suspected Ken tended to the fire more than she did, however, for by dawn the woodpile was nearly depleted.

The power wasn't restored until early afternoon the next day—around the same time the wind ground to a halt and blue skies rolled in. And then it was perfectly still—a hushed, bluish white. Within the hour, the yard was latticed with rabbits' prints, birds' tracks, and marks from whatever other little creatures had finally crawled from their hovels to forage for food.

Pamela, too—happy and surprisingly refreshed for all the time she'd spent shut up inside—emerged from her shelter, camera in hand. Her shutter clicked the remainder of the afternoon, capturing the beauty of a scene she believed God had painted just for her. Every so often, she looked back at Ken, who was shoveling the driveways and paths between their homes.

Something subtle had changed between them. Not that anyone else would know it. But she felt it—and by the contented smile Ken sent her way as he leaned against his shovel, Pamela was certain he felt it, too.

January 6

Dear Journal,

I love this city and the work I'm doing with the kids—mostly I'm tutoring kids at the shelter who have fallen behind in school. I've never felt so right about anything in my life. I'm only a freshman— and I know I don't have to declare a major until next year, but I *know* I want to teach. What's more, I know I want to do it here. In Chicago. And if there were any way I could work with homeless children, teaching them for real, I'd absolutely love it.

Tonight Jason and I had this huge conversation about our professional futures, and something tells me he doesn't really like the idea of me pursuing this whole inner city teaching deal. Not that he said anything. I just felt like he got all cold on me or something when I started raving about my job here. He's thinking about going into plastic surgery—which is new information to me. I heard about this organization that goes into third world countries and does operations on children who have harelips and other correctable deformities. I thought maybe that might be something Jason could do. But he wasn't all that thrilled with the third world idea. Or the children.

I hate even writing this, but lately I've been wondering if maybe he and I aren't as suited as I thought. And it bothers me a bit because I *really* like him. But maybe our life goals are too opposite. I don't know—I've got so much time before I have to think about serious stuff. It's not like I intend to break up with him. I guess it's just this inkling I have…Who knows? Things might change.

Dad got some great flight deal on the Internet and is flying in tomorrow instead of at the end of the month like he originally planned. I can't wait for him to see what I'm doing here. I can only imagine the conversations we'll have...I bet I'll have a novel to write in a few days! I'm scared to death—but then part of me is a little excited, too.

Fifty

PAUL WASN'T FEELING well when he unlocked the door to his room at the Chicago Marriott. He dropped his bag on the floor and collapsed on the bed, kicking his shoes to the floor.

Breathe deeply, he told himself. He felt achy—especially in his arms and chest—from sitting too long in the cramped airline seat. And he was just plain exhausted.

Think positive thoughts.

Optimism, however, wasn't an easy thing to muster these days. Dana—his wonderful, beautiful Dana—was still holding strong to her resolve to keep things casual between them until after the divorce was final. And unless the legal system moved amazingly fast, he could be in for another two- to three-month wait. Even a day seemed like an eternity without her!

To make matters worse, just yesterday Phil had called him into his office to share the latest news. Bank of America was attempting to acquire Liberty. And if that happened, Paul couldn't be certain of a job. Any sort of change was at least a year down the line, Phil allowed, but he felt it only fair to warn Paul now.

Just in case he wanted to cover his bases and get on with another headhunter.

As far as Paul was concerned, no other job could match what he had going for him at Liberty. At this point, he was going to hold out for the possibility that nothing would happen. And if it did? Paul intended to do his best to make himself indispensable to Bank of America.

But right now, he *had* to do something about this nausea and the headache that had started to pound on his skull. *Breathe*, he reminded himself as he got up and dug through his shaving kit for a bottle of Advil. *Deep, cleansing breaths.*

He needed sleep. In the morning, just a few hours from now, he was having breakfast with Angie. The thought made him smile. She'd been less caustic whenever he talked to her lately— almost friendly at times. Once she'd even called him just to talk. Maybe there was hope.

Hope is the promise of things unseen, Dana had said when he called to tell her about this trip. And she was full of advice as to how he should approach Angie. *Just admit that you've made mistakes and try to build a different sort of relationship with her now. I'll be praying for you both.*

Paul groaned at the sudden pain that started in his stomach and worked its way upward to his left shoulder. The ache accelerated into shooting bursts of fire up and down his arm. It was so bad, it took away his breath.

Paul clawed at the collar of his shirt as he fell against the hotel room door.

Fifty-One

PAMELA REACHED OVER and fumbled for the phone that jangled into her awareness.

"Hello?" she moaned.

"Mom, it's Angie! You need to come right away!"

"What?" She sat up, shocked now into wakefulness. "Are you hurt?"

"No—it's Dad. He had a heart attack and I'm at Central Hospital...downtown Chicago. I don't think it's good, Mom. Can you come?"

"I'm on my way." Pamela slammed down the phone only to pick it up again and make a reservation for a flight leaving Minneapolis in just under three hours. Then she made a quick call to the hospital and checked on Paul's condition. Instinctively, she told them she was his wife. The doctor explained he was on life support and they weren't sure he was going to make it. How soon could she be there? they asked. By eight A.M., she said. I'm booked on a six o'clock flight.

A little after eight, a cab dropped her off in front of Central Hospital, and Pamela made her way to the intensive care wing. Angie was alone in the waiting room, her face devoid of makeup, painted instead with exhaustion and dried tears.

"Oh, Mom," she said and collapsed into Pamela's arms. "It's really bad. He's been unconscious since he got here. They're doing all they can for him."

"You've been in to see him? I'd like to go in if we can."

"Dana just got here."

"Oh…" She stood up, nervous at the unknowns. "Maybe I should go. Find a hotel or something."

"No, Mom." Angie squeezed her arm tight to pull her back down to the vinyl couch. *"Please.* I need you. I'm so scared…and they told me I should just wait here until they know anything. Please don't leave."

"Okay, honey." Wordlessly, she held her daughter in the hospital waiting room, completely at a loss. Theoretically, she was no longer Paul's wife—but legally she still had that responsibility. Pamela's mind forbade her to worry, but her shattered emotions said otherwise.

Very briefly, she entertained a runaway notion of relief: If he dies, I will never have to wear the dreaded label *divorcée.*

"Did you get a chance to talk to your dad at all?" she asked after a while.

"Just on the phone before he left Los Angeles last night—his flight was late leaving. He was going to take me out for breakfast. But then a clerk at the hotel called sometime after midnight. Someone walking by heard him pounding on the door of his room and called the front desk. By the time I got here, he was completely out of it."

Pamela kept her eye on Paul's room, watching for Dana, but mostly willing the doctor to come out and tell them what was going on.

"Mom?" Angie indicated the sudden activity going on near Paul's room. Dana walked out and turned to go down the hall the opposite direction from the waiting room. "I'm gonna go see what's going on."

Frustrated she couldn't join her daughter, Pamela went to a window that overlooked a snowy courtyard. Footprints crisscrossed the snow. People passing time. Just like her.

"Dad's awake."

Pamela turned around at Angie's voice.

"They're doing some more blood work right now, but the nurse said it would be okay if I went in for a bit."

"I'll come too," Pamela said.

"You sure you want to?"

"Dana's not there anymore, and I'd like to see him. Yes."

The two women went back through the waiting area and entered Paul's room. He was lying on his side, facing the window. A doctor stood at the foot of his bed jotting something on a clipboard. And then the curtain around the bed moved slightly, and Pamela realized that Dana was seated beside Paul, holding his hand, bent over so her head rested beside his on the pillow.

"I'll give you some time," Dana said, rising quickly and exiting the room before either Pamela or Angie had a moment to think. Her eyes were red-rimmed and tears streaked her face.

Pamela stood off to the side, out of Paul's sight, but Angie went immediately to her dad's side. "How are you feeling? Oh...stupid question...sorry, Dad."

"I'm gonna make it, Angie. Dana told me you've been here all night."

382

Angie nodded. "I don't get why you had a heart attack. You're so careful."

"Doesn't always matter, honey. It could've been worse. My heart is strong. That's what they tell me, at least. Sorry I ruined our weekend."

Angie smiled. "Better be."

Pamela felt tinges of envy as she witnessed their interaction. She so badly wanted to join Angie beside her father—to be a family as they fought for Paul to regain his health. Pamela wanted to take care of him.

"Mom's here," Angie said, looking across the bed toward Pamela. "Would it be okay if she came and said hi?"

Pamela moved into Paul's sight. "Hi," she whispered, watching Angie as she slipped out the door. "Are you...are you comfortable enough?"

"They're taking care of me. Thanks for coming."

"I needed to. For Angie."

He nodded and closed his eyes.

"You tired?" Pamela asked.

"Yes."

"Well...I should go."

He didn't answer, and for a moment, Pamela thought he'd drifted off just that quickly. She headed for the door.

"I...I'm sorry..."

But when she turned around, Paul had rolled his head back toward the window.

February 26

Dear Journal,

I can't believe I haven't written for a month. I scribbled stuff down a ton of times…and who knows? I may end up tearing this page out just like the rest of them.

Dad's back in LA. And I think I'm glad for that. We're talking on the phone quite a bit and he's doing well. Mom doesn't say much, but she had it in her head that the heart attack was some sort of wake-up call God wanted to use to get Dad to go back to her.

Dana and I have talked briefly once or twice since Dad was here, too. It's hard to admit this, but she's really nice. That's the hard part for me. If I were to ever admit to my mom that I liked her, I think my mom would flip. Dana hasn't said a lot, but I know she's really sorry for the pain she caused our family. Neither of us wants to bring it up, but I think we both want to talk about the whole thing between her and my dad.

Second semester is going well school-wise, and maybe it's because I've not been seeing Jason as much since Chicago. We're heading in different directions and neither of us wants to say anything, but I've been praying that God will give me the strength to break up with him. I need to. Though I still care about him…

March 4

Dear Journal,

What a week.

First off, Jason and I broke up. And even though I knew it was the right thing, all I can do these days is cry. I've got a big test in Philosophy tomorrow and a paper due in American Lit—and as well as I've been doing up until now, I'm hoping I can stop being miserable long enough to study.

Next, Mom called. She's selling our house. Talk about mixed feelings...I keep telling myself I won't be back there for more than vacation times anyway. It's not my house anymore really, because I'm not a kid anymore—it's an odd feeling to suddenly come to terms with. And like Mom explained, she'll be so much better off in a smaller place without all the memories.

And then today, I was offered a summer internship with the shelter I worked for in Chicago. It's a real job this time—not something I have to raise support for. It would mean I wouldn't be home for the summer, but then again, that wouldn't be all that bad.

Fifty-Two

"MAYBE INSTEAD of buying another place in Minneapolis, you should just stay up here, Pamela," Ken suggested quietly one evening when spring had begun to shrink the leftover drifts of snow between his cabin and hers. He had stopped by to help fix a leak in the kitchen faucet. "You're up here all the time as it is."

Much to her surprise, Pamela's home in Minneapolis sold the first weekend it was listed. And now, with the closing only three weeks away, she was nowhere near finding a smaller place in Minneapolis she liked enough to buy. She planned to stick all her furniture in storage and temporarily move to her cabin, commuting south only when Jim needed her.

"Move up here permanently?" Pamela smiled in amusement. "Oh, I couldn't, Ken. I'm not a real northerner. I still belong in the city."

"How much more real can you get? You were born here."

"But I couldn't possibly move back."

Ken met her response with silence.

"Sunset Lake is my vacation place, Ken. Not my home."

"It could be. Angie's not home anymore…not until summer."
He crawled halfway into the cabinet to tighten the pipe he'd just
replaced.

"Not even then. She accepted a paid internship in Chicago
with that inner city organization she worked for in January. She
leaves right from school."

Ken eased his head and shoulders back out and stood up. "All
the more reason. Want a few others?"

"No."

"Your mom is an hour away. You're calling my church your
own these days. And as great of friends as you and Starla are, she's
got her plate full with this wedding…which is going to be up here
anyway. You'll probably see her more now than you have all
winter. Your divorce is final, and you're free to start an entirely
new life if you want. And think about it—your job isn't really a
job anymore, right?"

Pamela pursed her lips. "Stop."

"I mean, couldn't you keep driving back there the few times
a month you do work for Jim?"

"Ken, it's not that easy. I just can't pick up and move after
nearly twenty-five years!"

"Why not?"

"I just can't, that's why. I have a life…"

"And I'm here." The blasé look on Ken's face was hard to
interpret. "In my opinion—and you can take it or leave it—you
have more of a life up north than you do in Minneapolis."

"Ken…don't *do* this."

"I just think it's worth considering."

"All right. I will do that. I'll think about it."

But the month wore on, Pamela gave up possession of her home, and frustration got the best of her when it came to finding another place in Minneapolis.

"What would you think if I moved to my cabin?" Pamela asked Starla the first weekend of April when she drove back to Minneapolis to shop for a bridesmaid dress. The wedding was the eighteenth of August, so plans had jumped into overdrive.

The two women had seen little of each other the last few months, though they were never completely incommunicado. Never that. There were weekly, sometimes daily phone calls to update each other on the status of the wedding, on Pamela's book, on the divorce. And they tried to meet for coffee or breakfast whenever Pamela was in town.

The day they went shopping for a bridesmaid dress was one of the most pleasant afternoons the two of them had shared in months. For the first time since Paul left her, Pamela was free of the need to talk about him and immersed herself completely in Starla's joy.

"Move up north?" Starla laughed. "Don't worry, you'll find something around here, Pammi. It just takes time."

"No. *Really*." Pamela took a knee-length tangerine shift off the rack and held it up for Starla's perusal.

"You're serious?"

"Right. Wrong color."

"About moving."

Pamela turned her head to catch the wide-eyed expression on Starla's face, then hung the dress back on the rack. "Believe me,

I'm as shocked as you are that I'm actually going to do it."

"You've actually made up your mind to do this?"

Pamela nodded. "I feel like I've been in every suitable place that's for sale in the Twin Cities. Not one was anywhere close to what I've already got with my cabin. I'm sure it must sound like I've lost my mind, but I know this is the right thing. It's a new start, Star."

"What about your job?"

"I can keep doing it the way I am now, but Chad thinks I should quit. Go completely freelance."

"Chad, huh? Things heating up there?" Starla grinned.

"Oh, Star…" Pamela's eyes turned serious. "I can't help but be bowled over by him. He treats me like a queen."

"Not to mention that he's incredibly gorgeous…and persistent."

"He wants more than what I can give. Not that I don't enjoy spending time with him, but I keep picturing the future and I see myself doing the simple things—curling up by the fire with a good book, going to church, taking walks in the woods. Chad's goal is to travel the world, spend time in all the great cities of the world, write the great American novel. He's not simple, Starla."

"He's been good for you, though, Pamela. He's helped to draw you out. But I agree with you. And there is the bigger issue of where he stands with the Lord."

"For a while, his open-minded view of God appealed to me. I didn't want to be bound by any particular denomination. But that's changed."

"I think a *lot* has changed in you. For the better, Pammi. And, for the record, I don't think moving north is crazy at all. You've been heading that way for months now…you've just finally made it all the way home."

Home?

"That's a little like something Ken said," Pamela mused aloud.

"Now *that* is one wise man."

Fifty-Three

OVER THE NEXT month, the winter-gray sky gave way to a newly washed blue. And Pamela watched the bravest of her daffodils and tulips push their minty tips through a prison of dirt. By the end of May, her garden was a wash of color—the final masterpiece shot for the book—with all the early spring annuals blooming and a few summer plants that had bravely burst into flower.

Scary as it was, Pamela resigned from *TCM*—though at first Jim wondered if she was having a nervous breakdown. When she explained her plan to go out on her own, however, he applauded her courage and offered freelance anytime she needed the extra cash.

What thrilled Pamela the most, however, was turning her final pictures over to Chad so he could submit their manuscript to the publisher. It was, in some way, a rite of passage for her.

"Congratulations, Pamela," said Chad when they went out for dinner to celebrate. "We did it! And I couldn't be happier with the final product."

Their table, perched as it was near a broad expanse of windows, offered a twenty-second floor view of Minneapolis. The two of them were seated on a sofa facing the window, and Chad's arm was thrown casually across her shoulders. Soft piano music played in the background, and a trio of candles flickered in front of them. A waiter arrived and uncorked a bottle of champagne. He poured it, bubbling and popping, into two crystal glasses and then walked away.

Pamela turned her eyes to Chad's in curiosity.

"I ordered it ahead of time. This is a celebration, right?" He smiled and lifted his glass. "To Pamela. To the beauty of your pictures. And the beauty that is you." He leaned toward her and casually brushed his lips over hers.

Pamela's heart hammered in her ears, and she felt a flush move across her chest and face. "Thank you. But I owe every bit of it to you."

She couldn't deny that she loved this, being here with him, the magical feelings Chad inspired within her. She loved it and didn't want it to end. But it was a dream. And people always woke from their dreams.

"Not at all," he ran a finger down the side of her face. "I mean every word. Come with me to Spain for the summer, Pamela."

"Chad!"

"Please? It's beautiful, and we could travel to France and Italy. I could show you—"

"I can't...you know that."

"Why not, Pamela? Do you have any idea what I feel for you? Any clue of the things I've been waiting to say?"

"No. Don't. It will change things, Chad. For me. For you.

You've been so entirely patient with me. But I'm not sure I can let anything happen with us."

"It's already happening, Pamela."

"But if you tell me how deeply you feel…and I listen…"

"So listen. And come with me. We'll see the world. Dance under the stars. Stay in the most exquisite hotels money can buy. I'll write. You photograph. It'll be perfect." Chad's words were gentle and light—as if he'd known ahead of time what she would say.

Pamela looked into his eyes. "I can't. But you know that, don't you?"

He pulled her close for a moment. "I desperately wish I didn't."

"Years ago, I ran away to Minneapolis to be free—and ended up trapped by so many things that weren't really me. I know now what God wants me to do. For the first time in my life, I can see that clearly. I could give up my home on the lake, but it would be settling for something that isn't me. I can't do that anymore. And I gave up something in my marriage to Paul that I can't afford to sacrifice again."

"What's that, Pamela?"

"He and I viewed God differently. Too differently. If I marry again, my husband will have to be on the same page as I am spiritually. It's not that I'm criticizing you, Chad—"

He put a finger to her lips. "Shhh. I understand."

Pamela smiled. "You've given me something very special, Chad. You've given me confidence in myself—not just professionally, but as a woman."

"Ah, Pamela, you've had that all along."

After dinner, they talked a while longer about Pamela's plans, about the novel Chad was nearly finished with, about their own book. "What happens now, Chad?"

"The publisher received our manuscript—photos and all. I spoke with him on the phone last week, and he's thrilled. We should be seeing some money from the advance any day now."

"How long until we see a finished product?"

"Nine months or so."

"You've done so much of the groundwork, Chad," Pamela said. "There must be something I can do to help? I feel guilty!"

"Keep in mind that my work was finished over a year ago. You've been using all your extra energy and resources to complete your part. Now we can both sit back for a while and enjoy the process. And maybe start on something new."

"You have something in mind?"

"Maybe…" He grinned. "The publisher does, actually. When I talked to them this week, they asked if we'd team up on another project for them. I've never been one to write on command, but this is definitely something that interests me. It isn't poetry this time—they want a history of the Minneapolis lakes and the homes surrounding them. They saw the piece we did for *TCM*."

"You're kidding! I move north, and now I've got to come right back here?" Pamela couldn't help but laugh.

"That's the life of a photographer. You interested?"

"Of *course* I'm interested!"

June 18

Dear Journal,

Is it possible to age a lifetime in one year? I feel thirty years old.
It's not bad, though. I just look back at where I was this time last
year: in Mexico with all my Hoyt friends, completely oblivious to
what was going on at home. I remember thinking then about how
nice it would be to get back home—to my bed, to my stable family,
to my church.

Nothing of that life exists anymore.

Here I am, living in downtown Chicago all by myself, working
with homeless kids. My dad is half a nation away. My mom has up
and moved to northern Minnesota. And despite the way it may
seem, I'm happy.

Dad's invited me to go to LA the last week of August and I
think I'm gonna go. I've talked to Dana once or twice on the phone,
and she's different than I thought she was. Different even than what
she was before I knew any of this. I don't think she's had an easy
time of it. Not that she didn't choose it.

Mom never said a lot, but I think she's always thought Dana was
promiscuous. Like the harlot Proverbs talks about. The one who
lures men into her home, whose lips drip honey and all that. And it
feels weird, but I'm willing to give her a chance. She's going to be a
part of my life if she marries my dad, and there's not much I can do
about it.

Fifty-Four

"COULD I INTEREST you in an evening swim?"

Pamela grinned at Ken—all decked out in wildly patterned swim trunks that reached past his knees. "Love to," she said. "I meant to go this morning and kept putting it off."

Pamela's goal by the end of summer was to swim the half mile to the island and then back once a week. This past week, she'd made it out there, and Ken fetched her in the boat about halfway back. Tonight, however, the two of them just swam laps across the front of their two beach areas. As could be expected, Pamela outlasted Ken by a long shot.

Finally, she too crawled out of the water, dripping all over the dock where Ken was already sprawled in exhaustion. She wrapped a towel around her, and together they watched the sun dip beneath the horizon. By a half past nine, it was so dark the island was only a hint. A loon warbled from a dark corner of the lake.

"I wonder if it's one of ours?" Pamela said.

"The loon? Probably. I haven't seen more than just those two out on the lake this year."

The night sounds were loud around them, and neither said a word for a while.

"I hate swimming at night," Pamela said finally, gathering her towel more tightly around her.

"Afraid the fish will get you?"

"No! It just means I have to do it again in the morning. Let's go in. I'm getting chilly. Want some ice cream?"

"You just swam half a mile and you want ice cream?"

"I swam *three-quarters* of a mile," Pamela corrected with a smile. "And I *always* want ice cream."

Ken followed Pamela up to the house, and she pulled a T-shirt over her head before dishing up the mocha chip ice cream she'd been craving all day. He grabbed the first bowl and leaned on the countertop across from her.

"I don't know why I let you get me addicted to this stuff," he said, shoveling the first spoonful into his mouth.

"First you blame me for getting you in shape. Then you pin your dependency on ice cream on me? Think of it this way, other than that occasional and very odd fetish you have for liver, you have very few vices that I know of. And everyone needs something to keep them humble. Me? I have more than enough to pass around!" She savored another spoonful and then looked up. "By the way, I'm driving down for the final fitting of my bridesmaid dress this weekend. Would you like to come along? Maybe go to a play or something?"

Ken's spoon stayed in his mouth a moment longer than necessary. "You sure?"

"Absolutely sure. It's time I started getting over what other people think when they see us together. It's my business who and when I choose to fall in l—" Pamela's eyes opened wide. "We're *friends*. And Starla understands that."

"Rewind, Pamela. Tell me what you were really going to say."

"I can't, Ken...I'm not ready."

He shook his head and moved closer to her. "How much more ready do you need to be, Pamela?"

"I don't know."

She finished up the remainder of her ice cream. Ken set his nearly empty bowl beside hers and reached to take her hands.

"I love you, Pamela." He paused, then pulled her gently into his arms and kissed her. His lips were warm and not a bit demanding.

"Mmmm," he moaned. "I've wanted to do that for months now."

Pamela pursed her lips to hide a smile, but stayed comfortably quiet within Ken's embrace.

"The only reason I've hesitated is because I knew you were afraid," he continued. "But I'm not sure that's a reason to hold back. And I know...well, I'm pretty sure that you love me, too."

Pamela took great care with her words before answering.

"Yes...but I'm not sure I know what it all means anymore—not after over twenty years of loving someone and then being told I was never loved in return. How am I supposed to live my love out...what does it look like? Is it more than a simple emotional or physical attraction? Sure, that's there but—"

"But you aren't ready to get married again. You aren't sure you even *want* to get married again?"

"Yes," she said quietly, searching his face to see if she'd hurt him. But Ken only smiled, so she continued. "For a long time after Paul left me, all I wanted was for us to get back together, to be a couple again. I hated it when Starla first met Adam. It even bugged me that Angie was dating. When I finally admitted to myself that Paul was never coming back, all that attention from Chad was flattering...But I know now that just being *with* someone isn't the answer."

"And that's a *good* thing. You're stronger now. More self-assured than you were before. I understand that, Pamela. And I respect it."

"But if we get serious, and eventually get married, everything would be different. Can't you see that, Ken? I'd have to sacrifice that independence. Maybe that's why we like each other so much now—we aren't dependent upon each other. As close as we are, we still have our own separate lives."

He shook his head. "You've just confused losing independence with losing individuality. You can be dependent, actually interdependent, upon someone—need someone who needs you—and still hold on to your individuality. Are you afraid I'll try to change you?"

"Not exactly. You're nothing like Paul. He tried to make me into who he wanted me to be—and I tried so hard to be that for him. But it never really worked. The 'me' part still kept coming out. And he never really liked that part."

"You're right. I am *nothing* like Paul. I love *you*." He smiled. "I love you! And I don't expect it's going to stop anytime soon. If we take the next step, it will be when the time is right. And we'll both want to."

Thursday, July 14

Dear Angie,

We haven't spoken for a few weeks, but I've been thinking about something you said and finally decided that I needed to write. You mentioned that I wasn't like you had expected me to be. And when I asked what that was, it seemed to have embarrassed you.

But from a few other comments you made, I think I have a clue as to what you meant. And with that in mind, I want to share something with you. If you'd like, we can meet for lunch and talk some more when you visit your dad next month.

Prior to moving to Minneapolis, I was married for nearly five years to a man I met in college. A Christian man who was very respected and trusted. He was everything I ever wanted.

Except for the fact that I became his prisoner.

Oh, not literally, but emotionally and sometimes physically. I was not allowed to spend money on anything other than what he had planned for or go out with friends outside of his knowledge or approval, and I was even manipulated to give up the job I had in the first law firm I worked for. All this so we could spend more time together, so I could meet his needs and fit my life into his busy schedule.

I should have recognized the signs then. But in other ways, he was kind and good. And I was able to live with the rest. Every few weeks or so, however, he would go through a particularly bad spell. His need for control would get the worst of him and he was so verbally explosive I could hardly breathe. At first, his temper was only directed toward other people—those who dared to disagree with his ideas or way of doing things.

But as the stress of life worsened, so did his ability to control his anger. More often, I received the brunt of it. And it was for dumb things. The house not clean enough, dinner too hot or too cool, the grocery bill higher than it should be.

But I always told myself it was my fault. That I was the one who needed to do better. I learned that as long as I did everything his way, life would be good. And after he exploded—especially when it was in a more physical way— he was always so sorry. He would take me out, bring me flowers, and do all he could to woo me back with the kindness that had captivated me in the first place.

I never told a soul about this, mostly because I didn't know what to say. All anybody else ever saw was how kind he was. How romantic he always was in public. What made confession even more difficult was that I was struggling with my own problems as well. I lived a pretty isolated life and had gotten in the habit of telling lies and partial truths in order to cover for my loneliness and misery.

This is where the story becomes painful and messy. Later, I can share the details of my divorce with you if you would like.

Later, I met your dad. He was the first person I had ever been completely honest with about my life. He picked me up and helped me to stand on my own two feet. He got the interview with the law firm in Minneapolis I ended up working for. And together we started Lifelines. In the first few years, this friendship was the extent of our relationship.

But I fell in love with him.

Angie, I so badly want to apologize to you for the part I played in destroying your family. I still hurt inside thinking of the pain you and your mother went through. And though I know she is the one to whom I owe a far greater apology, I feel that since you and I have talked, this is an easier place for me to begin.

During the months preceding your dad's heart attack, God began to lead me through a process of repentance. I'm not trying to excuse what I've done, but I need to tell you this much: Because of the pain I'd experienced, I was living in a fog. My own need for your dad became so strong, I could hardly see anything else. After we moved to LA, I sank into depression. But that was God's way of getting me into counseling.

You pretty much know the rest. As a part of working through my past to find wholeness, I began to look to the Lord for guidance instead of to your dad. I confessed how sorry I was for betraying your mother—and for the sin of my involvement with your dad. And though your parents' marriage ended, I have no doubt that God's grace has been enacted in my life. I possess a joy and peace that I've never known. One that goes way beyond the circumstances of my life.

Your dad is just beginning to go through the same process that I did—and I really see some amazing things happening. We still spend time together as friends. And someday, maybe, we might both have the assurance that we can take the next step.

I wish with all that I am that I could right the wrongs I have done. And I don't expect that your mom will ever forgive me. I need to do it face-to-face—and that is utterly terrifying to me. But sometime soon, I intend to apologize to her as well.

For all I have done, I am sorry.

Sincerely, Dana

Fifty-Five

ON FRIDAY MORNING, the weekend of Starla's wedding, Pamela drove to the Cities to pick up Angie at the airport. The two of them hadn't seen each other since Paul's heart attack, and though they still chatted each Sunday, the changes Pamela saw in her daughter were nothing she could have detected from Angie's voice. Something shined from the inside and colored Angie's features with a mature, quiet beauty.

"It's just the job, Mom," Angie responded when Pamela commented on the change. "When you face poverty and the effects of it day in and day out like I'm doing, it kind of makes you think more about what really matters."

Pamela smiled. "I'm so proud of you."

"Guess what else? I declared a major."

"Elementary ed?"

Angie nodded. "You think I'll be a good teacher, Mom?"

"Angie, I think you'll be good at whatever you do. But I do see you as a teacher. You still thinking about working in the inner city schools?"

"Yeah…this summer is making that clearer than ever to me. Chuck, that's my boss, he's offered me a standing internship on vacations and during the summer for as long as I'm in school— and he'll also help me line up my student teaching assignment there when the time comes. His wife is a principal at a school I'd just love to work for."

"I'm so proud of you, Angie. And I'm sure your dad is, too. You have his gift, that's for sure."

Angie didn't answer, and when Pamela looked at her daughter, she could see tears running down her face. "Angie? I didn't mean to make you cry…"

"It's okay." She smiled through the tears. "All my life I wanted him to be proud of me. I am a little like him in that way, aren't I?"

The morning of Starla's wedding dawned clear, if just a little on the hot side. Starla arrived at Pamela's cabin before nine to shower and do her makeup. Her own cabin had been usurped by Adam and Vernon and the other men so they could complete the traditional preparations for the Jewish ceremony.

"Help yourself to some breakfast," Pamela said after Starla emerged from the shower. "There's bagels and fruit and coffee set up on the table."

"Ah, Pammi, I'm so sorry. I forgot to tell you I'm fasting! Can ya believe that? I'll take some coffee, though."

"Fasting? You! Don't tell me—it's tradition."

"You guessed it. Adam and I both, although I'm paranoid one of us is going to pass out. It's supposed to symbolize a cleansing from all our past sins." She lowered her lids and looked through her eyelashes: "I guess I shoulda been starving myself a lot longer than one day, huh?"

"So what are the guys doing at your place, anyway—besides fasting and getting into their tuxes?" Angie asked. "I take it your rabbi is there, too? I really liked meeting him at the rehearsal dinner last night. He reminded me of Abraham Lincoln."

"Don't tell him that. Rabbi Goldenstein thinks he's a dead ringer for Dustin Hoffman!"

"Oh, brother," Pamela said.

"And yes, Angie, he is at my cabin. He and Adam are completing *kinyan.* And you should be impressed that I can even tell ya what it is. Basically it's just the process of formalizing the marital obligations. My dad, Adam's dad, and Adam's brother are all there as witnesses. It's a little like signing a marriage license but with more ceremony."

"Man, Starla, I feel like I need one of those little dictionary things to carry around with me at your wedding. You know, the ones people buy when they visit foreign countries so they know how to ask for a bathroom."

Starla smiled back. "I know. It's taken me a while too, but I'm starting to get it. The *ketubbah* is the marital contract Adam wrote—and then paid a Hebrew scribe an arm and a leg to make into a calligraphy wall hanging. My dad still has the one he gave to my mom—and knowing Adam, mine will be just as beautiful."

After the three women were powdered and primped, Pamela helped Starla into her dress—a simple linen shift overlaid with antique ecru lace. The gown hugged Starla from bodice to hemline with a complimentary fit that emphasized her height and made you forget she was even a pound overweight. Her black hair, crowned with a simple pearl band, was piled in a loose tumble of curls on her head, with a few feminine tendrils hanging down her neck. The whole effect was that of an antique, porcelain wedding doll.

Pamela's dress was a simple complement to Starla's: a sunflower-colored shift with a decoratively stitched square neckline and a closely fit skirt that barely brushed the knee.

When the women had finished dressing, almost on command an old-fashioned white limousine pulled up to the cabin. Ken was waiting outside and eagerly took over for the chauffeur, opening doors and seeing them into their beautiful transport. He discreetly kissed Pamela's cheek and whispered conspiratorially, "You're even more beautiful than the bride!" She glared at him happily.

All the guests were already seated in the white, slatted chairs on the lawn by the time the limo dropped them at Starla's cabin. And the string quartet was playing softly from a white platform near the lake. Pamela glanced over the small crowd and spotted the *huppah* planted at the front of the guests.

"Oh, Starla!" she gasped. "Look at that!"

"It's definitely the crowning touch to your wedding decor!" said Angie to a beaming Starla.

The rest of Starla's yard was beautifully adorned with planters and pots of gold flowers and greens scattered here and there—but Angie was right about the huppah, a spectacular portico fashioned entirely of sunflowers and marigolds and trailing vines.

"I need to duck back a bit so no one sees me until I walk down the aisle," Starla said.

Angie found an empty seat next to one of the other guests,

and Pamela took her place in the back listening for the music to grow louder.

Adam's parents, who were waiting just to Pamela's right, met him as he exited Starla's cabin and escorted him down the center aisle, leaving him to stand in front of the white podium beneath the huppah. Each parent stood next to one of the poles supporting the canopy. Then Rabbi Goldenstein led Pamela and Adam's brother David down the aisle, where they split and took their spots at either side of the huppah.

Finally, Starla's dad, his eyes already overflowing with emotion, took his daughter's arm and led her to stand beside her groom. He took his place at the third pole of the huppah, leaving the fourth, symbolically, for Starla's mother.

When the music took on a slower, marchlike beat, first Adam's mother and then Starla began to slowly and reverently circle Adam—one, two, three…seven times.

As the stringed quartet brought the processional music to a close, the rabbi came from the side to welcome the guests. He joked a little, and then read in his wonderful, lilting voice:

> "Blessed is he who comes in the name of the Lord. From the house of the Lord we bless you. The Lord is God and He has made His light shine upon us. With boughs in hand, join in the festal procession up to the horns of the altar. You are my God, and I will give You thanks: You are my God, and I will exalt You. Give thanks to the Lord for He is good; His love endures forever!"

In the background, loons were calling, and a pontoon full of curious neighbors slowly motored past. The sounds of summer, of nature and man, were welcome accompaniment to Starla's wedding. Into the tranquility of the afternoon, Rabbi Goldenstein chanted a hymn that had been uttered at Hebrew weddings since medieval days:

"He who is strong above all else
    He who is blessed above all else
He who is great above all else
    May He bless the bridegroom and bride."

When he finished, he recited the traditional betrothal benediction—in Hebrew and in English—then retrieved a large chalice of wine from the small table behind Adam and Starla. Arching his hand back and forth over the wine, he prayed, and then lifted the goblet to Adam and Starla.

"Adam…Starla…you have chosen to join your lives today," said Rabbi Goldenstein, "and I agree with you that this is right and honorable. I have come to know the two of you and know how important it is for you to keep Jesus Christ the center of your home."

He spoke of how beautiful it was that in Starla and Adam's home, the saving grace of Christ would be wrapped around the Hebrew culture that was both of their birthrights. "I pray that in this, the genesis of your life together, that you will commit to serve the Lord always."

The rabbi then lifted a simple gold band from his pocket and handed it to Adam, who put the ring on Starla's index finger and recited solemnly, "Behold, you are consecrated to me with this ring according to the law of Moses and of Israel."

Then Adam turned back to the rabbi to accept the document

the two of them had formalized earlier—the kettubah Starla had described—and put it into Starla's open hands. Pamela could see the tears welling in her friend's eyes as she saw the gift for the first time.

"I give this to you, my love, my wife, to protect and keep, knowing that it is my promise to you that will last all the days of my life."

"You abound in blessings, Lord our God, source of all creation, Creator of the fruit of the vine, symbol of human joy," said Adam's mother, the first to offer one of the special prayers. Though she was teary-eyed, her voice was strong and filled with love.

"You abound in blessing, Lord our God, source of all creation, all of whose creations reflect Your glory," recited Adam's father.

"You abound in blessing, Lord our God, source of all creation, Creator of human beings," said Vernon. Pamela had been watching him carefully and she could see how close his emotion was to the surface. No doubt he was remembering his own wedding and Starla as a little girl.

"You abound in blessing, Lord our God, source of all creation, who created man and woman in Your image that they might live, love, and so perpetuate life," said David. He grabbed his brother's hand in spontaneous affection, and Adam pulled him into a hug. From where Pamela stood, she could hear Adam's husky, "I love you, David!"

"We *all* rejoice as these two persons, overcoming separateness, unite in joy. *You* abound in blessing, Lord, permitting *us* to share in others' joy." Pamela was fighting back tears at the beauty of the ancient words she recited.

Ken smiled at her from the congregation, and she marveled that she still believed the words spoken today, was confident in God's blessing despite the great pain she'd gone through.

After so many years alone, Starla had been given the desire of her heart! *God is so good*, Pamela thought as she took her place beside David.

Rabbi Goldenstein closed: "May these lovers rejoice as did the first man and woman in the primordial Garden of Eden. You abound in blessings, Lord, source of joy for bride and groom."

At this final word, Adam gulped down the last of the wine and threw the goblet to the ground, stomping on it theatrically, as did every groom in this concluding ritual of Jewish weddings.

The music began again, a bouncing tune that reached into Pamela's heart and lifted high pure laughter and celebratory joy.

In the midst of applause, the rabbi nearly had to shout as he pronounced Starla and Adam, man and wife. Starla threw her arms around her groom's neck and planted a big kiss on his lips— much to the amusement of Rabbi Goldenstein, who hadn't yet told Adam to kiss the bride.

"Adam," he said, "seeing as how this wanton woman has already taken such liberty with you, it's now *your* turn! Go ahead—kiss your bride."

Adam dipped Starla low and deep and sealed their union with a prolonged, slobbery kiss for the benefit of his laughing audience. Then he summoned everyone to the wedding feast, and he and Starla hurried down the aisle, shaking hands and grinning at everyone.

The wedding feast was an enormous offering of food and drink, laid out on long tables behind Starla's cabin. Long before the food was gone, the dancing and celebration began, with Starla's dad giving lessons in traditional Hebrew dance to anyone who was interested. He began with his daughter, whirling Starla about and leading her in the steps that seemed to come back to her from somewhere in her memory.

And when Adam took over, he continued the graceful movement without error, holding her in his arms and smiling into her eyes. Pamela had never seen a happier bride or groom—or father of the bride, for that matter!

When finally the sun began to set, the newlyweds rode off in the white limousine, and the reception started to break up. It had been a magical afternoon and evening, they all agreed.

Ken drove Angie and Pamela home to Sunset Lake through the darkening night. And as tired as they all were, conversation was slow and limited—each content with his or her own thoughts.

Angie was the first from the car and headed sleepily toward the cabin, eager for bed. But then she turned back to where Pamela and Ken stood in the yard.

"You know, Mom," she said with a barely concealed yawn and catlike stretch. "It's just too bad *you* didn't catch that bouquet."

"Angela!" But Ken was laughing so hard Pamela could hardly help but join him. "Oh, you!"

"Good night, Mother dear. Good night, Ken." Then she winked playfully and left Pamela and Ken alone.

Fifty-Six

"I CAN'T BELIEVE this," Pamela whispered, dropping the letter Angie had given her onto the beach towel she was sitting on.

She sat still a long while, saying nothing at all, just letting the tears fall and then dry upon her cheeks. Neither woman said a word, though Angie, seated on the chaise across from her mother, was watching like a hawk.

But how could her daughter even begin to read the emotion, when Pamela couldn't understand her own mixed-up feelings? Part of her wanted to believe the letter was Dana's pretty little attempt to put a nice spin on this whole ordeal. But the other part…the part that trusted in the Lord's ability to bring people into repentance…that corner of Pamela's heart yearned to reach out and tell Dana that she was forgiven.

Pamela feared the oodles of times she had played the fool during the years Dana and Paul had dallied with each other behind her back. *Lord*, she prayed, *let me know if this woman is sincere or if her letter is an attempt to get away with sin.*

Pamela glanced down at the water and then scanned the lake. The sun was making way for the long shadows and fading light of the August evening. The trees framing the lake were already hinting at autumn's yellow. All was at peace.

Angie had been right to wait until tonight, the evening before she left, to show the letter to Pamela. An earlier revelation would have changed the tone of the entire weekend.

"So," Pamela finally said, "what was your reaction, Angie?"

"Honestly?" Angie paused, searching her mother's face. "We'd spoken a few times on the phone, and I kinda saw it coming. And I've been praying for her. I think she's truly sorry, Mom."

Pamela listened with her eyes closed, weighing it all in her heart.

"What about you, Mom? What do you think?"

Pamela opened her eyes and smiled at her daughter. "I think you are a very wise woman." The light had mellowed, bathing the lake with muted pinks and blues. "*And* I think I promised you a sunset. Come down to the water with me?"

There were no words between them as they walked out to the end of the dock. Angie sat down first, and Pamela sank pretzel-style beside her and wrapped her arm around her daughter's waist. A curious buoyancy had begun to well up inside—a levity that had much to do with the lessening of the ugly burden she'd carried for so long. Vengeance. Hate. Anger.

Time had eased the worst of it. But it wasn't completely gone.

Was Pamela, too, ready to forgive Dana?

And maybe even Paul? Even though he'd probably never come to her and ask for it?

Try as she might, her own human nature could *never* forgive

Paul for all he'd done. She had settled for putting his betrayal out of her mind and simply moving on with life. So what was this willingness she now had to actually forgive?

Pamela knew exactly what it was: This ability to offer grace—this wellspring that had occurred at just that moment—was from God. But the difficult conversation Dana hinted at in her letter would come. And Pamela dreaded it nearly as much as Dana evidently did.

But she could do it.

Pamela breathed deeply and smiled. "I'm free," she whispered to her daughter and wiped away the tears that had tracked down her cheeks.

The sun was approaching its familiar intersection between lake and sky. Silently they watched the uppermost silver clouds blush pink and then, more languidly, darken to stains of crimson. With closed eyes, Pamela saw the image in negative. A snapshot of memory to pull up and cherish much, much later.

Peace. Contentedness. This is what freedom feels like, she acknowledged. *God's gift to those who heed His call to forgive.*

The sun touched the lake. Pamela smiled at her crazy wondering: If she listened really carefully, could she hear the sizzle as that great round ball of fire hit the water?

Then, just before the sun was completely submerged, Pamela felt the dock shake behind them and turned to see Ken, swim trunks on, towel in hand. He stopped at about the halfway point and flashed his familiar, scrunch-eyed grin—a grin Pamela could no longer imagine living without. Angie laughed to see it.

Pamela's heart swelled. "What are you doing?"

"Watch out!" Ken yelled as he galloped toward them, bobbing

the dock up and down so hard both women had to place their palms at their sides for balance. He leaped from the end of the dock, all curled up in a cannonball, and soaked them both.

Dear Readers,

Many Christian authors consider writing to be their ministry. Though, for me, it has definitely evolved into that, my initial purpose in writing *Jumping in Sunset* was more self-directed. The earliest version of this novel was my way of working through the pain and hurt and failures of my own life.

Years ago, when my parents' marriage and, secretly, my own were falling apart, I desperately sought fiction I could relate to— with characters whose lives reflected the struggles I faced. My primary choice had always been Christian fiction. But as my daily walk became more tumultuous and less "normal," I had little in common with the happy endings and lily white heroes and heroines that often crossed the pages of my favorite genre.

I wondered why there weren't more authors like Patricia Hickman, Francine Rivers, and Karen Kingsbury. Or plots that addressed such things as emotional or physical abuse, infidelity, or divorce. I longed for characters who were not perfect, but like me, were fallen Christians desperate for the wholeness only the Lord can provide.

I have attempted in this novel to honestly portray the two sides of a broken marriage. And though it was difficult at times to keep my opinions to myself, I tried to allow each character to live his or her life and make decisions separate from "shoulds" and "woulds." I've found that to be one of the greatest challenges of being a Christian author—to write without preaching.

The simplest thing to communicate is that divorce is wrong, so why write about it at all? Two reasons: First, because it happens in our Christian circles just as regularly as it does outside the

Church. And second, because even when a marriage ends in divorce, forgiveness and grace are available to *both* partners. If there is one theme running through my novel, that is it.

My prayer is that God will use *Jumping in Sunset* to touch your heart with the amazing truths of His grace and love.

Dawn Ringling

Discussion Questions

1. Read through all of Matthew 5. In this passage, commonly referred to as the Sermon on the Mount, Jesus explores six topics. It is clear that Jesus has something more in mind than just following the rules; He desires a heart that yearns completely after Him. It is also interesting to note the many figures of speech and graphic images He uses to get His points across. Jesus' sayings on divorce follow his statements on lust and on anger. Should we take His discourse on divorce more seriously than we do the others? What light do these other passages shed upon how we should interpret and follow the divorce passage? Did Jesus forbid divorce under all circumstances?

2. Did Pamela do all she could to save her marriage?

3. Dana's struggles are understated, but they raise some good questions, especially in light of what was finally revealed about the emotional abuse of her first marriage. Read through the story of the woman caught in adultery found in John 7:53–8:11. Do you see any parallels between Dana and this woman? What would Jesus have to say to Dana? Jesus' final

words to the woman in John were, "Then neither do I condemn you. Go now and leave your life of sin." What about Dana? Did she leave her life of sin when she cut off the adultery, even though she was still in contact with Paul? Some people would say that remarriage in her case would be ongoing sin. What is your view of this?

4. Angie's position is a hard one. She loves both of her parents and, despite the past, desires a renewed relationship with her dad and can even do so with Dana in the picture. If you were Angie, how would you have handled the situation?

5. *Jumping in Sunset* leaves the reader wondering whether or not Paul and Dana, both believers struggling through the process of repentance, will get married. Assuming they eventually marry, how would you (knowing them as you do) respond to them if they were to become a part of your church? Would they be shunned or welcomed? What would Jesus do?

6. What if Pamela remarries? Would there be a difference in the way you would respond to her compared to how you would respond to Paul and Dana?

7. From the very beginning, Paul was committed to the institution of marriage, even though he never felt love or attraction for Pamela. He "needed" a wife to complete his world. Once he met Dana, he realized there was such a thing as romantic love. Should he have stayed with Pamela out of commitment to her and the history they had together? Do you think counseling would have helped teach Paul to love Pamela?

Visit

www.letstalkfiction.com
today!

Fiction Readers Unite!

You've just found a new way to feed your fiction addiction. Letstalkfiction.com is a place where fiction readers can come together to learn about new fiction releases from Multnomah. You can read about the latest book releases, catch a behind the scenes look at the your favorite authors, sign up to receive the most current book information, and much more. Everything you need to make the most out of your fictional world can be found at www.letstalkfiction.com. Come and join the network!

DO YOU KNOW WHO YOUR FRIENDS ARE?

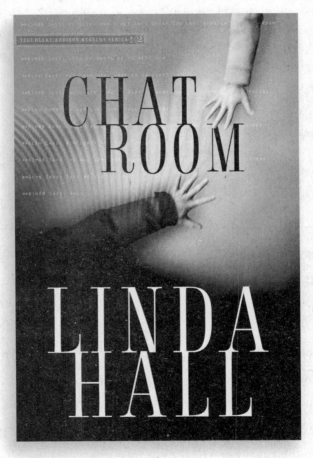

Lonely, nervous Glynis Piggot hires Teri to find her only friend, who disappeared after meeting a man on the Internet. Soon a simple missing persons case leads to a suspected cult compound, a hostage crisis, and a ritual murder—echoes from Teri's own past on the police force. This threat may be closer to home than she realized...

ISBN 1-59052-200-1

THE COLD ATLANTIC OCEAN
SWALLOWS OLD SECRETS

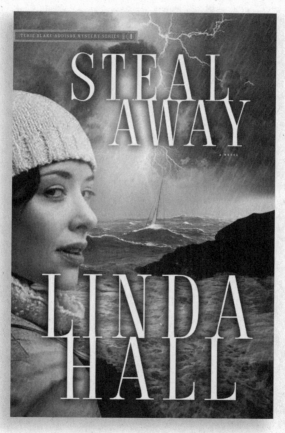

Dr. Carl Houseman, celebrated minister and speaker, is determined to find out what really happened to his wife, declared dead five years ago after her sailboat washed ashore on a coastal island of Maine. Private investigator Teri Blake-Addison must piece together the life of this woman who felt she didn't know or understand the God that her husband so faithfully served. Did Ellen really die in those cold Atlantic waters? When a murder rocks the island, Teri knows more is at stake than just the puzzling life of an unhappy minister's wife.

ISBN 1-59052-072-6

A MYSTERIOUS DISAPPEARANCE…A FAMILY IN TUMULT…VOLATILE SURROUNDINGS…CAN ONE WOMAN CONNECT THE PIECES IN TIME?

When nine-year-old Ally Buckley turns up missing, fear spreads throughout the New England fishing village where Sadie and her family live and worship. But when Sadie discovers one of Ally's drawings among her husband's possessions, she suspects danger may be closer to home than she had ever known.

ISBN 1-57673-659-8

A DESPERATE QUEST...

This rerelease of Randall Arthur's bestselling novel presents the hypocrisy of Christian legalism and a man's search for the only surviving member of his family. The story's hero, Pastor Jason Faircloth, embarks on a journey that lasts eighteen years and takes him through four countries in a quest to find the granddaughter who is being hidden from him. In a process that mirrors our own spiritual journey, he discovers a rich relationship with God and the peace that finally comes with true faith.

ISBN 1-59052-259-1

VENGEANCE DEVOURS A PASTOR'S HEART

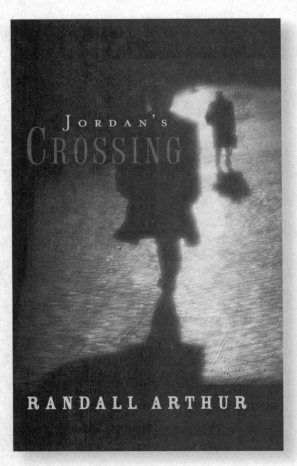

JORDAN'S CROSSING

RANDALL ARTHUR

When pastor Jordan Rau accepted a position with a European missions agency, his decision was based on money, not on an opportunity to serve God. However, shortly after his family's arrival in Germany, Jordan's priorities dramatically change—his young son, Chase, has been murdered. Abandoning his faith in God, Jordan becomes obsessed with finding Chase's killers and delivering justice. He sets out on a course of action that will destroy not only the murderers, but his own family as well—and only a miracle can stop him.

ISBN 1-59052-260-5

SINNER, DON'T COME HOME...

BROTHERHOOD OF BETRAYAL

RANDALL ARTHUR

"Your love for one another will prove to the world that you are my disciples," Jesus said (John 13:35, NLT). Why then are Christians noted for their hateful judgment of each other? *Brotherhood of Betrayal* illustrates the ugliness of the betrayal syndrome that festers inside the Christian church. Respected missionary pastor Clay McCain leaves his family and growing church in Sweden for a beautiful, wealthy woman. But the Christian community reacts cruelly—even to his innocent abandoned family...

ISBN 1-59052-258-3

OTHER FICTION TITLES FROM MULTNOMAH® PUBLISHERS

AN EXOTIC DANCER IS A STRATEGIC PAWN IN A SPIRITUAL BATTLE

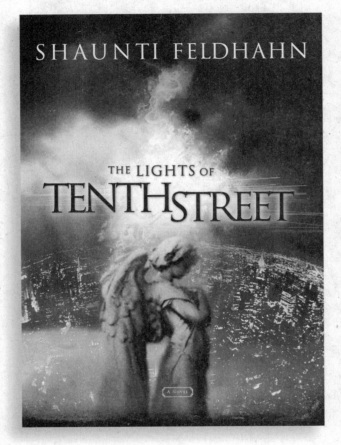

They have the house, the two kids, and the minivan. They have a well-meaning but shallow church. What Sherry doesn't know is that Doug has a shameful struggle with his thought life. When an exotic dancer's life intersects theirs, this suburban couple has to make a hard choice: Do they risk their convenience and security for her sake, or do they cross to the other side of the road? The dark forces will not easily give up their most important pawn. But Ronnie must come out of the darkness, for only she can unravel a plot of devastating destruction.

ISBN 1-59052-080-7